# The First Cut

MARY BIRK

Copyright © 2015 by Mary Birk

ISBN-13:978-1539936275

ISBN-10:1539936279

Cover Design by JT Lindroos

*For Lydia, Brave and True*

*The first cut is the deepest.*
CAT STEVENS

# SATURDAY, APRIL 4, 2009

# Chapter 1

Glasgow, Scotland

ON THE LAST DAY OF HIS LIFE, Richard Ramsey slid his shiny silver Mercedes to the side of the deserted lane and killed the engine. The sudden stillness made what he was doing startlingly real. He sneaked a nervous glance at the tantalizing woman seated next to him. Tonight he had taken the first step down a forbidden, but unbearably enticing, path. The kind of path every man knows he shouldn't go down, but the kind of path few men can resist.

She tilted the bottle of whiskey to her mouth, then grinned, a grin that flashed a hint of wickedness so devastatingly delicious his chest hurt. She slowly flicked her tongue around the bottle's rim in a teasing dance and a throbbing, aching sensation flooded his groin.

"Why here?" He loosened his death grip on the steering wheel and drew his hands along its contours, wishing it was her supple body he was touching. He wanted his hands on her more than anything he'd wanted for years, but he wasn't exactly sure how to proceed. He had not done anything like this since—well, ever. He had never before been unfaithful to Barbara in the nearly eighteen years they'd been married, quite an accomplishment, especially through the past few years.

He wasn't sure why he'd remained faithful until now. His colleagues didn't hesitate to take mistresses or just get a bit on the side. It wouldn't have been difficult—money had a way of making any man attractive to most women, but he hadn't wanted a woman who wanted him because of his money.

This woman didn't want his money. She wanted him and, God knew, he wanted her, wanted her with a hunger that had become all consuming. Right now, with the night wrapped protectively around them, it was like they were the only two people alive.

Dark hair swirled around her neck as she shrugged, passing the bottle back to him. "No one can see us. The road's been closed for a month." She pouted with soft pink lips so full they looked almost swollen.

It was those lips that had tempted him, those lips that had filled his dreams, and those lips that had finally convinced him. She'd made it clear that she wanted him, hinted she wanted to use her mouth and that agile tongue on him. He couldn't remember the last time his wife had done that; generally, by half seven she was passed out, sloshed as a sailor.

He took a swig of the whiskey, firmly capped the bottle, and let it slide down to the car floor. A glance out the window convinced him she was right about the place being private. Silhouetted trees hid the road from view on one side, and although a short expanse of rough grass lay between them and a double set of railroad tracks, access to the other side was blocked by heavy brush and a chain link fence that glinted in the moonlight. No need to be nervous, he told himself.

"Here it will be, then." He leaned in to kiss her. Her smell intoxicated him—fresh, clean eucalyptus and something else, something earthy sweet. "You look so incredibly sexy like this."

"You like it?"

"Love it." He threaded his fingers through the dark silken strands of her wig, then fisted a handful of hair to pull her closer. He crushed her lips with his, pried her mouth open with his tongue, felt her teeth against his own. She tasted of warm whiskey and wanting and woman. Waves of desire flooded him.

She pulled away slightly, using her hand to loosen his hold, and alarm gripped him. Was she having second thoughts? Surely not. Surely she wouldn't back out now. He had to have her. Then he realized what she must be thinking.

"Not to worry." Fumbling, he took a condom out of his pocket. "I brought this." He'd actually brought several from the box he'd bought as soon as she'd agreed to meet him, but he didn't want to look too presumptuous. Just in case, though, he had the extras stashed in the glovebox.

She wrinkled her adorable nose. "I hate those. I want to feel you, not a nasty rubber."

He couldn't believe his luck. "I just thought . . ."

"And they taste awful."

A shudder of excitement ran down his spine, and he dropped the packet. She was going to use her mouth. His heart thudded against his chest as he tried to think what he should do next. Should he suggest they get into the backseat right now? Or maybe he should kiss her again, get her ready first, then suggest the move to the backseat?

To his surprise, she took control. "Let's do it outside." The mischievous tone in her voice both thrilled and terrified him.

"Bit cold for that, isn't it, sweetheart?" The early April weather in Glasgow was cold and damp, not making for an ideal shagging venue. He wanted to convince her to stay in the car, but she had already opened the door, reaching around first to the backseat to grab the tartan blanket he kept there. He took off his fedora and threw it in the back; his bald head would be cold without it, but it seemed ridiculous to wear a hat under the circumstances.

"I'll warm you up." Her smile held a promise of pure pleasure that made his heartbeat accelerate wildly and his cock twitch like he was in his twenties again.

He got out of the car, and followed to where she was laying out the blanket. She carefully arranged what was to be their bed, sat down, then motioned for him to join her. He hesitated, then decided why the hell not? He couldn't remember when he had last done anything so wild. He'd wasted so much time, but not anymore. He wanted this passion, this excitement, this vitality in his life again.

Kneeling down beside her, he found her mouth with his own and took her in what he hoped she would think was a tender kiss. He caressed her breasts through her soft red sweater, felt her nipples peak. He drew in a deep breath, inhaling the rich, spicy perfume that clung to her skin, slipped one hand under the neckline of her sweater, and shuddered at the satiny soft feel of female flesh. Ah, this is what had led him here. Worth it. It was all worth it.

He felt himself swell; his desire and his potency were still there. At sixty-four, he had just needed something to catch his interest again, and this beauty with her nipples hardening under his touch was just the thing. He could tell how much she wanted him. Why had he waited so long?

He swallowed, easing his other hand under her skirt, skimming his fingers up between her legs. The feel of the smooth skin of her thighs sent the blood rushing to his head. Yes, she was exactly what he'd needed.

She reached to unfasten his belt, interrupting the progress of his hands on her body. Hard as it was to not feel frustrated when his fingers had been so close, he was also gratified. He couldn't remember the last time he'd been with a woman who was so eager. She wanted him as much as he wanted her.

She flicked her nimble tongue around her lips, her eyes half hooded with desire, and pushed her index finger against his chest. "Down."

Obediently, he lay back on the blanket. From far away in the background, he heard the low vibrating rumble that signified the advent of a train. He strained his neck slightly to see the tracks. "Shouldn't we get back in the car? We'll be giving them a bit of a show, won't we?"

She shook her head, teasing, playful. "Those trains go by so fast they can't see anything. Not at night, especially. Or if they do, they won't be able to see who we are."

He nodded. He sure as bloody hell wasn't going to do anything to dissuade her from doing what they both wanted her to do. How had he let himself miss out on this all these years? There were women out there, beautiful women, who really wanted, and liked, sex. Women who wouldn't lie there like a dead trout when a man wanted her.

She unzipped his pants and his cock sprang toward her, seeking. A frisson of anticipation rippled through his body at the possibility of strangers getting a glimpse of this beautiful woman with her mouth on him. The thought of them being seen like that both excited and terrified him. The cold air hit his skin, but the warmth of her tight grasp quickly protected him.

She moved her fingers along the shaft, appraising him with a catlike intensity. He was glad he'd thought to see his doctor beforehand. Stay hard, he instructed his cock, hoping that the willful bastard would listen for once. He heard her inhale, with what? Lust, anticipation, desire? He prayed it wasn't disappointment. Stay hard.

"You're so big, so thick."

Pride inflated his chest like helium filling a balloon. "It's all yours, sweetheart."

"Lovely." Her delicious pink tongue circled her mouth again. "I'll take you as deep as I can."

He chuckled, his old confidence in his virility returning. He'd never had a woman complain, had he? "Just take what you can."

He closed his eyes, waiting in breathless anticipation for the clasp of her mouth around him. He braced himself. Waited for her soft, warm mouth to take him in. Soon, it would be soon.

Nothing happened.

What was taking her so long? He should be feeling those tenderly voracious lips by now. He felt her move closer, her hand still holding him, and he groaned in agonized anticipation.

"You're torturing me. Come on, sweetheart, get to it."

Suddenly, a searing pain gripped his chest. God, not a heart attack out here in the middle of nowhere, with his pants open and him so ready. Not now. Not when he was so close. The pain ebbed. He opened his eyes and gingerly touched one hand to his chest, felt the wet warmth soaking his shirt.

The thundering onslaught of the train on the nearby tracks was the last sound he heard, the woman's departing figure, illuminated by the train's garishly blaring lights, the last thing he saw.

# SUNDAY, APRIL 5, 2009

# Chapter 2

SUPERINTENDENT TERRENCE REID crossed from where he'd parked his car on the road to the railroad tracks, fingering the rosary in the left pocket of his wool coat as he walked. The chill of the early spring wind slapped across his face, and his feet crunched the thinly iced dew on the grass. Neither the hopeful green of the newly leafed out trees nor the smattering of blue flowers in the grass told the truth about the weather. It might be April, it might be spring, but it was freeze-your-bone-marrow cold.

His day had just gone from bad to absolute bollocks. He'd had bad days before, bad weeks before, even bad years before, but he'd never felt so much like a failure as he did right now. Every aspect of his life, from his marriage to his career, was careening out of control. And now this. His star witness. His star bloody witness.

A glance around the crime scene told him he wasn't the only one having a bad day. The morning sun, even filtered as it was by the typical haze of gray clouds, revealed that the newest member of his elite police team wasn't dealing well with having to confront the battered and bloody remains of what had been a man before she'd even had breakfast.

At twenty-two, Detective Constable Allison Muirhead was still raw when it came to the business of death. She was bundled up in a red down jacket, her curly brown hair mostly covered by a white knitted hat, but underneath all that, Reid recognized the look on her face; she was concentrating fervently on not being sick. The gruesome sight of the mutilated body alone could have turned anyone's stomach. At least, thanks to the cold air and being out in the open, the body didn't stink yet, but Reid suspected the greasy tar smell clinging to the railroad tracks wasn't helping Allison's stomach any.

"A'right, Allison?" he asked.

"A'right, sir." Allison would throw herself in front of the next train rather than embarrass herself by admitting that the crime scene bothered her. She put on a brave face, Reid thought. An oddly yellowish-green face, but a brave one, nonetheless.

Reid nodded at her, then turned his attention to Detective Sergeant Harry Ross, the senior member of his team.

"You're sure it's him?" Even a cursory inspection of the carnage on the tracks revealed the utter impossibility of making an identification based on the man's mangled face, and Reid allowed himself to feel a brief flicker of hope that a mistake had been made.

"As sure as we can be." Harry's innocent face with its sea of freckles and messy cap of ginger hair did not look like it belonged to a man who was one of the best electronic crime detectives in Great Britain. "There's not much left of him." Harry gestured toward a silver Mercedes sedan parked on the side of the road. "But that's Ramsey's car, his jacket is folded up on the front passenger seat, and his wallet was in it."

Reid nodded, making sure his demeanor didn't reflect even a hint of the weariness or frustration he felt. Richard Ramsey, a prominent industrialist, had finally agreed not just to act as an informant, but also to give testimony against the man Reid believed was the chief Scottish conduit in a pipeline financing a string of violent terrorist attacks on British and European universities. Ramsey's cooperation had been kept quiet so they could make sure the noose around Walter Von Zandt's neck was looped good and tight before bringing charges against the wealthy financier.

In the six weeks since he'd left California—since he'd left Anne— Reid had worked ceaselessly on the investigation, trying to make up for the time he'd lost by being away. Much of that time had been spent recruiting Ramsey. Without Ramsey's help, the chances of getting the evidence needed to implicate Von Zandt were next to impossible. The chances of Reid being able to find a replacement informant in time to stop the next attacks were even worse.

Reid walked over to the Mercedes to get a closer look at the number plate. Harry was right, it was definitely Ramsey's car. Reid was well-acquainted with everything about Richard Ramsey: his car, his family, his business, his house. He'd burned every blessed fact into his brain when he'd been trying to get Ramsey to turn informant. And it had worked, for all the good it would do now.

Reid felt a veil of depression sink over him. It wasn't just Ramsey. It was Ramsey and Anne and California and nights spent sitting by a phone that wouldn't ring. He fought the urge to yell, to lash out, to drive his fist through the sedan's window. None of that would help. It never had.

He unclenched his fist and walked back across the grass to rejoin Henry and Allison by the railroad tracks.

Harry popped two sticks of gum into his mouth and squinted at Allison. "This is your first dead body, isn't it, ducks?" Chewing his gum with a little too much enthusiasm, Harry peered into her face with more amusement than concern. "You're not looking so good, lassie. Green, almost." Although he was actually from Dundee, Harry, chameleon-like, had adopted a broad Glaswegian accent.

"Stuff it. I'm fine."

Harry widened his eyes in mock surprise at her prickly response, then shrugged, a demonic grin on his face.

Reid shot Harry a warning look. Usually Reid was mildly amused by the banter between his detectives, but not today. "Allison, breathe through your mouth until you get your bearings."

She swallowed, inhaled deeply, then nodded.

"Where was the surveillance that was supposed to be on Ramsey?"

"Don't know, sir. It was supposed to be DC Parsons, but it looks like he ditched it."

Reid frowned. "When exactly did DC Parsons leave his post?"

"Sometime after eleven, sir," Allison said. "According to the computer records, that's when Parsons reported in saying that the house lights had been turned off a half hour before, and he figured the family had turned in for the night."

Reid shook his head, disgusted. This forced liaison with the Glasgow Criminal Investigation Division, and particularly with CID's DI Mark Lawrence, had been nothing but trouble. Lawrence had tried to undercut Reid at every turn. No doubt the arrogant bastard would find some way to shift the blame for this mess back on Reid. "So are you saying DC Parsons left off the surveillance when the family went to bed? Ramsey was supposed to be under watch around the clock."

"From what I was able to winkle out of one of the other CID lads, DI Lawrence has been letting his people make a judgment call as to whether they needed to stay after Ramsey looked to be home for the night." Allison obviously didn't relish being the one giving Reid this news. "I guess Parsons decided to call it a night."

Reid tried to reconcile what he was hearing with what he knew about the young constable who had approached him several weeks ago, asking to join Reid's team. Reid had let him know that he'd be under consideration, depending on his performance on this investigation. So why would he throw away his chance like this? "How did he explain himself?"

"Don't know, sir. No one's been able to get hold of him."

Reid forced down the cold dread that clamped around his chest. That Parsons would abandon his duties last night and then ignore efforts to contact him made no sense. "When you get him, have him call me directly."

"Yes, sir." Allison said, a little faintly. She was staring at the body again.

Harry snapped his gum, and Allison rolled her eyes in disapproval.

Reid gave his sergeant a mildly reproving look, not at the gum snapping, but because Harry was doing it to annoy Allison. Harry caught Reid's look, raised his eyebrows, and gave a slight jerk of his thumb toward Allison. Reid finally realized his sergeant had been deliberately annoying Allison to distract her from being sick. And to Harry's credit, she did look less green.

Harry, completely serious now, said, "The local coppers say he did it on purpose. Got soused and plunked himself down across the railroad tracks." He pointed to an empty bottle of whiskey that looked to have rolled a few feet down the embankment. "What do you think, guv? Drunken accident or a desperate act of remorse?"

Reid didn't answer, just frowned, pacing closer to where the mutilated body lay across the tracks. He let his eyes slowly assess the entire site, taking in the access road, the trees and other thick vegetation screening the small grassy knoll on the other side of the tracks, and the location of the Mercedes, while he analyzed the possible scenarios that might have led to Ramsey's end.

He looked at Allison. "Your thoughts, DC?"

The young woman's face blushed a wild pink, which was a marked improvement, Reid decided. He could tell Allison was trying desperately to think of an insightful comment to make. "I'm not sure, sir. Maybe suicide? Or it could have been an accident, I guess." She shook her head. "I don't know, sir. Suicide, I guess."

Reid let his gaze wander from the car to the tracks and back again.

"You said he was pretty shook when he realized the money he was helping launder was being used to finance terrorists," Harry said. "Maybe he just couldn't live with himself."

Reid made a noncommittal sound, still deep in thought. After a moment, he looked over at Allison. "Who found the body?"

Allison gestured at an elderly man, thin and almost certainly hung over, who stood away from the scene, quietly waiting, an old woolen jacket wrapped around him and a red plaid cap with ear muffs keeping his head warm.

"Have you taken his statement?"

"Yes, sir. He was walking home after a night out with his mates. He lives just past there." She indicated an area away from the tracks where the trees were thick. "After he found Mr. Ramsey's body, he went home and rang the local police. They brought him back here so he could show them where the body was."

"You can let him go if you've got his contact information." Reid glanced at the old man, registering the bowed shoulders and uncertain posture. "Make sure he has a lift home if he wants one."

"Right." She moved away to speak to the old man. Reid watched, saw the man shake his head at Allison's offer and then shamble across the field to the trees.

Harry picked at his teeth with a piece of dried grass, but his attention was on Allison who was hurrying back toward them. "I wouldn't have wanted to be the poor sod who found him. At least we knew what to expect when we showed up. Stumbling across a sight like this had to suck."

Reid ignored the comment. His voice low, he said, "For Ramsey to want to kill himself, he'd have to either be unable to face his involvement being made public, or be overcome with guilt. But he'd already figured out the spin he'd take to excuse his involvement and he didn't blame himself. His story was that he was a victim as well."

Harry made a face. "Right. Like he didn't suspect. What did he think the money was being used for? To help starving orphans?"

Reid shrugged. He had learned never to underestimate the ability of people not to see what they didn't want to see.

"An accident, then?" Harry asked. "Passed out while taking a piss?"

"Then what was he doing here in the first place? This road goes nowhere, and he's lived around here long enough to know that."

"What if it wasn't guilt or shame? What if it was fear? Maybe he decided killing himself would be less painful than getting crosswise with Von Zandt. When you've let the devil get you by the balls, it may get a mite uncomfortable when he twists them. Could be Ramsey decided offing himself was preferable to what he was going to get from Von Zandt."

Reid didn't mind his conclusions being questioned. But Harry hadn't been there, hadn't talked to Ramsey, hadn't seen the man's outraged demeanor. Ramsey wasn't a man who let himself be beaten by anything or anyone. Something wasn't right.

He leaned toward the mutilated and mangled body to get a closer look at the torso. Then he gave a low, thoughtful whistle, and squeezed his eyes to better focus. When Reid was sure, he gestured at Harry to come closer.

Harry obliged, squatted down, and looked at where Reid was pointing. "Ah, bugger me, but I think you're right."

Reid straightened up. "We were meant to think suicide, or at a stretch, a drunken accident. The killer must have expected the train would make more of a mess than it did."

Allison poked her head from behind Harry, then cleared her throat as if preparing to speak. She didn't say anything, but Reid felt her question.

"See, Allison? Just there." He pointed to what had been the body's chest. "I'd be surprised if the medical examiner doesn't tell us that that hole in his chest was made by a sharp instrument. He was stabbed and then dragged to, or thrown on, the tracks. Already dead when the train hit him, I'd say. Harry, have Ramsey's car towed in and get the SOCOs to go over it carefully. Whoever killed him may have been in the car with him."

Harry gestured toward the Scene of Crime operatives milling around taking photographs and samples. "Already gave the order, guv. And I told them to check for tracks to see if another vehicle was here."

"Good." Reid said. "Either Ramsey met the killer here, or the killer drove here with Ramsey, dead or alive. Had to have been picked up by someone else afterwards or had transport hidden somewhere nearby." He studied the desolate area around the tracks. "Make sure they look for motorbike and bicycle tracks as well. Also, for any signs the body was dragged."

Harry nodded.

"And get warrants to search Ramsey's office and home. I want you to personally take charge of looking at all of the electronics—computers, mobile phones, everything. Quickly, before Von Zandt figures out a way to get there before we do."

"On that, guv. I'm sure Ramsey's been holding out on us. The bugger had to have more info on the accounts they were using than he admitted." Harry's freckled face folded into a grimace, a sign of concentrated thought. "And if he's got it, we'll find it."

"I want anything that could help us find who killed Ramsey, whether it leads to Von Zandt or not. But most of all, I want Von Zandt."

"Understood. All I need is one small end of the string to follow it somewhere else. Eventually we'll get there." Harry's self-confidence, justified as it was by the results he customarily got, gave Reid a small measure of hope.

Reid was suddenly anxious to leave. "I'm heading out now to update the Chief Constable. Let the local police know they're to make no statements to the press or anyone else about this, and that we'll be handling the investigation ourselves. I want the details kept quiet unless and until I decide to release them."

Harry held up a hand in acquiescence and headed toward where the scene of crime operatives were setting up.

On his way back to his car, Reid reached inside his coat pocket. Pressing the beads of his rosary together so hard he thought his fingers might bleed, he numbly marched the Latin words of the accompanying prayers through his mind.

At least the day couldn't possibly get any worse.

# Chapter 3

CID HAD MANY superbly competent detectives, but, in Reid's opinion, Detective Inspector Mark Lawrence was not one of them. DI Lawrence was arrogant and lazy. Unfortunately, he was also politically connected within the police force.

Reid had thought he'd minimized the damage Lawrence could cause by assigning the detective inspector parts of the operation that he was least likely to foul up. Something as simple as the round-the-clock surveillance of Richard Ramsey, a man who had a fairly regular pattern of activity, should have been easy. Even if Reid hadn't given explicit instructions that the surveillance on Ramsey was to be continuous, giving someone as junior as DC Parsons the discretion to make the decision to suspend surveillance was inexcusable. Any young officer would, no doubt, rather be tucked up in his own bed than sitting in a cold car all night, although Reid still found it difficult to believe Parsons had dropped the surveillance on his own. It just didn't jive with the young man's fervently expressed ambitions.

Reid glanced down from the road to check his mobile for text messages, something he knew he shouldn't do while he was driving. Nothing from Anne. He looked up quickly to make sure no cars were approaching, then hit the button for voicemail. Nothing. He put down his mobile as he merged into the roundabout.

Yesterday had marked six weeks exactly from when he'd left California, and six weeks had been their agreement. A cold hand squeezed his heart and his throat closed up. He knew what it meant that she hadn't called. After all, he'd been through this with her before. It was just that he'd been so sure this time. This time things between them had felt so right, like they were finally on the same page with what they wanted out of their marriage. But then he'd left California without her. That had been a mistake. A huge mistake in a long line of mistakes he'd made with his wife.

He hit speed dial for CID at Glasgow City Centre station, confirming with the officer answering calls that DI Lawrence was, uncharacteristically, actually in his office on a Sunday. Reid next made a quick call to Chief Constable McMurty to let him know he'd be by after he'd gotten some questions answered. At the moment, he had things to discuss with DI Lawrence. But to be honest, discussing things wasn't what Reid wanted to do. He wanted to beat the bloody hell out of the sabotaging arsehole. If they weren't able to stop the next terrorist attack in time, it would be down to Lawrence's idiocy.

The street outside the police station was Sunday city quiet. Without the bustle of people going to and from work and many nearby stores either closed for the day or opening late, the neighborhood had the feel of a deserted movie set. Quiet, empty, closed down.

Inside the station, Reid made his way to CID, his steps seeming oddly loud in the semi-deserted halls. He nodded curtly to the few people he passed. In the way he'd now become too familiar with, Reid saw the faces first merely register recognition, then snap back with more interest—the result of his recent descent into tabloid hell.

He spotted DI Mark Lawrence through the half-glass of the door that led into the main CID bullpen. Lawrence's dark blond hair was slicked back in the smug, vain, way favored by men who fancied themselves dangerously attractive, and the muscles that showed through his black too-tight t-shirt all but announced steroid use.

Reid opened the door in one swift move, the noise causing heads to turn toward him. DI Lawrence looked up from his position at the center of a circle of officers who were apparently hanging on his every word. None of the faces that turned toward Reid looked friendly, but DI Lawrence's expression was insolently hostile.

"Well, if it isn't Lord Reid, the golden wunderkind. What brings you to our humble abode? Slumming, are we? Or did you get lonely over in your private headquarters?"

The reference to his title had been made to rankle him, Reid knew, as well as to brand him further as an outsider to the watching officers. Reid wondered what lies Lawrence had been telling his audience.

"A word, DI Lawrence?" Reid kept his voice calm and expressionless as he sized up the situation. Definitely an enemy camp. The large room was broken up into work stations divided by chest-high partitions, but no one seemed to be working. The air reeked of bacon butties, burnt coffee, and political bullshite. With efforts in play to unify the Scottish police force, the jockeying for position and power had intensified, and along with it, the intricacy of political stratagems. The City Centre Police Office, the largest in the Strathclyde district, held more than its share of influential officers. Rumor had it that DI Lawrence's mentor, Chief Superintendent Steynton, a man known for his ruthlessness, was maneuvering to land the position of head of the new national force.

"Certainly. Go ahead, my lord." The mocking tone in Lawrence's voice made Reid want to dispense with all pretense at civility himself.

"Go ahead, Superintendent." Reid deliberately reminded the other man that he outranked him, even though DI Lawrence didn't actually report to him.

"Aye. Superintendent." The title came out as a sneer.

"In your office."

"Feel free to speak in front of my men, Superintendent. I don't keep secrets from them."

"In your office."

Something in either Reid's tone or his manner sent Lawrence's minions scurrying back to their cubbyholes.

Lawrence shrugged. He led Reid into a small office that had a window with a view of the street on one wall and three walls whose upper glass portions allowed the officers sitting in the general area to see inside. Lawrence took a seat behind a desk cluttered with piles of papers and file folders and motioned for Reid to take one of the two metal chairs on the other side. "So what's got your silk knickers in a twist this fine morning, Superintendent?"

"Richard Ramsey was murdered last night."

Muscles tightened visibly around DI Lawrence's eyes. "So I heard."

Reid wasn't surprised. Even though he'd tried to keep the news of Ramsey's death quiet, DI Lawrence had a lot of connections. Probably someone from the local force or even one of the scene of crime team. "Your boy Parsons, the one who was supposed to be watching him, wasn't anywhere around."

Lawrence hit a button on his computer's keyboard, displaying the investigation database. "According to the surveillance log, at eleven, Parsons reported that the cars were all garaged and the house was dark. He must have left after that."

"When exactly did he leave?"

Lawrence glanced at the screen, not seeming to be cognizant of the enormity of his team's failure. "Dunno. The log doesn't say."

"When was the next shift supposed to start?"

Lawrence looked at his watch. "Started at seven this morning. Brady was in front of the Ramsey house at seven on the dot, but I called him off once we got the news."

"And Parsons?"

"He's likely planning to update the log when he gets in."

"Which is when? I need to talk to him now."

"He's not scheduled back until tomorrow, but I left him a message to call in."

"Get him in here right away."

The detective inspector's glare could have sliced steel. "I don't see what you need to say that can't be said over the telephone."

"I want to talk to him in person."

Lawrence shot Reid an exasperated look, but pulled something up on the computer that looked to be a personnel directory, then dialed the telephone. Reid heard the faint ring on the other end, then a droning tone that he knew was saying to leave a message. After instructing Parsons to call in immediately, Lawrence hung up. "I'll send someone round to his house to rouse him."

"Now."

Lawrence clamped his jaw shut, but nodded. He hit the intercom and barked out an order.

When Reid had Lawrence's attention again, he said, "Dropping the surveillance was a major mistake, DI."

"No one dropped the surveillance. The man was in for the night."

Reid struggled to keep his voice calm. "So?"

"I give my men the discretion to terminate surveillance when it's clear the subject's tucked up for the night. Saves wear and tear on them and on the overtime budget."

"Ramsey apparently wasn't tucked up for the night as his body was on the railroad tracks on the edge of town this morning."

Lawrence thinned his lips, his eyes glowering at the implied rebuke. "And I suppose you blame Parsons."

"No, DI Lawrence, I blame you. Ramsey was supposed to be under surveillance around the clock."

"I don't recall anyone saying it was a protection detail. Simple surveillance is how I understood it."

"Around the clock surveillance or protection, neither one means your people take the night off and go home to watch the telly."

Lawrence shifted in his seat. "You can't expect me to make a man stay all night watching after everyone's gone to bed for the night. That would be a waste of manpower."

"That was not your call to make, DI Lawrence."

"Maybe you should be more clear about your expectations next time."

"More clear?" Reid spoke through clenched teeth, incensed by the other man's cavalier attitude. "More clear? How could I be any clearer than to say there was to be someone around the clock on Ramsey?"

Lawrence's back visibly stiffened. "As I recall, your orders were that the man was to be under surveillance when he was likely to be away from his home or office."

Reid tried to breathe back his anger while he scoured his memory for exactly how the order had been given. What exactly had he said? He'd been distracted by his worries about Anne, he knew, but he was fairly certain he wouldn't have mucked up such an essential order. No, he distinctly remembered saying the surveillance was to be around the clock. He tried to think. Who else had been there when he'd given the command? Then he remembered. DC Parsons.

"You and I both know that's not true. And Parsons knew as well."

"Superintendent, explain to me how anything Parsons could have done would have stopped Ramsey from committing suicide. He could have slit his wrists in his bathtub and having my man sitting outside the gate of his house wouldn't have stopped him."

"Who said it was suicide?"

DI Lawrence's face took on a wary look. "That's what I heard."

That narrowed Lawrence's probable source down to someone from the local cops, Reid thought. The SOCOs would have had better information.

"I'll be waiting to hear from DC Parsons. Have him call my mobile as soon as he's located. You'll be lucky if I don't decide to file a formal complaint against you for this."

"You're not exactly in the best position to do that right now, are you, Superintendent?"

Reid raised his eyebrows in a question, searching his mind for what DI Lawrence's snide comment signified.

The other man didn't make him wonder long. "A little birdie told me that this operation might not be yours much longer. I understand some of the brass isn't taking your recent notoriety well. They don't like the idea of one of their superintendents starring in sleazy tabloid stories and true crime shows about love triangles, kidnapping, and murder. So you'd best be nice to me. You need all the friends you can get."

Reid stood up to leave, letting the fantasy scene where he punched Lawrence hard in the face run through his mind, then drop away. "I doubt I'll ever be so hard up as to need you as a friend."

"Don't be so sure." Lawrence barely bothered to hide his smirk.

Something in his manner gave Reid an uneasy feeling that the other man knew something he wasn't telling.

# Chapter 4

"LOSING RAMSEY is a serious setback, but you'll have to find another way to get the information we need. We're chasing a lit fuse line." Chief Constable McMurty sat behind the ubiquitous government-issue blond wood desk chewing on a fat unlit cigar. Although in his late fifties, the chief constable had an athletic build that made his only average-sized body seem more powerful than that of many larger men. His mustache was bushy though his hairline had receded. Despite McMurty's outward compliance with the smoking ban, the telltale smell of cigar smoke hung in the room. Outside, the sound of sirens made a steady stream of background noise, police vehicles pulling out to respond to calls in regular intervals.

"Understood." Reid nodded, feeling more tired than he wanted to let on. He'd no sooner returned from California, exhausted emotionally and physically, than he'd been thrust into the middle of one of the worst international disasters in which Scotland had ever been involved. In a hideously brutal attack, over seventy innocent students had been killed, and dozens more wounded and maimed in an early morning bombing of a student residence hall at the university in Heidelberg, Germany. German authorities uncovered evidence tying the funding of the terrorist group responsible to a Scottish money connection, and when Interpol intercepted intelligence that a more coordinated attack on universities all over Europe and Great Britain was being planned, they'd known that there was a good chance the connection was the same man Reid's team had already been investigating—Walter Von Zandt.

"We can't afford any more delays." McMurty, the ranking officer overseeing the Strathclyde Police, had an air of comfortable and intelligent authority that inspired confidence and loyalty in the officers that served under him. Not a small feat, considering that the

Strathclyde force made up almost half of Scotland's police officers.

"No, sir."

McMurty expelled a sigh. "So now explain to me how someone got to Ramsey when he was under surveillance."

"The surveillance was dropped." There was no pretty way to say it.

"I'd figured that out. Why?"

"My question exactly. As you know, the surveillance detail was put under DI Lawrence's management." Reid had argued against having the CID team involved, but the urgency and high priority nature of the investigation meant internal politics came into play, and he'd been stuck with them.

"You've talked to DI Lawrence?"

"Aye, right before I came here. Lawrence tells me that he told his people surveillance could be discontinued once they decided the man was tucked up in bed for the night."

"That wasn't the plan."

"No, surveillance was to be around the clock." Reid tried to control how furious he was about the balls-up the CID team had made of the surveillance, and consequently, of the operation, knowing any show of emotion would weaken his position, but his words came out clipped and harsh.

"So DI Lawrence countermanded your order?"

"He did." Reid said, "And not for the first time. I know this situation is rife with political implications, but he needs to be taken off the operation. We can't afford these kinds of mistakes." Reid weighed whether to bring up what DI Lawrence had said about the brass's uneasiness regarding Reid's suddenly very public and messy personal life, and try to gauge from McMurty's response how much damage to his career the whole California debacle had caused.

"How did he explain going against your orders?"

"He doesn't agree that my orders specified it was to be round the clock."

"And did they?"

"Yes." Reid had hesitated for a mere fraction of a second before answering, but he knew McMurty had seen it. Although he was fairly certain he'd made his command that the surveillance be around the clock clear, if he were being brutally honest with himself, he couldn't be absolutely sure if he'd said that the surveillance was also for

Ramsey's protection. He took a breath, let it out. Surveillance was surveillance. Whether the purpose of the surveillance had been spelled out didn't matter.

"Were your orders in writing?"

"No, nor would they be expected to be."

"Was anyone else there that can back up what you told Lawrence?"

Reid nodded. "The young officer who was on duty was there when I gave the instruction. DC Parsons. We're trying to track him down and find out what happened."

McMurty pressed his lips together. "Let me know when you find him. If we can prove Lawrence disobeyed your orders, I'll go to Steynton and tell him we're pulling Lawrence off. Until then, it won't help you to ruffle any more CID feathers. Steynton hasn't forgiven you for getting the superintendent position he was championing Lawrence for. It's colored his support of not just you, but also of the task force. I wouldn't be surprised if he's hoping you'll fail." The unlit cigar went in and out of McMurty's lips. "I'm not saying he wants the human carnage that will result, mind you. He just doesn't want you to be the one to get the credit for resolving things."

"Understood." Reid's struggle to gain acceptance with his colleagues in law enforcement was an unending uphill battle. Reid's family was not only titled, but Roman Catholic in a country where that religion was a disfavored minority. To make matters worse, they were rich—filthy rich, some would say, due to owning one of the most prominent whiskey distilleries in the world. Some thought Reid's social rank and wealth gave him an advantage over his peers, but in truth it did just the opposite. He had to work that much harder to prove himself, besides being on constant guard for potential political attacks.

Since he'd returned from California, he'd worked just as hard as he always had, but he knew he'd been preoccupied on a visceral level. Reminded, he glanced at his watch, calculating what time it was in San Francisco. Maybe he should just call Anne. Better to get the bad news sooner rather than later.

McMurty misinterpreted Reid's interest in the time. "I know you need to go. What's your next move?"

"That's a good question. Obviously, Ramsey's death changes everything." In the weeks since Heidelberg, Reid had focused his efforts on recruiting Ramsey to turn informant, feeling the urgency to get the information in time to stop further attacks. In addition to showing Ramsey graphically horrific photographs of the carnage from the attack—the bodies of blameless young people lying slaughtered amongst the wreckage of the old building—he'd pressured Ramsey with threats to put a word in the ear of his contacts at Inland Revenue who would initiate an uncomfortable investigation into Ramsey's financial affairs if he refused to cooperate.

Faced with the horror of what he'd help fund, as well as fear of tax evasion charges, Ramsey had agreed to supply the information about the numbered accounts into which he'd been feeding his payments to Von Zandt. There was no guarantee that those accounts would be the same as those being used to fund the terrorist cells, but as Harry had pointed out, the information would have given them a valuable start at unraveling the thread that would lead to the information. The bitter taste of failure, like old onions and burnt garlic, coated Reid's tongue, and he remembered he hadn't eaten yet today.

Most importantly," Reid said, "We need to stop the rest of the attacks. And right now the best way to do that is to get the account information. Finding the accounts will help us trace where the money originated and where it ended up, or is supposed to end up. That could give us not only the conspirators ordering these attacks, but the actual bastards carrying them out."

"You think you can find the accounts without Ramsey?"

"I hope so. We're doing everything we can."

"And then?"

"Once we get the actual account numbers, we can confirm that the destination or the origination of the monies is tied to known terrorist factions. Then we can shut off the money spigot, trace it to the conspirators, and force them to turn over the dates and locations of the next attacks, so we can stop them from happening."

"If they even know the details. Often things are too compartmentalized."

"Aye." As he thought, Reid traced one of his fingers around the cold metal that edged the chair's arm. "We have to get someone high up enough to know."

"You're still sure Von Zandt's involved?"

"Up to his rotten neck."

"And you think Von Zandt actually knows names?"

"I do. If not, he'll likely know who does."

"Have you talked to Schilling?"

"Aye. I've kept him advised." Reid officially answered to two men: Chief Constable Martin McMurty of Strathclyde Police, and the Director General of SCEDA, the Scottish Crime and Drug Enforcement Agency, Deputy Chief Constable Rex Shreve. Unofficially, he also answered to Nelson Schilling, who, as the Deputy Director General of the Security Service, also known as MI5, was largely responsible for counter-terrorism for that agency. Schilling had been Reid's commanding officer when he was in the military intelligence service early on in his career, and had been instrumental in placing Reid in the position he was today.

"And does MI5 have any more intelligence?"

"They still think the next attacks are planned for right before classes adjourn for the summer—probably on the same day or at least close together."

"Any more clarity on locations?"

"The next targets are most likely Paris, London, Munich, and Florence. Which institutions in those cities, we don't know. Precautions are being taken under the assumption that it could be any of the universities in those cities."

"It's still not been on the news."

"No, they don't want to cause general panic, but the authorities are all in the loop, and the universities have been advised. No one thinks shutting every university in Europe is a practical alternative. But to be safe, all colleges and universities in Europe and the United Kingdom have been advised of the increased threat and are on alert as well."

McMurty nodded his head. "So being as you are stuck with him for the time being, what are you planning to do about DI Lawrence?"

"I'll keep an eye on him."

"Might be wise to keep your opinion that he bollocksed things up to yourself until we talk to Parsons. It's important that you're able to work well with CID. Having a special operations team as a liaison between our standing divisions only works if we get cooperation and buy-in from those divisions. There are too many who fought having a task force with as much independence as yours has. Bureaucrats are nothing if not territorial, but keeping them on our side is vital."

"I understand. Truth be told, I'm not anxious that the balls-up becomes common knowledge. We're working with a lorry load of international agencies, and if word gets out that we botched this by dropping surveillance on Ramsey at such a critical juncture, it could seriously undermine our credibility."

McMurty pondered for a moment. "At least perhaps DI Lawrence will realize he's under heightened scrutiny, and that he'd better cooperate."

"Maybe." But Reid knew Lawrence would never play nice. The remark the other man had made about the operation not being Reid's much longer thrummed against the back of Reid's mind. He resisted the urge to ask McMurty if there was any basis for Lawrence's insinuation.

McMurty shook his head in disgust. "And even though I think it's best that we leave Lawrence on the operation right now, I'll speak with Chief Superintendent Steynton and express my displeasure, which in turn, I expect, will result in Steynton calling DI Lawrence on the carpet. I'll make it clear that if anything like this happens again, Lawrence will not just be off the operation, he'll be lucky if he keeps his rank." McMurty slowly twirled the ill-used cigar around in his fingers.

"I appreciate that, and rest assured I'm taking measures to make sure Lawrence doesn't have the chance to foul things up again."

"Do what you need to do to protect the operation." McMurty lips formed a thin smile. "Whatever you need to do."

Reid nodded.

McMurty put the cigar down on top of a small plate that bore a suspicious dusting of ash. "How do you think Von Zandt knew Ramsey was talking to you?"

"No question someone is feeding him information. Not just about Ramsey, but also about the leads we've gotten on financial institutions where we've tracked down suspicious accounts. Every time we've gotten close to being able to pin down account locations, Von Zandt seems to have gotten wind of it, and suddenly, the money's moved."

"You think that someone in our organization is letting Von Zandt know when you're close to getting something." It was a statement rather than a question.

"It's the only explanation considering we've had problems no matter which of the various financial institutions were involved. Von Zandt has his fingers in many different pies, and informants in some of those places, I'm sure, but it stretches credibility to believe he has an informant in every bank or financial institution, or that Ramsey just happened to get himself killed this weekend."

"That does seem far-fetched. And there's no question that Von Zandt has his own political connections."

"Aye, I know. I also know that Von Zandt is ruthless with anyone he suspects of betraying him. We know Ramsey met with him on Friday, but we don't know what transpired at that meeting. I'd hoped to find that out when I met with Ramsey tomorrow morning."

"That's out now. Do you think there's any chance the leak is coming from DI Lawrence?"

"That might make sense if the information about Ramsey turning informant was the only thing that had been leaked. But Lawrence didn't have the information about the accounts we'd located, so I don't know how that could have come from him. So, as things stand, I don't have any reason to suspect it's him."

"Then who?"

"Everything that's been leaked was in reports that went to those in command in CID."

"You think the leak is from someone high up?"

"Not necessarily. All of those who are privy to the information have staff who may also have been given access to the reports."

"Obviously we need to make some changes. What exactly are you suggesting?"

"We need to limit access to information even more stringently than we've been doing, and minimize the amount of information we put in writing. I'll give you oral reports and you can share to those you deem necessary on a need-to-know basis, with the caveat that no one else—however trusted—be told."

"Agreed."

"Also, I'd like to bring in someone from Interpol to work with us on the international financial aspects. I want to be able to concentrate on Ramsey's murder and Von Zandt himself. When the news gets out about Ramsey's murder, we'll have the press all over us. The death of an industrial tycoon like Ramsey is news, and if it's murder, it's front page news."

McMurty frowned. "Interpol has a way of trying to take over our operations. They seem to consider Scotland a third world country."

"I know, but we could use their resources. I thought I'd suggest they send my sister. At least we can be sure of her loyalties."

"Good idea. Go ahead."

"Thank you, sir." Reid stood to leave. "I'd better be on my way."

McMurty got up from his chair as well. His face was grave. "We haven't had a chance to discuss what happened in California."

Reid felt his face heat. "Nothing to discuss. Everything is under control." There had been nothing in the tabloids for a few weeks now, and Reid was determined they'd have nothing else. No matter what happened.

McMurty nodded. "Good, I don't have to tell you that kind of publicity isn't something the department likes to see."

"Understood."

"We don't want you distracted."

"Understood."

"Don't let us down. There's too much at stake."

Reid took a deep breath, nodded. "I won't."

# Chapter 5

REID SWUNG BY the High Street office in his black SUV to collect Allison for the notification of Ramsey's wife. Allison was standing on the curb, waiting for him, a packet in her hand. The storefront of the narrow red brick building that housed their offices was covered with a discreet frosted glass treatment so that passersby could not see inside. There was no sign on the front of the building to announce what kind of work went on there: just the building number in simple black letters. The front door, like the back, was kept locked so that no one could wander in by mistake. Bordered by the urban camouflage of Johnnie's Fish Bar on one side and an Evangelical Mission office on the other, the High Street office garnered less than no attention from the casual observer.

For strategic reasons, Reid had not wanted to be situated in any of the various buildings that housed the different law enforcement agencies with which he worked. The entire police system in Scotland was in a state of flux, and Reid preferred to be out of the line of political fire.

Luckily, because of overcrowding at all of those locations, he'd had no difficulty in convincing his superiors that his team be headquartered elsewhere. The seizure of this narrow three-story building for illegal activities serendipitously occurred at just the right time, and Reid ended up with the High Street shop for his team's offices.

Reid's was an unconventional position. He was part of CID, yet apart from it, liaised with SCEDA, yet apart from it as well, and the location of his offices accentuated that separateness. That he was also affiliated with MI5 was known to only a select few. If and when the looming specter of a national police force became real, the Lord only knew what would happen to his job.

Allison opened the car door, bounced in, and fastened her seat belt immediately. As soon as Reid heard the click of the buckle, he pulled into traffic. Once he was safely in a lane, he glanced at the young woman in the seat next to him.

"Any word from DC Parsons?"

"No, sir."

Reid frowned. "Nothing?"

"I talked to his mum. She said he didn't come home last night."

"Did she think he might just be off with some friends?"

Allison gnawed on her lip, shaking her head. "She says he would have told her. She's that upset, sir."

Reid considered. It was very possible Parson's mother didn't know him as well as she thought she did. If Parsons didn't think he needed to report back to work until tomorrow, perhaps he'd gone to ground with a young lady and wasn't checking his mobile.

"And you checked in with the station again?"

"Yes, sir. They've still heard nothing."

Reid had a bad feeling. "Did they check with his work mates to see if they knew anything?"

"Yes, sir. No one has any idea where he is. It's like he's just vanished. I told them you wanted them to send someone out to search the area where he was last seen. They gave me grief, but I think they're doing it."

"Good." Tomorrow, if Parsons didn't report for work, Reid would make sure to escalate efforts to find him. For now, he decided to change the subject.

"This will be your first notification, won't it?" Reid had been given free rein to choose all of his team members. Allison was the newest, the youngest. She'd been a good addition to his team. He'd picked Allison out from the crime analysis unit of the Scottish Crime and Drug Enforcement Agency to be on his team. Her evaluations at SCEDA indicated that she was outstanding in her mastery of the required courses and skills, and although she was still green, he'd recognized in her a quickness that he knew would work well with the other team members he'd selected.

Learning that she had four older brothers with whom she seemed to be able to hold her own had sealed the deal for him. He'd wagered she would be able to also hold her own with the rest of his all-male team, even though they had more experience than she did. So far the young woman had not dis-appointed him. As a result, he'd been sending her to as many advanced training courses as came available, as well as trying to make sure she got all of the practical experience she needed to rise in the ranks.

"Yes, guv." Allison's face was somber, but her voice betrayed her excitement. As ever, she was eager to learn. "Thanks for bringing me along."

He grimaced. "Don't thank me yet. It's not going to be much fun." She would soon learn why this was one of the hardest parts of the job, and a part that most officers tried to avoid. But in a murder investigation, the notification of death could be one of the most important ways to get an impression of the real relationship the family had with the victim—before they'd had time to readjust their perceptions of their deceased family member. People not much loved during life often acquired the glowing qualities of a saint after death.

Allison didn't seem fazed. "All the same, I'm glad for the experience." She held up a large envelope. "Sir, Frank sent a packet of things he thought you might want to review before tomorrow morning. I told him I thought you'd be coming back to High Street, but he wanted to make sure you had them just in case you went directly home."

"Just put them in the glovebox." Frank Butterworth ran the administrative end of the High Street office from the wheelchair to which he'd been confined since he was injured in the line of duty as a Detective Sergeant with the Strathclyde police force. After Frank was injured three years ago, he'd undergone vigorous rehabilitation, but nothing he could do would enable him to use his legs—or his lower body—again. Consequently, his wife of fifteen years had left him for one of his able-bodied colleagues.

The thought of Frank's wife sent Reid's mind skittering back to his own wife. He resisted the urge to pull out his mobile again and check for messages or missed calls, running their last morning in California through his mind for what had to be the millionth time. Had she changed her mind about giving their marriage another chance?

Allison interrupted his thoughts. "Guv?"

"Yes?"

"I said, how do you decide what to say to the family?"

"Good question. Each situation is different. It depends on what you know about them and about the crime when you go in. Some of it is just playing it by ear. Experience helps."

She blew out a breath. "I wish I had more experience."

"That will come in time."

"Yeah, I guess."

"I promise you, it will."

"Sir, even without Mr. Ramsey's help, we'll be able to stop the next attacks, right? We won't let what happened to those poor students happen again, will we?" Her face searched his for confirmation, as if he actually could know the answer, and Reid wondered if he'd ever been so young.

"We're all doing our best, but I'm afraid there are no guarantees."

"When do you think they're planning to try again?"

"I wish I knew." They'd tried to figure out a likely date, but still had nothing more certain than that it would be this summer. The Heidelberg bombing had taken place on the day that many Sunni and some Shiite Muslims celebrated the birthday of the prophet Muhammad, so speculation was that the next attacks would also occur on a date of particular significance to the terrorists. From the few credible intelligence reports they'd received, it looked as if the Heidelberg bombing had been in the way of a practice run for the larger, more coordinated attacks being planned, and that likely the next attacks would occur simultaneously at different targets.

"Harry says that the group that actually did Heidelberg might have been one of the Hamburg jihads."

"Maybe so."

"Harry says that group was involved in the 9/11 attacks in the States."

"He does, does he?" Reid hid a smile at the repeated invocations of what Harry said, but was pleased to hear that Harry was taking his assigned role of mentor to Allison seriously. He'd noted some tension between the two early on, and had wondered if perhaps he'd made the wrong choice. But the brash young electronics expert was Reid's right-hand man and knew what Reid wanted often without him having to say a word, so Allison couldn't have a better teacher.

Allison frowned. "So, the Hamburg jihad blokes, are they German?"

"Probably not. Likely they're Muslim from a variety of

nationalities—but they organize out of Hamburg, and were probably trained in one of the terrorist camps in the Pakistani-Afghanistan border region. MI5 thinks a Nigerian extremist Muslim faction may be involved, and using the terrorist groups to do their dirty work."

Allison nodded. "So why now?"

Reid reached for the takeaway cup of tea in the drink holder next to him. He took a sip, screwing up his face as he swallowed the bitter, lukewarm brew, knowing his empty stomach would rebel at more acid being sent its way. "No idea, but they seem to be perpetually at war."

"Why target students? What did they ever do to deserve it?"

"I don't know why, Allison, but I suspect that it's because those kinds of attacks hit a country hard emotionally. Murdering so many young, innocent students garners more publicity than random, unfocused bombings. The publicity helps them recruit others to their cause."

Reid had arrived in Germany while the bodies were still being recovered from the rubble, and the horror of the grisly scene was burned into his brain, running just under his consciousness during the day, and erupting into his dreams at night. Night and day he'd been haunted by the urgent need to stop the next attacks.

"Why does a man like Von Zandt get involved in something like this? He's not Muslim, is he?"

"No, for him, it's all about money. He takes a healthy cut of the money as he launders it, and on anything else he does for them, such as supplying other items they want. Arms, in particular." There had been rumors that Von Zandt had a pipeline to munitions, and Reid suspected that Ramsey had known a lot more about that than he'd let on, and that perhaps the subsidiary of Ramsey International that manufactured supposedly legitimate arms, was being used by Von Zandt for his own nefarious purposes.

"It almost seems worse to do it for money than because you think you've got a holy mission."

"Money or religion, the result is the same. A blood bath of innocent people."

# Chapter 6

THE RAMSEY HOUSE, nestled securely in a prosperous neighborhood on the outskirts of town not far from the railroad tracks where Richard Ramsey's body had been found, was large, imposing, and tastefully whispered old money. The front drive was circled with beds of vibrantly orange tulips emerging from beds of soft white flowers. Reid could recognize a tulip, but he couldn't put a name to the white flowers. Anne would know, he thought automatically. He slipped his mobile out of his pocket as he got out of the car, quickly checked. Nothing.

The societal circles of the privileged in Scotland were tight enough to ensure that a family such as the Ramsey family would be in at least occasional contact with Reid's own prominent family. But that wasn't why Reid knew this house inside and out. He'd studied blueprints of the Victorian gray stone manor, as well as its security diagrams. He also knew a great deal more about Richard Ramsey's business dealings and family details than a mere social acquaintance would have known.

A young maid led Reid and Allison to the drawing room, a spacious room carpeted in plush oriental carpets and appointed with ornate antiques. Even before they entered the room, the sounds of a piano accompanied by a woman's voice singing an achingly poignant blues song reached them, pulling them in. Reid recognized the piece as one he'd heard on recordings by Billie Holiday, an American jazz singer. He knew the song. *Lover Man.*

Barbara Ramsey had a voice that made an ache spread through Reid's chest. She sat on a cushioned bench in front of a mahogany grand piano at the far end of the room. Long green sofas were positioned near a dark stone fireplace, and around the tastefully furnished room were additional groupings of chairs and tables. Vases of orange tulips punctuated by voluptuous white roses filled the room with a thick peppery fragrance that seemed to suit the mood of the music.

Mrs. Ramsey was probably fifteen years younger than her husband. She was attractive, her sable hair styled in a dramatic swinging cut, her dark eyes framed with softly thick brows, but something about her seemed blurred, almost ghostlike. Reid remembered hearing that she'd been working as a professional singer in a small club when she'd met Ramsey.

Reid signaled to Allison with his hand to let her know they were going to wait until Barbara Ramsey finished singing before trying to talk to her. He let himself feel the music, feel the emotion it held, knowing his news was going to change the woman's life forever.

The last words of the song still hung in the air, *Lover man, oh where can you be*, when she finally turned to them, her face almost instantly changing from the sensual softness it had while she sang, to a tentative, questioning frown. She stood up, came over to where they stood. Her glance took in Allison, registered puzzled, then went back to Reid.

"Lord Reid?" She smiled. "I'm so sorry, but my husband isn't here right now."

Reid took a deep breath. Telling Barbara Ramsey that her husband was dead wasn't going to be easy, but there was only one way to do it: state the facts and offer condolences. He led the woman over to a sofa, and sat down beside her.

"I have bad news, Mrs. Ramsey, and there's no easy way to tell you. Richard is dead."

"Dead? He can't be." She looked helplessly at Reid. "You must be mistaken."

"I'm afraid there's no doubt."

Stunned, she just kept shaking her head. "I need my son. I need Bert."

"Of course, we'll get him. Is he here?"

She nodded. "Upstairs."

Reid motioned to Allison to take care of finding the son.

While they waited for Allison to return with Bert, Barbara Ramsey hugged her arms against her chest and rocked back and forth, keeping her eyes tightly shut.

Allison came back in and nodded to Reid, indicating that she'd accomplished her mission. Not long after that, a young man appeared in the doorway, quickly crossed the room, and Reid stood up, vacating the seat next to Barbara Ramsey to allow her son to take his place.

Bertram Ramsey sat down next to his mother. She fell against him, and her face instantly folded into tears.

"Mother, what happened? What's wrong?" The young man pulled his mother close. He looked up at Reid in expectation of an answer. "Lord Reid?"

Reid sat down on the opposing sofa. "I've brought bad news about Mr. Ramsey. He's dead."

"Dead?"

Reid nodded. "His body was found on the railroad tracks just outside of town early this morning. We don't have a lot of details right now, but his body was hit by a train."

Bert Ramsey took the news in silence, rubbing his mother's back as he held her. But Barbara Ramsey suddenly seemed to become alert. She pulled her face away from her son's shoulder. "On the train tracks? In his car?"

Reid said, "No. His car was nearby, but not on the tracks."

"Then why . . ." She shook her head. "No, that can't be. He wouldn't kill himself, if that's what you're thinking. He absolutely wouldn't." Her voice took on a pleading tone. "You won't say he did, will you? I couldn't bear everyone thinking that."

"We're still investigating. We should have a report from the medical examiner by tomorrow, and we'll know more then." He wanted to tell her that it had definitely not been suicide, but he wasn't going to rush his forensic fences. He did need to give her something, though. "Right now we don't have any reason to think he did it deliberately."

She leaned back against her son, and started to cry again. "What am I going to do without him?"

Bert seemed at a loss for words to comfort his mother. He just held her while she cried.

Finally, her crying stopped, and she gulped in a breath. "I need a drink, Bert. Please get me a drink."

Reid remembered hearing that Barbara Ramsey had a drinking

problem, although needing a drink after receiving such news certainly didn't do anything to confirm that. Reid could have used a drink himself.

The young man hesitated just a moment, then got up.

Barbara Ramsey's soft sobs resumed, hiccupping through the room. She quieted only when her son returned and handed her a tall glass filled with vodka. She downed almost half of the glass's contents before stopping for air.

Bert's face was somber. "I think I'd better call the doctor and let my mother rest. This has been a shock. Can the rest of this wait until tomorrow?"

"I'll come back tomorrow, but I have a few questions that can't wait."

"What questions?" Bert's voice was neither impatient nor particularly interested.

Reid didn't answer, but instead directed his first question to Barbara Ramsey. "When did you last see your husband, Mrs. Ramsey?"

She looked at him blankly, then said, her voice quavering, "Last night."

"What time?"

"I'm not sure, but it was at dinner. I wasn't feeling well so I went up to bed right after the soup, I think?" Her eyes went to Bert as if for confirmation of her statement, and Reid realized she'd probably been many sheets to the proverbial winds and wasn't sure of her movements.

Her son nodded. "Actually, it was before the soup. Dad took her upstairs, then came back down to finish dinner."

"Did he mention to either of you that he was planning to go out later last night?"

Bert shook his head, answering for them both. "No."

"When did you see your father last, Bert?"

"I didn't see him again at all after dinner. My girlfriend was here, and we went up to my apartments directly after we finished eating."

Reid directed his next question at both Bert and Barbara Ramsey. "And this morning? Were you surprised he wasn't here?"

Barbara Ramsey sniffled and gave her head a little shake.

Bert gave more of an explanation. "He usually goes in to work early, even on the weekends. He and Mother have separate rooms, and she sleeps late, so he's generally gone when she gets up. I usually go in to work early as well, but not on Sundays, though this morning I was up early to take Patty home."

"Did Mr. Ramsey mention to either of you that he was assisting the police in an investigation?"

Bert frowned. "I don't understand." He looked at his mother for her answer. Her face tightened as if she were trying to comprehend what she'd heard, then she shook her head and tilted the glass to her lips, draining it.

Reid rose to leave. "We can talk about that later." He motioned to Allison to follow him. "I'll call tomorrow morning to set up a time to come back." He hesitated, then spoke, his tone deliberately nonthreatening, "Would you be agreeable to letting my people examine Mr. Ramsey's office, and other parts of your home, for evidence?"

"Evidence?" Barbara Ramsey turned confused eyes toward her son.

Reid focused his attention on Bert, knowing it would be him from whom permission would come. "It's routine in an unexplained death of this nature." He blessed the power of bureaucratic double-speak when no one questioned this bouncer.

Bert shrugged. "Go ahead, Mother, let them."

Barbara Ramsey looked into her empty glass as if trying to will it into refilling itself. "If Bert thinks we should."

Bert patted her hand, then took the glass from her. "I do, Mother." Then to Reid, "Will it take long?"

"No. They're just outside. I'll have them come in now." Reid moved quickly toward the door so as not to give the family the opportunity to reconsider. A warrant would take time, but with permission there was no need to delay. And he wanted Ramsey's computer before anyone else could get to it.

Bert Ramsey put his mother's empty glass on the table next to the sofa, then bent toward his mother and helped her to stand. He turned to Reid. "Will they need to go through her room? Father had his own room."

Going through anything other than the man's office and bedroom would have been unusual in the event of a suicide, but Reid knew this was a murder, and he wanted everything he could get before anyone called in lawyers.

"Yes, but why don't I have them start in there, then she can go in as soon as they're finished. It won't take long. Then they can move on to the other rooms and she can rest."

Bert considered, then nodded. "I'll keep her in here until they're through."

"Thank you. I have to leave now, but Detective Constable Muirhead will stay here."

Barbara Ramsey retrieved the glass her son had taken from her, and whispered something in his ear. Bert shook his head, and she frowned and said something Reid could not hear. Bert shook his head again and reached to take the glass from her. She waved him back with an unmistakable leave-me-alone gesture, marching over to the drinks table by herself.

Reid moved away and motioned to Allison to come closer so they could talk without being overheard. He kept his voice low. "I'm leaving you in charge. I'll be on my mobile if you need me. One of the search team can give you a ride back when you're finished."

Allison nodded and beckoned the waiting officers to start the search.

Reid went back over to where Bert was watching his mother fill her glass almost to the rim with vodka, his expression resigned.

"Bert, I'll need to speak to Moira also. Would you like me to call her and tell her about Mr. Ramsey, or would you prefer to do so yourself?"

The young man rubbed his temple. "I'll do it. If you'd gotten here just a little earlier, you could have talked to her yourself."

"She was here this morning?" Reid's scalp prickled.

"She didn't have classes today, so she came to work on Dad's computer. He was having some problems, and Moira's good with computers."

Reid's chest burned with the acidic knowledge that he'd arrived too late. Richard Ramsey's computer would have been wiped clean.

Moira was not just Richard Ramsey's stepdaughter.

She was also Walter Von Zandt's mistress.

# Chapter 7

REID MANAGED to make the last Mass for Palm Sunday at St. Andrew's Cathedral, and had even arrived in time to go to Confession. He'd taken a place in the back of the church, away from other worshippers. He'd not wanted to meet anyone's eyes, not wanted to have to shake their hands, or to mouth wishes for peace to be with them.

Back at High Street, Reid nodded in acknowledgement at Frank's news that there was still no word from DC Parsons, then closed his door and began reviewing last week's surveillance reports. He needed to figure out what Ramsey had been doing last night that had gotten him killed. Reid doubted the man had been kidnapped from his home and taken to the railroad tracks in his own car. He had to have been meeting someone.

Reid's mobile rang, startling him out of his concentration. His heart leapt as it had with every call he'd gotten since last week, when he'd begun expecting Anne's call. He glanced at the screen expectantly, but when he saw what the caller i.d. said, or rather what it did not say, disappointment swamped him once again. He hit the talk button and forced a lightheartedness he did not feel into his voice. "Hello, brat."

"Big brother."

Despite his ennui, he smiled at the sound of his sister's voice. "Ah, Darby. That was quick." He checked his watch. His younger sister, these past two years an operative for Interpol, had wasted no time in calling after Reid sent the request to Interpol headquarters in Lyon, France.

"I've just been given the assignment to work with your team.

Finally, it's paid off for me to have a brother in the same line of business. Did you really ask for me?"

Reid closed the file he'd been reviewing. "I may have mentioned that I'd prefer if it was you they sent to work with us. Better the devil you know and all that. Apparently you've been angling to get in on anything related to the Heidelberg bombing." His stomach growled and he realized he'd missed lunch. Breakfast as well. He'd just finished his morning run when he got the call about Ramsey's body being found. He'd been planning on going to the first morning Mass, so he'd waited to eat so he could take communion, then with one thing and the other, he'd never gotten around to eating. He could have ducked into his flat after Mass this evening to get something to eat as he lived directly next to the Cathedral, but his flat was devoid of food. Maybe he'd get a takeout curry on his way home.

"I was, yes."

"Great. Darby, just so you know, I asked for you specifically because I want to make sure that we get the right kind of help. This isn't Interpol's investigation, it's ours, and Interpol is only assisting."

"Whatever. I understand. You're in charge." Her exasperation bled through her excitement. Darby was the youngest in his family, and had been indulged perhaps a little too much. She was bright but had a tendency to be arrogant and headstrong. Reid had never had the same kind of issues with her that his parents or siblings had, though. She'd put him on a pedestal of sorts, and had always been fiercely loyal and protective of him. However, he had a feeling that it was just a matter of time before Darby's strongly competitive tendencies outweighed any youthful hero worship.

"Just so."

"You do seem to have a great deal of influence with my agency, Terrence. My stock went up immediately when people realized you were my brother. I didn't know you were so connected."

Of his family, only their father, the Earl, knew the extent of Reid's involvement in the intelligence community. "I've had occasional dealings with Interpol over the years. I've quite a few years on you."

"Ten, to be exact. You're practically an old man."

"Thanks so much." Reid felt old. Old and tired. Not like a thirty-six-year-old man should feel. Looking around his office, he thought, if this were a crime scene, no one would be able to discern anything about him from his surroundings. No family photographs, no diplomas or certificates, no art work, not even a personal mug. He'd had a photograph of Anne on his desk right after they got married, but when things between them went south, he'd taken it back to his flat. No need to invite unwanted comments or speculation.

"Don't mention it."

"Just so you know, it will be hard work and long hours. I expect it from everyone on my team, and you'll be no exception."

"Of course." She brushed off his words. "Hopefully we'll be busy past Easter. Mum's been on me to come home, and I've been putting her off. I'm guessing she's been on you as well. She says you haven't been back since Christmas, and not much before then."

Reid took a deep breath before answering. He'd avoided going to Dunbaryn since he and Anne had separated, though he'd always made a brief appearance for the major holidays. Last Christmas had been a nightmare with the lies he'd had to tell to explain Anne's absence for yet another holiday. He hadn't wanted to share his failure at marriage with his family. Of course, they all knew now.

"I don't expect either one of us will be able to get away for Easter."

"Good, gives me an excuse to give it a miss. You'll be wanting that as well, I'll bet. I don't envy you having to explain why you didn't tell them about being separated so long. Did you know Anne had a lover before it was in the news?"

"Darby, I'm not going to discuss this with you."

She ignored him. "I miss a lot being in France, but Pippa says the tabloids were putting it out that you two are back together. I told her she was bonkers if she thought you'd take the slag back. You won't, will you?"

"Darby." Reid knew his voice was harsh, but didn't care. "I'd better never hear you use that word about Anne again. What is between my wife and me is none of your business."

An exasperated sigh came from the other end of the line.

"All right. Keep your secrets; you always do. It's not like we're family or anything." A resentful tone in Darby's voice hinted that there was something more than simple sarcasm to her comment, but Reid didn't have the stomach to pursue it at the moment.

"Darby, do you want to talk about the case or not? I haven't got all night to chat."

"I do. So, did Ramsey really commit suicide?"

Reid wondered how that rumor had gotten to Interpol. "Doubtful. I'm still waiting for a report on the post mortem examination, but I suspect someone helped Ramsey on the way to hell and that the body was thrown on the railroad tracks to hide the fact that it was a murder."

"No kidding? Murdered?"

"Aye. There's no report from the medical examiner yet, but that's what I expect to hear."

She whistled in appreciative anticipation. "Brilliant." She stretched out the word triumphantly. "Much more exciting to have it be a murder."

"God, you're young."

"Stuff it."

He laughed. "Are you still in Paris?"

"Aye, but I'll be in Glasgow by tomorrow. You have a room I can stay in for a couple of days till I find a place of my own, don't you?"

He hesitated. "You want to stay with me?"

"Don't sound so enthusiastic."

"It's not that." He didn't know quite what to say.

"You've never minded before." Her voice instantly turned suspicious, and she exhaled loudly. "Oh, Jesus fucking Christ. Don't tell me it's Anne? Don't tell me she's there? Terrence, are you daft?"

Reid didn't say anything, trying to decide how much he absolutely needed to share with his sister.

"She is, isn't she?"

"No. And I don't appreciate your language."

"Then why can't I stay there?"

"I may have to go to the States for a few days."

"The States? Oh, I suppose the FBI's getting involved in the case. Don't worry, I don't mind staying at your flat by myself."

Reid wasn't going to correct her assumption that the FBI's interest in the Von Zandt investigation might necessitate his trip to the U.S. And he certainly wasn't going to tell Darby that he'd promised to fly to California to help Anne with her move to Scotland. If she moved to Scotland. At this point, the possibility of him needing to go seemed unlikely.

"Fine, then. You can stay with me for a couple of days." Even if Anne did call, it would take him a few days to go to California, get her packed up, and bring her back to Scotland. By then, Darby would be in her own place.

They discussed the case further, but right before the call ended, Darby's voice took on a studiedly casual tone. "So, is John Stirling in town?"

Reid smiled to himself. His old friend had long been a source of fascination for his hard-hearted sister, a fascination that was probably intensified by his friend's refusal to take any serious notice of her.

"Not that I know. Last time I spoke with him he was in Aberdeen. He's giving us some assistance on this investigation, though, and should be coming to town soon. You looking to see him?"

"Just asking. He's always fun to be around, unlike some people I know."

"Thanks for nothing. He's too old for you—and has a reputation where women are concerned."

"If I'm to mind my own business about your love life, perhaps you should mind your own about mine."

He had asked for that. "Deal."

"Besides, he's the same age as you are, and I'm about the same age as your precious Anne, so I don't see that you have any room to talk."

"Just so. I'll take my own advice then, and mind my own business." He'd seen no sign that Stirling was inclined to start taking notice of Darby, but she was right. It was none of his business. Through the glass on the top half of his office wall, Reid saw Harry directing placement of the electronic equipment that had presumably arrived from Ramsey's home, and occasionally conferring with Oscar Browne, the other electronic expert on Reid's team. He silently prayed they'd find something, but his expectations weren't high. "Come to my flat when you get in. The guest room is yours until we find you somewhere where you won't be bothered by your ancient brother."

"Sounds good."

"Safe travels." As Reid switched off his mobile, his office door opened and he heard the whirring of a wheelchair motor.

Frank held up a folder. "SOCO's report on the findings at the crime scene."

# Chapter 8

**R**EID TOOK THE REPORT from Frank without much
optimism. If Von Zandt was behind Ramsey's murder, Reid doubted
there would be anything much to find.

"You've read it already?"

"It only just came in while you were on the phone, but I looked it
over while I waited for you to get off the phone." Frank Butterworth
reminded Reid of a centaur from Greek mythology. His upper body
was overlarge, the muscles overdeveloped, but instead of the half
horse component, Frank's torso melded into the shiny metal
wheelchair that seemed to be part of him. After his injury, Frank, not
wanting to spend the rest of his life on disability, had returned to
work at a desk at Strathclyde Police Headquarters in his wheelchair.
When Reid was given the command of the task force, he asked that
Frank be assigned to work with him, and immediately delegated
responsibility for the day-to-day running of the office to the other
man.

"Anything interesting?"

"Some strands of dark human hair—no follicles, so no probably
no DNA for testing. And our man Ramsey was bald as a baby pig's
bum."

"From someone else, then."

"Actually, SOCO seems to think they're likely from a wig or
hairpiece. There are bends on the top of the strands from where they
were woven onto the fabric."

"A toupee."

"The strands look too long for most toupees, and from all reports
there was no sign of a hairpiece at the scene. I called Allison to tell

her to have the search team look while they go through the Ramsey house to see if there's any indication he used one."

Reid perused the report. "It looks like the Mercedes was wiped clean of prints. The unopened condom packet left on the floor of the car is interesting."

"The only prints on that are Ramsey's. There were also several more condom packets in the glove box with just his prints on them. Allison called and said they found what looks to be the rest of the box in Ramsey's bedroom. The bag they were in had a pharmacy receipt time stamped Friday afternoon."

Reid considered what he was hearing. "Surveillance had him at his doctor's on Friday afternoon before his meeting at Von Zandt's. No mention of a pharmacy visit, but I believe there's a pharmacy in the lobby of that building, so if Ramsey stopped in there after or before his appointment, surveillance might not have noted it."

"Makes sense."

"No sign of a murder weapon." Reid thought. "Did the ME call?"

"Aye, Tessa confirmed it was a stabbing, said you'll have to wait until she finishes for anything else. The body's too much of a mess for it to be easy."

"I thought that might be the case."

"You have an idea as to what the murder weapon might have been?"

Reid shook his head. "I'm not sure. The hole in the chest seemed to be more like a puncture than a cut. Whatever it was, it wasn't left on scene, so the killer must have taken it with him."

Frank frowned. "Him or her. What do you make of the condom packets?"

"Hard to have more than one interpretation on that, isn't it? The packets in the glove box don't necessarily signify, but the one on the floor is different. Ramsey had hopes of using it, either right then, or at some time between when he bought the box and when he died." Suddenly aware that this subject could be hard for Frank, who although only in his late thirties, was unlikely to ever need such items again, Reid quickly moved on. "And they had no luck with tire tracks, I see."

Frank looked levelly at Reid. They'd been friends since Reid's early days with the force at Strathclyde. "I don't want your pity,

Terrence. Nor do I want you walking on bleeding eggshells with me every time the subject touches something I can't do anymore. In return, I'll do you the favor of doing the same when it comes to topics that hit too close to whatever is going on in your life. And as that's bound to happen more often, you'll be getting the better side of the deal."

Reid gave a wry smile. "Agreed."

"Good." Frank went on with summarizing the evidence. "No on the tire tracks. Another car had been there, but they weren't able to get any usable tracks. The ground is too sandy and between the disturbance in the air from the trains rushing by and the wind itself, it doesn't lay quiet for long."

Reid flipped through the pages of the report. "Anyone see anything?"

"No, the officers canvassing the area couldn't find anyone who'd seen or heard anything helpful."

"Did the old man who found the body check inside the car?"

"He said not. We've got his prints, though, and we'll compare those with what we find on and in the car."

Reid raised his eyebrows. "You don't sound like you believe him."

"Don't know. Best to check."

"Aye. Tox results?"

"Not yet."

"Any news on the whiskey bottle?" Reid knew it could have been thrown down by anyone at any time. They needed to link it to Ramsey for it to mean anything. "The local cops' theory that he wandered, drunk, on to the tracks doesn't sync with the obvious evidence of him being murdered. He wasn't much of a drinker."

"Maybe not, but I'm thinking if Ramsey was going to that spot to have a bit of fun, there's a good chance he'd have brought some refreshments along for his partner and himself. Anyway, that's what I would have done, and I assume most men would do."

"Really?" Reid never would have thought of that. But then, he'd never taken a woman to a deserted lane to make love. He'd had lovers before Anne, of course, but he'd always conducted his brief affairs with discretion and decorum. He'd grown up in the detritus of his parents' marital scandal and the last thing he wanted was more of that.

Frank shook his head. "You're bloody socially backward, Reid."

Reid sighed. "Right. So, still no news from Parsons?"

"Not a word."

"Give DI Lawrence a call. Make sure he's had a search team out to where Parsons was last heard from. He should have called in by now, even if it is his day off."

"Got it."

"Then put together a statement for the press. I'll have to send it to McMurty for approval, but I've a meeting to brief Carolyn Caspary set up for Tuesday to put out the story we want the press to have." Reid had worked with the reporter for years and had made sure to give her regular exclusives so he'd have her ear when he needed it.

"First thing in the morning soon enough? By then we'll have more on what Allison's finding and maybe something from Harry and Oscar on the electronics. And hopefully the tox screen will be back."

"Morning is fine."

"I assume you're doing something about DI Lawrence?"

"Aye. First priority."

Frank gave a satisfied smile, turned his chair, and motored out, leaving Reid alone with his thoughts. He looked down at his mobile where it lay on his desk, willing it to ring, but it stayed silent.

Bloody socially backward.

# Chapter 9

"FUCKING BASTARDS!" Allison slammed the door of the High Street office behind her just before six that night.

Harry looked up, taking a quick inventory. She was practically trembling with anger; tears threatening to escape from her eyes. He looked over at Frank, who just shrugged. Oscar studied Allison from behind his thick eyeglasses, with no expression, as if she always burst in like a tsunami.

"Us, duck?" Harry ventured, trying to think what they could have done. He didn't think he'd committed any fresh outrages.

She flounced over to her desk, throwing her shoulder bag on the floor, and landing heavily on her chair. "Not you lot, though you're all the same."

"Ah, men in general, I'm assuming?" Harry relaxed. He'd heard this particular accusation before.

"Yes, and in particular, those stupid bastards doing the search. The Super left me in charge but they ignored me when I said anything, or rolled their eyes and said things like, don't worry your pretty little head about it, luv, we know what we're doing." She mimicked them, and Harry had to stop himself from smiling. "The worst was that prick Michaud who I ended up having to get a lift back with."

Harry tried to think what to say. "Don't let them rattle you, sweetcakes. So what did you do?" He marveled silently on how quickly this minister's daughter had picked up her colleagues' habit of profanity when agitated. She'd primly reprimanded him about his language for the first month she'd been on the team, then the first bloody had slipped out of her mouth and there'd been no turning back.

She puffed out a breath. "I told them, quite calmly, that it was my job to make sure the search was done the way the Super wanted. They just smiled at me in their stupid way and pretended to agree, then went on doing whatever they wanted. I had to practically pitch a bloody fit to get them to do what I needed done."

Harry rummaged around in his mind for what she would expect—no, want—him to do. "Do you want me to talk to them?"

She screwed up her face in horror. "Are you kidding? That would just make it worse. Like I went crying about it to my big brother or something. Absolutely not. I'll handle it." She looked over at the closed door to Reid's office. "Is he in?"

Harry nodded. "He'll want your report."

Her back stiffened, and he could see her donning the professional poise at which she worked so hard to present to the guv. "Right. I know. I'm just getting myself calmed down, then I'll go in."

Oscar went back to his computer screen, but Frank brought Allison a cup of tea, motoring his wheel chair automatically, rather than the manual mode he preferred when he didn't have his hands full.

She nodded. "Thanks."

Frank handed her two sugar sachets. "I imagine it's rough being a woman in this business sometimes. Being young doesn't help, but it'll get easier."

"I know. Still, it's a lot of aggro."

Harry said, "I'd have . . ."

She interrupted, her voice impatient. "It doesn't matter what you'd have done. It's different when you're a man. You lot have your own ways of letting each other know who's in charge or that you'll beat each other's brains out or something. I can't do it the way you do it—or how the Super does. I have to find my own way. I just wish I wasn't so young."

Frank shook his head, his face serious, though Harry saw the flicker of a smile before it was skillfully suppressed. "Don't wish that away too soon. Eventually you won't be."

"Or so small." She added.

Frank pondered, then said, "You could eat more and get fat."

Allison gave a rueful smile. "Might be an idea." She pulled her notes out of her bag and stood up. "At least then maybe the bastards wouldn't ask me out after not giving me any respect on the job." She pushed her hair back from her face. "On that subject, if that arsehole Michaud calls while I'm in with the Super, tell him I'll call back when hell bloody freezes over."

Harry cocked one eyebrow. "He asked you out?"

"Him and Boyle and Wolfe as well. Not in front of each other, of course."

He shook his head and stood up. "You're right, you'll have to figure out your own way. That never happens to me." He motioned to Reid's door. "I'll go in with you—I want to hear about the search."

Allison made a face, marched to the door, and knocked. After Reid called to come in, she opened the door and went in, Harry following behind. He leaned against the wall while she took the chair Reid indicated.

"All finished?"

"Yes, sir."

"Everything went all right?"

She nodded. "Fine. They didn't find much. No papers or anything. Nothing in his room or his wife's of too much interest. No hairpiece. His son said he'd never seen him wear one. But Mrs. Ramsey had about a dozen wigs in the attic from when she used to sing professionally. We took those to compare against the strands. Also, there were some prescription meds there—I bagged them for the medical examiner to compare with whatever she finds."

"Good."

"There were some porno mags and a collection of DVDs of the same ilk. Nothing too deviant." Her voice was businesslike, but spots of bright pink dotted her cheekbones.

Harry almost smiled. What would a curly-headed milkmaid like her know from deviant? No wonder the lads had a hard time taking her seriously.

"You checked the DVDs to make sure they were what they said they were?" Reid asked, his face patient and noncommittal, although Harry assumed the guv had the same thought as he had.

"I brought them back with me. The lads were a little too interested in playing them and I didn't want to waste time in the house doing that." Allison's cherubic face registered disapproval. Harry pursed his lips in restrained amusement; they hadn't completely corrupted her yet.

Reid nodded. "And the computer?"

"I had them copy anything remotely promising, but nothing seemed of any interest to us. The hard drive was new. It looked to have been replaced recently and the files seemed to be ones that had just been transferred over from the old one."

Harry wasn't surprised at that after what Reid had told him he'd learned from Bert Ramsey.

Allison went on. "I asked the son about it. He said his father had mentioned having to replace the drive because of a virus."

"Did he say when?"

Harry knew Reid had heard Bert's story already, but was asking because he wanted to make sure the young man's explanation had stayed consistent.

"His father complained about it last week, but Bert thinks it got fixed this morning."

"By whom?"

"His sister." She glanced down at her notes. "Moira."

Harry made a face, and Allison gave him a quick puzzled look. He raised his eyebrows in a tell-you-later look.

Reid's face, however, didn't show any reaction. "Where's the drive that was supposed to have the virus?"

"Bert didn't know."

"You had the search team look for it?"

Harry watched to see if Allison would betray any of the trouble the officers had given her, but she didn't blink or hesitate.

"I did. They weren't able to find anything like that."

"Any other computers in the house?"

She shook her head.

"Bert lives there as well, doesn't he?"

"Yes, but he says he uses his work computer. A desktop at the office."

"Likely anything on Ramsey's computer implicating Von Zandt, if it ever existed, isn't there anymore."

"I'm afraid not, sir."

"Anything from the other family cars that looked like they had been at the crime scene?"

Harry held his breath, wondering if Allison had thought to have them checked.

She gave a satisfied nod. "I knew you'd ask that. Those lads on the search team thought that was overreaching with no suspects and the house likely not being the crime scene. But we checked, and no, there was nothing. All in all, the search was a nonstarter."

"Can't be helped. If there's nothing to find, we can't find anything. The search team was thorough?" Reid raised his eyes, appearing to seriously gauge Allison's response.

"Yes, guv."

"Good job, then." Reid smiled his approval and Harry saw Allison relax, pleased and proud.

"Thank you, sir." She stood up, all efficient and eager. "I'll just get on with things, then. Bert Ramsey signed a consent to search his father's office at work as well and called security to tell them to give us access. I think we should just bring Richard Ramsey's work computer back here so it can be gone over thoroughly. We've got overtime approval."

Reid frowned. "It's Sunday afternoon, Allison. I doubt that you'll be able to get enough officers . . ."

She waved her hand airily as she moved to the door. "The lads from the search are waiting for my call—I warned them they might be needed again. We'll just go out and get it done quickly. I may have to stand them a round after, though."

"That's fine. Get a chit and have Frank reimburse you." Reid looked at Harry as the door closed behind her. "So she had no trouble with that lot?"

"Nothing she couldn't handle, looks like."

"Any joy on the bottle?"

Harry was glad he could report some progress, paltry as it was. "Ramsey's prints. Some lipstick on the rim. They're running more tests to see if it can be i.d.'d."

"Good."

Harry moved toward the door. "By the bye, Lawrence has called three times asking if he was needed to help with things."

Reid raised his eyebrows. "And?"

"The first two times I told him he and his lads weren't needed just yet. The third time, I assured him they'd done quite enough to help and that we would call if we needed any more surveillance dropped or anything else fed up."

The telephone rang. Reid picked it up and motioned for Harry to stay. He listened and his face turned grim. After he hung up, he looked at his sergeant, and Harry knew the news was bad. "Parsons?"

"Aye."

"He's been found?"

"Aye."

"And?" Harry knew what Reid was going to say next, knew in that way you feel when hope swirled down a sucking drain.

"He's dead."

# Chapter 10

REID AND HARRY spent long hours at the High Street office that evening going over how to reconfigure the operation in light of Ramsey's death, and as a secondary goal, to figure out whether, or perhaps more to the point, how, DC Parson's death was related to Ramsey's. Having both the man being watched and the man watching him, turn up dead was more of a hard lump of coincidence than either of them could swallow.

The search team had found Parsons' body hidden in some brush along a road not too far from where he'd been stationed to keep an eye on the Ramsey house. According to the report Reid got, it looked as if the young constable been hit by a car—a victim of either a deliberate or accidental hit-and-run. Reid leaned heavily to the deliberate.

Reid's desk phone rang. He answered, not very surprised to hear DI Lawrence's angry voice on the other end.

"Not only did you get one of my lads killed, but you've left me the dirty task of dealing with his family. Thanks ever so much, Superintendent."

Reid restrained himself from saying what he wanted to say, that whatever had happened to Parsons could, at least in part, be traced back to DI Lawrence's irresponsible manner of managing his team. If Parsons had been expected to check in periodically throughout the night, when he failed to do so, someone would have gone to check on the lad. Maybe he could have been saved if he'd gotten medical attention in time.

"We're all grieved by the loss, Mark. I'll talk to Parsons' family if you'd prefer."

Reid could almost see the other man's surprise through the telephone.

"Yes, well, maybe that would be best. I've a lot to do here trying to keep the rest of my people calm. They're blaming you, of course."

Of course they are, Reid thought. With DI Lawrence's encouragement.

"What exactly am I being blamed for?"

A pause, then Lawrence spit out, in a voice that held more bluster than sense. "It's your operation, isn't it?"

As the Reid family's longtime cook would say, that was the outside of enough. He heard the snap in his own voice. "Actually, the surveillance portion was yours, as I recall. I'd hope that in the future, you'd make sure your surveillance teams have a check-in and back-up routine. But I don't see that this discussion is getting us anywhere. Give me the family's contact information and I'll reach out to them. Have they been informed of his death?"

"Yes." The sulk in the CID officer's tone was unmistakable.

"I'll make a visit." Not that anything he said could make things better. Nothing could blunt the tragedy the young man's family was living right now. Reid thought about all of the young people killed and injured in the Heidelberg bombing and their families. If he wasn't able to stop the next attacks, the death toll would be unimaginable.

The mood at High Street was somber. No one complained about working late on Sunday, but then they never did.

Allison, back from the Ramsey office search and a quick visit to a pub to reward her team, was still shaken by the news about Parsons that had greeted her on her return. She was working with Frank to set up two crime boards—one for their eyes only, and one that could be used when DI Lawrence or his people were around. Reid was not going to let Lawrence damage this operation any more than he already had. If there were more screw-ups, they would be his own.

Implementing the plans they'd developed, Harry, earbuds tucked in, sat in front of the computer screen. His fingers flew along the keyboard and he bounced in his seat, presumably in accompaniment to the music being pumped into his head. Harry Ross haled from a lower middle class family in Dundee, but had as much confidence as if he'd been descended from the Royal Family. After serving in the British Army's Special Forces, he'd joined the Glasgow police. When he'd heard about Reid's task force, he'd shown up one day at Reid's first makeshift office in the basement of SCEDA headquarters to sell himself as a prospective team member. Reid quickly ascertained that the young man's cocksure attitude was justified, and Harry soon became Reid's de facto second-in-command.

Harry pulled the earbuds out. "Guv, got a moment? I'd like to show you the extra security I've set up for our ESI." More and more, electronically stored information had become the heart of any investigation, and it most especially was for this one.

Reid went over to Harry's computer station to watch, taking a place next to Oscar.

"Enlighten me."

Harry beckoned to Allison. "Come on over here, little bird, so I don't have to repeat myself."

Allison scowled at the appellation, but nonetheless joined them.

Reid inclined his head toward Frank. "You, too, Frank. We all need to know what's what."

When Frank maneuvered his wheelchair over to the computer, Harry began. "I've set up the site to look like whoever gets on with the password they've been given has full access. What DI Lawrence and his minions won't know is that certain passwords open up a broader version of the site. He doesn't get one of those passwords, of course, and won't even be able to tell that more information is here, but hidden."

Reid nodded. "I want you to make sure the firewalls are impenetrable from outside our team—no one, no matter how high up, gets access to our files. Von Zandt obviously knows we're on to him, and if he was involved in what happened to Ramsey and Parsons, I'd guess that somehow he found out that Ramsey was talking to us and decided to stop him. Parsons was most likely collateral damage."

Harry said, "I'm guessing either whoever killed Ramsey spotted Parsons, or Parsons spotted them." Harry's conjecture made sense, Reid thought, but there was another possibility. "They might have known about the surveillance and known to look for Parsons."

"The leak?"

"Aye. The more I think about it, the more convinced I am that the leak is somewhere higher up the chain. Maybe from the reports that we've been sending to the brass at CID. McMurty's given the okay to stop the reports, and we'll keep things closer to our vests."

"If the leaks were coming from someone getting into our computers, that's not going to happen anymore. No one will get in but us now, guv. I've sewn it up tight as a virgin's . . ." Harry stopped, glancing at Allison. "Tight, anyway."

Allison rolled her eyes.

Reid pretended not to notice Harry's slip or Allison's reaction. "I want you all to assume that he or someone on Von Zandt's behalf may try to get to one of us, either by bribery or by threats, to get information or to dissuade us from what we're doing. If anyone approaches any of you, I want to hear about it immediately."

Harry narrowed his eyes at Allison. She glared back at Harry, giving a little warning shake of her head, and Reid wondered again if assigning her Harry as a mentor had been a good idea.

Reid watched the exchange. "Something you want to say, Harry?"

Harry feigned nonchalance. "I was thinking if they tried threats on anyone, they'd try the bird first." He gestured toward Allison, who swatted his hand away.

"Sod you." The coarse words coming from Allison only elicited a grin from Harry.

"Stop it, you two. This is extremely serious." After quick apologies were mumbled from both transgressors, Reid went on. "It could be any one of us. I want you all to be especially mindful of your personal security. If they're murdering witnesses and cops, they're taking this investigation very seriously and very personally. Harry, I'd like you to help Allison get firearms qualified as soon as possible."

The red haired man's mouth went agape, and alarm flashed in his eyes. "She's a baby, guv."

"She's police. Start tomorrow." Unlike in some other countries such as the United States, not all police officers in Scotland were firearms qualified. That qualification was limited to those officers who were actually expected to have a need to carry or use a firearm. The regulations kept getting tighter and tighter, but because of the unique character of the High Street taskforce, Reid's people were approved for firearm qualification eligibility. Allison was the only one on his core team not yet qualified.

Allison's face could hardly conceal what seemed to be something between excitement and a smirk. Reid wanted to smile at her youthful enthusiasm, but didn't let himself. Frank, however, smiled widely. Oscar, who was almost as good a shot as Harry, just watched.

Reid made sure his voice carried the seriousness that his message implied. "All of us need to be careful. These people are not to be taken lightly and they most definitely do not like what we are doing here. I do not want any of you to end up like DC Parsons."

# Chapter 11

IMMEDIATELY UPON entering his flat, Reid tensed. Something was off. He could not say exactly what alerted him, but he knew that he was not alone. He did not turn on any lights, but instead allowed his eyes to adjust to the dark. Artificial city light, coupled with moonlight, filtered in through the wall of windows spanning the entire length and breadth of the side of his flat facing the Cathedral, providing enough illumination for him to make out shapes and shadows.

He briefly considered leaving and calling for back up, but for reasons he couldn't explain, instead closed the front door quietly behind him. He listened, his senses on hyper alert. A clock ticked in the background, the refrigerator hummed, a faint clicking signaled the radiators at work. Nothing else, but he knew. He was not alone.

Cautiously, he pulled his gun out of the pancake holster that nestled on his belt against the small of his back. He moved through the flat in the dark, his firearm at the ready, going through each room, starting with the kitchen. The kitchen, dining room, and lounge, all open to each other, made up the central part of his flat. A loft, tucked against the second story of his flat opposite the glass wall of windows, functioned as his home office. Down a short hallway at one end of the lounge was a guest bedroom and bath. On the other side of the main living area, down another short hallway, were his own bedroom and bath.

He saw no signs of an intruder as he passed through the main living area toward the hallway down which the guest bedroom was located. He opened the door slowly, looked around. Nothing seemed to have been disturbed. He approached the closet, and, standing to the side, opened the door. Nothing. He checked the bathroom. Again, nothing.

Silently, he returned down the hall to the main living area and quietly ascended the stairs to the loft. Seeing nothing amiss, he checked the drawers of his desk. Still locked. He went slowly back down the stairs and crossed the lounge to the hallway toward his own bedroom. The door was shut. He frowned. He was positive that it had been open when he'd left that morning. He took a deep and silent breath, turned the door knob, and carefully pushed the door open.

Nothing happened.

Reid turned his body sideways to look inside the room without making himself too easy a target. He let his eyes adjust to the deeper darkness of this room, shrouded as it was with thick shades closing out any light from the windows. Now the sense of another person's presence was overwhelming. He stopped breathing for a moment so he could hear better, but he couldn't stop his heart from hammering furiously.

He drew in a breath, fingered the trigger of his gun, preparing himself to react instantaneously. Scanning the room quickly, he stopped at the sight of a large suitcase lying open in one corner. His tension evaporated immediately, and he smiled.

In his bed, fast asleep, lay the intruder—a beautiful blonde, her face softly hugging one of his pillows and one of her long, bare legs flung outside of the covers.

He replaced his gun in its holster. Going over to the bed, he bent down and kissed his wife, enjoying the sleepy arousal of her soft lips.

"Goldilocks, I presume?" He moved his lips back to hers, kissed her again.

"Terrence." She put her arms around him, pulling him close.

He moved back just enough to see her face. "Lass, you should have told me you were coming. I've been half mad with worry." He reached down past the lacy front of her nightgown to cup her breasts. "God, I missed you." He kissed her again, long and deep. She smelled of sleepy clean woman. His woman. His fingers traveled through her silky hair, trying to convince himself that she was really here, that the waiting and worrying was over.

"I need to talk to you." She was struggling to speak through his kisses, but he couldn't wait.

"No talk just now," he whispered as he slipped into bed with her. "Time enough for that in the morning. Right now it's not talk I'm wanting." He felt her yield to him and his mouth and give up on conversation.

# MONDAY, APRIL 6

# Chapter 12

**R**EID RETURNED to the bedroom with two steaming mugs of tea. This morning he'd reached for her, and once again she willingly and enthusiastically opened to him with that melting response he loved. The utter luxury of having his wife in his bed was something he didn't think he would ever take for granted. Two years married, and it had not happened often enough.

Anne, her eyes still languid with sleep, patted the space next to her. "Come back to bed. I missed you."

"I'm coming. Here's tea. Regular for me, and herbal for you, as requested. Is this something new you like, girl?" He gestured to the mug that smelled to him disgustingly like wet, hot grass.

She made a face. "It's supposed to be healthier."

"Ah, well, then, drink up. I certainly want you to be healthy." He put the mugs down and took her soft body into his arms. "God, Anne, those were the longest six weeks I've ever known."

She ran her hand through his hair as she softly kissed his face all over.

He smoothed her hair down, then formed a ponytail with his hand. "You've let your hair get longer. I like it." He twisted her hair gently into a rope and lifted it up so he could kiss the spot on the back of her neck that always made her breathless. He loved that spot.

She shut her eyes and he saw her go weak, loving her predictably sensual response. One of the loveliest qualities of this woman was her easy arousal. He ran his fingers down her back to where her body touched the bed. She arched to him, and he held her.

"I've got something I want to show you as soon as I can stand to let go of you for a moment."

"I really need to talk to you, Terrence."

He smiled and lay down next to her on top of the sheets. "And I, you. We have a lot to talk about, and years to talk about it now that you've come. But just now I've something to show you. Indulge me for a minute."

She nodded and leaned over to pick up her nightgown from the floor beside the bed. When she started to put it back on, he caught her hands to stop her.

"Oh, no, you'll not cover up that pretty body just yet. I've been a man alone on a deserted island too long. Stay naked for me." He trailed his hand across her breasts and down her stomach as he watched her eyes slip back into that lovely unfocused look she got when she was aroused. She put her arms around him, and took his ear lobe into her mouth. Shivers went through him. Releasing her mouth from his ear, she pulled him to her.

"It's chilly without you." She lifted up the sheets invitingly. "Come under the covers with me. You don't want me to freeze."

His eyes went to those naked legs, momentarily focusing on the mound between her thighs. Oh, God, was she really his? He swallowed, "I'll join you in a minute, I promise. Back under the covers, but stay naked, if you please."

She smiled. "I please."

"You please me, indeed."

He took a folder from the table beside the bed and handed it to her. "There now, open it." Reid studied her face as she took the folder from him, her mind still obviously on sex. Her eyes did not look at what she held in her hands, but instead stayed on him. She caught her bottom lip with her teeth.

"Don't bite that lip, Anne. That's my job." He leaned down to her, took his finger to release her lip from her teeth, then moved his mouth to hers. Her lips parted and she met his with the intensity he adored. When the kiss finally ended, he pulled her bare body against his so her back curved into him. With more self-control than he'd known he possessed, once again he put the packet in her hand. He wanted to see her reaction, to please her with what he'd done. He could look over her shoulder as she read, and while he was at it, kiss her neck.

"Go on, open it." His hands caressed her breasts and then roamed down her body. He felt her relax for him as he touched her softest parts.

"I can't concentrate while you're doing that, Terrence." She closed her eyes and her lips parted slightly, and he sensed her breathing slow in receptive invitation of his kiss. "But don't stop. Can't we look at this later?" The papers fluttered to the floor and he gave up, with no real regret for her inability to disregard passion for practicality.

Later, much later, he watched her lovely bottom as she reached down to the floor and gathered up the papers that had fallen out of the folder. She hopped back into bed and leaned back against the pillow, propping the papers up against her naked legs so she could review them. He leaned toward her and caught her nipple lightly in his teeth.

"Terrence, if you start that again, I'll never be able to look at these." She laid back and closed her eyes, her hips arching up almost automatically.

He moved his mouth to her other breast. "Why can't you do both?"

"It's too distracting—but in a wonderful, lovely, achy way. I've missed you too much, and if you do that, I can't think. So make your choice. It's up to you."

Reluctantly, he released her. "All right. No hands, no mouth. I want you to look at what I've brought you—for a few minutes, anyway."

She smiled, and started examining the papers he had given her. When she spoke, he heard her confusion. "A house?"

"Aye, our house. I bought it for us directly after I got back from California. It's a good location—perfect for us—and I knew if I didn't snap it up, it would be gone. It's on a little cul-de-sac called Aytoun Lane." He took her hand, pressed it to his mouth. "I'd like to take you to see it today."

He studied her face, and not seeing the happiness in it he had hoped for, worried about her silence. He'd wanted to do something concrete to show his faith that she would actually be coming back to him. Buying a house for them to live in together had been the only thing he could think of that even came close to expressing how he felt. But now he realized that selecting it by himself might have been a mistake. "Are you upset I chose it without you?"

She shook her head. "No, it's beautiful. Absolutely lovely." Her eyes, huge and deeply blue, looked up at him, and his heart swelled with his love for her. But it worried him that she still did not smile.

"Not large like Dunbaryn. We have that, of course, to go to, but in town we don't need anything so immense."

"Terrence, this house is huge. Dunbaryn is a castle." Still, she did not smile, and his heart fell. He definitely shouldn't have chosen it without her. When would he ever learn? Bloody socially backward.

"Lass, if you don't like it, we'll sell it. You can choose something else you like. I'll want anything you like." He kissed her. "As long as you're in it, it will suit me fine."

"No, it's perfect. I love it." Now she smiled, and he was instantly relieved. He wanted her to be as happy about the house as he was. He could tell she meant it, and he went on to describe it to her.

"It has a large garden—I thought you'd like that. And rooms, lots of rooms for children."

She suddenly looked stricken and the smile fell from her face. He cursed himself. He'd scared her before when he'd brought up the idea of having children too suddenly. He ran his finger around her mouth and kissed her. "When you're ready, girl. I'm not rushing you. Not until you're ready. I've learned my lesson. I'm thick, but I'm learning."

She put his face in her hands and kissed him back, her eyes moist with emotion. "Oh, Terrence, I love you so much."

"And me, you. It's truly all right with you?"

"It's perfect. I love it."

"Wonderful. Let's go see it. I can take some time this morning before I need to get back to work." He patted her on the bottom, letting his fingers wander until she slapped at him playfully.

"We'll never get out of bed if you keep doing things like that."

"Get dressed, then, my beautiful wife, before I can't stop myself."

Anne stood up and she suddenly looked sick. Her face was pale and there was a bead of moisture above her lip. Instantly, worry filled him. "What is it, girl? Are you ill? You look a bit off."

She shook her head but hurried to the lavatory. "No, I'm fine. I'll just go wash up."

He let his eyes follow her, pushing away the thought of the visit he would make to DC Parson's family that afternoon. Time enough for that later. For now, he could be happy.

# Chapter 13

ANNE QUICKLY closed the door of the bathroom, flipped on the fan, turned the taps on full bore, and threw up as quietly as she could manage.

When her stomach was completely empty, she slumped to the floor and sat with her face in her hands. Her face still felt clammy, but at least the nausea was gone. Momentarily, anyway. How long did morning sickness go on, she wondered.

She had wanted to tell him, knew she had to, but she just couldn't. He looked at her with so much love. He'd bought them a house. Oh, God, a house with rooms for children. His children. He was going to be so crushed, so angry, and what if she lost him forever this time? She knew she couldn't avoid telling him much longer, and when she did, he would know instantly that there was a good chance the baby wasn't his.

She washed her face and brushed her teeth. Better, but the smell of her sickness still hung over the room. Cranking open the window to let in fresh air, she tried to think what to do. He had a right to know, and it wasn't fair to let him think things were okay when they weren't. But she'd missed him so much. She needed time with him.

A knock on the door startled her.

She cleared her throat. "Yes?"

"Are you all right?" Terrence's voice was full of concern.

She drew in a deep breath, put a smile on her face, and called out. "Fine. I'm just going to take a quick bath and get ready to go."

"Okay if I come in?"

Her eyes assessed the room quickly for any signs she'd been throwing up. Seeing nothing, she opened the door. "Of course."

He gave an apologetic grin. "I'd make breakfast but I haven't any food. I can run down to a shop and get something. What do you want?"

She wrinkled her nose before she could stop herself, and he misinterpreted her distaste at the thought of food for disapproval.

"Hey, I didn't know you were coming."

Arching her eyebrows, she covered her gaffe. "I'm not hungry yet, but if you don't have food here, you probably haven't been eating properly."

He leaned in to kiss her. "I eat fine. Just not here."

She met his lips, kept hers closed. If he tasted her mouth, even though she'd brushed her teeth, she was afraid he'd be able to tell she'd been sick. "Liar. You've lost weight."

"I've been busy." He kissed her again. "We'll get something to eat on the way." He pulled her to him, but she playfully pushed at his chest.

"Bath."

He laughed and closed the door.

She turned on the taps to fill the bathtub, sat on the edge and looked around. The bathroom was spacious, but like everything else in the flat, austere. Even though she knew he'd bought the place years ago, it still looked like a model flat. Furnished but not lived in. Except for the Crucifixes in every room, the small holy water fonts by the front door and near the light switch in the master bedroom, and his books. And the photos of her that occupied every available surface. She bit the side of her forefinger to keep from crying.

Later, she would tell him. Just for today she would pretend everything was okay. She would cherish every second of this time with him. When he knew, she was afraid, no, she was sure, everything would change. He wouldn't be able to handle the thought of her carrying another man's child.

Tonight. She would tell him tonight. She would let herself have one more day with him before crashing their world down around them.

# Chapter 14

REID'S MOBILE rang just as Anne and he were ready to leave. He frowned, then looked at Anne to reassure her. "I need to take this, but don't go anywhere and don't worry. I'm taking the morning off even if it's the Lord God himself."

"Answer your phone. I'll wait." Anne smiled and sat down on the edge of the sofa nearest the door. She wore long brown leather boots over close-fitting jeans that hugged her long legs, and she'd wrapped a soft camel colored shawl kind of thing over a silk shirt and thin brown cashmere sweater. He shook his head, still incredulous that this beautiful creature was really his.

"You look amazing."

She pointed to his mobile. "Answer your phone."

Reid hit the talk button. The voice of the Medical Examiner, Tessa Marcon, sounded tired. She would have had to work through the night to be finished with a report by now.

"Superintendent, I have your rush on Richard Ramsey."

"Much appreciated. Results?"

"No surprise. Confirmed what you and I both thought preliminarily. He was stabbed to death—a narrow, sharp blade right into the heart. Not so much a blade, perhaps, but a sharp pointed object. You suggested an ice pick, but I believe this weapon would have had to have been thinner and sharper than that. The train messed up his body, but he was dead already when it hit him. There could have been other, lesser, injuries, but frankly, it's almost impossible to pick them out with the body as impacted as it was. He could have been bashed about a bit before he was killed, but I don't think so and I can't tell you that for certain."

"Tox screen?"

"Shows evidence of alphaprozam, an anti-anxiety drug, blood pressure and cholesterol medicine and, here's a bit of a surprise considering where he was found, sildenafil citrate, commonly known as Viagra."

"A surprise because?"

"Generally, you don't take a drug like that until you're planning to have sex."

Reid thought about that, remembered the condom. "That actually makes sense considering some of the other evidence. So he was either getting ready for or getting back from a woman, then. How long does Viagra stay in the blood?"

Tessa puffed out a breath of exasperation. "Not necessarily a woman, Superintendent. Could have been another man."

"Ah, yes. Any signs he'd had sex with a man in the past?"

He glanced at Anne who arched her eyes at him. He shrugged.

On the other end of the line, there was a pause as Tessa considered his question. Then she said, "Actually, no, so you're probably right. No anal fissures or characteristic stretching. I'd say no. Viagra lasts about four hours, but we can see traces of it for a short time after that. From the level we found in his body, it looks like he took it no more than an hour before he died."

"Could you tell if he'd had sex recently?"

"He hadn't ejaculated recently, so whatever he was getting ready for, didn't happen."

"Thanks. Send the report to me only. Keep the tox results quiet. Don't let it get about over there in your shop."

"In the vault."

"Thanks. Would you do me a favor and take charge of the autopsy of DC Darrin Parsons?"

"Hit and run, right?"

"That's what I've been told."

"No problem."

"Later, then."

Reid briefly told Anne about his case as they drove, not mentioning the connection to the Heidelberg university bombing because of the confidential nature of the information, but gave her a general idea of what was keeping him occupied, especially because the Ramseys had attended the party Reid's parents had given for

Anne and him at Dunbaryn after they were married. She'd actually met the family, he reminded her.

Her face stilled as she tried to remember. "Can't picture them right now. There were so many people there."

"There were indeed."

"So you're investigating a murder? But I thought your task force was working on something involving financial crimes right now."

He was pleased that she'd remembered. "Aye, but we think this might be related." He went on with what little he felt comfortable sharing with her about the investigation, but not mentioning any names.

She listened attentively. For the first time he thought about the fact that Anne would really be a policeman's wife now. And she would be in his bed every night. Just the thought of that made him feel like he'd received a reprieve from some undetermined life sentence. Another thought, not as welcome, came into his head, and he knew he needed to warn her. He put his hand on her leg.

"Anne, Darby will be in town soon. She may show up at the flat. I didn't know you'd be here, so I told her she could stay here a night or two."

She made a face, dismayed. "Oh, no."

He ran his hand along her leg, trying to reassure her. "If she makes herself disagreeable, I'll see that she leaves. Better yet, when she calls to let me know she's arrived, I'll ask her to get a hotel."

"I don't want you to do that because of me. She's your sister."

"You're my wife."

"She can stay with us for a few days. I'll try really hard with her. Maybe she's mellowed about me." She looked up at him with those lovely blue eyes that always made him want to give her a small country.

Reid smiled back. "Maybe so." He knew his sister had not mellowed one bit, but Darby would behave, or he would send her packing. For him, Anne came first; his sister would have to accept that and be civil to his wife. "Anyway, I'm sorry. I thought I was supposed to be going to California to help you with the move."

"I know."

"When are your things coming? Did your sisters help you pack your condo?"

Anne waved her hand noncommittally. "Let's not talk about that right now. I have enough with me for a while."

"One suitcase?" He knew she was an efficient packer, but she wasn't like him. She needed her "things" around her to feel at home, as she always told him: her knickknacks, her books, her endless collection of boots, shoes, and hats, her gardening tools, her drawing materials, her cookery gadgets.

"One very big suitcase, Terrence."

He made a face to let her know she hadn't fooled him. "If you like the house, we'll have the rest of your things shipped right to it. No point in moving things twice."

"I love you, Terrence." She leaned against his shoulder, put her hand on his leg, and he thought everything they'd gone through had been worth it.

They drove up to large black iron gates that led to a driveway that split off into two directions: one part wrapped around the side of the house to a garage, the other part became a circular driveway in front of the house. Reid pushed a remote control. The gates opened and he guided the car through them to the front of the house, hitting the remote control to close the gates behind them. He parked the car, then leaned over and kissed her. "We're home."

She unfastened her seatbelt and wrapped her arms around him, holding on to him so tightly that a dark cloud of unnamed worry suddenly spun around him. His mind quickly paged through possible causes. Not Grainger, or she wouldn't have been with him like she had. Not her family, she'd told him they were all fine. Not the house, she seemed to like the idea. Not the sex, no, definitely not the sex, it had been unbelievable. He dismissed the worry as unfounded, and kissed her again.

# Chapter 15

THE HOUSE was perfect. Large open rooms, airy and light, greeted her as soon as they entered. Spying French doors at the far end of the living room, Anne immediately headed in that direction. A house was one thing, but the yard, or garden as they called it here, was to her, the main thing.

Terrence, apparently tuned in to the purpose of her detour, followed in her wake and moved in front of her to unlock and open the glass doors. Anne looked around the garden and its potential sprang to life in her mind, first as a set of drawings, then as a finished landscape. The property was completely fenced in with aged gray brick walls that caused additional issues with blocking out what she suspected was, based on what she knew of Glasgow weather, limited sunlight in the first place. Mentally, she refurbished the stone and glass greenhouse, added trees in a bare spot, and calculated where to move the rose garden so the plants would get more sun.

She spotted an extensive perennial garden border around the entire backyard—back garden, she mentally corrected herself. Recently, in anticipation of her next project, she'd immersed herself in the work of the garden designer Russell Page and his principles of order and simplicity. Her own personal tastes tended more toward a voluptuous garden display, but she saw the wisdom of wedding the two schools of design. A restrained voluptuous garden display, then.

A clock rung out, presumably from a nearby church. Noon. Terrence would find a quiet spot and disappear for a little while, she knew. At noon he always prayed the Angelus. But then he'd come back, always calmer, always happier. She turned around, and he was gone, just as she'd expected.

Her attention went back to the garden. An inviting spot that would be perfect for alfresco dining sat between some boxwood shrubbery and an impressive lavender hedge. Pea gravel for the base, she decided. What color for the shade umbrella?

She must have been lost in thought there for a quarter of an hour when she heard Terrence clear his throat. "Do you want to see the house, Anne? Or would you be happy with a tent out here? I could have saved a lot of money if I'd known you wouldn't require an actual house. Perhaps just a camping spot would do?"

She turned and smiled.

He raised his eyebrows in a question. "I take it you like the back garden?"

"It needs some work, but yes, it's wonderful."

"And the house?"

She glanced up at the back view of the house. It looked to be three stories. The upper portion of the walls were stucco, but the lower portion was a soft gray stone. "It looks beautiful. Big, but homey."

"Don't you want to see inside? The rooms? The kitchen? The baths?"

She laughed. "Of course I do. And the front yard, I mean, front garden."

"The house first." He took her hand and playfully pulled her along.

Terrence seemed so happy to be showing her around, explaining where her studio would be, where his office would be, the kitchen. There were rooms for staff to help with the house, he said, and with the children.

He smiled when he told her that part, but rushed to reassure her again. "No hurry for the children, though. Now that I have time to consider, and having been apart from you so much, I don't mind having some time with you all to myself."

Anne held his hand and smiled, but inside she was a whirling mass of worry. She did not want this time to end, did not want to shatter everything he had planned for them. But she knew that as soon as she told him about the baby, the sweet, almost boyish pleasure he was showing about finally beginning their life together would be gone.

She couldn't remember the last time she'd seen him so playful—

no, actually, she could. He had been like this on their honeymoon and, she remembered, when they'd reconciled in Bodega Bay she'd had a brief glimpse of this more carefree side of Terrence again. He was such a self-contained man; this joyfulness was something she had not seen in him when they first met and married. He had pursued her, courted her, and married her with a determined single-mindedness that was almost scary in its intensity. The lightheartedness she saw in him now had to be coming from his relief that they had rescued their marriage from almost certain destruction. Her news would almost certainly send them hurtling back against those awful rocks again. She felt guilty letting him go on being happy, but also greedy to feel his joy in her for as long as she could.

He was businesslike now. "We'll get a designer in. You'll want to choose the furnishings, the wall colors, all that. I chose the house, but everything else is up to you. I want you to make it your—and our—home. I didn't want to do any of that without you. I've the name of a designer who comes highly recommended. A woman who is used to dealing with homes like this. I've seen some homes she's designed and liked them. I think you will, too."

She said nothing, and he looked abashed.

"I've done it again, haven't I, girl? Made the decisions? If you don't like her, we'll find someone you like."

Anne smiled and squeezed his hand. "I'm sure she's wonderful." She wanted so much to do as he was saying: furnish their house, make it their home. Her heart hurt at the thought of telling him, of spoiling all of this for him and for her—for them. There was little chance he would want her to stay with him when he knew. She wished the news about the baby could be something joyful for him, but realistically, if the baby was Andrew's, she knew Terrence would be devastated, and her marriage would be over. But she couldn't wish her baby didn't exist; the child was already so real to her. Don't worry, little one. I love you.

He took her hand and pulled her down the hall upstairs, opening double doors into a large bedroom with a fireplace. "This is our bedroom."

One more day. She'd wait one more day to tell him. Maybe how we are together today will make it easier for him to stay with me no matter what, she thought. She took his hand and pulled him close and kissed him with everything she felt for him.

As their lips separated, he murmured to her, letting his mouth trail down her neck and his hand run up and down her back. "Lassie, don't be kissing me like that unless you mean to do something about it." He pressed himself against her and she felt him ready for her.

"Well, it is the bedroom."

"True, so true." He ran his hand under her silk top, unfastening her bra, and then traveling across her breasts. He unzipped her jeans and slid his hand down to her, sighing. "Ah, girl, you're ready. Ready again. I love you so much."

Without dislodging his hand, she reached down and unfastened his belt, then slipped her blouse over her head, losing the bra, opened his pants, and moved her mouth down to him.

# Chapter 16

ALONE IN THE FLAT after Terrence went to work, Anne walked around, examining where her husband had lived so long without her. It was a large, modern flat, in a large, modern building. He had the corner penthouse, so there were two solid walls of double story windows, both opening to glass-barriered balconies, one looking right over the Cathedral's sculpture garden, the other to the river. The place had an almost monastic feel to it, the only ornamental objects being either religious or the photographs of her that seemed to occupy every available surface. A photograph of them the day they were married sat on a corner table next to the sofa.

She picked up the framed picture. It had not been a formal wedding—just the two of them at a small chapel in Virginia—but it had been wonderful because they were in love. So much had happened to complicate their lives since then that she wondered if things would ever be right again.

When she went to the kitchen to make herself some tea, mint this time, she was surprised to see a note to her from Terrence on the counter by the electric teapot. When had he done that? She read the first part of the note, puzzled, and then examined the stack of things underneath the note. A checkbook, credit cards and health card, all in her name. Well, not actually her name, as she'd never changed her name to add his surname, although all of the documentation he left for her had her name listed as Anne Michaels Reid.

His note said he'd opened accounts in her name, and wanted her to use them to start making their house a home. She flipped open the checkbook, saw that the staggering amount entered as an initial deposit had been made shortly after they were married, almost two years ago. He'd never told her, and there were no other entries after the initial deposit.

She looked back at the note and finished reading it. "I've left the designer's business card on the counter. I've given her a heads up and told her to make our house a rush job. She'll be by at half two to collect you to go to the house. Love, Terrence."

Her head hurt. Would he want a home with her after he knew? She went back to the bedroom and lay on the bed. She also needed to work on the garden plans for Lynstrade Manor, but she didn't think she could concentrate. Tonight after dinner she would tell Terrence about the baby. He loved children, maybe he wouldn't care whose baby it was. But she knew he would.

Her cell phone rang. She checked the caller i.d. even though she knew who it would be. She couldn't talk to Andrew right now. Not until she knew what Terrence's reaction was to her news. She rubbed her stomach lightly, again trying to reassure the little person inside. Don't worry, I love you.

She turned off the phone's ringer and pulled the book she was reading out of her bag: *The Education of a Gardener* by Russell Page. Page was the original designer of the gardens at Lynstrade Manor, and the owner wanted them restored faithfully. Luckily, the estate's manager had been able to locate a copy of Page's design plans for the house's gardens. Still, there were some slight changes she wanted to suggest, nothing that would compromise the integrity of the project, just some things to make the gardens easier to maintain. After all, there had been a lot of advances in gardening and technology since Russell Page's day, and it made no sense to ignore progress.

She would read, then sleep a little, take a nap. After that, she would do some work. Being pregnant made her so sleepy. She'd never been much for naps, but now she could easily take several in one day. She changed into the shirt Terrence had worn to see the house, loving the smell of him that came from it, and climbed under the sheets.

Closing her eyes, she remembered what Terrence had said about Darby coming. Yuck and double yuck. Now she couldn't sleep. She couldn't concentrate on her book and couldn't concentrate on her work.

She'd cook. Always a good plan when she was anxious. She scrambled out of bed, went to the kitchen, and examined the meager contents of his refrigerator (a bottle of HP sauce), freezer (ice) and pantry (a half bottle of red wine that looked barely drinkable, some dried up garlic, and olive oil). What in God's name did this man live on?

So she'd shop, then she'd cook.

# Chapter 17

ARRIVING AT THE Ramsey home, Reid realized that for the first time in ages he wanted the workday to end earlier, rather than later. While he and Anne had been apart, he'd filled his days and, as often as not, his nights, with work. Although such a schedule had positively impacted his career, he was well past ready to have a life in which he could look forward to going home at night.

The afternoon was clouding up and rain looked to be inevitable. He had hoped for sunny weather today to make a good impression on his California girl, but eventually and inevitably, she was going to realize that rain was a frequent visitor to Glasgow. Still, given time, he knew she would love this country, this city, as he did. Perhaps next weekend he'd take her to the Botanic Gardens. He'd not been there for years, but he remembered some very nice woodland walks.

He reached the Ramsey front door just as the first few drops of rain started to fall, and he thought of how vastly different this grand house was from the last home he'd visited that afternoon. The Parsons lived in a small, crowded flat. There'd been no lush gardens, no sweeping driveway, no servants. Just two people whose hearts were irreparably broken.

Reid was ushered into the Ramsey drawing room as he had been the day before. A young woman Reid recognized immediately greeted him. Moira Ramsey. Moira was a pretty girl, very much like her mother, though she wore a little too much make-up for Reid's tastes. She wore low-waisted black jean shorts and a small tight shirt that exposed her midriff. A silver-studded belt encircled the top of the shorts, set off by a diamond belly button ring.

Her eyes appraised him with frank interest. "We've met before, Lord Reid. The party at Dunbaryn after your wedding. Two years ago, wasn't it?"

"Aye, I remember. Almost exactly two year ago. I'm sorry that our meeting this time is under such sad circumstances."

"Thank you. Please sit." Moira indicated the sofa, and sat across from him on another. "We appreciate that you came personally to tell Mother yesterday."

"It was the least I could do. I am sorry to have to intrude on your family's grief today, but I need to ask some questions."

"Do you know any more about what happened?" Moira's tone was matter-of-fact, and more adult that he'd expected. But then, at nineteen she was leading a very adult life. Reid felt a wave of dismay for the girl—nineteen years old and kept by a man who held almost unimaginable depths of evil.

"We're still investigating."

Moira's voice was hesitant, low, and now she sounded young. "Mother's afraid he might have done it on purpose. Killed himself. Is that what happened?"

He shook his head. "We're waiting for the medical examiner's report, but it doesn't appear to have been suicide."

She took his answer in stride. "An accident, then?"

"I can't say any more than that right now. I need to talk to your mother first."

"But you'll let us know? Mother is very worried about that. About everything of course, but about that in particular."

"Aye, I will."

"Mother was in shock yesterday. The news hit her super hard. She depended on Richard for pretty much everything. She's practically helpless without him."

"It had to be a terrible shock. How is she today?"

"Better. My aunt came over to help and the doctor gave Mum something. She's still a little out of it but Bert's bringing her downstairs to talk to you."

He nodded. "I'm sure having her sister, as well as you and Bert, to help her cope, will be a comfort. Does your aunt live in Glasgow?"

Moira nodded. "Downtown—not far from me." The luxurious flat where Moira lived was maintained for her by Walter Von Zandt. In fact, Von Zandt did not seem to go to the trouble of trying to hide that he had a mistress. He apparently didn't care if his wife or anyone else knew.

She sat down and crossed her legs, voicing what he'd been thinking. "I expect you know I'm Walter Von Zandt's side bit. It's his flat I live in." Her eyes challenged him as she spoke.

Reid shrugged as if what she said was of no importance. He sensed she was disappointed in his lack of response. Still a typical teenager, for all that, wanting to shock the grown-ups.

"Walter says you're trying to put him in jail."

Reid made sure his surprise didn't show. He'd assumed Von Zandt knew he was under investigation, and that Reid was involved, but somehow he'd not expected the man to be sharing that information with others.

"Actually, Moira, I wanted to talk to you about your father. I've some questions you may be able to help with."

She furrowed her perfectly shaped eyebrows. "I doubt it, but ask away."

"Did you happen to see him the night he died?"

Moira nodded, looking directly at him. Uncrossing her legs, she leaned back on the sofa, then folded her legs up beside her. "I had dinner with my family here Saturday night. Walter had something he had to do with his family—his wife's birthday dinner." She made a wry face. "I wasn't invited."

Reid stayed silent and the girl gave him a knowing smirk. "Elisa knows about me, of course, but she's not broadminded enough to include me in family functions. Not that I'd want to go. Boring, I'm sure."

"What time did your family have dinner?"

"Eight-thirty. Then afterwards, Walter's son, Frederick, came to collect me and take me back to the flat. He does things like that for Walter. Drives Walter or me, or does other kinds of errands." She motioned to some vague location outside of the room they were in. "He's here now, waiting to take me back later."

"When was it that you left?"

"Ten-thirty, maybe?"

"You don't have a vehicle of your own?"

"No. Walter doesn't like me driving."

"How did your father feel about your relationship with Mr. Von Zandt? You're considerably younger than he is."

She looked amused. "It was my father who introduced us, you know. They are—were—business colleagues. Richard thought Walter would be a good influence on me." She raised her eyebrows, smiling the smile of a woman decades older. "I've been living with Walter since I was sixteen."

Reid knew that, but had not known of Ramsey's role in bringing about the relationship. What kind of man would encourage his sixteen-year-old daughter to become the mistress of a man like Von Zandt?

"You don't seem overly distressed by your father's death."

She got up and moved to join Reid on the sofa where he was sitting. "Not my father. My stepfather." Moira looked at him lazily from behind her heavily made up eyes, and Reid got the definite impression that she was trying to vamp him. He acted as if he did not notice and went on with his questions.

"You have his last name."

"Yes, but he was just my stepfather."

"How did he seem Saturday?"

She shrugged and relaxed her gaze, changing from seductive to matter-of-fact. A child playacting, and not quite able to figure out what role to play.

"The same as always. Dull as dirt. I'm not sure what my mother saw in him. Other than the fact that he was filthy rich." Then she smiled. "Dirt and filthy. Funny. I didn't even plan that."

Reid gave a small, perfunctory smile, a smile he did not feel. "You've lived with him most of your life, haven't you?"

She nodded. "My real father was a worthless bastard who left us basically penniless. My mother was working at some club singing when Richard met her. His first wife was dead, and he married Mum and here we are." She waved her hand around their opulent surroundings.

"Did you talk to—should I call him your father?"

"Richard. I call him Richard."

"Did you talk to Richard at dinner?"

"I guess so. We all talked." She studied her long red nails, as if trying to determine if they needed a touch up.

"Any particular subjects?"

"Not really. Bert talked about his job—he works for one of Richard's companies, so they talked about that. We talked about Mum and him going on vacation. They were thinking about Spain. I told them about our trip to Toledo last fall, and said they should go there. Have you been there?"

Reid nodded.

"It's great, don't you think? Anyway, we talked about that and that Walter was taking me to Greece next month—to Rome and then to the island. Walter's island." She slanted her eyes toward him. "Where do you go on vacation, Lord Reid?"

"Wherever my wife wants to go." It was certainly handy to finally have his wife around to invoke for protection. His last vacation had been their honeymoon, but he'd often thought about where they would vacation if they were together. Now they would actually be able to do it.

"Lucky woman."

Reid shook his head. "I'm the lucky one. So, did Richard say anything about your trip to Greece?"

"He asked me how long I'd be gone."

"And?"

She shrugged. "I never know. Walter decides all those kinds of things. It depends on when he needs to be where. I just tag along to be with him."

"Anything happen at dinner that struck you as unusual or that indicated Richard had a meeting later?"

She shook her head and went over to a cabinet and poured a drink. Vodka and cranberry.

"Oh, sorry, do you want something?" She turned around and held up her glass. "I figured you probably wouldn't since you're working, but I still should have asked. Walter always gets annoyed when I do something thoughtless like that with guests. He says it shows lack of breeding."

Reid shook his head. "No, thank you." A nineteen-year-old girl from a family such as this one should be at university, studying and cavorting with people her own age—not playing house with a man old enough to be her father.

Moira went over to the piano, sat down, and began softly trilling a melody with fast fingers. "He didn't say anything about going out again later. Dinner was boring. Probably as boring as the one Walter went to." She spoke just loudly enough for him to hear over the music. "My brother was here."

"Yes, he told me."

"He lives here. Do you know this song?"

Reid shook his head. "Was anyone else at dinner Saturday night?"

She stopped playing and took a long pull from the glass she'd placed on top of the piano. "Just our happy little family. Oh, and Bert's girl."

"What's Bert's girl's name?"

"Patty something. You'll have to ask him her last name. She works at Richard's company. She's a typist or something."

"I'll get her full name from Bert. Did you go straight back to your flat from here?"

Moira nodded. "Walter told Frederick to deliver me directly home afterwards—even though Walter was spending the night with Elisa. How unfair was that?" She made a face. "Frederick didn't think it was fair either."

"What did you do after you got back to your flat?"

Her eyes glittered with suspicion. "Why do you want to know?"

"I don't know. It's no fun to be left on your own, I'd guess, if your . . . what exactly do you call Walter?"

She shrugged, tapping out a melody on the piano keys. "It depends on who I'm talking to, but I usually call him my boyfriend."

An oddly innocent term for someone like Von Zandt. "It can't be very amusing to have your boyfriend spend the night with his wife instead of you."

"No shite."

"So what did you do after you got back to your flat?"

She made her lips into a little pout. "You won't tell Walter, will you?"

"I can't imagine that happening."

"I went clubbing. Dancing. Walter doesn't like going to clubs or that kind of music. There are several places within walking distance so I changed clothes and headed out. I got home late—probably around three."

"Were you alone?"

"No, of course not. I danced with lots of people. I might be able to give you some names, but probably just first names."

"I meant did you go to the clubs with anyone?"

"I don't really have anyone to go with. It's hard to keep in touch with people my own age with the kind of life I have with Walter, so I don't have many of my old friends left, but when I have a night off, I like to party." She tilted her head and studied him. "What about you?

Do you like to party?"

Her use of the term "night off" made her relationship with Von Zandt sound like a demanding job, which Reid had no doubt it was. "You're sure Richard didn't say anything about going anywhere after dinner?"

"I'm sure. I think he might have even said he was going up to bed early. Mum didn't even make it through dinner before she fell asleep."

"Moira, do you know whether Richard was involved with any other women?"

She frowned. "No, but he'd hardly tell me."

"Walter's never mentioned anything like that?"

"Not to me. You don't like Walter, do you?"

Reid gave a mirthless smile. "What do you think?"

"He doesn't like you either."

"Not a surprise."

"I love him, you know. He's the best thing that's ever happened to me." She closed her eyes and hummed as she played.

Reid recognized the melody, but couldn't remember the name of the song. If going to live with a man thirty years older than she was when she was sixteen years old was the best thing that ever happened to Moira, he couldn't imagine what her life before that had been like.

The door to the room turned and Moira pulled her hands from the piano keys as if they'd burned her fingers. She quickly got up from behind the piano.

As the door opened, Moira drew in an audible breath, then relaxed. She whispered. "That's my Aunt Glynnis."

Glynnis looked amazingly like a young Barbara Ramsey, or an older Moira Ramsey. These women could almost all be one woman, shown at different ages.

Reid felt a click of recognition. He'd seen her before.

# Chapter 18

REID CALCULATED that Moira's Aunt Glynnis was a good fifteen years and oceans of booze younger than Barbara Ramsey. The curvy body topped with a gamine face and short cropped brown hair definitely looked familiar, and not just because she so closely resembled her sister and niece. He delved around in his mind, but couldn't place where he'd seen the aunt before. Socially, maybe?

Bert Ramsey accompanied his mother over to greet Reid, and put out his hand. "Lord Reid, thank you for coming. We appreciate the fact that you're handling Father's death personally. It makes a difficult situation a little easier."

"I know this is hard for all of you." Reid shook Bert's hand, not allowing himself to feel guilty about the younger man's misinterpretation of why he was personally involved. What Ramsey had been doing had enabled the murder of many innocent people, no matter how removed he might have been from the actual crimes. And their families grieved for them as well. Suddenly, the image of DC Parson's grief-stricken parents filled his mind. Their only child, dead; their dreams for him, dead; their hopes for a grandchild, dead. No, Reid did not feel guilty.

Bert motioned to the woman standing next to his mother. "This is my aunt, Glynnis Taylor. She's staying at the house for a few days to help Mum."

Glynnis Taylor offered her hand to Reid with calm composure. He took it, using the moment to study her face closely.

"We've met before." He disguised his inquiry as a statement, hoping she'd fill in the circumstances.

"Met?" Her eyes twinkled.

He nodded.

"Your memory must be better than mine." An evasive note in her tone alerted him she was not telling the truth, or at least not telling the whole truth.

He gave her a knowing half-smile, a look meant to imply he remembered exactly the circumstances in which he'd seen her before. He'd remember eventually.

Reid turned his attention to include the entire group, and, after they were seated, started the interview.

To Barbara Ramsey, he said, "Tell me everything you can remember about the last time you saw your husband."

"I told you, Lord Reid. It was at dinner on Saturday."

"Yes. I'd appreciate it if you'd go through exactly what happened that night now that you've had more time to think about it."

She plucked at the sofa fabric on both sides of where she sat, rolling the peaks she made between her fingers. "Richard came home from work sometime before dinner. Then we gathered in the drawing room for drinks before going in to eat."

"Was it his habit to work on Saturdays?"

"Yes."

"Who all was there?"

"Richard and I, Bert and his friend, and Moira."

"Did Richard talk to you about his day?"

She looked blank. "I don't think so. Bert, do you remember?"

For the first time, Bert Ramsey's impatience with his mother began to show. "Father almost never talks about work at home, and never to Mother."

Reid held up a hand to stop Bert from interrupting his mother again. "Did your husband say anything about planning to go out later?"

Barbara Ramsey's eyes slid over to where the drinks table was set up. "I don't remember anything. Bert, can you get me a small drink, darling?" Her fingers hadn't stopped their worried attack on the sofa fabric.

Bert ignored her request for a drink.

Reid prompted, "Mrs. Ramsey? What else can you tell me about that night?"

"I had a headache, and Richard took me up to my room. I went to sleep right away." Her eyes lifted to briefly meet his own. "As I told you yesterday, we have separate rooms. He keeps irregular hours—works late and gets up early. He doesn't—didn't—want to disturb me."

"I see." Reid couldn't even fathom wanting to have a room separate from Anne. How had the Ramseys' marriage gotten to that point? "And you didn't hear him leave the house?"

"No."

"Bert?" Reid turned his attention to the young man.

"My girlfriend was here. We went upstairs together, and I didn't hear anything."

"Did she stay all night?"

Bert nodded. "I took her home in the morning."

"What time?"

He considered. "About seven. We went out to breakfast on the way to her mum's house."

"Did you notice your father's car gone when you left?"

"Yes, though that didn't mean much to me. He works most days, including Sunday, so I just assumed he'd gone into the office."

Reid got Bert's girlfriend's name and contact information. After he finished here, he'd send Harry and Allison to interview her.

"Do any of you know of anyone who might have wanted to harm Mr. Ramsey?"

Barbara Ramsey's head went up, her nervous plucking stopped. "What do you mean?"

Reid kept his voice gentle, sensing her fragility. "We're investigating the possibility that someone intentionally killed your husband."

"You think he was murdered? Not suicide?"

"Not suicide."

Mrs. Ramsey shook her head. "No, no one."

Reid looked over at the others. Moira lifted her shoulders in a slight who-knows gesture, but Bert seemed genuinely troubled.

Glynnis Taylor gave Reid a bored look. "I wouldn't have any idea."

"I can't think of anyone who would want my father dead," Bert said.

Interesting that Richard Ramsey was Richard to Moira but father to Bert, yet neither one was Ramsey's biological child. "Couldn't it have been an accident?"

"No." Reid didn't explain. "I have a few questions I'd like to ask

Mrs. Ramsey privately. Can you let us have a few moments?"

Barbara Ramsey frowned. "I want my sister to stay."

"I think it would be best if it was just you, Mrs. Ramsey."

She hesitated, but the younger woman said, "I'll be right outside. You'll be fine." Glynnis gave her sister a quick embrace and turned to go.

Moira, obviously miffed at being dismissed, sauntered over to refill her glass before leaving. Bert sent his sister a disapproving glance, but stood by the door waiting for her. After making her drink, Moira gave a dramatically exasperated huff, and exited through the door being held open by her brother.

Alone now, Barbara Ramsey darted a look at Reid. "It's such a relief to me that he didn't kill himself. All night I laid awake wondering if anything I did made him so unhappy that he wanted to end his life."

Reid gentled his voice. "That's normal. Was there anything in particular you were thinking you had done?"

"Not really." Her hands fluttered together, then apart. "At least nothing specifically. We weren't as close as we used to be, but I'm not sure that Richard cared. He had his life and I had mine. I took care of the house and the family. He took care of his business."

"Ramsey International." The company Richard Ramsey had built was a huge conglomerate with tentacles in many different industries, from pharmaceuticals to paper goods.

"Yes."

"Was he having any problems at work?"

"I don't think so." She hesitated, then added. "A few years ago, I think the company had some difficult times. Nothing serious, Richard said. Nothing for me to worry about. Just a cash flow problem. He got all of that worked out."

"With the help of Walter Von Zandt?"

"I don't know much about what happened, but things are fine now." She rolled her palms along the upholstery of the sofa. "At least I think they are. I haven't met with our lawyer yet, but I expect I'm taken care of—that things are fine."

From what Reid knew of Richard Ramsey's financial situation, things would be more than fine, and someone would be inheriting a great deal of money. Money that could be a strong motive for murder. Reid could not discount the possibility that someone besides

Von Zandt had a motive for killing Ramsey. "Did your husband have a will?"

"I think so."

"Do you have any idea what the terms are?"

"No, but Bert called Richard's solicitor, and he's coming over later today to go over things with us."

"What's the solicitor's name?"

She gave a slight I-don't-know shake of her head. "Bert will know."

Reid handed her his card. "Here are my contact numbers. I'd appreciate it if you could ask the solicitor to call me."

She took the card without reading it, and nodded.

Reid changed the subject. "Mrs. Ramsey, was your husband taking any medications?"

She considered, then nodded. "High blood pressure and high cholesterol."

"How about an anti-anxiety drug?"

"No, he'd never take anything like that. He disapproved of those kind of drugs. He thought people should be able to will themselves out of depression, or anxiety, or anything like that."

Reid could imagine how that had come up between the couple. Barbara Ramsey must have seemed weak to her husband, and he'd apparently let her know.

"We found traces of a sexual potency drug in his blood. And there was a plastic vial containing the same medication in his bathroom cabinet. What can you tell me about that?"

Barbara Ramsey's face changed from soft to stone. "Nothing."

"You didn't know?"

"No."

"I'm sorry to have to ask such personal questions, but was he having trouble in that area?"

She shrugged. "He hadn't touched me in almost four years. He blamed it on me." Barbara Ramsey spoke, her voice and manner remote. "He didn't like my drinking. Speaking of which . . ." She went over to the drinks table and poured a tall glass of vodka. She drank half of it without pausing, then placed her hand just beneath her throat. "I hadn't guessed that there was someone else. But I shouldn't be surprised, should I?" She looked at him with eyes that seemed half-dead. "Do you know who it was?"

Reid shook his head. "I don't know that there was anyone else. Just that the drug was in his bloodstream."

"I'd appreciate it if you would keep that information private. I assume if this was really a murder, there'll be stories about it in the news." She regarded him with an intensity that surprised him, coming as it did from a woman who seemed so adrift. "I'm sure you understand better than most how awful the press can be."

Reid knew all too well the destruction that could be caused by the press on the hunt for a sensational story. He didn't know if Barbara Ramsey was referring to the stories about Anne and him, or to the ones from years ago about his mother and father. Either way, he never wanted to have to endure the humiliation of having the sordid details of his private life made the subject of other people's prurient curiosity.

"I'll do my best to keep the details private. Mrs. Ramsey, if there was another woman, do you have any idea who it might have been?"

"No. I don't. Maybe it was someone at work, that's where he spent most of his time."

Reid saw her glance toward the door through which the rest of her family, including her sister, had just left. He wondered about Glynnis Taylor—a younger, more vibrant version of Barbara Ramsey. Could Richard Ramsey have been dallying with his own sister-in-law?

"Are you thinking of anyone in particular?" Even if a spouse didn't actually know their partner was having an affair, Reid knew that they often had a feeling about his or her attraction to a particular person.

She gave him a lost look. "No idea. I rarely see anyone from his office. We quit entertaining years ago, and he stopped taking me to office parties. My drinking embarrassed him, he said."

As painful as he knew this topic must be for the woman, Reid had to persevere. "Another hard question. Do you know if he ever engaged the services of a professional?"

She clasped one hand against her throat, softly kneading her own flesh. "He never mentioned it, but then, I would suppose most men don't tell their wives if they are visiting prostitutes, do they?"

"Depends. Sometimes they do."

A canny, cagey look flickered across Barbara Ramsey's face. "So you think a woman killed him?"

"We don't know, but with the presence of the drug in his

bloodstream, it's certainly a possibility." Then Reid remembered the other route that could have been taken, regardless of what the medical examiner had found. For all Reid knew, Ramsey could have decided to try something new. "I know these questions are difficult, but I have to ask them. Is there any possibility your husband could have been meeting another man for sex?"

"Richard? Absolutely not. He disapproved of that, along with a lot of other things. And until the past few years, he was . . . we were . . . active that way." She made a face, and tears filled her eyes. "In spite of my drinking." As if the reference had reminded her, she drained her glass, then went over to the drinks table and refilled her glass. "Is that all, Lord Reid? I don't think I can answer any more questions right now." Without waiting for him to answer, she crossed to the piano, and put down her glass. Reid heard sobs start to bubble out of her just as her hands hit the keys with a rush. She closed her eyes, and with deliberate movements pounded out what sounded like a funeral dirge.

A movement by the door caught Reid's eye, and he looked over to see Glynnis Taylor standing there. She gave him a time-for-you-to-leave look, and he knew his visit had come to an end.

They walked to the front door in silence. Before she opened it, she said, "Superintendent?"

"Yes, Ms. Taylor?"

"I wouldn't waste too much time on this if I were you. Richard Ramsey deserved what he got."

"Why do you say that?"

"He was a bastard."

"Indeed? What did he do to you?"

"Nothing. Not to me."

"To whom, then?"

Glynnis's shoulders lifted nonchalantly. "He was just a bastard in general."

Reid waited for her to elaborate. When she didn't, he asked, "Where were you Saturday night, Ms. Taylor?"

"You want my alibi." Her mouth twisted in a slight smile. "I was home. I had an early supper and watched telly." Her tone was arch and teasing.

"Alone?"

"Alone. Alas. Goodbye, Superintendent."

# Chapter 19

"PATTY CADY?"

The young woman turned instantly, her short hennaed hair swinging around her head. Seeing Harry and Allison, she stopped in mid-step, just as abruptly as if she'd put on an emergency brake. She squinted, chewing a mouthful of gum. "Who wants to know?"

Harry resisted the urge to mimic Allison and roll his eyes at the hackneyed expression, and instead flashed his warrant card. "I'm Detective Sergeant Ross and this is Detective Constable Muirhead. We have some questions we'd like to ask you."

The girl puffed out her cheeks, then let out her breath in a sigh. "About Richard Ramsey, I suppose?"

Harry tilted his head in a nod.

"Not here. It'll upset my mum. Let's go across the street." She gestured to a sandwich shop whose windows featured painted pictures of less than appetizing food. "We can get coffee over there. Let me just tell my mum I'm back from work and where I'll be so she won't worry. I'll meet you over there in a wink."

Harry and Allison found a table toward the back that afforded some semblance of privacy and ordered coffee, which arrived at the same time as Patty Cady. Harry saw Allison turn up her nose at the weak-looking swill, and suppressed a smile. She'd gotten spoiled by the excellent brew they'd all gotten used to at High Street.

Patty quickly shed her purple coat and arranged it on the back of her chair. "Mum's waiting our tea for me, but it'll hold. What do you want to know?"

"Seems Mr. Ramsey's gone and got himself murdered, and we're trying to find out who did it." Harry felt Allison's tension next to him, as if she were absorbing into her body every vibration in the air. He wished she'd chill. She was the most intense DC he'd ever seen, desperate to learn everything she could as fast as she could.

Patty's mouth made a perfect O. "Murdered? We all thought he'd topped himself."

"Is that right?"

She nodded. "That's what we heard."

"Any ideas why he'd want to do that?"

She looked at him blankly. "Me? How would I know?"

"How about any ideas about who'd want to kill him, Ms. Cady?"

The young woman waved away the formality. "Call me Patty."

"Right. Patty, then. Any ideas?"

She wrinkled her forehead in thought. "Can't say as I do. Not that anyone loved him—but I don't know anyone who cared about him enough to hate him. Harmless old fart, to my mind." She reached for the cup of coffee in front of her and doused it with milk.

Harry took a drink of his coffee, trying to square how a man who'd been shrewd enough to build a business empire as impressive as Ramsey International could quality as a harmless old fart. "What do you mean, exactly?"

Patty shrugged. "I dunno. Just what I said, I guess." Stirring her coffee, she added two sachets of sugar.

"Can you be a bit more specific?"

She pursed her lips. "He never yelled or anything at anyone. Unless it was about work, he didn't even pay much attention."

"Did you see him outside of work?"

"Only with Bert. Like for dinner sometimes, or just when I came over with Bert. Bert's rooms are at his folks' house, you know, separate, but no private entrance."

"I assume you stayed over sometimes."

Her eyes studied her coffee. "Sure, sometimes."

"Only sometimes?"

"There are only so many nights my mum will believe I'm staying over with a girlfriend. So I couldn't stay with him as much as I wanted. But I did when I could."

"Was that awkward?"

"No. Bert's mother's out of it most the time, and the old man never paid any attention to me."

"But he knew you were staying over?"

"Sure. I'd have to come downstairs to get out of the house. If he was down there, he'd give me that look like, I know what you've been up to, but not like he cared one way or the other."

"You were at dinner there Saturday night?"

"Yeah."

"When did you leave?"

"Next morning. My mum thought I was staying at my girlfriend's." In response to questions from Harry, Patty explained how she'd spent the night with Bert, and that he'd brought her home after giving her breakfast at a café. She denied knowing anything about Richard Ramsey leaving the house after dinner, and said Bert had been with her all night.

"Ever hear, did Richard have a bird on the side?"

Patty mused. "Don't know, do I? Why would he tell me?"

"But you work at Ramsey International?"

"Yeah, I'm in the office pool. That's how I met Bert."

"So you hear the gossip?"

"Sure, but I never heard anything about the old man getting any. Everyone knows he's—was—a cold old coot." She sipped her coffee and made a face, then added two more sugar sachets.

"Bert get on with his father?"

She narrowed her eyes, warily assessing the thrust of Harry's question. "I guess."

"I'd bet the old coot was hard to work for—especially for a son. Bert ever say?"

"Bert's smart, knows where his bread's buttered."

"Meaning?"

"His da was the boss there, but everyone knew who made Richard dance, didn't they?"

"Who?"

"Walter Von Zandt, of course." Patty rolled her eyes, exasperated by his ignorance.

Harry hoped Allison was getting as annoyed by Patty's eye rolls as he got at Allison's. "So Bert got on with Von Zandt as well?"

She nodded, then seemed to notice Allison for the first time. She inclined her head toward the other woman, then asked Harry, "She's like your assistant?"

Harry saw Allison bristle. Suppressing a grin, he said, "Definitely not."

"You're higher up than her, though? Right? She's a constable and you're a sergeant."

"We work as a team. So, did Walter Von Zandt come to RI often?"

Patty shook her head and looked down, playing with her cup. "No, but his son did. Henry has his own office at RI. He's on the board, you know, him and his father."

"Do you ever work for Henry while he's there?"

"No, Henry brings his own girl." She gave him a knowing look. "If Richard was hot for anyone, I'd say that would be the one."

"Henry Von Zandt's secretary?"

"Yeah, Glynnis. Bert's aunt."

"What's her last name?"

Patty screwed up her face. "Taylor, I think."

So that answered Reid's question to Harry about whether he could think of where he might have seen Glynnis Taylor before. They'd not paid much attention to who Henry Von Zandt's secretary was, and she'd had a different last name than Ramsey. Still, they should have caught this. No, he should have caught this. Chagrined at his lapse, Henry made a mental note to check out all of Von Zandt's staff, no matter their position.

"But you don't think Ramsey was doing this Glynnis?"

"Not on your f'ing life. Henry wouldn't stand for that. She's his girl in more ways than one, if you know what I mean," Patty said.

Interesting, Harry thought. How hadn't they known that? "Patty, tell us about your relationship with Walter Von Zandt."

She pointed to herself. "Me? I don't have any relationship with him."

Harry locked eyes with Patty's. "That's not quite right, is it?"

Her whole body seemed to tense and she leaned back against the seat. "What do you mean?"

"You used to work for him, Patty."

Her face blanched. "Not me." Her voice came out quiet, scared.

Harry didn't let his gaze waver, knowing if he let her go now, she might never talk to them again. "Not directly for him, maybe, but you worked for him."

Patty hissed at him, looking around to make sure no one else in the café heard. "Shut up, you. That was a long time ago." She turned her face away and stood up. "I'm leaving. I don't have to talk to you."

Harry let out a breath of exasperation. "Sit down, Patty, or I'll just go have a chat with your mum."

"You shite."

"Sit down."

She sat down, shaking her head. "You're going to ruin everything for me, aren't you? You're going to tell Bert, and he'll not have anything to do with me ever again."

"No matter who tells him, he's not likely to be happy to find out his girlfriend's a former prozzy—or that she worked out of a whorehouse owned by Walter Von Zandt."

Patty put her hand on her forehead, despair deflating her. "Do you have to tell him? He's the first nice guy who's ever cared about me." Tears gathered in her eyes, and Harry felt lower than a worm's arse.

"We don't have to tell him. Not if you work with us. Start with telling us how you came to work at Ramsey International."

She wiped tears from her cheeks with a paper napkin. "Henry got me the job."

"Henry Von Zandt?"

She nodded.

"Why?"

"He told me if I could get Bert Ramsey to go for me, all they'd expect from me is to tell them if I heard anything that Mr. Von Zandt would want to know."

"And did you tell them things?"

"Sometimes."

"Like what?"

"Not really that much, but sometimes there was something, and I'd tell Henry, just to get him off my back." Patty put her face in her hands. "Don't tell Bert."

"Maybe you should tell him yourself. Better than if he finds out from someone else."

She looked up, her eyes suddenly huge. "No way. I'm already so beneath the kind of girl his family and friends think he should be dating, it's a miracle he's stuck it out. If he finds out about what I used to do, he'll get rid of me for certain."

"Maybe not." Harry thought about his boss's American wife. The guv was good at hiding his feelings, but Harry had studied him long enough to be able to see what others couldn't. Watching them together on the news films after her lover's daughter was kidnapped, Harry could tell that his boss was still beyond crazy about his wife. Crazy being the operative word. Harry wouldn't have put up with that kind of thing for one moment from any bird, much less a wife.

Patty shook her head. "What planet are you from? He'll drop me so fast my head will spin off."

Harry shrugged. "Up to you. What kinds of things did you tell Henry that you learned from Bert?"

"Nothing important."

"Nothing important? Funny they'd want nothing important."

She twirled two fingers in her brassy hair, frowning. "Financial stuff, mostly. Sometimes Henry would ask me for stuff, and I'd look for it and get it for him."

"What kind of financial stuff did Henry ask for?" He used her word. After all, stuff covered everything, didn't it?

"I can't remember exactly. He'd give me the date of something he wanted me to look for, or names on the papers, and I'd look for it."

"Did Walter Von Zandt himself ever ask you to get stuff from RI for him?"

She made a horrified face. "Walter? Fuck, no. I tried to stay away from him."

"You knew him—from before, didn't you?"

She flinched, her face a study in abject misery, then jerked her chin in Allison's direction. "Does she have to stay?"

Harry motioned to Allison, who gave a disgusted look and an unprofessional huff, but got up and left the table.

After Allison was out of earshot, Patty went on, her voice tortured. "He was there, you know, at Rebecca's. She was the woman who ran the place. She did this training thing, and when she thought you were ready, he came. For different parts of the training."

Harry nodded. He did know. Rebecca was infamous for the variety of sophisticatedly depraved offerings her girls provided.

"And it was filmed. God, I can't believe I did that. But the money was so good. We needed that money, my mum and me. She'd been sick . . ." Patty shook her head in despair. "Bert can't possibly understand. His life is so different."

"I'm not planning to tell him, Patty. Not unless there's some reason I need to."

"I'll never be free of it. They still have those films."

"How do you know?"

"One time, Henry called me into the office he uses at RI, and he had one of them playing on the telly. He told me to lock the door and take off my clothes and . . ." She started to cry. "And I did. I did what he told me to, so he wouldn't tell Bert. And every time he looks at me, he does this, this thing with his eyes." She shuddered. "To remind me."

"How many films?"

"Four. One at each stage of training." She gave a mirthless laugh. "I'm well trained—maybe that's what Bert likes. But he wouldn't like how it happened. Want me to tell you the stages?"

Harry shook his head. "I can guess. Do you think Henry has all the copies?"

"I don't know. Rebecca uses the training films for the new girls. There could be dozens. It could be on the internet for all I know."

"Does Walter's face show on any of the films?"

Tears were now streaming down the girl's face, and she shook her head. "He always wore a hood. A black hood that covered the top part of his face." She blew her nose into her napkin, then crumpled it in her hand.

Harry made a promise he hoped he wouldn't regret. "If we find the films, we'll get them to you, okay? Then you can destroy them yourself."

"Really?"

"Really."

She nodded. "Then yes. Please."

"Your mum's probably wondering where you are. Get on home with you now." He handed her his card. "You call me if you think of anything or if you think you're in trouble, okay?"

Patty sniffled and slipped the card into her purse. "Yeah. You're not going to tell Bert?"

"Not me, pet."

"He'll find out, though."

"Not from us."

"You think maybe he'll understand?"

Harry nodded, but both of them knew that wasn't bloody likely.

# Chapter 20

ONCE SHE HAD the garlic and onions sautéing, Anne began to feel better. By the time she'd added browned Italian sausage, ground beef, and pepperoni to the rich tomato sauce simmering on the stove, the air was thick with the comforting good foods smell, and she felt completely calm. Everything would work out. At least that's what she told herself.

When the flat's telephone rang, Anne answered automatically. As soon as she lifted the receiver to her ear, though, she wondered whether she should have. After all, it wasn't her telephone or her flat, and no one would expect her to be answering. Briefly, she wondered about other women, in spite of Terrence's unequivocal assurance that there had been no one else while they were separated. Of course, she certainly wasn't in any position to say anything to him if there had been.

All of those thoughts flew out of her mind when she realized it was Terrence on the line. She smiled when his lovely Scottish brogue filled her ear.

"Lass, I'm just calling to see whether you want to go out to dinner, or whether I should bring something home."

"Terrence." His voice made her melt inside. "I just love picking up the phone and having it be you."

He laughed, and she wanted to hold him. "I love it being you, girl. So are you hungry?"

"Actually, I cooked. Nothing fancy, as I was at the house all afternoon with the designer. Just spaghetti with meat sauce, salad, bread."

"Sounds great, and I happen to know your spaghetti with meat sauce is fancy. I'll bring wine."

"If you like. I used the bit you had here in the sauce. Are you coming soon?" She wasn't drinking, of course, and she'd made dinner more to keep busy and fight down the nervousness about telling him, than because she was feeling particularly domestic. Panicked is what she felt. But she wasn't going to tell him that. At least not yet.

After dinner, they could talk. She'd explain, and he'd understand, and they'd work things out together. She squeezed her eyes shut. She really, really, wished she could have wine.

"On my way. I'll just stop at the wine shop, then I'll be there. I've missed you."

"I've missed you, too. Hurry home."

She put down the phone, mixed up a bleu cheese dressing she knew he liked, and finished setting the table. Terrence's kitchen things, although unadorned, were well-organized and complete, down to candles for the table. He was an organized man. Anne was the only messy thing in his life, and she'd caused havoc ever since she met him. Inadvertently, perhaps, but havoc nonetheless. And what she had to tell him now was worse than anything else she'd done. But maybe he could handle it. Maybe.

After she'd done all she could do to get ready for Terrence's homecoming, she settled down on the sofa and pulled out her design sketchbook to try to get some work done while she waited for him. This was the other thing she needed to talk to Terrence about. Her boss from California, Jonas Reveille, had accepted a job close to Glasgow for which the client had specifically requested Jonas to bid on because Jonas—with Anne's assistance—had done the restoration of another Russell Page garden last year. She had tentatively agreed, pending discussing things with Terrence.

Anne had promised Terrence that they would have a normal married life when she came to live with him; they both now realized that they could not make a long distance marriage work. To be honest, Terrence had never thought it would work, which is probably why it didn't. But this job was just an hour from Glasgow, and if, after she broke her news, he still wanted her to stay, it would be perfect. She could either commute every day or stay in the hotel where her boss would be staying and Terrence and she could be together on the weekends.

Or if he took the news about the baby badly, she could just stay at the hotel and work on the project. That way she'd be close by in case he changed his mind after he got over the shock. She wanted to be close to him, no matter what. He might need some time to adjust to her news, but if she were nearby, it would be easier for him to come to her after he did.

She spread out the photographs Jonas had taken of the Lynstrade Manor garden, compared them with the original design plans, and considered in what order the major changes needed to be made. Engrossed in her work, she was startled by a knock at the door. Then she realized that Terrence's arms were probably full and he needed her to get the door. She ran to open it, smiling.

To Anne's dismay, it wasn't Terrence, but instead a tall, rangy young woman dressed in black jeans, black shirt, and a black leather jacket. Her rich brown hair swirled to her shoulders in that way that only the most expensive stylists could achieve.

Anne managed a smile, despite her consternation at seeing this unfriendly sister-in-law. Although she and Anne were almost the same age, they seemed to have nothing else in common.

"Hello, Darby. Terrence said you might be coming. It's nice to see you." Good thing polite lies were excusable, otherwise Anne would be in danger of being struck dead by lightning.

Darby's green eyes were as cold as glass in winter. "I talked to him yesterday and he said you weren't here."

"I wasn't. I just got here late last night."

Darby moved without hesitation into the room past Anne, and tossed down a black leather duffel bag, the kind of horribly expensive thing rich people think of as casual luggage. Anne's own suitcase, though five times larger, had probably cost at least five times less than Darby's Italian designer bag.

"Where's Terrence?" Darby Reid might have the same last name as her brother, but she had none of his diplomacy or maturity.

Anne tried to hide her discomfort at having to entertain Darby by herself, albeit for a short time. Mentally, she sent Terrence a message to hurry home.

"He's on his way. He's picking up wine for dinner. Have you eaten?"

"Not yet. I was going to make Terrence take me out. He never has any food."

"We're just having spaghetti. I'll set another place." Anne smiled, trying in vain to elicit a return smile from her cold sister-in-law.

Darby didn't respond, but looked around the flat as if she were trying to find evidence of something. Did she think Anne had been stealing the silver or something?

Nonetheless, Anne continued to try to be hospitable. "Would you like something to drink? The wine's not here yet, but there's . . ." Anne didn't know what it was about Darby that made her feel so uncomfortable. Generally, she was confident of her social skills. She may not have been born with the Reid money and status, but she had never doubted her equality in any situation with anyone. Nevertheless, Darby seemed determined to try to make Anne feel like she was some kind of gold-digging country hick—or whatever the Scottish equivalent of that would be. How was she going to be able to talk to Terrence about the baby tonight with his sister here?

"Don't worry. I know my way around Terrence's flat. I've probably been here more than you have, come to that." Darby moved to an antique chest Terrence used as a drinks table. "I'm having a whiskey. I don't suppose you want one?"

"No, thank you." Anne answered automatically. She pulled additional dishes and silverware out of the cupboards, and began to set another place at the table while Darby made herself at home on the sofa.

Darby leaned back on the sofa, curling her long legs underneath her. She studied Anne, her gaze like a surgical examination.

"So what happened to your boyfriend?" Raw enmity pulsated in Darby's words.

Anne flushed and momentarily couldn't think of anything to say. Her breeding may not be equivalent to that of Lady Dominique Reid, Darby for short, but Anne was sure that her manners were better. She decided to ignore the question. Rise above it, she told herself.

Folding the extra napkin, she said, "Terrence said you would be in town, but he didn't mention why. Are you here for work?"

"I'm working with him on an investigation." Darby stretched out her arms and yawned. "But I'm not really surprised he didn't mention it—I doubt he's had much time for conversation with you. As I recall, it's not your conversation that has him acting like a fool. I'm surprised you let him out of bed long enough to go to work." Darby didn't even try to disguise her contempt.

Anne could not remember anyone ever acting like this to her.

Certainly she and Terrence had been passionately involved in each other when they'd come to Scotland together—they'd been on their honeymoon, for heaven's sake. She couldn't even fathom how to respond to such antagonistic comments, but then her temper rose to her rescue, and words rushed out, even as she made sure her voice was cool and her face confident.

"Of course I do, Darby, but just long enough for him to go to work, then it's back to bed for him. Sometimes I even allow him enough time to eat a meal, as long as he makes it quick."

Anger radiating from her, her sister-in-law raised a finger, coiled to strike, a rattlesnake with sharp scarlet fingernails. Darby had just opened her mouth to respond, no doubt with more poisonous words, when she was interrupted by Terrence opening the door and walking in, carrying the promised wine. He put his keys and the wine down and looked first at Darby, then at Anne. Anne could feel his gaze assessing her; he knew she was upset.

He came over to where Anne stood and kissed her. "Hello, my darling. Hello, Darby." With his arm around Anne, he looked back at Darby. "How long have you been here?"

"Not too long." Darby's face looked bored, the dangerous rattlesnake temporarily dormant. "Anne's cooked. Pasta." She said the last word as if it were gruel.

Terrence grinned. "Indeed, I know she has. Anne makes great pasta. And she's had a long day after her trip from the States, so I'm going to make her sit down now." He led Anne over to a chair. "Would you like some wine, my love?"

Anne smiled at him. "Not right now. I have some sparkling water in my glass over there."

He brought it to her and kissed her again. "I'll just open the wine. Darby, some Chianti?"

"In a bit. I'm having a whiskey." Darby took a drink from the cut crystal tumbler. "So, Anne, what exactly have you been doing with your long day?"

Anne bit her lip, not wanting to talk about the house with Darby. If it turned out that Terrence didn't want her to stay after he found out about the pregnancy, having Darby know about their house would just make everything worse. Anne had no doubt that if Terrence ended things between them again, Darby would be thrilled.

"Not much." She hoped Terrence would get the signal that she did not want Darby to know about the house.

Terrence brought his glass of wine and sat on the edge of Anne's chair, his arm around her. But he'd missed her signal in his effort to show his solidarity with her. "Not true. She's been meeting with the designer at the house all afternoon, then came home and made dinner."

"House?" Darby's eyes narrowed at Terrence, but then shifted to Anne. Anne made herself stay steady, and let Terrence talk.

He kept his arm around her as he spoke. "We've bought a house here in town. The painters are lined up, Anne?"

She nodded, and felt him squeeze her shoulder in support. He had to know his sister was a bitch, and he was showing them both clearly whose side he was on. She looked up at him and smiled. "They should be finished this week."

Terrence raised those dark eyebrows and shot a look at Darby that made Anne shiver. His tone was ominously calm. "We'd be pleased to have you visit us there when it's finished, Darby. Just check with Anne to make sure your visit fits with our schedules."

Darby looked at the two of them, then shrugged. "Fine. Should I look for a hotel for tonight? Obviously I didn't know Anne would be here when I made my plans."

Terrence's gaze caught Anne's. "Would it be convenient for you if Darby stayed here?"

Anne managed a thin smile. "Of course. You're more than welcome, Darby."

"That's settled, then. Shall we eat?"

# Chapter 21

IT WAS ONLY A GUARDED TRUCE between Darby and her, Anne knew.

Dinner went well enough, with Darby keeping her scarlet-tipped claws hidden and concentrating on talking to Terrence about her job and family news. Darby inquired whether they were going to Dunbaryn for Easter, and Anne could tell her sister-in-law was dying to know if the rest of the Reid family knew Anne was here. But Terrence didn't bite, simply shook his head and said with the case at the stage it was, he couldn't leave town right now.

He hadn't mentioned that their wedding anniversary this year fell on Easter, and Anne wondered if he remembered. She had his present hidden in a closet in the guest room where Darby would now be staying. She hoped Darby wouldn't go snooping and find it. Maybe she could move it later before Darby had a chance to go to the room.

After dinner, Terrence insisted that he and Darby do the dishes as Anne had cooked. Anne heard them talking about the investigation as they worked, but she didn't bother to listen, instead using the opportunity to move the present from the guest room closet to under Terrence's bed. Surely he wouldn't have any reason to look under the bed tonight. She smiled, unable to think of any possible circumstance in which Lord Terrence Reid would crawl under a bed.

When the present was safely stowed away, she settled herself on top of the bedspread. To keep her mind off of problems that couldn't be resolved without first talking to Terrence, Anne spread out her design papers again and tried to concentrate on her work. But her mind wouldn't cooperate. Her thoughts kept going back to her awkward situation and how she could work things out with Terrence. There was no way to have the conversation about the baby tonight with his sister in the flat. The discussion was bound to be volatile and they would need privacy to work things out. Maybe one night was really all Darby would be staying with them.

Finally, Anne was able to make herself focus on her design sketches. She didn't know how long she'd been working when she looked up to see her husband closing the bedroom door behind himself.

"Kitchen is in order, and I've shown Darby to her room. Shall we go to bed?" Terrence buried his face in her neck, kissing her in a way that made shivers run through her.

She dropped her pencil and wrapped her arms around his neck. "Wonderful idea."

"Lord, you smell good. I've been thinking about you all day. I can't believe this is legal—having such a beautifully delectable wife at home to love every day and night. Has to be a crime of some sort."

She laughed, then closed her eyes, tilting her head back as he nibbled on her neck. "I've been thinking about you, too—but can I talk to you about something first?" Although she couldn't tell Terrence about the baby until they had more privacy, she could talk to him about the job now.

"Of course. What is it?" His hand was under her shirt, his fingers tracing paths up and down her middle, stopping before touching her breasts or traveling far enough south to take away her power of speech.

Almost breathless, she explained about the job and added, "It's called Lynstrade Manor. It's just outside of Glasgow. Jonas has been dealing with the estate manager of the corporation that owns it."

He looked up and smiled. "A job in Scotland—and close to Glasgow? It sounds perfect. Our house will be in upheaval with the decorators, anyway. We can work out the details, but perhaps we could stay somewhere halfway between for part of the time." He ran his fingers along her side, tracing the curve of her waist down to her hips. "I told you there would be work for you in Scotland. Does it start soon?"

She nodded. "The consultation meetings will be at the end of the week, and work is scheduled to start next Monday. They've offered for us to stay at the house, but Jonas said no. He likes to have his independence when he's on a job—otherwise he says the work is all-consuming. The client will pay for us to stay at hotel near the estate. Maybe you and I can stay there together part of the time and here part of the time." She relaxed her legs, hoping he'd notice and accept the invitation.

"We'll need to get you a car, and you, my love, will need to learn to drive on the left side of the road." His fingers trailed down, down, so close, then changed course and went slowly up her body. Anne murmured an assent in response to his remark about the driving, but her mind was on where his fingers were, and wondering why he just wouldn't go where she needed him to be.

"Is Jonas there yet?" His fingers continued their tortuous path, arousing but never actually going anyplace that could satisfy.

"No, not till Thursday." She made herself breathe.

"We'll have to take him to dinner or something."

"That would be nice. Thanks, Terrence." Touch me just further down a bit.

"Girl, I want you to be happy. You love your work, I love you, and I am just damned happy you're not on another continent." He pulled her close and nuzzled her neck again, this time using his tongue to send ripples through her. She giggled, knowing that now he would fulfill the promises he'd made with his teasing.

"You're tickling me."

"I'm going to do more than tickle you." His hands left the restricted area they had been patrolling and went north, then south.

"Oh, God, I've missed you." She wrapped her arms around his neck and let him explore. "But we have to be quiet. Darby is . . ."

"Her room is on the other side of the flat. Besides, she can leave if she doesn't like it." He reached over, taking his hand away for one unbearable moment while he turned off the lights.

# TUESDAY, APRIL 7

# Chapter 22

REID WENT DIRECTLY to the office from early Mass, before which he'd gone for a run. Anne had been sleeping soundly when he left. He'd made coffee and, not knowing if her herbal tea of the day before was a regular habit now or something she just liked occasionally, put the tea things on the counter and left her a note.

He quickly thumbed through the report he'd pulled from his email inbox on the testing of the wigs from the Ramsey house. No match with the hairs in the car. Well, that would have been too easy.

This morning his first order of business was to deal with the press, something he generally disliked because he begrudged the time away from his actual work. However, talking to the press was an integral part of the strategy on a case. He had taken care to build strong relationships with both the print and the broadcast reporters. And now he intended to use those relationships to carefully leak the information that he wanted dispersed.

He gave a professional smile when Allison led Carolyn Caspary into his offices.

"Superintendent Reid, lovely to see you." The reporter, dressed in a sleek silk suit the color of antique bronze, a color that set off the highlights in her deep auburn crown of hair, kissed him on both cheeks.

"Ms. Caspary, thank you for meeting me so early this morning."

"I'm always happy to accommodate you." She beamed at him. "I'm still collecting accolades from the last story you gave me."

"My pleasure." He turned to his constable. "Allison, would you please see whether the reports we're expecting from the lab are in?"

"Yes, guv." Allison moved to the door, closing it after her.

Without an audience, Carolyn's manner instantly relaxed. "So,

Terrence, how are things?" Then, apparently sensing his guard going up, she added, "Off the record."

"Off the record?"

She held up a hand. "I swear, absolutely off the record. What's going on with you and Anne? I haven't heard anything new since you got back from California. Much to my frustration, you've both stayed out of the press since then."

Something squeezed his heart, something like joy, something like flying. Like a besotted schoolboy, he wanted to tell someone, anyone, about his sweetheart.

"Off the record, then, as we'd like our personal life to continue to stay out of the press. Anne is here. In Scotland." He pressed his smile into an acceptable, conservative, barely curved line, not letting it burst into the ludicrous display of exhilarated excitement he felt.

Carolyn raised her eyebrows in a question. "After everything? I'm a bit surprised."

"That was my fault as much as hers. I'm not the easiest husband, as you may surmise."

"Indeed, I can." She crossed her legs, waggled her foot.

Guilt swamped him. "I'm sorry . . ."

She waved his apology away. "I don't need to hear it again. It was a long time ago. I'm glad for you. Really."

"Thank you. What about you? How are you doing?"

She tilted her head, casting her eyes down. "As a matter of fact, Ian is moving in next week."

Guilt lifted, and he smiled. "You're getting married?" Ian Stevens, one of the top executives in the news organization for which Carolyn worked, was a solid, good man.

She made a face. "No. Moving in as in living in sin."

He felt his face flush. "I didn't mean . . ."

"You forget; I happen to know you're no saint." She gave him an annoyed look. "Though not for lack of trying."

Reid stiffened. "I've never professed to be a saint."

She flapped her hand in an airy gesture. "Forget I said that, Terrence. It was a shitty thing to say. So Anne's really back this time? For good?"

He kept his emotions hidden behind his eyes, wary now. "She is, yes."

She swatted him on the side of the arm. "Smile, you beast. You know you want to."

He gave up and flat out grinned.

Carolyn smiled in return, touched his cheek. "She must be something special. I hate her."

He nodded, moved away from her hand, uncomfortable. He shuffled some papers on his desk. "The reason I called you is that I have a story for you. I can give part of it to you now, and if you work with me, I'll give you an exclusive when things are at a point where we can let more information out."

Carolyn looked interested. "About the Ramsey death?"

"Aye. Are you interested?"

"Definitely."

"You've heard that Richard Ramsey was found dead yesterday morning?"

"Of course, I've heard. The head of RI. On the railroad tracks. Speculation is that it was suicide."

He shook his head. "Not suicide. Ramsey had agreed to provide evidence regarding money being laundered to fund terrorist cells. We suspect that may have led to his murder."

Her eyes zeroed in on his. Now she was all business. "Murder? You're sure? That's been determined?"

"Aye. Yesterday the medical examiner gave me the preliminary report and I expect to get the final by tomorrow. Ramsey was stabbed through the heart and then thrown on the railroad tracks to disguise the cause of death."

"Terrence, I think I love you." When he frowned, she clicked her tongue in exasperation. "A figure of speech, you jerk. You're married. I get it. Just give me the rest of it, and I'll do what I can to figure out any other background information."

"And you'll share with me whatever you find out as well?"

"Right. You first. Start with why Richard Ramsey would even know anything about the whole business. Money laundering, terrorism, all that. It doesn't sound like anything he'd be mixed up in."

"Ah, well." Reid proceeded to dole out the story he wanted told, making sure he did not let on who was behind it all. Not yet.

# Chapter 23

ANNE RUSHED to the bathroom, and with no time to close the door, leaned over the toilet and threw up. She weakly reached her hand to the lever, flushed, keeping her head curled above the toilet as she waited for the next wave of nausea to hit, thankful Terrence had gone to work hours ago. The next onslaught came, after which she flushed again immediately, but the disgusting smell of vomit still clung to the air. She shivered, then scooted the bathroom rug under her as protection from the cold tile, wondering if she could make it back and forth to the bedroom to get her robe before she threw up again. Deciding not to take the chance, she rested her forehead against the ceramic bowl and closed her eyes.

A voice brought her to attention, and Anne looked up, momentarily confused.

"Something you ate?" Darby was standing by the door, cool disdain oozing from her like slime from a snail.

"I guess." Anne wiped her mouth, relieved that her empty stomach had started to settle down. She swallowed. "I thought you would have left when Terrence did."

"He gets up too early for me. I'll see him over at High Street later."

Anne nodded. She felt wrung out and her mouth tasted awful. She wished Darby would just go away.

"Do you have everything you need in the other bathroom? I didn't get a chance to check." She felt a little ridiculous, acting the hostess while practically hugging the toilet.

"I have everything I need. Do you think it's the flu?" Before Anne could think of a reply, Darby went on, "It can't be food poisoning; I feel fine and I assume Terrence didn't get sick or he

117

wouldn't have gone to work."

Anne brushed her hair back behind her ears, trying for nonchalance. "It must have been something I picked up on the trip over."

"Or something you picked up before you left. Anyway, there's coffee made. Apparently, Terrence made it before he left. Want me to bring you some?"

Beware of Greeks bearing gifts. If Darby brought it, it would probably be poisoned. Besides, Anne was off caffeine for the duration.

"No, thank you. I'll just get into the shower. If you like, I'll make breakfast when I get out." God, why had she said that? The thought of cooking eggs or sausages made the nausea rise up again, but her empty stomach had nothing left to retch up, and she willed it to calm.

"Not for me. I'm a yogurt-and-granola girl. I'll leave you to your shower." Darby closed the bathroom door.

Anne let the hot water run over her, feeling whole worlds better after she was done. She got out of the shower, looked around the bathroom and realized she hadn't brought her toiletries bag in with her. Bundled in a towel, she went to the bedroom to get her things. Her heart caught in her throat when she opened the door. Sitting on the bed in front of Anne's open toiletries bag, was Darby, looking smug and holding a bottle of prenatal vitamins.

Anne's heart sunk from her throat to her stomach. "What are you doing?"

"Good news, Anne. You're not sick, you're pregnant." Darby's voice dripped with gleeful contempt.

"How dare you go through my things?" She couldn't believe Darby's flagrant disregard for her privacy. "This is not your home."

"Not really yours either. I was fairly certain that bout in there was morning sickness. I remembered you didn't drink any wine last night, so I thought I'd take a look."

"You had no right to go into my things."

Darby made a pretend pouty face. "Oh, no. Are you going to tell Terrence on me? Go ahead, tell him; he doesn't know about the baby, does he?"

"This is none of your business."

Darby put a finger to her temple in pretend concentration. "I'm a trained investigator, so I should be able to figure this out. Let me think. Terrence has wanted children all his adult life, but only with the right woman, his perfect woman. He stupidly thinks that perfect woman is you. Ergo, if he thought you were pregnant with his child, he would be announcing it from the bloody rooftops."

"Get out of here." Anne's voice was barely a whisper.

Darby threw the vitamin bottle on the bed, and stood up. "Not just yet, you little bitch. I'm not finished."

Anne leaned weakly against the door frame. "Finish then."

Darby's eyes shone with malice as she continued. "You saw how happy he was just that you are working on putting a home together with him. A baby—correction, a baby with you—would have him delirious. As he doesn't seem to know, my deduction is that the baby isn't his. All of this, coupled with the knowledge that I share with most of the civilized world, that you were another man's mistress until, what, less than two months ago, leads me to the conclusion that the baby is your boyfriend's, not Terrence's."

Anne absorbed Darby's tirade in silence, trying to remove herself emotionally from what was happening. She couldn't think of anything to say in her own defense.

Darby, her face flushed with unleashed anger, didn't seem to care if Anne responded or not. She held up Anne's phone. "So then I checked your mobile . . . oh, please don't look so righteous, Anne. Regular calls from Andrew Grainger. Who is—I presume—the baby's father?"

"Get out." Anne finally managed a response, then closed her eyes as currents of agonizing pain swam around her head. "Get out of here. Leave me alone."

"I'm going. I'll stay somewhere else tonight. But you had better tell him, and you'd better do it soon. If you don't, I will. Can you imagine what this whole mess with you has already done to him professionally? After everything he's done to build his career, you tear it down and make him look a fool." Darby spit her words out like poison darts, then slammed every door between the bedroom and the front door on her way out.

Anne slumped to the floor, put her face in her hands and wept.

# Chapter 24

DARBY STRODE into the High Street offices, her mind still reeling from her discovery about her slag of a sister-in-law's pregnancy, and passed a familiar looking redhead who was on her way out. The television newswoman. Interesting.

Terrence was leaning over a computer terminal where another redhead, this one a man, was intently working. She couldn't imagine two redheads who looked less alike. Carolyn Caspary defined the word elegance, and the computer jockey looked like he just fell off an old farm lorry.

Her brother looked up, saw her, and frowned. "Nice that you could join us. Had a bit of a lie-in, did you?"

Darby brushed him off. Maybe Terrence should have stuck around longer. He could have learned all kinds of interesting things about his wife. But she just said, "We don't all get up at the crack of dawn. What was the telly news girl doing here?

"Carolyn is an investigative reporter."

"Excuse me, investigative reporter. Don't want to slight her profession. I should have said bloodsucker. So what's she doing here?"

"I'm feeding her some information I want put out on the case."

"You really think you can trust her?"

"We've worked together before. There's a quid pro quo, of course, but she's trustworthy."

Something clicked in her memory, and Darby smiled. "Didn't you used to have a thing with her?" Heads turned toward them, quick interest in their faces, and her brother shot her a warning look.

She lowered her voice. "Oops, wasn't I supposed to mention

that? So sorry, are we keeping secrets?" Served him right. He'd kept secrets from her, secrets he should have shared with her, secrets she'd deserved to know. He needed to be taught a lesson about what keeping secrets could cost.

He ignored her question, but Darby didn't need his answer. Carolyn Caspary's name had been tied to her brother's a few years ago, before the woman that was before Anne. Past lover once removed. Mr. Holier-Than-Thou had carnal needs, too.

Her brother indicated the man sitting at the computer next to him. "Darby, this is Harry Reid."

The ginger-haired bumpkin gave her a slight, distracted wave, then returned his attention to his dual computer screens.

She didn't bother with a greeting, just let her eyes scan the rest of the group. Hopefully there'd be someone more interesting than the bumpkin. But no. A guy in a wheelchair who looked like he used to be a circus acrobat, a guy who would have been passable if he didn't wear black-rimmed glasses as thick as scones that made him look like a human owl, and a young woman with hair desperately begging to be styled and who goggled at Darby with obvious awe. Where did he find these people? But Darby smiled and made nice while her brother recited their names. She might need them on her side.

Introductions complete, Terrence said, "This is the first time you've been to our new offices, isn't it?"

"Aye. Last time I was here you were still in the basement of that building over in the Osprey House complex." She looked around, her eyes taking a quick survey of the large room. The main floor of what obviously used to be a shop was open except for an office in one corner with half glass walls that gave the occupant of the office, Terrence, she assumed, a view of the open room where the rest of the detectives worked, another room she could tell from the open door was a conference room, and an alcove with a small kitchen.

The desk of the man who apparently ran the administrative side of the office, the one in the wheelchair, was set in the main area near the entrance, appearing to double as almost a reception desk, although Terrence explained that Frank spent a good deal of time on the lower floor where the records and other more space-intensive administrative areas were housed. The rest of the open area held assorted desks boasting what looked to be top-of-the line computer stations. A staircase at the back of the room appeared to access both the upper and lower floors, and a small glass-walled elevator ran beside the staircase. For the wheelchair, Darby assumed.

"What's upstairs?"

"It used to be the building's above-shop living quarters, but now it's a state-of-the-art computer and surveillance paraphernalia lab. Oscar's got a full house up there right now working on the computers. Right, Oscar?"

"Aye. They've been at it over an hour already this morning." The owl man gestured upstairs. "We've four officers who've been seconded to the team to help review account information and analyze bank and financial institution intelligence."

Terrence said, "As you can probably tell, we spent the bulk of our budget on the electronic component of the offices. Consequently, the furnishings might have been a bit shortchanged, but Frank got us some bargains from secondhand stores."

Darby wrinkled her nose. "Shortchanged is an understatement. The place looks more than a wee bit shabby." She didn't miss the flash of contempt in the ginger-haired farmer's face at her remark, before he turned his attention back to his computer screen. The owl likewise turned away, returning to his machine, and the circus acrobat wheeled his chair over to his desk. Apparently they all liked the furnishings.

"We spent money where it was best spent for what we need. Elegant office furnishings weren't a priority. Our equipment was."

Darby could tell Terrence was annoyed at her. What did she care? She was more than annoyed with him.

But Terrence seemed to get past his pique quickly, and was all business again. "Allison, will you give Darby a full tour?"

"Yes, guv." Allison beamed.

Darby shook her head. "I'm good for now. I'm sure I can find my way around." No way was she going to be forced into a tour of this rattrap led by Allison in Bloody Wonderland.

Terrence nodded. "DI Lawrence should be here any moment. You're clear on what I want you to do?"

She nodded. "Crystal."

* * * * *

Darby didn't have to wait long for her assignment to show up. DI

Mark Lawrence entered High Street not a quarter hour after Darby finished going through the file. Terrence closed the door of his office, motioned for Lawrence to take the seat next to Darby, then resumed his place behind his desk.

Lawrence was an attractive man: sandy hair that was obviously professionally styled, regular features, and a well-maintained body set off by an expensive suit that fit him perfectly. But it was equally obvious that he knew exactly how attractive he was, and that his smile was calculated to melt the knickers off most women. Luckily, she was not most women. Nonetheless, when he flashed his smile at her, she sent him a sidelong glance that let him think she just might be interested.

Terrence said, "This is Darby Reid, Interpol. She's come to assist in some of the financial aspects of the investigation that have been being pursued by her agency. And yes, she's my sister, but she gets no special treatment for that."

Darby could feel DI Lawrence's deep blue eyes appraising her. She had a good sense of when a man was attracted to her, and she knew without a doubt that she had Lawrence's full attention.

Darby spoke, not bothering to even look at her brother. "Nor do I want—or need—any."

DI Lawrence grinned. "I'll bet you don't."

She smiled, putting as much coy in her voice as she could get by with in front of her brother. "Thank you very much, Detective Inspector."

"Don't mention it, angel."

Terrence's icy voice broke into the flirtatious banter. "I met with DC Parsons' family yesterday. Has your team been able to find any more evidence about what happened to him?"

Darby remembered what her brother had told her about the young constable who'd supposed to have been watching Ramsey turning up dead.

Lawrence looked suddenly subdued. "Not really. Hit and run most likely. Looks like he was walking on that dark lane after he left his post, and just was unlucky to get in the way of a car. The lane leads to a popular spot for shagging. My guess is whoever hit him had someone he shouldn't have had in the car with him, and moved the body so it wouldn't be found for a while. We've got bulletins out looking for information, but I doubt if there's any connection to what happened to Ramsey."

"Maybe not, but it's too early to rule it out. I've reminded everyone on my team to be careful. You might want to do the same with your people."

Lawrence nodded. "Aye."

Terrence picked up his mug of tea and took a long drink. "Right, then. We'll be continuing our interviews today on Ramsey's murder. I'll interview the Von Zandts myself. DI Lawrence, if you and your team could finish interviews of the people in Ramsey's office who he worked with most closely, maybe we'll get a lead there. Also, I'd appreciate it if you would brief Darby on the Ramsey surveillance history—who he was in contact with regularly, etc., and try to determine who else needs to be investigated for possible involvement in his death."

"Happy to." Lawrence cocked his head at Darby and gave her a smirk that told her he still had no idea with whom he was dealing. But she could play impressed female when she needed to, as long as it suited her purposes.

"Darby has access to some deep background information that can save some time, so work with her on that. Other than the Von Zandt interviews, I'd like to leave following up on the Ramsey murder leads chiefly to the two of you. Frank will get you copies of the reports from the interviews that we've done already, as well as information on the evidence we've collected. Use your people from CID to do any additional legwork you need done."

Lawrence's eyes widened briefly, and Darby could tell he was surprised he was still going to be allowed to be involved so deeply in the investigation, especially after the reprimand her brother told her Lawrence had likely received from his own guv.

"I was just thinking that perhaps my men and I should work out of High Street while we're on this investigation. Might improve communication." Lawrence watched for Terrence's reaction to his suggestion.

Not bloody likely, Darby guessed. She doubted improving communication was actually what Lawrence wanted; more likely he wanted to make sure he wasn't excluded from anything important. But, just as she'd surmised, her brother wasn't going to go for that.

Terrence said, "Let's leave things as they are for now. We're a bit short on space."

Lawrence gave a just-trying-to-help shrug.

"Meanwhile, the rest of the task force will continue to concentrate on trying to find the terrorist funding source. I'm beginning to think we were misled on the Von Zandt connection, and I have some other ideas I want to follow. I have no doubt he's had some minor involvement, but as many dead ends as we've hit makes me think that he's not who we're looking for." Terrence spun the tale he'd explained to Darby earlier. She knew he was hoping the false information would get back to Von Zandt and that the man would consequently be more likely to drop his guard.

DI Lawrence face registered his surprise. "You're bleeding kidding me."

"We've found some other leads on possible conduits for the terrorist financing, and I've decided to shift our resources in that direction. Harry and Allison will continue working on the electronic transmissions evidence, and Oscar and the officers he has helping on computers will keep focusing on tracing financing trails." Terrence turned to Darby. "If you'll meet with Oscar on that later, I'd appreciate it. Your lot at Interpol may have some resources we don't have, and you can help him out with that."

DI Lawrence cleared his throat. "I'm not quite following why the task force is still on the Ramsey murder if you don't think Von Zandt was involved. Doesn't that mean whatever Ramsey was going to give you on Von Zandt was bogus?"

"Might be, but he was our informant, so his murder is ours."

Lawrence gave a short laugh. "Maybe his wife killed him."

Terrence's somber expression didn't change. "Stranger things have happened."

# Chapter 25

DARBY AND DI LAWRENCE exited the High Street office into the chill of the cloudy Glasgow morning. Terrence had asked her to get the CID officer out of the way so his own team wouldn't have to be on guard about what they were actually doing. So, after they left Terrence's office, she'd suggested the two of them find someplace they could talk besides the crowded quarters at High Street.

"Thanks for agreeing to brief me, DI Lawrence."

"My pleasure. And call me Mark."

"All right, Mark."

"Should I call you Darby? Or is it Lady Darby?" He was trying to make his manner mockingly casual, but she could tell it was bravado. The title impressed him. The title that wasn't really hers.

She shook her head. "Just Darby. I don't use the other for work. Too off-putting." She didn't use it at all anymore, but she didn't tell him that.

"I think Lady Darby has a nice ring to it."

She'd always thought it did, as well. Before she'd found out the truth, she'd loved the title, loved the way it sounded, loved the way it set her apart. She'd felt like it was part of who she was.

"Just Darby, okay?" She kept her face friendly, but it took an effort. Was it possible he knew the truth about her and was just taunting her?

"As you like, Darby." He touched her arm lightly. "Want to get some coffee? We can talk and I'll fill you in on what we've done, and what I'm planning to do next. The coffee at CID is sheep piss, but there's a café down the street here that's not half bad."

"Do they have food? I didn't have time for breakfast and I'm starving."

"Full breakfast menu. I could do with a fry up myself." Then he squinted at her, considering. The fine laugh lines at the edges of his eyes didn't detract from his good looks one bit. Slime or not, he was definitely hot. "Or are you the granola and yogurt type?"

She laughed and made a face. "Not me. Fry up as well."

"A woman after my own heart."

"So I'm taking it that you don't think I'm too much like my brother?"

"Nothing like your brother."

"What do you mean?" She posed her question, listening carefully for any hidden meaning in his answer.

He snorted. "I'm not into men. I could very easily be into you."

She breathed a silent sigh of relief. So he didn't know her secret.

Lawrence opened the door of the café and let her pass in front of him. Darby led the way to a vacant booth and slid into the battered red vinyl seat. He took the seat across from her. The air hung heavy with the smell of fried meats and coffee, and Darby knew her clothing would reek when she left. Ah, the price of devotion to duty.

A tired waitress in a pink uniform with lemon yellow frizz for hair handed them menus. Noting the grimy condition of the laminated cardboard, Darby hastily declined the one offered to her. God, didn't they ever wipe the bloody things off. Hadn't they heard of disinfectant?

"I'll just have what you're having, Mark."

He nodded as if he were used to women deferring to him, and rattled off their order. She wanted to puke. How much animal fat did he shove down his self-satisfied gullet every day? The thought of puking reminded her of her sister-in-law's miserable condition. She didn't feel any sympathy, though. The bitch deserved to be sick every second of every day, and Darby hoped she was.

When they each had a cup of what apparently passed for coffee here in front of them, Lawrence and Darby went over the status of the investigation into Richard Ramsey's death, as well as the reports on both Ramsey and DC Parson's deaths.

Darby frowned when he finished. "So, nothing yet. That's disappointing."

"It is."

"So do you agree with Terrence that it's unlikely Von Zandt was involved?"

"I never thought he was, but Reid was keen for it. I'm glad he's finally seen the error of his ways."

Darby heard the note of self-satisfaction in Lawrence's voice and resisted the urge to kick him under the table. "What about the suspicious timing—the day before Ramsey's supposed to hand over information implicating him?" Terrence wanted her to make sure DI Lawrence had bought the story about the change in the investigation's focus.

"We don't actually know that Ramsey really ever had anything. He could have just been bluffing to cover his own involvement. He might have just been saying what he thought your brother wanted to hear."

"Good point." The insufferable bastard. Her brother would never have signaled what he wanted to hear to a witness.

"I think from what he said about changing the direction of the investigation that Reid finally agrees with me."

She nodded. "You must be right."

In a voice that was just a little too nonchalant, Lawrence said, "So, are you staying with big brother?"

She took a drink of her coffee. "Just last night. I'm staying at the Blythswood Square for the rest of my time here."

Lawrence gave a low whistle. "That's spendy, isn't it? Why not just stay at his flat?"

She let just the hint of a coquettish smile dance on her lips. "Staying with a big brother can be difficult for any more than a night or two, if you know what I mean." Especially when she was so angry with Terrence she could hardly stand to be near him. Her brother's betrayal still felt so fresh.

"Protective?"

"A little. Disapproving . . . you know." She'd trusted Terrence above all others, adored him, no, idolized him. But he hadn't trusted her with the truth. Even if he hadn't known right away, Terrence had to have eventually figured it out. After all, he'd been ten when she was born.

DI Lawrence grinned. "I understand. He has a reputation as being a bit straitlaced."

"He's rigid about certain things. He's very much like the Earl. Very Catholic." Until now, Darby had loved the strong, steady predictability of the two men who anchored her life. Now, she knew everything she'd thought about her life had been a lie. Terrence should have told her the truth; he should not have let her go on blithely thinking she was as much a part of the family as her brothers and sister were.

"The earl?" Lawrence blinked. "Oh, right, your father. Who would have thought I'd be sharing my breakfast with an earl's daughter?"

She wasn't going to tell DI Lawrence that the Earl wasn't her father. The report in her file had said their mother had left the Earl, taking her two younger children with her, almost two years before Darby was born. Only Terrence had remained with the Earl. Juliette Reid had returned to her husband two years after she'd left him, and just a month shy of giving birth to Darby. No, the Earl wasn't her father.

Darby said, "Terrence and the Earl are equally devout, which, believe me, is saying something." That was an understatement. Not just devout, but Opus Dei devout. But that was none of Lawrence's business. "We all had to go to daily Mass when we were kids, but I think Terrence is the only one of us who continued after we didn't have to."

"Unusual isn't it, for a Scottish earl to be Catholic?"

"It is." Darby set her coffee cup down. If the food was as bad as the coffee, they were doomed. "One of the previous earls fell in love with a Catholic woman who talked him into converting."

"And your mother?"

Darby shrugged. "She's Catholic, but she's French. Church once a week is enough for her." She didn't want to talk about her mother. Or to her mother. She'd avoided going home or even talking to anyone there since she'd found out the truth about her parentage.

"And you?"

"I only go when I'm home and can't get out of it." She realized she was probably telling more about their private family life than Terrence would like her to do. But nothing she'd said was a secret.

"What about your brother's wife?"

Now here was a subject Darby knew unequivocally Terrence would not want her talking about. His precious Anne was sacrosanct topic number one. Ironic that he'd marry a woman that was doing to him just what their mother had done to his father. Served him right.

"Anne's Catholic. At least nominally, if you know what I mean."

DI Lawrence nodded. "I saw the stories. She's more of a sinner than a saint, looks like. So what's going on with them?"

Darby stirred her coffee, a better alternative than actually drinking it. Terrence would kill her if she talked about Anne to Mark Lawrence. She was ballsy, but she wasn't crazy. On the other hand, she wasn't going to stick up for the bitch.

"You'd have to ask Terrence."

"Not likely. No one talks to him about that. Verboten subject."

"You're telling me." She gave a wry smile. "Why all this interest in Terrence's wife?"

"Just making small talk." He motioned his head indicating the approaching waitress who deposited their plates in front of them. Resuming the conversation when the waitress was again out of earshot, he said, "So, tell me, what clever new ideas does Interpol have about the investigation?"

Darby pretended to butter her toast, scraping off as much as she put on. She tried to block out the disgusting sight of undercooked eggs and fatty bacon on her plate. Even the tomatoes looked greasy. "We're just here to help."

Lawrence started to tuck into his fried eggs; the half-cooked whites and rubbery bacon didn't seem to bother him. Between mouthfuls, he said, "I've heard your brother is tied in with MI5. Rumor has it he's slated to take over MI5's Scottish office when Schilling steps down."

Darby concealed her surprise, even as she realized that it made perfect sense. So there was yet another secret her brother had kept from her. But Lawrence didn't need to know that she'd been clueless, so she gave him a knowing look. "Let's not go there."

"Did Interpol think Reid was on the right track when he was targeting Von Zandt?"

She paused, a piece of barely buttered toast raised halfway to her lips. "As I say, we're just here to help. We're not involved with every aspect of the investigation until we're actually brought in. Now that we have been, we agree with Terrence's conclusion that Von Zandt may be a sleaze, but that he's probably not who we're looking for."

DI Lawrence stopped shoveling in his food long enough to take a drink of coffee. "We've been wasting our time, and the government's money, then. Are you sure Reid means to give up on Von Zandt after all that we've invested in that line of investigation?"

"Unless something new comes up to tie Von Zandt in again, I'd say that lead will be dropped." Darby averted her eyes from the congealing and disgusting mess of her breakfast. If she had to, she'd cut it up and push it around her plate to make it look like she was actually eating it.

"The brass can't be too happy about this. I'd guess Reid got an earful when he told them."

Darby swallowed a drink of the bitter coffee. "It's not unusual for leads that seemed promising at first to dry up later. You think they'd blame him?"

"It's Reid's operation. He chooses the directions to follow. So I guess it's fair for him to take the flak when he's wrong."

"I'm getting the distinct feeling that you're not fond of my brother." She silently pondered the implications of what Lawrence had said. Her own boss wanted Interpol to take over the investigation. He'd implied she'd be rewarded if she could make it happen. They'd been hoping she could get Terrence to agree, but she knew that would never happen. She'd have to go around him. Doubtless, DI Lawrence was looking for the same opportunity she was.

"We have differences of opinion, you could say. Some say that he's been given the position he's in because of who he is."

"Obviously." She held back from telling Lawrence that a piece of tomato skin was caught between his top front teeth, enjoying how ridiculous it made him look.

Lawrence vigorously shook a grubby salt shaker over his food. How had this place not been shut down for health code violations?

"I mean because of who he is outside of being police. That he's been given preferential treatment because of, well, your family's money and his title."

Mad as she was at her brother, she didn't like hearing him be disparaged by someone else. "I can't imagine there's anyone who works harder than Terrence does, or who is more dedicated."

"I'm just saying not everyone thinks that way." Lawrence's glance slid to her plate. "You're not eating."

"Stomach's still queasy from the flight last night. Choppy air."

He looked chagrined. "Sorry." After a pause he said, "You're not going to eat your bacon?" He gave her a smile she thought he must consider his endearing-hungry-growing-boy smile.

"Help yourself." She pushed her plate toward him. "So, impress me with your ideas of how you'd do things better."

He shook his head, jabbed his fork into the wiggly bacon on her plate, and preening like the prick of a piggish peacock he was, started to talk.

# Chapter 26

VON ZANDT'S ULTRA-MODERN offices all but shouted money-making mojo. Stark, sleek granite floors, white walls splashed with blood red paintings, and steel framed furnishings upholstered in violently expensive black leather. Reid could have sent someone else to do the interview, or could have brought someone else with him, but instead, he'd come alone, reasoning that a meeting alone would send more of a message.

An elegant young brunette dressed in a red that matched the paintings perched on a space age chair behind a metal and glass desk. She looked up, bored, then her mouth fell open and her face blossomed into an inelegant, genuine smile. "Oy, you're Lord Reid, aren't you?"

He'd started to recognize that look on strangers, but he still wasn't used to it. Those damned tabloids apparently had quite a following, especially among young women. Good thing he didn't work undercover anymore.

He inclined his head in acknowledgement and forced a smile. "Just Superintendent Reid today. I'm here to see Walter Von Zandt."

"I'll see if he's available, Lord Reid."

She punched some buttons, spoke into her headset, then listened. She fluttered her eyelashes at Reid and smiled. "He'll see you now. His office is . . . never mind, I'll just take you there." She took off her headset and, standing up, she motioned for him to follow her. "It's this way."

Reid followed, idly wondering who was going to answer the telephones in her absence. As she walked, the young woman chatted nonstop—asking him his opinion about the weather, the upcoming Easter holidays, and even made a brief reference to the events in

California. He fingered his wedding ring, trying not to let his discomfort show. When they reached their destination, she reluctantly let him go, but not before reminding him of her name with what he thought was meant to be a soulful look, and telling him to let her know if there was ever anything she could do for him.

Lord save him.

Von Zandt's private office was decorated in the same manner as the reception area. He sat behind a vast glass desk that held only a silver laptop computer. Not one scrap of paperwork was in evidence. Bare as it was, it was a legitimate-appearing office for someone who dealt, however indirectly, in terrorism and murder.

Walter Von Zandt stood up from a glossy black leather chair and came over to shake Reid's hand. At fifty-seven, Von Zandt was still in good shape. He had a full head of steel gray hair and hard, cold eyes. He dressed impeccably, his clothes obviously expensive, and he sported a tan that shouted French Riviera.

"Please have a seat."

Von Zandt motioned to the chairs in front of his desk, then went back behind his desk and sat down. "It's been a while, Superintendent Reid—though you weren't a superintendent last time we spoke. To what do I owe the honor of this visit?"

Reid took a seat. "We're making inquiries into the death of Richard Ramsey."

"An unfortunate business." Von Zandt shook his head. "Suicide is an ugly thing. Richard must have been very unhappy to have done something like that to his family."

"Actually, it wasn't suicide."

"An accident?"

"Murder."

"Murder? How terrible." Von Zandt's voice didn't even try to express actual dismay or surprise. He sounded bored.

"Yes."

"I hadn't heard that the police suspected murder."

"We just got the autopsy report today." Reid said, noting that Von Zandt seemed to feel entitled to have received the correct information earlier. "As you'd expect, we're talking to people who knew him. Do you know anyone who would have wanted him dead?"

Von Zandt's reptilian eyes held Reid's gaze, then blinked slowly and deliberately. "No, I don't."

"Tell me about your business relationship."

Von Zandt gave an elegant shrug and stood up, moving out from behind his desk. "We had business dealings with each other, profitable for both of us." He walked over to an Oriental cabinet that served as a drinks trolley. "Would you like a drink? Your family's label." He held up a familiar bottle of whiskey.

Reid shook his head, but noted the bottle was from Dunbaryn's first reserve.

Von Zandt poured himself a whiskey and went back to sit behind his desk.

"You also had a personal relationship with him?"

"I'm not sure how to answer that. We were business colleagues, not friends." Von Zandt steepled his fingers, ignoring the drink he'd just poured, and Reid realized the man hadn't had any intention of actually drinking it. "Though I'm sure you're aware that I have a relationship with his daughter."

"Yes. I've spoken with Moira."

Von Zandt blinked slowly. "This has been upsetting for her, of course, but she and Ramsey weren't close."

"Did Ramsey object to your relationship with Moira?"

A cold smile played over Von Zandt's hard features. "Hardly. He introduced us. You might even say he encouraged us to get to know each other. He thought I would be a good influence on Moira."

"A good influence?" Reid could hardly keep the disbelief out of his voice.

"Yes, and he was right. With me, she finished school, and her marks greatly improved. She's studying at the university now. Part time, of course, as she frequently accompanies me on my travels. Which is educational for her, as well."

"You've been involved with Moira for some time, as I understand it."

"Three years. She moved in with me on her sixteenth birthday." Von Zandt would never admit to having been involved with Moira before the legal age of consent.

"Tell me more about your relationship with Richard Ramsey."

"I thought your task force concentrated on organized and financial crimes. Not murder."

"You're well-informed. CID is actually taking the lead on investigating the Ramsey murder. But I have an interest in Richard

Ramsey with regard to one of my own investigations." As he had this information planted to come out in tomorrow's news, Reid decided not to play coy.

"I've been receiving reports of your task force's interest in me." Von Zandt took a drink of his whiskey.

"Receiving reports?"

Von Zandt seemed to realize how close he'd come to admitting he had an informant in the police ranks. "Just an expression. Glasgow's a small town in many respects."

That was true, Reid thought, but just said, "You shouldn't believe everything you hear."

"Let me assure you I am a legitimate businessman and any attempt to paint me as anything else I will consider to be defamation and harassment."

Reid ignored Von Zandt's threat. "Today I'm just here to talk about Richard Ramsey. Asking a good citizen for information that can help us catch his murderer. I'm sure you want to help us in our inquiries. Let's start with what exactly were the business interests you two had in common."

Von Zandt opened a gold cigarette case and took out a cigarette. He offered one to Reid, who shook his head. Von Zandt lit the cigarette with a matching thin gold lighter, and inhaled deeply before answering. Only a man not brought up with money needed such trying-too-hard trappings, Reid thought.

"It was a mutually beneficial business relationship."

When Von Zandt said nothing else, Reid prompted, "How so?"

"A few years ago, Ramsey International needed an influx of cash. I provided the cash, gained an interest in the company. You might say, a significant interest."

"You're on the Board of Directors of Ramsey International."

"I am. That was one of the conditions of the investment I made."

"As is your son. Henry?"

"Yes, my eldest. His seat on the board was also one of the conditions." Von Zandt blew out a cloud of cigarette smoke.

Reid silently apologized to his lungs. "How will Ramsey's death affect the structure of the board? Who will be in control of the company?"

"No way to know." Something sinister slithered from Von Zandt's eyes.

Reid suddenly realized what he should have seen all along. Why Von Zandt had gotten involved with Richard Ramsey. Von Zandt wanted control of Ramsey International. Out loud, he said, "With the control of Ramsey International comes the control of millions of pounds and many different businesses."

Von Zandt's smile was glacial but he didn't say anything.

Reid went on. "One of those businesses is a pharmaceutical company."

Von Zandt said nothing.

"And one an aeronautics company."

Again, no response.

"Weapons?" As Reid said the word, a chill froze his body and the truth exploded in his mind. This was what Von Zandt was after.

"I don't think you need me to tell you what companies Ramsey owned. Look it up."

Reid's mind was churning feverishly. Von Zandt had more of a motive to kill Richard Ramsey than just because he'd been about to spill Von Zandt's secrets. It might also explain the real reason Richard Ramsey had agreed to help Reid.

"When's the vote?"

Von Zandt shrugged.

Reid kept his voice placid. "It won't be hard for me to find out. You may as well tell me."

"The meeting is next week."

Reid considered. "Who is the solicitor in charge of the estate?"

"Really, Superintendent, I'm surprised you didn't get that information from Mrs. Ramsey."

"Why don't you just tell me?"

"Ramsey used the same solicitor as I use. Cyrus Rothman."

Reid absorbed the information, then asked, "When did you last see Ramsey?"

"Friday afternoon. We met on some issues concerning the company. Henry was there, as well. The meeting ended at half five."

"We have reason to believe Ramsey was planning to meet a woman the night he was killed. Do you have any idea who it could have been?"

Von Zandt raised his eyebrows in a parody of surprise. "None."

"Did he have a girlfriend?"

"How would I know?"

"Where were you Saturday night?"

Von Zandt looked amused. "I was with my family for dinner, and spent the night with my wife at our home here in the city. It was her birthday. My sons were both there, and Henry's wife as well, in case you need to know that—although my son Frederick did leave to take Moira to her parents and then back to the flat afterwards, as I believe Moira told you."

Reid inclined his head in assent.

"On the off chance that you think I might have had something to do with Richard's death, please accept my reassurances that not only would I never be involved in such a thing as murder, but I would be a fool to do so when it would focus the police's attention on me. I am not a fool."

Reid stood up and moved toward the door. "I'll let you get back to work."

Von Zandt stood up. "Superintendent, always a pleasure. Perhaps next time we meet it will be a more pleasant occasion. We could have dinner. I'll bring my wife, and you can bring yours—or," he frowned, "is she still with her lover?"

Reid didn't say anything and kept his face impassive.

Von Zandt smiled. "That must be awkward for you, but every marriage has its challenges, doesn't it? Seriously, I'd like to meet her. I enjoy beautiful women."

Reid opened the door to leave. "I thought teenagers were more your style. Believe me, there's a world of difference."

# Chapter 27

DARBY LEANED OVER to see Oscar's computer screen, making sure the V of her shirt revealed a generous glimpse of cleavage. She'd been trying to ascertain the man's exact position on her brother's team. Terrence was undoubtedly not telling her everything, and she needed another source of inside information if she was going to take over this investigation.

Oscar indicated some columns on the screen. "Four times we've located accounts suspected of being used to launder international funds. Four times, we tied them to Von Zandt, and four times, right before we got in, they're cleaned out and closed down."

"You're right; there's definitely a leak." Darby put her hand lightly on Oscar's arm, in a way she often did to invite intimacy and interest from a man.

No reaction.

"Do you think the leak's plugged now?"

He turned to her, and she parted her lips in the soft signal of receptive female.

Oscar didn't look at her lips, didn't steal a peek at her chest, didn't register any sign of being aware of her being just slightly too close. His face was all business. "We hope so, but now they're making the accounts harder to find."

"Any new leads?" She looked intently into his eyes, and put all the heat she could muster without being ridiculous into her voice.

"Maybe. The guv's friend, John Stirling, just deciphered some encrypted transmissions that might help."

Darby's heartbeat sped up at the mention of John Stirling. God, she really might see him soon. But she breathed down her excitement. Right now her focus had to be on Oscar. "Where's the money coming from that's feeding into the accounts?"

Oscar shrugged. "That's the question, but we're pretty sure it's coming from Muslim extremist supporters. The guv says MI5 thinks the faction behind the university bombing plot is Nigerian, although we're not entirely certain about that."

Darby didn't need a primer on money laundering. She knew the backers couldn't give the money directly to the terrorists because then they'd be tied to the attacks—so they went through people like Von Zandt who cleaned up the money and redirected it to the people actually doing the dirty work. And presto, once the money was cleaned, the tie between the givers and the receivers became invisible. "Then the money sitting in the accounts isn't Von Zandt's."

"Most of it isn't, but he takes a cut of what's there as a fee for the wash job."

Darby tapped her fingers. "If the money disappears from the account, I assume both ends of the transaction will be annoyed at Von Zandt. That wouldn't be so bad."

"Not as long as we've followed the trail each way from the middle before that happens. Otherwise, they'll just find another way to wash the money."

"Right. So this is where I might be able to help. Interpol has some sources that might be helpful. Okay to take the controls?"

Oscar nodded, got up, and let her take over his computer. She talked while she accessed the websites she needed, but dropped her flirtatious maneuvers. She would never be able to recruit this man to ally with her, or to keep her informed of things Terrence didn't share with her. Oscar was not vulnerable to her at all.

The man was either the coldest fish she'd ever met—or he was gay.

# Chapter 28

"TERRENCE REID came to see me today." A large, rather mangy, calico cat with one ear half chewed off, wound its way around the burgundy leather chair that was reserved for Walter Von Zandt's exclusive use in lounge of the City Centre flat. Von Zandt moved his legs to avoid letting the animal shed its hair on his clothes, then gave it a hard kick with his foot. He spoke curtly to the bodyguard nearest to him. "Throw Moira's fucking cat in her room."

The girl was in her bedroom doing whatever it was she did when she was alone. She was supposed to be studying, but he still could not understand how she could concentrate on her schoolwork when she had ear pieces plugged in her ears, feeding her the raucous noise she considered music. At least she wasn't singing again. He remembered Reid's remark about teenagers and was irritated again, thinking how close to right the man had been.

The bodyguard moved swiftly to remove the disgusting creature. Von Zandt motioned to the man seated across from him. "How much exactly does Reid know?"

Before DI Lawrence could answer, Von Zandt nodded to the largest of his bodyguards. "Stay at Moira's door, and make sure she doesn't come out while we're talking." His eyes moved around the room, checking that his other two bodyguards were in place: one at the flat's front door and the other by the glass doors to the balcony. Then he brought his attention back to Lawrence, and waited for an answer.

"Nothing for you to worry about, Walter." The cop's jaunty attitude grated on Von Zandt. He was bought and paid for, and Von Zandt expected the man to show him respect.

"Tell me why I shouldn't be worried."

"There's not much to tell." Lawrence's eyes darted toward the bar, but Von Zandt doubted the cop would be brave enough to ask for a drink. "He knows Ramsey was murdered. They suspect a woman was involved."

"I got that much from his questions. But that's not what I want to know. Any reason to think he suspects you of being involved with me? Or that you're providing information to me?" Von Zandt regarded Lawrence with a steely gaze and saw a muscle twitch in the other man's jaw. Good, at least the shite knew enough to be afraid.

"Not a chance. I'd know if he did."

"You think so?"

"Absolutely. As you know, I have connections. Besides, Reid says he now thinks he was wrong about you being involved in funding the terrorist attacks. He says he's refocusing."

Von Zandt narrowed his eyes. "Bullshite. Tell me another."

"That's what he said."

Von Zandt pursed his lips. "You're sure?"

"Positive."

Von Zandt motioned to one of his men to bring him a drink. He didn't bother to ask Lawrence if he wanted one. He might need to use Lawrence, but he didn't have to drink with him. "Maybe he's not telling you the truth. I'd heard there'd been trouble between you and him."

"Nothing to worry about. He's just cheesed off that I didn't direct my men to stay with Ramsey 24/7, and the idiot got himself killed. Reid went up the chain to complain about it, but as I'm still on the task force, I'd guess they gave him short shrift. He may be their golden boy, but I've got Steynton looking after me."

"I heard you'd been reprimanded." He could tell Lawrence was surprised that he knew about that. "You're not my only source of information, you know."

The cop's face went red. "It was nothing. A slap on the hand to keep Reid pacified."

"Are you certain?" Von Zandt didn't bother to keep the skepticism from his voice.

"Yeah, it was just for show." The detective looked uneasy.

Growing up as stinking poor rubbish in the seedy part of Glasgow, Von Zandt had learned the vicious rules of survival. As a young man, to give himself courage, he'd imagined himself as a ruthless tiger. Right now he let his mind toy with the idea of being that tiger and tearing Lawrence's throat out. "I'm not sure you're much of a detective. I'll wager you don't even know that Reid's wandering wife is back."

DI Lawrence squinted, apparently trying to register the news. "She's here? In Scotland?"

"She's been in Glasgow since Sunday night."

"With him?"

"Yes, with him."

"Are you sure?"

Von Zandt gave him a withering glance. "Don't insult me."

"Right. You know everything."

Von Zandt made a mental note of the man's sarcastic tone. He'd pay for that. "As a matter of fact, she and the man she works for are meeting with me Thursday about the renovation of the gardens on an estate I purchased. They've just accepted the job."

Lawrence's jaw actually fell open. "You're fucking kidding."

"Not at all. They'd been offered the job a few weeks ago, but Lady Anne wouldn't accept until she cleared it with her husband. She was concerned he wouldn't want her to work so far outside of Glasgow, but apparently he's given his consent."

"And he knows she'll be working for you?"

Von Zandt smiled. "Not yet. The estate is still named for the family that owned it originally, and it's titled in one of my more obscure companies' name. The contacts have all been through our estate manager, and I gave instructions that my name wasn't to be mentioned."

"He'll never agree to have her work for you."

"The contract is signed."

Lawrence gave a rough laugh. "So apparently she doesn't have a brain in that fucking gorgeous body."

Von Zandt was unaccountably irritated. "On the contrary, apparently she does. The man she's working for is probably the best historical garden restorer in the world, and she's his star protégé."

"She's probably doing him."

The cop's response was pathetically predicable, Von Zandt decided. His analytical thinking seemed to consist of jumping from one stereotypical cliché to the next. "I doubt it, as he's gay. And that's beside the point. It will be hard for her to walk away from the job, even when she learns I'm involved. It's going to drive Reid crazy."

"Yeah, you're right. I wouldn't have guessed he'd take her back."

"Hard to fathom, I agree." But convenient. Von Zandt had plans for Lady Anne. Screwing Reid's wife would be a fulfilling way to stick it to Reid as well. And if she wasn't agreeable, well, she just might not get a chance to say no. "I'm looking forward to meeting her. You haven't, I take it?"

"I'm not in Reid's illustrious social circle." Lawrence's tone was sour.

"Nor am I. But that's going to change." With control of Ramsey International, Von Zandt's world would have endless possibilities. Neither Moira nor, for that matter, Elisa, fit in his vision of his future. He deserved more, and by God, he would have more.

"Is that why you bought the place? So you could get Reid's wife there?"

Von Zandt shook his head. "No, that was just one of life's unexpected ironies. My estate manager presented me with a couple of choices of garden designers that would have the experience to restore the estate's garden, but he said that the top choice, if I was willing to pay for the best, would be Jonas Reveille and Anne Michaels. Then he reminded me who Anne Michaels was. That made the choice easy."

The cop grinned. "You're going to fuck her, aren't you?"

Von Zandt gave the idiot cop a withering glance. "Don't be coarse."

Lawrence flushed at the reprimand, then smoothed back his hair. "Speaking of Reid women, Darby Reid is here working with the task force. She's with Interpol, you know."

"I am aware of her affiliation. When did this happen?"

"She showed up this morning. I think it's safe to say that she's someone I should have no trouble keeping an eye on, if you get my meaning." Lawrence's smile was as contrived as his slicked back hair.

"Don't be too sure of yourself."

DI Lawrence didn't back down. "If there's one thing I know, it's women."

"You wouldn't be the first man to make the mistake of believing that. You'd better make sure."

The cop scowled. "I'm sure."

"Do not disappoint me. I'm warning you, I am not nice when I'm disappointed."

"Nor am I." DI Lawrence's posture stiffened, and he stared back, but Von Zandt knew he'd won.

He was ready to dismiss the cop, but decided to break the tension, and end the meeting on a better note. No point in having unhappy stooges wandering around causing trouble. "Good work, then."

The tension left the cop's spine, and the man relaxed, his customary jauntiness returning. "So, did you get a chance to talk to Ramsey last night? I went through a lot of trouble to make sure he could get away to meet you without being followed."

Von Zandt glared. "I told you Ramsey didn't show up. Henry and I waited for an hour, then gave up."

Lawrence looked at him, his skepticism barely concealed. "So you didn't have anything to do with him getting killed?"

"Absolutely not. I gave strict instructions that none of my men were to touch a hair on his head."

Lawrence seemed to retreat into thought, an odd smile playing on his lips. Von Zandt finished his drink, wondering how long he needed to put up with the idiot. Who knew what beetlebrained thoughts were wandering around his head? Keeping him around was getting more and more risky.

Von Zandt stood up, signaling the meeting was at an end. "And for your information, nor did I have anything to do with that cop getting killed. I didn't get to where I am today by being stupid. Whoever killed that poor young man did not have my blessing. And if I find out that one of my people had anything to do with that, they'll be sorry."

# Chapter 29

ALLISON STARED at her computer, but she wasn't concentrating.

How did Darby Reid, who was just a few years older than she was, manage to always look so self-assured and competent? The guv had that same self-assurance, but he was older and had been in positions of command for many years, so that was to be expected. Would she ever be able to acquire that kind of polish, or was it something you had to be born with? Certainly the blokes on her search detail at the Ramsey house wouldn't have treated Darby the way they'd treated her. They wouldn't have asked Darby out, either. Even they would have seen she was out of their raggedy-arsed league.

And Patty Cady wouldn't have ever made the mistake of thinking that Darby Reid was Harry's bloody assistant. She wouldn't have had the cheek to insist Darby go away just when the interview was getting down to things.

The telephone next to Allison's computer rang. Her mother. Frustration made her want to cry. Did anyone else at High Street's mother call them at work? She wanted to ignore it, but if she did, everyone would wonder why she let her phone keep ringing. Besides, if she didn't pick up, her mother would ring her mobile. And if Allison ignored that, her mother would probably call the Superintendent to find out if Allison was all right.

Allison's mother worried about Allison being police, even though her job never involved anything dangerous, worried about Allison being around so many men all day, even though she barely dated, and even, ludicrously, worried about Allison working for a Catholic, even though the Superintendent never mentioned his religion.

"Busy here." Allison kept her voice low. Maybe no one would

realize it was her mother. She tried to look businesslike and nodded, pretending to take notes as she listened as if it were a work call. The whole family still treated her like she was a little girl. While her mother nattered on, Allison mentally reviewed her finances. In a year, maybe she'd be able to move out. She'd still have her older brothers hovering around her, but it would be harder for everyone to keep tabs on her if she didn't live at home.

Finally, Allison decided she'd listened long enough. "Right. I need to go now." She hung up, glancing around the room to see if anyone had been paying attention. Everyone seemed intent on their own work. Good.

She let her eyes drift over to the Superintendent's office where he was meeting with his sister. Maybe money had something to do with their confidence. Those boots Darby was wearing today must have cost more than Allison made in a month. Two months. On the other hand, Harry was confident, and he wasn't rich. So, money, and what went with it, the right schools and connections, certainly didn't hurt, but it wasn't what really made the difference.

It was attitude. They all had that same confident attitude. Trying to emulate the guv was a bit of a stretch, and trying to imitate Harry would be idiotic. It was bloody hard to translate what worked in a man's demeanor to what worked for a woman. But she could try to adopt Darby's confident attitude.

Allison arranged her face in an imitation of Darby's self-assured, superior expression, tilting her computer screen so she could see her reflection. She definitely looked more confident, but not really like herself. She needed a more sophisticated haircut to go with the attitude.

Harry's voice interrupted her thoughts. "What's got you so cheesed off, sweetcakes?"

She looked over at him hastily, hoping he hadn't noticed her looking at her reflection. "I'm not cheesed off. And stop calling me that."

"You look cheesed off. Your nose went into the air, and you look like you've been sucking on a salty lemon."

She tried to give Harry the withering look she'd been practicing at home. "I was thinking."

"About lemons?"

"You're hilarious. About work. Maybe you should try doing that as well."

"Aren't you little miss la-di-da?" He seemed to think, then grinned. "Oh, I get it. You're trying to act like Lady Interpol." He gestured to the Superintendent's office.

"You're an arse. Leave me alone." Her face flushed at being found out so easily. She hated Harry.

Frank wheeled his chair over and handed Harry some reports, then turned and looked sympathetically at Allison. "Harry, leave the poor kid alone."

Allison knew he was trying to be supportive, but it annoyed her to be called a kid. She bet no one called Darby Reid a kid, let alone poor kid. They wouldn't dare. Putting on her most aloof manner, she said, "Frank, I can handle DS Ross and his insulting behavior on my own."

Frank blinked in surprise at the rebuke in her voice. Quickly recovering, he nodded. "I'm sure you can, DC Muirhead. Excuse me for interfering." He turned his wheelchair toward the lift.

No one spoke until the door to the lift closed and the machine whisked Frank away.

Then Harry looked over at her, his face showing his disappointment. "I wouldn't have thought it, Allison but you can be a right bitch."

His words stung, but she kept her face impassive. He'd started it, and she hadn't meant to sound snooty to Frank. "I'm sure I don't know what you mean. I'm just trying to do my job without personal comments from you. We're colleagues, not friends, so I'd appreciate it if you would keep your remarks to me professional, and I'll do the same for you."

"Sod off."

\* \* \* \* \*

Still feeling the sting of Harry's words, Allison watched as the door to the Superintendent's office opened and Darby came out, followed by her brother. The Super motioned to Oscar and Harry, and they all went into the conference room to go over what Allison suspected was some new account information the two had uncovered. Normally if the Superintendent forgot, Harry or Oscar would ask that she be included so she could learn. But this time neither Harry nor Oscar even looked back at her.

She'd felt like an outsider ever since her outburst to Frank. She couldn't remember ever feeling so tense an atmosphere between her and the others, and she hated it. Why had she snapped at Frank? He'd been nothing but good to her. It was Harry's fault. He'd goaded her into it. But still, she felt like shite.

Lost in her self-recriminations, Allison almost fell out of her chair when Darby's imperious voice interrupted her thoughts

"You're to come with me, DC Muirhead. I've a meet with someone from my agency who's working with the Germans on the investigation about the materials used to make the bombs. Some of the purchases were made with credit cards that were paid by offshore accounts. We'll get what they have and try to match it with what we're doing here. With any luck, it'll lead us somewhere."

Allison swallowed, nodded, trying not to show her relief. Maybe she hadn't been left out deliberately. Probably everyone had known she was going to be needed elsewhere.

"What are you waiting for? Get your coat."

"Aye." Allison wasn't sure she wanted to be quite like Darby Reid; no one else talked to her like she was a mere lackey. When the blokes teased her, it might be patronizing, but it at least seemed affectionate. "I'll be right with you."

Darby frowned, tapped her watch. "We need to leave now."

"Right, be ready in a tick. I just have to tell Frank something." Knowing she was risking the other woman's displeasure, Allison ran down the stairs to the bottom floor.

She found Frank studying schematics of the reconstruction of the bombing scene at Heidelberg University. He looked up as she came in, but didn't say anything.

Allison felt her face get hot, but decided there was nothing for it but to eat shite. "I'm that sorry about how I acted, Frank. I'm just tired of having to prove myself every moment, and Harry's teasing, and everything, but I shouldn't have taken it out on you."

He shrugged, and then smiled. "I shouldn't have called you a kid. I'm sorry about that, as well."

"That's okay. From you I know it wasn't meant as a put-down." She nodded toward the stairs. "I'd better go. Lady Interpol awaits." She pushed the tip of her nose up with her finger.

Frank laughed, and she ran over and hugged him before flying up the steps, her heart lighter.

Her day got even better. After that rough start, Darby Reid treated her like she was, if not an equal, as something close to it. A protégé, maybe. Darby was nothing like Harry. She was complimentary about Allison's work, listened to Allison's opinions, and commended Allison's ideas. And now they were on a first name basis.

After they'd finished their meeting with Darby's Interpol colleague, Darby dropped Allison back off at High Street with the data they'd collected, before going on to another meeting.

"Thanks for taking me with you."

Darby smiled. "No thanks needed. I think we're going to make quite a team."

# Chapter 30

OSCAR PRINTED OUT a screenshot from Richard Ramsey's work computer. "We're not going to find any deleted files here. This hard drive was replaced just like the one on the home computer."

Harry groaned. It had been a long day. Already it was dark outside the High Street office, and so far, they'd made little progress. "With Von Zandt senior and junior going in and out of Ramsey International like they owned the place, that's no surprise. What about on the other computers there?"

"Big fat nothing. There's no trace of anything except routine Ramsey International business."

Harry nodded. "Someone made sure we'd find nothing. The guv will be disappointed, but I don't think he was really expecting much. These credit card purchase records might pay off, though."

"We could use a break. That might make bringing in Interpol worth it." Oscar didn't say what Harry expected they were both thinking. Darby Reid was trouble waiting to happen.

Harry grunted. "I don't think we'll hear back on the cardholder information until tomorrow. I expect they'll be held in the name of some trust set up in an offshore bank, but that information is easier to get than it used to be."

"Easier, maybe, but still a bleeding pain."

"Looked like you were getting special attention from the guv's sister." Harry shifted his eyes to his computer screen, suppressing a smile.

"Lucky me."

"What did she want?"

"I'm not sure. Not me, I'm sure, but she tried to act like it."

"Dangerous, that one." Harry weighed his next words. He'd

never acknowledged that he knew Oscar was gay, and Oscar had never shared anything that would invite inquiry on the subject. "Not too bright if that was the route she took to get to you."

Oscar shot an assessing glance his way. "No." His eyes behind the thick glasses didn't waver.

Harry grinned, sending the message that it didn't bother him, and that he wasn't willing to pretend he didn't know anymore. Oscar gave a tight smile, but Harry thought his message had been delivered.

"We need to keep an eye on her."

"Do you think the Superintendent sees it?"

Harry shook his head. "She's family. And he's distracted."

"Yeah, something's not right with him. Like where'd he'd go off to so early? And taking the morning off yesterday? It's not like him."

Harry shrugged. "He was watching the clock all day and shot out of here at six on the nose. If it were me, I'd say it was a bird. Being it's him, I'd still say it's a bird. For him that means it's his wife, and that's unlikely given there's no indication she's even in the country. But the evidence points that way."

"Good for him, then."

"Why do you say that?" That Oscar even had an opinion on the subject surprised Harry.

"He works more than all of us. Whether it's his wife, or someone else . . ."

Harry interrupted. "It wouldn't be someone else. It's her or something else entirely. Nothing was on his calendar for tonight, so it's not one of his regular do's like those dinners and things he's always going to." They all knew those social commitments were part of Reid's job. The guv hated going to them, but as with everything else that was expected of him, he just did it. Gruesome life, Harry thought. Church, run, work, stiff-collar parties with stiff-arsed people, and no sweet, soft bird to sink into at night. Then the same thing over and over, day after day.

Oscar nodded. "If we could find the old hard drives, I could restore them. But I doubt that's going to happen."

"Tomorrow I'll check with Patty Cady. Maybe she saw something, or heard about Ramsey's work computer hard drive being replaced."

"Great." Oscar logged off. "I'm calling it a night. There's only so much disappointment I can take."

"Me, too. I'm meeting a dolly bird five minutes ago. Where'd Darby and Allison get off to?"

"Darby left to go to dinner with DI Lawrence."

Harry raised his eyebrows. "A meeting of giant egos. I'd like to be a genetically enhanced fly listening to the two of them talk. And Allison?"

"She's below with Frank working on something."

"They made it up, then?"

Oscar nodded.

"That's good. I'll just pop down and tell them we're leaving."

# Chapter 31

TERRENCE RAN HIS FINGERS down past Anne's naked breasts to her flat, taut abdomen. "I'm enjoying the sight of you like this. Your legs, girl—and what they lead to. I'm just damned glad Darby took herself off to a hotel. Making love before dinner is difficult to manage when you have a houseguest."

Anne put her hands on his face and kissed him. The lovely man-smell of him filled her nostrils. Her husband. Her love.

He pulled her on top of him. "I'll need a bit of recovery time, but we can do this again after some food. I'll order something delivered. Indian food sound good to you?"

She winced at the thought of spicy food with the way her stomach had been acting.

"Not yet, Terrence. I need to talk to you."

"You can do anything you like with me, girl. I'm entirely in your power." He smiled and held her head against his chest. For a moment she lay still against him, enjoying the feeling of him stroking her hair.

After a time, she moved off and rolled over beside him so that they were facing each other. Her fingers trailed along the side of his face.

"I've got something to tell you."

He smiled. "So tell me."

"I've been trying to figure out what to say, but I can't think of any way to tell you that isn't going to be awful."

"Just tell me." He kissed her gently. "It can't be that bad, Anne. You've come to me, you've not chosen Grainger. Anything else you tell me has to be better than that." He ran his fingers along her neck, and then down further to caress her body.

She swallowed. "I hope you say that when you hear what it is."

"Whatever it is, we'll deal with it." He placed soft kisses all around the edges of her lips.

Anne closed her eyes and received his blessings, afraid they would end as soon as she told him. But maybe not. They would deal with it, he said. Whatever it was, they would deal with it.

"Go on then, lassie, tell me what's wrong."

Her heart clenched as she struggled to get the words out, and when she finally did, her voice trembled. "I'm pregnant."

He pulled back slightly, and she saw him go pale, saw him swallow, knew he was praying.

"And that is bad news because?"

"Oh, Terrence, don't make me say it." Her voice caught.

"It's Grainger's baby?" He pulled farther away from her, and she felt a cavern open between them.

"I . . . I don't know."

She saw a fog of disbelief and confusion overcome him.

"Terrence, I'm so sorry."

"Isn't there a test they can do?" The pain in his voice cut through her.

She shook her head. "An amniocentesis could tell us, but my doctor said they won't do one just for that. It's too risky. I asked him if there was some other way—I begged him, but he said no—nothing safe."

"Oh, God." He looked sick, but then she saw anger take over. "God." He expelled his breath loudly.

She felt her tears start to fall, and put her face into her hands, gulping in air. "I'm so sorry."

"I can't believe I have to ask this." She heard him swallow. "Weren't you using anything when you were with him?"

Anne flushed. "Most of the time."

"Sweet Jesus."

"Terrence, you and I didn't use anything at all."

He bit his words out through clenched teeth. "We're married, Anne. I want to have children with you. You know that. And I guess I stupidly thought that going in bareback was a husband's privilege, as long as the wife was willing. And you certainly seemed willing." He sat up and ran his hands through his hair.

"I've been in agony trying to figure out how to tell you this. I knew how much it would hurt you. It's been killing me to have to tell you."

He raised his face to her, and the hurt she saw in it broke her heart. "Now what? What in Christ's name do we do now?"

She was quiet for a time, composing herself, hoping whatever words she found would bring him back to her. She took a deep breath. "I know this might be expecting too much. And I understand if you say no, but I was hoping that you might still want me to be with you. That we could just go on together, and figure out how to handle it however it turns out."

He was quiet for what seemed an eternity, but finally spoke. "I think that is asking too much, and not just of me."

Anne said nothing; she couldn't think of anything to say.

He went on, his voice now devoid of emotion. She knew that tone. She'd lost him.

"Have you told Grainger?"

She nodded.

"Before me?" That same uninvolved tone hid the raw emotion she knew he was feeling.

"It was something I had to do in person, and I needed to leave California to come to tell you. I was hoping I wouldn't be going back there. That I would stay here with you."

"So, how exactly are you seeing this play out, girl? You come with me, and then what happens if the baby isn't mine?"

She twisted the sheet between her fingers. "I guess I was thinking that, if that was the case, I would just make sure Andrew could see the baby as much as possible. But the baby and I would live with you." She heard the pleading in her voice, but she couldn't stop, couldn't make her voice sound as uninvolved as his had become. "People raise children they had with previous spouses all the time. It will work out. I know this is hard, but we can do it." She tried to stop more tears from coming; she needed to keep as much composure as possible so that she could convince him that they could handle this together.

"Excuse me, but this is a little different. We were married to each other when you got pregnant. What if the child is Grainger's? What do we tell the child?"

She whispered, "I don't know."

They were both silent for what seemed like years. She had no answers to the questions he had asked, but she knew she needed to tell him about Darby.

"There's something else I need to tell you."

He closed his eyes briefly. "Go on. Tell me." His voice was flat.

"Darby guessed. She walked in on me being sick this morning, and then she went through my things. She found the prenatal vitamins my doctor gave me."

He nodded. "I see. She would have put it together about Grainger."

"I'm so sorry." Anne was miserable, trying to think of something to say that would make things better. "I know this is difficult for you, for everyone. If it helps at all, I think the baby is yours. But I just can't be sure."

"Doesn't help much right now, I can truthfully say. I had two nights with you. He had the rest of the time. I don't think the odds are in my favor." Finally, his pretense of detachment broke. He picked up the clock that sat on the bedside table and threw it against the wall, shattering it. "Goddamn it, Anne. Goddamn it."

There was a silence between them after the violence of his outburst. Then Anne spoke, trying to make her voice calm him. "I know this is a shock. I would have given anything for it not to have happened. But you love me. I love you. We can deal with this."

"Deal with this? How? Girl, you're my wife. I can't stand the thought that you're carrying another man's child. You know how much I want children with you."

The lump in her throat throbbed as she tried to swallow.

"I'm so sorry."

"Grainger will want that child, and you know he wants you. If it's Grainger's child, and you stay with me, how is the child going to feel knowing he was conceived from an affair you had when you were married to me? What about the rest of our children after him? Having a brother or sister in the house from when you were another man's mistress? Can you imagine what kind of treatment that will get on the playground, or at school from their classmates?" He put his head in his hands. "No, if this child is Grainger's, the best thing for you to do is to marry him."

She hadn't been prepared for that. Shaking her head, not believing he could tell her to marry another man, she reached for him. He moved away from her and her grasp came up empty.

"Terrence, I love you. I don't want to marry him. I want to be with you."

He got up and pulled on his jeans and a shirt. She thought he was ignoring her, or that he hadn't heard her, but then he spoke, his voice sounding as if everything inside of him was dead. "You may have to grow up, and accept that what you want may not matter as much as what is best for the child. And I'll have to accept that as well. Now, if there is no more catastrophic news you need to impart, I have to leave."

"Leave? Where are you going?"

He shook his head. His face was drained of any color, and he seemed unfocused.

She repeated, "Where are you going?"

"I don't know. Out."

"Please don't go." She reached for him again, this time catching his arm, but he shook her off.

"I can't stay here right now. I can't stay here with you."

"Can we talk when you come back?"

"Anne, for God's sake, have some mercy on me. I think it would be best if you leave."

"Leave?" Her throat hurt.

He moved away from her. "I'll leave some cash out on the counter for you so you'll have some money—and take the checkbook and credit cards. Could you please go stay at that hotel by your job?"

She swallowed, nodded. "Will you call me?"

He turned to leave, shaking his head.

She watched him go through her tears, feeling as if her world had been irredeemably shattered.

# Chapter 32

TWO HOURS LATER, Reid returned to the flat. He could tell as soon as he opened the door that she was gone. The place felt empty, unbearably empty. On the kitchen counter he found the checkbook and credit cards he had given her, along with the cash he'd set out. A short note let him know that she had indeed gotten a room at the hotel, and she asked him to call when he felt he could. He ran his finger over the note slowly, lingering over her name as if she were someone he'd known a long time ago, then turned away from it.

He walked aimlessly through the flat, thinking of the hours he needed to survive until it was time to go to work in the morning, and ended up in the bedroom. She had made the bed, taken her big suitcase, and tidied everything. The shattered clock had been cleared away. She'd taken all of her things, erased every sign that she had been there for a few unbelievably wonderful days. He could have just imagined she'd been here, he thought. He wished that it had just been his imagination, that she'd never come, never told him.

In the bathroom he washed his face, trying to stop the raging pressure in his head. As he reached for a towel, he saw with an inexplicable relief that she had forgotten her nightgown. It still hung on a hook on the back of the bathroom door, waiting for her to float it over her head and cover her lovely body. He touched the soft fabric tentatively, as if it might disappear, and then buried his face the scent of her. He would know that scent anywhere: a mixture of her citrusy floral perfume and the sweet muskiness of her body's own natural scent. He could be put blindfolded in front of hundreds of women, and he would be able to pick out Anne just by that smell.

After taking the nightgown down, he got some paracetamol tablets from the cabinet. On the bottom shelf, between his deodorant and his shaving cream, sat a bottle of her perfume. He took it out, uncapped it, put it to his nose, and inhaled. Mechanically, he took the perfume and the nightgown with him on his way to get brandy to wash the tablets down. The golden liquid burned his throat as he swallowed it too fast, but he quickly poured another one. He suddenly thought of something and hurried to the bedroom.

He placed his brandy on the nightstand, opened the bottom drawer, and carefully put her nightgown and perfume inside. He pulled down the counterpane, exposing the sheets. Maybe he would be able to sleep if he could be surrounded by the scent of her.

But the sheets weren't the ones they had had just made love on. He realized she must have changed them before she'd left. Not yet defeated, he went down the hall to the closet that held the washer and dryer. The sheets would still be there. He'd just put them back on.

When he opened the door, he heard the dryer turning. He was too late.

He took his glass back to the brandy decanter, filled it to the top, climbed the stairs to the loft, and turned on his computer. He'd been alone before. He could do it again. He'd get through this as he'd gotten through every other disaster in his life.

He'd work.

# WEDNESDAY, APRIL 8

# Chapter 33

REID CLOSED THE door to his office behind his sister. "Sit if you like." He went around to his desk and sat down. Detached, he let his eyes take in this place in which he spent so much time. Never had the bare room seemed so desolate, so empty. Like his life.

Darby's gaze was cool, but not entirely unsympathetic. "I gather she told you."

"She did." He picked up his coffee mug and took a drink. He hadn't been able to even contemplate eating anything, but the coffee at least poured some warmth on the ice that had enveloped his body. "I trust you can keep your mouth shut."

"Yes, of course. Isn't that what we do in our family? Keep our mouths shut?"

"Thank you." He couldn't spare the effort to puzzle out what she was implying. Right now, his own pain was overwhelming. But soon he'd get over it, and it wouldn't matter anymore. It would all be in his past.

"You'll get an annulment?"

"That's none of your business." He shut his eyes briefly. But what choice did he have?

It had been different with his father and mother. They'd had their own children together first. If his mother hadn't come back, Terrence and his brother and sister would have grown up either without their mother, or without their father. Here, there was a better choice. The child wouldn't have to be split between two homes. Its mother and father could quickly marry before anyone knew Anne was pregnant. The child would not grow up being taunted about his mother being another man's whore.

"There'll be no trouble getting a divorce with what she's done. If you get a good solicitor, she shouldn't be able to bleed any money out of you at all."

"It's none of your business." He repeated, feeling his eyes glaze over. He knew he needed to let Anne go. Quickly. He knew it, and he'd do it, but he didn't want to hear it from his sister.

"Jesus, Terrence, you can't let her use you like this."

"Shut up, Darby. Shut the fuck up." He saw her reel from his rare use of the obscenity, but there was no other word that fit his frustration with her, and with the entire situation in which he found himself.

"I just can't fathom how you can have anything to do with her after this."

"She's my wife, Darby. Even with this mess, in any contest between you and her, she wins. So again—shut the fuck up. I would like to talk about the investigation, if you can focus." He kept his voice hard, but he wanted to cry—something he'd never let himself do.

Darby's face clouded over. "Of course. Why listen to me? Who am I to you, anyway?"

His head hurt. "What are you talking about?"

She waved his question away. "Never mind. I need to tell you what I learned from DI Lawrence last night."

He rubbed the bridge of his nose, trying to clear his mind. "Go on, then."

"All right, but don't yell at me. The first thing is about Anne. He knows she's here–with you in the flat. He mentioned it last night at dinner."

Now his head was pounding against his skull. He could hardly think. "How could he possibly know? The only place we've gone together since she's come was to the house. And the only other time she went out was with the designer." He narrowed his eyes at his sister. "You're the only one who's been at the flat since she came."

She shrugged. "I didn't tell him. I'm just telling you what he said."

He shook his head, hoping for the return of the protective sheet of ice over his heart. "It doesn't matter, but it's bloody odd he'd know. What else did you find out?"

"He's adamant Von Zandt's not involved in Ramsey's murder."

"Did he say why?"

"He said instinct. I had a feeling it was something else."

"Such as?"

"I'm not sure. It was just a feeling. He did say he thought if Von Zandt had done it, we wouldn't have been able to pin it down as a murder. That Von Zandt's people would have done a better job at concealing the actual cause of death."

"That crossed my mind as well. But even a professional makes a miscalculation sometimes–and even professionals sometimes use amateur help. Besides, if the train was going a bit faster, or the body position was just a little different, we wouldn't have been able to see the puncture mark."

Darby made a face, then asked, "Did you know Lawrence has a girlfriend that works at CID headquarters?"

Reid turned. "No."

"I don't think he advertises her existence."

"How did you find out?"

She smirked. "The cow came into the pub where we were having dinner. Made a bit of a scene when she saw him with me. He had to leave and go after her."

"What's her name?"

"Shelley something."

Reid mused. "There's a Shelley who works for Chief Superintendent Steynton, but it couldn't be the same one. Steynton's admin's not the not the type I'd have thought would attract DI Lawrence."

"Minger?"

"I don't like that word, but yes, she's unattractive."

"If she's downright butt ugly, then I'd guess it's the same Shelley. On the fat side of plump and disgustingly bad skin. Dresses badly and just plain mean."

"That's her."

Darby made a face. "Either she's fantastic in bed, or there's something else he's getting from her. He was embarrassed of her, but terrified when she walked out. He ran after her. Left me sitting there like yesterday's breakfast. That was a first for me."

Considering the memos and other information that would go through Steynton's desk, Reid thought he knew what DI Lawrence saw in the hapless Shelley. "I'll look into that. Just now, I'd best get going. I'm off to Ramsey's funeral."

Her face indecipherable, Darby said, "Terrence, about Anne—

you'll be fine. You're certainly not the only man who's ever been in this situation."

Reid flinched at the undercurrent of bitterness in his sister's voice. Although he knew Darby hated Anne, this seemed to be directed not just at Anne, but also at him. Something was going on. He would have to talk to Darby, find out what it was.

But not now.

# Chapter 34

ANNE'S CHEST, heavy with fatigue and hopelessness, kept her pressed to the bed. The taxi ride to the hotel last night—over an hour from her husband's flat—had been exorbitant, but she hadn't been able to face the prospect of negotiating the details of a train ride and then getting a taxi from there to the hotel.

She'd stayed up late last night putting all of her things away, hoping against hope—and, as it turned out, in vain—that Terrence would call. Finally, she'd gone to bed, keeping her cell phone right next to her. There had been no call, and when she'd eventually slept, it was fitfully.

When he had time to think about it, he would put things in perspective, wouldn't he? She put her head in her hands. No, he wouldn't. Couldn't. There was no perspective that made this workable for a man like her husband.

If she could have the paternity test before the baby was born, at least she would know. She'd tried to get her doctor to understand how important this was; he had listened sympathetically and with a promise of absolute secrecy—even agreeing not to include Anne's doubts about the paternity of the child in her chart—but he would not sanction an amniocentesis for that purpose only, and there was no indication she needed one for any other reason. She was only twenty-seven, too young to need testing for most of the problems for which amnios were used to screen older women.

Anne got out of bed long enough to let room service deliver her breakfast tray. She poured herself a cup of herbal tea—something she had disdained until she became pregnant and had to start watching out for things like alcohol, caffeine, and—who knew—lunch meat. She got back into bed with her cup and a piece of toast, trying to outsmart the morning sickness that had become her regular morning visitor. So far, so good. Her stomach was fine. At least there was that.

Her cell rang, and a wave of relief washed over her. Thank God. She picked it up immediately. But, instead of Terrence, Andrew's hesitant voice greeted her.

"Hello, Andrew." She forced herself to sound as normal as possible. This whole situation was difficult for him as well, and he'd been through so much. The loss of Lenore was still so fresh for him.

"Anne."

She heard the relief in his voice and knew it came for him because of hearing her voice. He was such a kind, caring man, and he'd been a good friend to her, despite what she'd done to him.

"Isn't it awfully late there for you to be calling?" She thought about where he was calling from. The house where his daughter had been kidnapped and murdered just two months before.

"I couldn't sleep. Can you talk?"

"Yes. I can talk." Hearing the note of weary resignation in her own voice, she resolved to make herself sound more upbeat for Andrew. In his grief, every day had to seem interminable.

"Reid's not there?" Andrew would know she couldn't have taken this call from him if her husband was there.

"He's not with me. I'm in a hotel near the job."

There was a short silence, and she knew he understood the implications of what she'd said.

"You told him, then?"

"Yes." She was close to tears, but she made an effort to keep control. "It didn't go well. But I'm all right."

"You're not all right. I can hear it in your voice."

"No, really, I'm all right." She sniffed back her tears. "I knew it would be a shock to him at first. I'm still hoping after he has some time to absorb the news . . ."

"Of course." There was another silence on the line, then he spoke. "How are you feeling? The mornings any better?"

She sighed. "They haven't been, but today so far I'm doing okay."

"Good. You're eating?"

"Yes. It's only the mornings that are bad. I'm trying herbal tea and toast right now. Please don't worry. How are you doing?"

There was a pause, then he sighed. "Not great. I thought I'd establish a memorial for Lenore, but I can't decide what kind."

Anne pushed back the strands of hair that had fallen in front of her eyes. "What were you thinking about doing?"

"Maybe a ballet scholarship? Or do you think something to do with art? Or critically ill children? I just can't decide."

"Any of those would be good. Why don't you wait and think about it for a while? You don't have to decide today."

"I just want to . . . I don't know. Do something, I guess."

"I know."

There was a silence, then he spoke, his voice so hopeless, it broke her heart.

"I miss you, Anne. Losing Lenore, then you. Sometimes it's more than I can stand."

She swallowed, the heavy weight of guilt on her for leaving him after he'd lost his daughter, and for her part in having left Lenore vulnerable to be kidnapped from what should have been a safe home. "Are you working?"

"Yes. I finished the painting. It's comforting to me to paint her. I'm doing another one of Lenore using that photo you took of her dancing."

"Good. That's good." She'd taken the photograph of Andrew and his daughter just hours before Lenore disappeared. "I want to see it when it's finished."

"Yes, of course."

She could hear him swallow.

"Do you want me to come, Anne? I can be there in a day."

"No, please don't. That would only make things worse."

"He's such a fool. If I had a chance for you, any chance for you, I'd never leave you."

"It's just a mess, isn't it?" She started to cry.

"Don't cry, babe. God, don't cry."

"Andrew, don't be so nice to me. This isn't fair to you."

"I just want you to know that whatever happens, I'm here for you. I want your child so much. I want it to be mine, but if it's his, that's fine, too. I want you, no matter what."

"Please don't. I know it hurts you for me to say it, but I love him so much."

"I can live with that. I don't need to be the one you love the most. If he chooses not to be in the picture, that's his loss. I'm telling you I'll be there no matter what—if you want me—or even if you just need me. That's enough for me."

"You need to get to sleep—it's so late there. What time is it?"

"Two-three? I'll go to bed. I just wanted to hear your voice. I worry about you—and about the baby."

"I'm fine, and the baby's fine, but it's better if you don't call. I'll let you know if anything happens. I promise."

"Are you getting a doctor over there?"

"Not yet. I'm waiting to see if I'll be staying."

"Do you need money? I can have some put in your account here for you, babe. No strings."

"No, please, I'm fine."

"I love you."

"Oh, Andrew." This was so hard. "Take care of yourself, okay? Go to bed now."

After they hung up, she felt like the biggest jerk in the world. Not only had she hurt Terrence, she had hurt this lovely man unbearably. As if in punishment, the rolling nausea of morning sickness rushed up her chest, and she ran to the bathroom.

# Chapter 35

THE MEDIEVAL CATHEDRAL was full to the proverbial rafters with mourners. How many were there out of true sympathy, and how many were there from a morbid curiosity about the circumstances surrounding Richard Ramsey's death, Reid couldn't tell.

He hated funerals. The last one he'd attended was for Andrew Grainger's murdered child. The mourners there had been cloaked with a deep, devastating sadness. The mood here was different. More formal, less personal. Richard Ramsey had been respected, but Reid did not get the feeling that there were many here who would actually mourn his death.

The Ramseys were Church of Scotland, and were apparently members in good standing of the Glasgow Cathedral, where the services were being held. The family was all there, dressed in appropriately somber clothing. Even Moira was in mourning, her black dress reaching halfway down her calves, and suitably subdued. Glynnis Taylor sat with her sister and her niece and nephew. Glynnis's own black dress was a more sophisticated version of what Moira wore. Terrence needed to talk to Glynnis again, now that he knew her relationship with Henry, though he doubted he'd get much information out of her.

The minister's voice filled the church with his recitation of the services, the congregation participating when required. Although heads were bowed in respect and sympathy, there was the usual furtive glancing around to see who else was there. Reid could almost feel the speculation of the putative mourners about the cause of the wealthy man's death.

He spotted the Von Zandt family and, taking the opportunity, studied them. Elisa Von Zandt may have been attractive when she was younger, but now what had probably been a generous figure when she was young, had spread. She was squeezed into a dress that was at least two sizes too small for her girth. He saw her pull surreptitiously at her waistband. Her hair was a yellow blonde, her dark lipstick harsh against her almost white skin.

Elisa spent most of her time living in Germany, apart from her husband. A marriage of convenience at this point, Reid suspected, considering Von Zandt's relationship with Moira Ramsey. Awkward for the wife, he mused, to be at the mistress's father's funeral. No wonder she looked detached. Von Zandt had to have more than a streak of cruelty in him to take his wife here, forcing her to pretend either not to know, or not to care.

On Elisa's right was the youngest son, Frederick, while to her husband's left stood the elder son, Henry. Coincidental, Reid wondered, or was this alignment significant? He stored the observation away for possible later use. When the congregation sat down at the minister's instruction, Reid slipped out the back.

At the obligatory reception held afterwards at the Ramsey home, Reid spotted Elisa Von Zandt standing alone by a long window and worked his way over to her. Her face was turned to watch whatever was outside. Reid glanced quickly in the direction she was looking, but saw nothing. To get her attention, Reid cleared his throat.

"Mrs. Von Zandt?"

When she turned, he saw she had a plate of food from the buffet in her hand and was shoving a cracker heavily frosted with pink salmon spread into her mouth. She sputtered in surprise and bits of cracker fell from her mouth. She covered her mouth with her hand, embarrassed. "Lord Reid, I'm so sorry."

"My fault, Mrs. Von Zandt, I startled you." Realizing she appeared to recognize him, he asked, "Have we met?"

She gave a rueful smile, brushing crumbs from her chest. "No, but I've seen your photograph in the news." The woman's German accent was thick, but her English was good, if a bit stilted.

"Ah, yes." Who hadn't? Damned tabloids.

"It was so sad about that little girl. The one in California, I mean."

"Yes, it was terribly sad." He motioned to the window seat and they both sat down. "Did you know Mr. Ramsey well?"

She shook her head. "He was a business colleague of my husband's."

"Are you friends with Mrs. Ramsey?"

"No." Elisa put her plate in her lap. "I live in Germany most of the time." She took a drink of her wine. "Besides, her daughter, Moira Ramsey, is my husband's mistress. I don't think it would be comfortable for either of us."

He wasn't sure what to say, so just nodded.

"Walter always has someone. I'm used to it." She shrugged as if she didn't care. "You know how it is. You go on. I have my own life. I have my sons, and my grandchildren." She picked up a cracker loaded thickly with brown liver paste. "I don't have my own lover, of course. Walter would never tolerate that." She blushed, stricken with sudden embarrassment. "I'm sorry."

Reid realized she must be thinking of his own wife and Andrew Grainger. If Grainger had slept with Von Zandt's wife, Reid had no doubt the man would have killed him, and probably her as well. And definitely if she'd gotten pregnant.

He forced a small smile. "No need to apologize. I'm sure he wouldn't. You're not in Scotland often, I understand?"

Elisa washed her cracker down with a drink of wine, then wiped her mouth with the back of her hand self-consciously before speaking. "I haven't been, but I think with our new house I will be here more. The garden is extraordinary, as I'm sure you've heard." She looked at him and he thought she was going to say something else, but they were interrupted by a large bald man Reid recognized as one of Von Zandt's bodyguards.

"Mrs. Von Zandt, your husband says it's time to leave."

"Yes, of course, Simon." She stood up and put her plate down. "It was nice talking to you, Lord Reid. Good luck."

He stood up. "You as well."

After she left, he sat down on the window seat, gazing absently toward the garden beyond. How had his father managed, he wondered. How long did it take before people forgot? He felt a hand on his arm, and looked up.

Glynnis Taylor sat next down next to him. "I had a feeling you'd want to talk to me, but I thought I'd wait until Elisa was gone."

"Aye." Reid felt fatigue overtake him, a product of his sleepless night, and wished he could just go back to his flat and sleep until next year. But he knew he needed to keep going. One day at a time. That was the only way to get through this hell on earth. "You didn't mention you worked for Henry Von Zandt when we talked the other day."

She smiled. "Or that I was sleeping with him?"

"That, either." He debated whether to ask her if she'd been the woman Richard Ramsey had been seeing, remembering Harry's report of the meeting with Patty Cady, and Patty's remark that if Ramsey had been interested in any woman, it would have been Glynnis. But if she'd been with Ramsey that night, she'd doubtless been involved in his murder, and she wasn't likely to admit it.

"You should have asked where I worked."

"Apparently."

"If you had, I would've told you."

"My fault, then." His heart wasn't in the exchange, but he forced himself to go through the motions.

"Actually, though, it wouldn't have changed anything I said."

"Does Henry's wife know about you?"

She shrugged. "You'd have to ask her. Why does it matter?"

"In general, or in specific?" Breaking marriage bonds almost always caused someone pain, and not always just the betrayed spouse. As a child, he'd endured the ribald jibes about his mother, and although he'd not quite understood them, he'd known enough to know she'd done something very bad, something dirty. Now, of course, with his mother as well as with Anne, he knew things were more complicated than that, but that didn't stop the pain.

Glynnis frowned, clearly confused at his answer, but apparently decided to ignore it. "You look tired, Superintendent. Is it the investigation about Richard's death? I told you he wasn't worth it."

He tried to assess what she knew and what she would take back to her lover or her sister, then decided it did not matter; he would be making a press statement on this soon.

"Richard Ramsey had just agreed to turn informant to help us find the people responsible for the Heidelberg University bombing."

She jerked her head back and stared at him. "You think Richard was involved with that? He was many things, but I'm sure he wasn't a terrorist."

"Not directly. But he had information on a money laundering scheme that funded the terrorists for that attack, and for additional attacks the terrorists are planning for this spring." Reid considered, then asked, "Were you involved with Richard Ramsey?"

Glynnis gaped. "Absolutely not. He was my sister's husband."

"Right." He didn't know whether to believe her or not. Undoubtedly she was a good liar.

Glynnis's mouth formed a tight line. "You think Walter's involved in this terrorist thing, don't you?"

Reid splayed his hands out and studied them as he considered his response. He should tell her no, in keeping with his plan to try to get Von Zandt to lower his guard, but he couldn't bring himself to lose the possible chance of getting another informant on his side.

Before he could decide what to say, Glynnis went on, "So Richard was going to help you, and he was killed. You think Walter's behind that, as well, I suppose?"

Still Reid didn't speak.

Glynnis leaned forward, and spoke in almost a whisper. "Why would Walter get involved in that?"

Reid raised his eyebrows, but still didn't speak. She'd figure it out on her own, he knew.

And she did. "For money, that's what you're saying, isn't it? That they get the money from the people supporting these terrorist groups and funnel through channels so it can't be traced back to them, and get it to the terrorists to help them do these awful things."

"I didn't say that."

"You didn't have to. And now you've lost your informant, and you need someone else."

He looked at her, but didn't speak, feeling remote from her but interested in where she'd go with this.

"I can't." Her voice was a hiss, but her eyes were floating in unshed tears.

"I didn't ask you."

"Because you don't think you can trust me."

Reid thought about Glynnis's situation, Barbara Ramsey's ruin of a marriage, and Moira's situation with Von Zandt. These three women were alike in more than looks. But in his mind, Glynnis Taylor had had more of a choice. Moira had been a teenager when she'd gotten sucked into Von Zandt's world, and Barbara Ramsey's life had driven her into living in an alcoholic haze, but Glynnis was where she was by choice.

No, he couldn't trust her.

She touched his arm. "I feel like you're disappointed in me and I don't even know you."

He stood up. "Nor I you, Glynnis. Nor I you."

"We could change that." Her voice was wistful.

"No, we couldn't. Now, if you'll excuse me, I have some other people I need to speak to."

# Chapter 36

STRONG MEN either raise sons who become men as strong as they themselves are, or sons who, growing up in the shadow of a larger-than-life father, collapse into weakness. Von Zandt seemed to have fathered one of each kind of son. The oldest son was much like Walter, strong both physically and in personality, whereas the younger son, Frederick, was not only a weak personality, but also physically weak. Reid had tried to set up the meetings with Von Zandt's sons separately, but had not been surprised when he learned that both of the brothers would be appearing at one meeting.

Briefly, Reid gave thanks for his own father, a strong man who had no problem allowing—even encouraging—his sons to be strong people in their own right. The Earl of Wynstrathe had no need or desire to overshadow his offspring, although his very presence was both quietly powerful and demanding of respect. Reid and his father had forged a strong bond early on, a bond that had gotten even stronger when his mother left them, taking his little brother and sister with her. His father had tried to explain that she hadn't taken her oldest son because she did not want to pull him out of his school and away from his friends. Reid had pretended to believe him, to understand, but even after she came back, although he loved his mother, he couldn't forget he'd been expendable to her.

As he'd been expendable to Anne.

Reid pushed his dismal thoughts away as he pushed open the door to the offices of Von Zandt's firm, VZ Capital. Reid preferred to interview witnesses in their own surroundings whenever possible. In a witness's own environment, one often got the added bonus of having other players wander in and out of the picture, and could observe interactions between the witness and others around him.

Those observations were often surprisingly useful.

Although the receptionist—Amanda, Reid remembered—seemed pleased to see him again, she was thwarted in her efforts at hospitality when he was taken back to Henry's offices almost immediately by a businesslike and taciturn Glynnis Taylor. Reid followed her neatly dressed figure down the hall, registering with detachment the expensive navy blue suit, five-inch heels, and the trail of sultry perfume wafting behind her.

Henry Von Zandt was taller than his father, but his face held the same stone cold eyes. His prematurely thinning hair was combed back tight against his head. His gray suit was expensive and well-tailored; the French cuffs on his starched white shirt were studded with platinum cufflinks, each holding a ruby the size of a raspberry.

Reid took the coffee Glynnis offered, nodding his head in thanks. Henry motioned for her to leave, then sat back and focused his attention on Reid.

"So, Superintendent, what can I help you with?"

Henry was thirty-two years old, a few years younger than Reid. According to the background file Frank had put together, Henry, until he was of age, had been raised chiefly in Germany. He, like his father, was married to a German woman. He had a house in the suburbs outside of Glasgow, where his wife stayed home to take care of their two young children.

"I wanted to talk to you about Richard Ramsey. I understand you dealt with him on behalf of your father's company."

"Our companies formed an alliance that was, I believe, mutually beneficial."

"How so?" Reid put down the coffee, having had no intention of drinking it. The day he actually drank anything a Von Zandt gave him would be the day he needed to resign.

"Richard had become overextended. His businesses were solid, but strained temporarily for cash. We had the cash." Henry's voice held just the hint of a German accent.

"You and your father were each given a position on the board of directors of Ramsey International as a condition for the loan?"

Henry inclined his head in an abbreviated nod, a mannerism reminiscent of his father's. "One of the conditions. There were others. With the investment of money, come conditions. As they say, there is no free lunch."

"Did Ramsey repay the loan when his situation improved?"

"Not quite. The terms were extremely favorable and I doubt he felt there was any hurry."

"Good investment for VZ Capital?"

"And for Ramsey. His situation wouldn't have been able to improve without the loan—or investment—of our money. Sometimes having an abundance of assets isn't enough if those assets aren't in the form of cash. Supplying cash for healthy businesses that need cash is a big part of our business."

"But it isn't actually your company's money that gets invested, is it?"

"Not usually. Most often it comes from investors who want opportunities to make their money grow. We help put the ones that need money together with the ones who want to invest money."

"How careful are you that you aren't matching up those needing investors with people who want to cause harm?"

"Terrorists, I assume you mean."

"Or those that fund terrorists."

"This sounds like a conversation for which I should have a solicitor."

Reid raised his eyebrows. "If you think you need one."

"This is a legitimate, law-abiding company. We scrupulously follow the UK's money laundering regulations."

"Then you needn't be concerned." Reid looked around. "I thought Frederick would be joining us."

"He'll be here. I wanted to talk to you first. Frederick is," Henry hesitated, then continued. "Frankly, he's disabled. Not just physically disabled, but challenged mentally. Both my father and I are concerned about distressing him."

"I have no intention of distressing him. I just want to talk to him. Is that a problem?"

"If it becomes a problem, I'll stop things." Henry reached over to the telephone intercom and hit one of the buttons. "Glynnis, send my brother in."

Frederick Von Zandt shuffled in, his pronounced limp giving the shuffle a little bounce at the end of each step. Frederick was nothing like his older brother. Where Henry was fit, Frederick carried a paunch. Where Henry was urbanely polished and immaculately groomed, Frederick dressed like an unkempt teenager. Where Henry was self-confident, Frederick, whose face was covered with an angry army of painful looking spots, was obviously self-conscious.

"Thank you for agreeing to meet with me. I appreciate it, Mr. Von Zandt." Reid had decided to be deferential to the younger Von Zandt brother, guessing that not many people would give him that courtesy.

Frederick seemed startled by being addressed as Mr. Von Zandt and nervously glanced at his older brother, who waved a hand at Frederick, as if to tell him to get on with things.

"Just call me Frederick." His eyes seemed to have difficulty meeting those to whom he was speaking, and his right eye seemed to continually water, necessitating him to keep wiping at it.

"Fine, if you'll call me Terrence."

Frederick smiled a bit uneasily. "All right."

Reid smiled, trying to put Frederick at ease. "Moira mentioned that you took her to her parents' home on Saturday night for dinner."

Frederick visibly relaxed. "That's right. I drive her around a lot. My father trusts my driving."

"Did you stay for dinner yourself?"

"No. I went back home for my mother's birthday dinner."

"Did you go back to the Ramsey house later?"

"To pick Moira up, yeah."

"When you and Moira left the Ramsey house, did you happen to see anything out of place? Unfamiliar vehicles, anything like that?"

Frederick thought. "No."

"Did you talk to Richard Ramsey at all that night?"

He shook his head. "Mr. Ramsey never talks to me."

"Where did you take Moira after you picked her up?"

Frederick's eyes slid toward Henry, who nodded. Having apparently been given approval to continue, Frederick said, "To the flat. Where she lives."

"Where she lives with your father?"

Frederick stared at his hands as if the answer to the question was written there, then sighed. "Yes."

"What did you do after that?"

Frederick hesitated, and his gaze this time went to his feet.

"Frederick?"

He looked up at Reid's question. "I kept an eye on her after I dropped her off."

"Kept an eye on her?"

"Yes. She walked down the street to a club. To go dancing."

"By herself?"

He nodded. "She went by herself, but there were men there who danced with her."

"You stayed with her?"

"Not with her. I watched her."

"What happened after that?"

"After a while, she left that club and went to another. Same thing there. Danced with some blokes."

"Did you watch her all night?" Reid tried to measure the creepiness factor of the young man following his father's mistress.

"Just until she went home to the flat."

"What time was that?"

"About half two. Maybe a little later."

"Then what did you do?"

"I was sitting in front of the building in the car, and she came over and talked to me before she went up to the flat. She knows I keep an eye out for her. She's only nineteen, you know. She's still a kid, and someone needs to take care of her."

Reid glanced over at Henry Von Zandt as his brother was talking. Henry was thrumming his fingers rapidly on his desk.

Reid turned his attention to the elder brother. "You don't agree?"

"What difference does it make if I agree?" Henry's fingers stilled, but then he picked up a pen, and started tapping it instead.

Reid waited.

"All right, she's a tart." Henry gesticulated with the pen in exasperation. "A slut. Her stepfather fobbed her off on Father first chance he got just to get rid of her."

Frederick's ears got bright red and sparks of anger flashed in his watery eyes. "That's a shitty thing to say about Moira, Henry."

Reid watched the exchange, appraising the tension between the brothers. He could tell from the way Frederick acted that his mental age did not match his actual age, hence Henry's description of his brother as disabled. Calculating everything he'd seen and heard, Reid would have put Frederick at about age fifteen mentally, and there was nothing more volatile than a teenage boy—especially when he was in love.

Henry looked disgusted and addressed himself to Reid. "You've seen her. She dresses like a tart, she acts like a tart."

Frederick shot a look of undisguised loathing at his brother and balled his fists as if he were restraining himself from using them, then stormed out of the room in galloping, uneven steps, muttering under his breath.

Henry shook his head, exasperated. "Freddie's an idiot."

Reid didn't respond.

Henry said, "So, Superintendent, if you were checking Moira's alibi, I guess you've got it. Freddie's as well."

"Since the subject of alibis is on the table, why don't tell me yours for Saturday night?"

In an exaggeratedly patient voice, Henry said, "I was at the birthday dinner for my mother, then my wife and I went home. The nanny was there with the children, so you can ask both her and my wife. I stayed home with my wife the rest of the night. The nanny lives with us, although I can't say whether she would notice if I left the house again. You can ask her, and my wife as well, for that matter, if you like."

"Thank you." Reid wrote down the nanny's name and mobile number as Henry Von Zandt dictated the information in a bored voice while studiedly checking his watch.

Reid asked, "Do you know if Richard Ramsey was involved with another woman? We have some information that he might have been meeting a woman the night he was killed."

Henry shrugged. "Not that I know of, but I can't think why he'd tell me. Maybe a prozzy?"

"Maybe." Reid switched subjects again. "As I understand it, your father has made a bid to replace Ramsey as the chairman of Ramsey's company. What kind of an impact will that make on your father's company if he's successful?"

"You're implying that my father and our company stand to benefit from Ramsey's death."

"I'm not implying anything. Both you and your father have already informed me that they would."

Henry stood up, suddenly seeming to sense he was out of his depth. "I've nothing else to say to you, Superintendent Reid. This interview is concluded. Please leave." He punched a button on his telephone and spoke a few sharp words Reid couldn't make out, but was fairly sure were a command to get rid of him.

And, indeed, Glynnis Taylor appeared within seconds to escort Reid out. In the hallway, she looked as if she wanted to say something, but Reid gave a slight shake of his head and murmured, "Not here."

She nodded, and he saw in her eyes that she understood. Any words they exchanged here would likely be overheard. Certainly she'd be questioned about them, and Reid did not want to endanger her.

In the lift, Reid reflected on what he'd learned. First, Frederick Von Zandt was in love with his father's mistress—just when you think you'd seen everything. But with regard to the investigation, Frederick Von Zandt gave Moira an alibi, and, he assumed, she'd give him one as well.

And he'd touched a nerve with his questions about the possible change of control of Ramsey International. That was something Von Zandt had to want very badly.

And something Reid could not let happen.

# Chapter 37

ON THE STREET outside the offices of VZ Capital, Reid regretted that he'd not bothered to don any type of a coat. But at least the cold bite of the wind made him feel like he might be alive again someday. This morning before Mass, he'd gone running, and for that blessed hour he felt as if he could get through the mess his personal life was in and eventually come out on the other side. During Mass, he'd prayed for guidance. Afterwards, he'd been even more certain that putting the child before what Anne and he wanted was the right thing to do.

Marshalling up the self-discipline that had helped him get through bad times before, Reid turned his thoughts to his work. First and foremost, he had to find the information they needed to stop the next terrorist attacks. To do that, he needed to pin down the details of Von Zandt's hidden financial operations. He thought about the ramifications of Von Zandt getting control of Ramsey International. Von Zandt had to be after the weapons subsidiary. If he controlled a significant supply of weapons as well as cash, Von Zandt's ties to terrorist factions would become even more formidable a threat. Reid hadn't been seeing the whole picture when he'd been focused solely on the money laundering.

He decided to stop in the first place he came to, get some tea and ring his friend, Peter MacTavish. He knew he could count on MacTavish, an investment banker, to maintain confidentiality and to do whatever he could to help. Reid pushed open the door to the small café and spotted a booth. As he headed toward it, he saw Frederick Von Zandt sitting all alone in a booth further back, huddled forlornly over a cup of hot tea. Reid drew a deep breath. Opportunity had presented itself. The weakest member was separated from the tribe.

Reid approached Frederick's table. "May I join you?"

Frederick started in surprise, but then nodded, gesturing to the other side of the booth.

Reid slid in, motioning to the waitress. "This is a coincidence. I was fancying a cup of tea myself."

"It takes the chill off."

"Aye. I apologize if I caused trouble back there between you and your brother."

Frederick shook his head. "Naught to do with you. He's a shite about Moira."

"You think he's wrong about her."

"Course he's wrong. Moira may dance with different blokes, but that's just because she likes to dance. But she doesn't cheat on Father. She wouldn't dare."

Reid nodded, listened without commenting, thinking about Elisa Von Zandt saying the same thing. The waitress deposited a cup and a small pot of tea in front of Reid without so much as a word. After she left, Frederick went on.

"Henry just doesn't understand. Moira doesn't have any friends her own age. She goes to school and takes care of Father. If she wants to go dancing, so what?"

"Your father doesn't mind?"

"Not as long as she's there when he wants her there. She works hard at school and deserves a break."

"Makes sense."

Frederick shook his head. "She's so smart, and she's genius at computers."

"Aye, I heard that."

The young man drank his tea and stared ahead, not speaking for a while.

Reid followed suit and sipped his own tea, waiting for Frederick to decide to talk again.

"Henry's got no right to say anything about Moira." He stirred his tea aimlessly. "He doesn't like her, but Moira and I are friends."

"Aye, she spoke fondly of you to me," Reid volunteered.

Frederick smiled, pleased. "She did?"

Reid nodded, then said what he thought Frederick wanted to hear. "She's a nice girl."

"She really is. She's just . . . incredible."

"Sounds like it."

Frederick seemed to relax. "I saw how you went to your wife in California—how you helped her. She needed you, and you were there for her."

Those damned tabloids again. Everyone seemed to know the story, or at least the story as the press put it out. As it had turned out, going to Anne had been a huge mistake—not just for himself, but for her as well. Reappearing in her life had caused Anne nothing but unhappy complications. She would have been better off if he'd stayed away. But he said nothing, keeping his eyes on Frederick.

Something flickered across the young man's face: pride and resolve. "How you feel about your wife—that's how I feel about Moira."

Poor sod, if that's true, Reid thought, but he said only, "You're in love with her."

Frederick nodded, miserable but armored in defense of his beloved. "I've tried to stop, but I can't."

"Not an easy thing to control. How is she handling her father's death?"

Frederick looked up, pulling himself away from whatever other thoughts were occupying his mind. "She's doing all right. They weren't close."

"You said he never talked to you. Why not?"

"He thought I was stupid." The astute look on Frederick's face told Reid that he'd underestimated the young man's intelligence. "I'm not. I'm not as smart as Henry or my father, but I'm not stupid."

"I know that. Were you at the meeting with Richard Ramsey on Friday?" Walter Von Zandt had said it was just Henry and himself there, but Reid had no reason to trust anything the man said.

"Friday?" Frederick shook his head. "No, I saw him come in, but I don't sit in on those kinds of meetings. It's usually just Henry and my father."

Reid nodded, thinking of what other information he could possibly elicit from Frederick. "Did Mr. Ramsey seem upset when he came to the offices? Or when he left?"

Frederick thought, then spoke, slowly formulating his words. "I think he was afraid of my father. Most people are. But Mr. Ramsey was not a nice man either."

"Why do you say that?"

Frederick rubbed the back of his neck. "What he did to Moira."

"What was that?"

Frederick looked embarrassed. "You know."

"Sending her to live with your father?"

Frederick nodded. "She was just barely sixteen. And she'd never . . . you know." The young man's face blushed bright red.

"How do you know that?"

Frederick started massaging his temples, as if what they were talking about made his head hurt. "My father showed me the blood spots on the sheets and explained what it meant. He said, this is how you know if you're getting what you paid for." His eyes, full of pain, though still watery, lost their unfocused look. "I hated Richard Ramsey for doing that to Moira. I'm glad he's dead."

Reid didn't blame Frederick; if he'd been Frederick, he'd have hated Walter Von Zandt as well. "What about Moira's mother? Why didn't she intervene?"

Frederick shook his head in disgust. "She knew her husband needed my father's money. Besides, she's always soused."

Reid tried not to let on how shocked he was. Moira had been part of the loan conditions. And apparently her mother had stood by and done nothing while her husband all but sold her daughter to Von Zandt.

"I'm sorry."

The young man grimaced and nodded. Reid couldn't even imagine how miserable it must be for him to be in love with Moira and have to see her with his own father. At least if Anne married Grainger, Reid would never have to see her again.

Reid stood up to leave, placing some money on the table to cover the bill.

The young man glanced up, his face anxious. "Don't tell my father we talked without Henry here."

"I won't."

# Chapter 38

BACK AT HIGH STREET, Reid buried himself in investigation reports and the results of the financial account searches. His mobile rang and he picked it up, distracted.

"Reid here."

"Aye, and Stirling here."

"What can I do for you, John?" Shite—the last thing Reid wanted right now was to talk to someone who knew him as well as John Stirling did.

"That's certainly an enthusiastic greeting for an old friend."

Reid kept his voice deliberately curt. "Sorry, mate, I'm in the middle of something."

"Right." Stirling put a world of amusement in his voice. "Of course you are."

Reid sighed, giving up. "Sorry. Are you in town?"

"Aye. For the Easter holidays. I'm going to be at MacTavish's for their annual Easter buffet Sunday. You going?"

Reid rubbed his hand over his face. This Sunday was indeed Easter. "Probably not. I've too much work to do."

There was a short silence, after which Stirling's cheerful voice came on again. "Then you'll have a pint with me tonight? And maybe a bite to eat?"

Reid hesitated. He didn't feel like being with anyone else and didn't want to go out, but Stirling lived in Aberdeen and didn't come to Glasgow that often. Besides, he was always quick to lend assistance every time Reid called him. Refusing to make time to see his friend would not only be ungracious, but would probably send up more red flags than Reid wanted.

"I could meet you for a short time. As I say, I've a fair bit of work to get done."

"All right then. Let's do it early rather than later. If you're not up for my company for long, I'll see if I can rustle up some young lady who's not so picky afterwards."

"I'm not meaning to be rude, John, but I'm just not in much of a mood," Reid said, feeling guilty that his response to his friend's invitation had been less than eager.

"Then we'll just keep it open. If I can't cheer you up and convince you to make a night of it, I'll toddle off and amuse myself elsewhere. Where shall we meet?"

"You choose."

"All right. Three Crows at six."

"What is it with you and that place?" Glasgow had a plethora of pubs and restaurants, but given the choice, Stirling always picked the same place.

"I like it." Stirling's confidence wasn't challenged by Reid's skepticism. He liked what he liked, what made him feel good, and he never made excuses. Stirling was probably the most naturally happy person Reid had ever met.

"Right then, Three Crows at six." Reid hung up the phone just as Allison poked her curly head in his door.

"You've got someone here to see you, guv."

"Who?" He searched his mind for any forgotten appointments, but nothing came to mind.

"Cyrus Rothman. He says he was Ramsey's solicitor. And Mr. Von Zandt's, as well."

Reid considered, then said, "Show him in." He stood up as his visitor entered and motioned for him to sit down. Cyrus Rothman's quick eyes appraised the office, but the man would see only what he was meant to see: a government office with some maps on the walls and folders on the desk hiding from view any papers Reid had there.

Reid waited until the man was seated, then asked, "What can I do for you, Rothman?"

Cyrus Rothman was a thin, balding man in his early fifties who, Reid knew, had worked for Von Zandt for many years. His metal rimmed glasses perched on a large beak of a nose, and his thin lips looked dry and chapped. Reid had no doubt that Rothman was one of the reasons Von Zandt had managed to stay out of trouble with the authorities for so long. The lawyer was no simple mouthpiece; he was clever and well connected. But how could Rothman be both Richard Ramsey and Von Zandt's solicitor when their affairs were so intertwined? How could that not be a conflict of interest?

Rothman cleared his throat. "I'm here about Richard Ramsey. I thought that perhaps you would like to speak to me. You understand I'm not at liberty to share any client confidences with you, but I know you're looking into his death and I thought that what I can tell you might be of some assistance." He reached into the small folder he held under one arm, and drew out a sheaf of papers. "I've brought a copy of his will."

Reid leaned back in his chair, making no move to take the proffered papers. "We appreciate any information we can get, although I do have other officers working on the investigation into Mr. Ramsey's death. Let me have one of them talk to you."

Rothman shook his head. "I'd prefer to talk to you."

Reid considered whether to challenge Rothman, and assign him to one of his subordinates, but decided not to play those kinds of games. Besides, he was dying to know what the will said. "All right. Go ahead."

The solicitor seemed to be swallowing his natural inclination to be offended at Reid's lack of interest. Reid assumed Rothman had to have been sent here on instructions from Von Zandt to talk to Reid, and the solicitor was not going to disobey those instructions and leave without doing so.

"I've had dealings with Mr. Ramsey for many years. I came to know him, or at least to know a considerable amount about his business, as well as about his business problems."

"Go on."

"Very few people knew it, but his business empire had begun to experience serious problems about four years ago. His businesses were interwoven, so when one thread came loose, everything was in danger of unraveling. He had considerable assets, but he also had a rapidly building debt that necessitated cash payments. He'd tried to expand too rapidly, and there was simply too much outlay before the infusion of profits began, and his obligations were all coming due at a time when his cash assets were temporarily tied up."

"Were you his solicitor at that time?" Reid asked.

"No. He hired me to help him get out of the mess he'd gotten himself into. He asked Walter—Mr. Von Zandt—for advice, and

Walter recommended he retain me. I set up some support lines between VZ Capital and Ramsey's businesses."

"Isn't that a conflict of interest?"

"Ordinarily, perhaps, but Mr. Ramsey and Mr. Von Zandt signed conflict waivers allowing me to work for them both."

"And?"

"I set up some emergency funding that allowed Mr. Ramsey to escape almost certain financial ruin."

"In exchange for?"

"VZ Capital was given certain non-monetary compensation and of course, some monetary repayment that would be put off until some future point when Mr. Ramsey had things under control again."

"The non-monetary compensation included seats on the board of directors of Ramsey International and what else?"

"Stock in Ramsey International and several of the subsidiary companies Ramsey owned."

"What else?" Reid had a bad feeling about the document in Rothman's hand. "Something in Ramsey's will?"

Rothman shifted in his chair. "Actually, yes. One of the conditions of the loan was that Ramsey make certain provisions in his will regarding Mr. Von Zandt in the event Mr. Ramsey passed away before the loan had been completely paid off."

Reid frowned. "And the loan wasn't paid off when he died?"

"That's correct." Rothman named the outstanding amount, an amount so small that Ramsey should have been able to pay it easily.

"So what does the will leave to Von Zandt?"

"Controlling interest of Ramsey International and the remaining assets of the estate in a trust to be administered by Mr. Von Zandt, with Mrs. Ramsey as the lifetime beneficiary of the trust." As he spoke, Rothman rubbed each fingernail of his left hand with his right thumb in turn, as if he were polishing them, then reversed with the opposite hand—one of the strangest tics Reid had ever noted in a grown man.

"Even though the loan had almost been entirely paid off?" This was unbelievable. Richard Ramsey had been a man of great wealth. Why wouldn't he have paid off the loan in full?

"Those were the terms of the agreement."

"But Ramsey was worth millions. He could have paid that loan off in full many times over, and he certainly could have made whatever the last few payments would have been." Ramsey must have been deceived into either thinking that the loan had been paid off in full, or as to what would happen in the event of any amount being outstanding upon his death.

"The loan obligations were staggered, and at this point, it had become an almost interest-free loan. Apparently Mr. Ramsey chose to leave it on the books and pay it off later. That was his decision."

Reid tried to keep his fury out of his voice, but he knew it leaked through. "You'll have serious difficulties getting this to pass muster in probate proceedings."

Rothman narrowed his eyes. "I don't think so. Mr. Von Zandt committed a great deal of money to Ramsey's company. It only makes sense that he'd need to get something of value back. Besides, I don't think Mrs. Ramsey will choose to fight the terms of the will."

"I assume you'll not be representing her." That would take the bloody cake, Reid thought.

"No, of course not. I'll be representing the estate and the trustee."

"And Mrs. Ramsey?"

"She'll have to engage separate counsel if she feels the need. But I expect she'll trust Mr. Von Zandt to see to her needs."

"What about Bert and Moira?"

Rothman pursed his lips. "Neither of them were actually Richard Ramsey's children, either by birth or adoption, and neither was named in the latest will. But Bert works for the company. He'll keep his position. Moira, well, Mr. Von Zandt provides for Moira."

When Rothman left, Reid read through the will, then picked up the telephone. This was not going to happen if he had anything to say about it.

# Chapter 39

REID SHOWED UP at the Three Crows at six. He glanced around until he spotted the tall blond man leaning against the bar, one hand resting lightly on the shoulder of a petite brunette. Another young woman—this one a redhead—sat on the next barstool apparently enthralled by whatever charming swill Stirling was dishing out. Reid thought about turning around and leaving, but was stuck when his friend spotted him and waved him over.

"Come meet these lovely young lassies, Terrence."

Reid went over reluctantly. "John, we can reschedule if you've made other plans."

Stirling shook his head. "We were just having a drink while I waited for you." Stirling looked down at the two women, his face radiating fondness. "I told the ladies that I was having dinner with a very married friend. Didn't I?"

The redhead dropped down from her barstool, and said in an awed voice, "I know who you are. You're Lord Reid."

The other girl's eyes widened as she studied him. "He is, isn't he?"

Reid looked over at Stirling, mutely begging for rescue.

Stirling frowned. "I'm not liking all the attention you ladies are giving my friend. Married, he is, did you hear me tell you?"

The redhead nodded. "We know who he is. He's been on the telly. Married to the American girl." She clucked her tongue. "Scottish girls treat their men better than that."

Stirling cocked an eyebrow. "I can see it's time we went in to dinner. Ladies, if you'll excuse us. Till next time." He smiled and moved Reid away to where the hostess was waiting with menus.

His friend leaned into him, speaking in a whisper. "Terrence, my boy, you're starting to steal my thunder with your tabloid appeal. This may be a problem in our friendship. I'm supposed to be the quine magnet."

"You can have it."

Stirling inclined his head. "Thank you. I accept. So, speaking of you being married, how is the fair Anne?" Stirling pulled a chair out at the table their hostess had indicated, and sat down.

Reid followed suit, now in more of a foul mood than when he'd arrived. He'd hoped to avoid any mention of his wife tonight. But at least his friend had always seemed to accept his irrational attachment to a wife who'd never really been his wife.

"She's fine."

"In California still?"

Reid beetled his eyebrows but said nothing. He'd not told his friend anything about what had happened in California.

Stirling sighed. "I'm not blind, min. I see the news. Few of my friends are featured, but lately, you and your lassie have been in the forefront."

A waitress brought their drinks, took their orders, and left them alone again.

Reid drank his whiskey in silence.

His friend did the same for a time, then finally broke the silence, "You don't want to talk about her?"

"No."

"So she stayed in California after all?"

Reid stared down into his glass, the dark honey brown elixir reflecting the light. "She's here."

Stirling, obviously surprised, quickly drained his glass. He motioned the waitress to bring another round.

"In town?"

"Aye. She has a job here for a few months."

They sat in silence again, until the new drinks came and Stirling raised his glass. "To Anne finally being in Glasgow."

Reid looked over at his friend but did not raise his own glass. Nor could he think of anything to say.

Not easily daunted, Stirling tried again. "No toast? I would think that would be good news."

Reid took a drink, letting the deep thick flavor fill his mouth, knowing that if he could confide in anyone, it would be John Stirling.

Reid had been eight years old, abandoned by his mother, sent to school by his distraught father, knowing no one, and the target for tormenting by other boys who said vile things about his mum, when he'd met John Stirling. They'd formed an instant bond, as only eight-year-old boys can do. Together Reid and Stirling did their best to beat the shite out of anyone who'd dared to bring up the subject of Reid's mother, which happened with some regularity as the news about his mother running away with her lover spread through the school.

Things hadn't gotten any easier after his mother had left her lover, coming back to his father with her stomach swollen in pregnancy. His classmates had left Reid no doubt about what she'd done that got the baby inside her. That fight had almost gotten him, Stirling, and the rest of their friends kicked out of school, but Reid's father had intervened and somehow smoothed things over. Reid suspected money had been involved.

Stirling waded back into the conversational bog. "Anne looked as bonnie as ever on the telly, and I got the impression from the later stories that you two were back together."

Reid nodded, finishing his whiskey. He couldn't think of anything to say, even to his best friend. How could he tell him that he'd chosen a wife who'd done to him what his mother had done to his father? It was like some kind of unbelievably horrible cosmic joke.

"But not now?" Stirling emptied his own glass.

This time it was Reid who motioned the waitress for another round. He was silent until his fresh drink arrived. This one he left untouched, pushing it away and taking up his glass of water. "Can we talk about something else?"

Stirling sipped his whiskey. "Of course."

"We've been intercepting some coded communications and we're having the devil's own time deciphering them. Darby sent them to Interpol, and they've come up with nothing. Could you take a look?" Reid took a folded set of papers from his pocket and smoothing them out, passed them and a flashdrive to his friend. While they had been in military intelligence, this kind of work had been Stirling's specialty. "I think we're close. We've decrypted the transmissions, and been able to trace them unofficially to an Islamic cell in Nigeria. But we've not been able to make sense of the messages. We need to get enough to determine the next target—then, at least we'd have a chance of stopping them. Searching in every European city with a university is unmanageably hopeless."

Stirling nodded. "I'll try."

"Thanks." Reid rubbed his temples. "John, about Anne—I just can't discuss it right now."

"Aye, I understand." Stirling gave the side of Reid's head a soft slap. "Let me know if I can help."

"Thanks." Reid doubted his friend actually understood, but, at least momentarily, he felt less alone.

"Order us some coffee." Stirling said, then pulled out his reading glasses and began perusing the papers Reid had given him.

Reid was on his second cup of coffee before Stirling spoke again. "I get what they're doing. It's like in Gibraltar. Like Llanito."

"What do you mean?"

"You know. The language they use there."

"I know what Llanito is, but what do you mean?" Reid and Stirling had spent their initial posting for military intelligence together in Gibraltar, where Stirling's natural genius for codes had emerged. Under the guidance of Nelson Schilling, now Deputy General of MI5, Stirling's talents had resulted in him being conscripted into rewriting the military code books.

"In Llanito, not only is the language already a combination of other languages, but they also do code-switching." He tapped the papers with his finger. "That's exactly what they did here. Combined languages, then used code-switching."

"Code-switching?"

"Right. That's not exactly what it sounds like. It's referring to language, not codes."

"Like using a word here and there from other languages?"

"No, it's more than that. You actually use more than one linguistic variety, keeping the syntax and phonology of each variety intact." Stirling signaled the waiter. "Let's order some food to take with us. I need to be somewhere I can set up my computer. I'm pretty sure I've got this."

"Got what?"

"Not what, where. For specifics, I need my computer, but I have some general locations."

Reid's mind finally tumbled to what Stirling was saying. He grabbed his friend's arm. "Where? For God's sake, where?"

"Paris is first, then London, then Rome, then Brussels, then

Edinburgh."

# THURSDAY, APRIL 9

# Chapter 40

REID HAD been up most of the night working with Stirling. He was exhausted, but at least now they knew the targets. When was still unknown, but they finally had some progress, and high priority alerts had been sent to the targeted cities and universities. The list was mindboggling: The Sorbonne; four targets in London in a simultaneous attack, including the London School of Economics, Kings College, University College, and Imperial College; Sapienza in Rome; Libre in Brussels; and, finally, the University of Edinburgh.

The walk to the car after the morning's press conference was far enough and windy enough to make Reid grateful for the efficacy of the car's heater during the drive to see Peter MacTavish. He wished it would start feeling like spring. The damp cold was beginning to depress him, despite the brave, shivering daffodils that poked up from the ground. They didn't look like they were really convinced it was spring themselves; rather, it was as if they'd been forced to show up to a place they neither wanted to be nor expected to be seen. Reid felt a bit like that himself.

He'd scheduled the press conference for a time that ensured the interview would make the midday television news. The positive side of Reid's tabloid fame was that the press seemed to be ready to pay more attention than ever to anything he wanted to release. He decided he might as well use his new notoriety if he had to be plagued with it.

The first question had come from Carolyn Caspary, and the rest of the interview went as they'd orchestrated. All in all, he was pleased with how things had gone. Without disclosing that they now had the specific targets identified, he'd focused on the plot to bomb more universities around Europe and the United Kingdom, and reminded people of the tragic toll of the Heidelberg University bombing. He wanted the immediacy of the danger to be clear as well as the vital importance that anyone who had information come forward. Then, without naming names, he'd discussed the discovery of certain funding sources and how the terrorists utilized the services of profiteers who laundered their money for a fee. With any luck, Von Zandt and his co-conspirators would feel the pressure and the attacks would be cancelled, or at least they might make a mistake which would expedite the efforts to locate and arrest those involved.

Reid entered the expensively decorated offices of the investment bank where his friend headed up the international investments division, and proceeded directly toward the back. He'd made no advance call for an appointment, but as long as Peter MacTavish was in, he wouldn't need one. In addition to managing a good deal of the Reid family investments, Peter was one of Reid's oldest and closest friends.

The slim, silver-haired woman that guarded MacTavish's offices wore a severe black suit and a competent manner that assured visitors that she was not just a gatekeeper. Her face broke out into a genuine smile when Reid walked in. Standing up, she came out from behind her desk to greet him.

"Lord Reid, it's good to see you. Is Mr. MacTavish expecting you?"

"I confess he's not, Mrs. Henning, but can you fit me in?"

Angela Henning went back to her desk and checked an appointment calendar. "I think so. As soon as this call finishes up. I'll just go slip a note to him that you're here. Would you like some coffee or tea while you wait?"

"Coffee, thank you." He motioned to where the coffee bar was set up. "I'll get it myself if you'll just let him know I'm here."

"Of course." She left, as silent as she was efficient.

Reid poured his coffee and went to the large window at one end of the reception area. There seemed to be hope that the sun would be coming out today. He thought of Anne working outside at Lynstrade Manor and hoped she would have good weather. It was getting easier to think about her again, but not easier to think about what to do with their situation. Their anniversary was Sunday, falling on Easter this year. Before she'd told him about being pregnant, he'd thought that was a good sign—the resurrection of their marriage on the day of Resurrection.

His thoughts were interrupted by Angela's return.

"Lord Reid, Mr. MacTavish asked that you go in whenever you're ready. He'll be finished with his call in a moment."

"Thank you. I'll do that." Reid passed back through the highly polished wood door into an office lined with more of the same.

Peter MacTavish motioned to Reid to sit down and held up five fingers, indicating the call would be ending soon. Reid sat down in a comfortable maroon leather chair and glanced around the room, letting his eyes rest for a moment on a photo of MacTavish's wife and three children. He looked away, sharp envy piercing his chest.

When MacTavish ended the call, he stood up and came over to Reid, clapping his hand on his friend's shoulder. "Terrence, how are you?"

MacTavish's naturally burly shape had thickened more around his middle as the years had passed. His round face, boyish in another age, was settling into the strong-jowled face of a man of consequence.

"Good, as ever. I trust your family is well?"

"Aye. Claudia wants me to make sure I pressure you to show up on Easter."

"I don't think I'll be able to make it, but please thank her for me. My sister, Darby, though, is in town. I think she'd like to come if there's room."

"I'll have Claudia call her."

"Thank you, she'll appreciate that. She's staying at the Blythswood."

"I'll tell Claudia. You're certain you can't make it?"

"I'm afraid not." Not only did Reid not feel like going to a party, but he didn't know if he could handle seeing his friend's happy family. Especially the children. "Can I bend your ear on something, Peter?"

"Indeed."

"I need some information on the institutions I think are being used to finance these terrorist attacks. The names are in here." Reid handed his friend a list he'd gotten from Oscar. "It would help if there was someone I could trust inside the banks to find out exactly what they require to set up the accounts, what kind of security they employ, and the timing of releasing funds by request. My people are good on this but new dodges keep popping up and throwing us off. I have a feeling that we're always one step behind the newest ruse."

"It's hard for us to keep up ourselves. Every time things tighten up in one arena, new schemes for eluding the authorities pop up in another. But you're not looking for those who are evading the Inland Revenue, are you?"

"Not really, but I presume our blokes want to do that as well as evade anti-terrorist tracking protocols. It behooves them to stay off either radar screen as one informs the other."

"Indeed."

"So here's our problem." Reid explained in more detail the difficulties they were having, and MacTavish opened the envelope, looked at the list, and nodded, thinking.

"So you want me to find you a contact in each of these institutions?"

"I do, yes."

"Let me make some calls."

"I'd appreciate that."

"No problem." MacTavish's voice took on a calculatingly casual tone. "So my friend, I saw your press conference this morning. You planning to stand for office?"

Reid made a face. "Not in my darkest of thoughts."

MacTavish laughed. "You've not taken leave of your senses, at least."

"No, not yet. And I've certainly had my fill of the press's interest in me."

Suddenly somber, MacTavish nodded. "How is Anne? Claudia asked me if . . . well, if things were better between the two of you."

Reid realized he'd inadvertently invited the inquiry, but he could no more share the news of Anne's pregnancy with MacTavish than he could have with Stirling. Anne and he had to carry this cross alone. "You'll forgive me if I'd rather not discuss it?"

"Aye, when do you ever?" His friend's eyes were sympathetic. MacTavish was also clearly trying to assess whether he should say anything else.

To forestall any more questions, Reid got up, putting out his hand to shake his friend's hand.

"Thanks for your time, Peter. I'll wait to hear from you on what you find out, and please tell Claudia I'm sorry I can't be there for her famous Easter buffet."

MacTavish gave a low whistle between his teeth, shaking his head. "You're a brave man. I wouldn't get on Claudia's bad side if I were you, but it's your head on the block."

Reid gave a wry smile. "So what else is new?"

# FRIDAY, APRIL 10

# Chapter 41

WALTER VON ZANDT put his hands in his pockets against the chill and continued his search around the gardens. She had to be out here somewhere.

He finally caught sight of her in a bed of bloomless perennials. His heartbeat quickened, and he smiled. She wore knee-high brown leather boots over brown pants, and a warm chocolate jacket. Her blonde hair—not the obvious dyed-straw color of Elisa's, but a honeyed wheat—was pulled back with a brown leather headband. She was concentrating on the garden bed, biting her bottom lip. He watched as she looked back down at her plans, intently studying them, and his chest hurt with wanting her.

He had seen her in photographs and in news reports, of course, but when he'd first met her in person yesterday, he'd realized they did not even come close to doing her justice. She was not just phenomenally beautiful, but soft, and she had a beguilingly natural charm that radiated with the brilliance of summer sunshine. No wonder Reid had been reluctant to end their marriage even after she'd gotten involved with another man.

She must have heard him approach because she turned and smiled just as he reached her.

"Mr. Von Zandt."

"Lady Anne."

She scrunched up her little nose in a gesture so endearing he could hardly stand it, then wiped a smudge of dirt away with the back of her hand. "Just Anne."

"Anne. And you must call me Walter." He smiled, then gestured to the plans. "What's the verdict? Can you restore the gardens to what they were?"

She nodded. "Absolutely. Jonas is a genius. They'll be spectacular."

"Not just Jonas. He tells me you're his secret weapon. But I can tell that myself."

"Thank you." She seemed slightly embarrassed. "Are you taking a tour of the gardens?"

Her modesty, so refreshing and rare, enchanted him. "Actually, I was looking for you."

She looked puzzled. "Is there something I can help you with?"

"Luncheon. Will you join me?"

She checked her watch. "Certainly. I can't believe it's noon already. Jonas is in the rose garden. I'll just go by and collect him. Where should we meet you?"

"No need for that. My estate manager has taken Jonas to the house for luncheon. I had something different in mind for us."

"Excuse me?" She looked wary, and he almost smiled. He liked that she wasn't naïve.

"I've had a luncheon set up for us at the folly across the large pond. My wife will be joining us there. I thought you would both enjoy it there. We've heaters set up. Elisa would be interested in hearing your thoughts on the garden."

Anne visibly relaxed. "That sounds lovely."

"Good. Shall we proceed, then?" Von Zandt took her arm, feeling the warmth of her body through the wool of her jacket.

"This is a lovely place, Walter. You were fortunate to find a home with such an impressive example of Russell Page's designs."

"Yes." He smiled at her, and resisted the impulse to bring her hand to his mouth to kiss it. Soon, though, that hand and this woman would be his. "I was not raised like this, you know."

Her eyes slanted up at him, teasing. "Rich, you mean? Or as a garden lover?"

He laughed. "Neither one. My father died shortly after I was born. He came here from Germany after the war and met my mother. She was left with two young children to take care of, and we grew up quite poor. We lived in a miserable few rooms in a part of Glasgow I'm sure you've never seen. And we had no garden at all."

She waved an arm to encompass the estate. "But now, you're successful and own an impressive place like this."

He glanced over at her to make sure she wasn't mocking him, and was reassured by the frank interest in her face. "Yes. I have an estate in Germany as well. In the Black Forest."

"Why Germany?"

He shrugged. "My father's people were from a small town there. I went back to see my roots, I guess you could say. That's where I met my wife." It had seemed a good idea at the time, marrying a nineteen-year-old woman with no ambition other than to be a wife and mother, but now, decades later, decades during which he'd polished his own image, Elisa's lack of education and sophistication galled him.

"That's nice."

He inclined his head slightly, enough to acknowledge Anne's comment, but not enough to signal his agreement. Nice wasn't the word he'd choose. Every time Elisa spoke, he had to grit his teeth to stop himself from saying something cutting. Too often, he wasn't successful and then there were her tedious tears.

"So you bought the house there for her?"

He'd actually bought the house in the Black Forest to get his wife out of his way. Elisa would never fit in with the types of social circles to which his wealth and position would eventually gain him entrance. Social circles that Anne's husband had been born into. Reid had had the foresight to marry a woman who could fit in anywhere, although Von Zandt imagined Anne's affair with the artist had caused the Reid family considerable embarrassment.

"Elisa feels more at home in Germany."

"But she's here now." Anne's tone made the comment more of a question.

Not for long, he thought, but he said only, "She misses our sons and the grandchildren."

Anne said, "Maybe that, combined with Lynstrade Manor, will entice her to stay in Scotland."

"Maybe. And you? You're planning to stay in Scotland now?"

"I'm not sure." A small smile wobbled across Anne's mouth.

Ah, so things weren't going well with Reid. He'd suspected as much when she'd moved into the hotel. Good.

He beamed at her. "Well, I, for one, hope you stay." At this stage in his life, Von Zandt thought, he deserved someone like Anne: educated, talented, and sexually vibrant. She would be able to give him more children—her figure combined a slim fitness with womanly curves, and was perfect for it. He let his gaze trail down her body, past her full breasts to her long, enticing legs.

Anne, oblivious to his thoughts, was surveying the various garden beds as they walked. "Thanks. I like it here a lot."

They would marry, of course, so he needed to get rid of Elisa. And Moira. Anne Michaels was a woman who needed to be owned. And, unlike Elisa, he didn't think Anne would tolerate mistresses. Besides, with Anne, he wouldn't need anyone else.

"I'm looking forward to talking to your wife about the design plans. You two can have a lot of fun with this garden."

"I'm looking forward to hearing your ideas." He'd tolerate being with Elisa this one last time, but no more. He had done his duty by her, but she had not been a good choice for him. She'd given him Henry, a son he could be proud of, but she'd also given birth to Frederick, whose physical and mental impairments were an embarrassment. There was nothing like that in his family; that could only have come from Elisa's side of the family.

"Have you seen other Russell Page gardens, or photos of them?" Anne asked.

"I confess I have not."

"I have some books you and your wife might want to look over. I'm re-reading a book he wrote right now."

"Re-reading?"

"Yes. It's a classic, but so much more exciting to read it when you can also immerse yourself in one of his actual creations."

"You enjoy your work." He smiled at her, loving her enthusiasm.

"Immensely. Page said something about a garden having a kaleidoscope of shifting garden pictures or scenes. I forget the exact words, but that's how it is to me. Everywhere I look, I see a new, perfect picture, or the potential for one."

Von Zandt encouraged her to expound, but his mind was not on gardens. He was trying to decide Elisa's fate.

Divorce or death?

# Chapter 42

**R**EID WALKED QUICKLY across the marble floor to the hotel reception desk and asked the desk clerk to ring Anne's room. His stomach was churning and his chest burned. It had been an impulse to come here without having spoken to her. He didn't know her room number, but at least he'd had the name of the hotel. His heart was pounding so fast that he forced himself to take deep breaths to slow it down.

The young man behind the desk, chubby and red-faced, nodded and rang the room. "I'm sorry, sir, there's no answer."

Reid looked at his watch. Just past nine. "Please try again. My wife may have slept through the telephone ringing. I didn't mention to her that I'd be coming tonight." He knew he shouldn't have come, but he hadn't been able to stop himself.

"Yes, sir." The desk clerk punched the number in again and waited. After a time, he shook his head. "Sorry, sir, there's no answer. Perhaps she's out for dinner. She may be in the dining room—let me call and check for you." He made a brief call, then shook his head as he hung up. "No, I'm sorry, sir. She's not in there."

"All right, thank you. I'll wait in the bar. Please leave word when she comes in that I'm here." He knew it was unreasonable to expect that she would be sitting in her room waiting for him. She certainly needed to eat dinner, and he'd given her no warning that he was coming.

"Your name, sir?"

"You can just tell her that her husband is here. She only has one as far as I know." There was an edge in his voice, a bitterness he momentarily could not keep back. How long would he be able to call himself her husband?

The clerk looked startled at his tone, so Reid softened his face into a smile. "I'm Lord Reid. I'll be in the bar." The title had the desired effect, calming the man, removing any worry that one of the hotel guests might be being bothered by an unwanted and unruly visitor.

Then he saw the man make the connection between his name and his beautiful wife. Apparently not just young women read the tabloids. "Yes, my lord. I'll tell her."

"I've forgotten her room number."

"321, my lord."

"Yes, of course. Thank you." He felt an irrational bit of comfort in knowing her room number. He ordered a whiskey and settled in to wait for her. He knew he should eat something, but he had no appetite.

More whiskies than he could count later, he finally saw her. Reid could not remember the last time he'd drunk so much, but he'd been waiting for over three hours and had nothing to do but drink. The chair he'd taken gave him a view of the hotel's lobby, and she was easy to spot. Her hair was caught up at the back of her head and cascaded down in a golden waterfall. She wore the black dress she'd worn the last time they'd gone out to dinner together, black high heels, and looked amazingly beautiful. Four men in business suits surrounded her, and she smiled and talked with them with that easy grace she had.

He recognized her boss, Jonas Reveille, a man of close to sixty years who looked like he'd spent thousands of hours outdoors, as indeed he had. Reid did not recognize either of the two men facing his way. A fourth man faced the other direction, his face hidden, his hand on Anne's arm.

Intense fury burned through him at the sight of the man touching her, even as Anne adroitly turned so that the hand was dropped. Her dress revealed an enticing glimpse of cleavage. Why couldn't she wear something more businesslike? Something like a suit and a high-necked blouse? He'd never been a jealous man, but finding out about the pregnancy seemed to have unearthed these strong, primordial feelings in him.

He watched her, torturing himself. He knew he'd had too much to drink, especially considering he had eaten nothing all day. He could tell himself he'd fasted today because it was Good Friday, but actually, he'd hardly eaten anything since he'd last seen her. She, on the other hand, had been out to dinner in a sexy dress with other men. There was no sign now of the distraught and tearful wife he'd last seen in his flat.

He rose and crossed to her. Surprise flickered across her face, and then pleasure, but he could tell that she recognized his mood. Poised nonetheless, she introduced him around. He knew Jonas, greeted him. When the last man, the one who had had his hand on Anne, turned and faced him, recognition hit Reid like a solid punch in the gut.

Walter Von Zandt.

The man bared his teeth in a cold, feral smile. Reid registered something familiar in the man's expression, familiar because he'd seen it in his own face many times lately: Von Zandt was jealous of Anne. Blast the woman. She had a way of causing that reaction in men without even realizing what she was doing. She should wear a bag over her head—or over her whole damned body.

Anne, seemingly oblivious, smiled at the other men as she made her excuses to leave them. "Thank you for dinner, Jonas. If you gentlemen would excuse us, please, I've not seen my husband for several days. He's been too busy to get away."

"By all means . . ." Jonas began, but was interrupted by Von Zandt's unctuous voice.

"Lord Reid—or should I say Superintendent Reid?"

Reid acknowledged the man with a nod. "I'm assuming you own Lynstrade Manor?"

"I do." Von Zandt looked unconvincingly sheepish. "Rather, it's owned by one of my companies."

Anne eyes went from Von Zandt to Reid, her confusion obvious. "You two know each other?"

"In a manner of speaking." Von Zandt glanced at Reid, but his attention remained on Anne. "We've greatly enjoyed having Anne with us at Lynstrade Manor these past few days."

"I'm sure you have." Reid bit each word out as if it were its own sentence.

"You know, I assume, that Jonas and your delightful wife have agreed to do the restoration of our gardens."

"Then you have the best there is." Reid, gripping Anne's arm tightly, smiled the briefest of smiles. "But I have missed her delightful company myself, and so, we'll say good night."

"Please allow me to buy you a drink. I'd enjoy talking to both of you some more."

Reid remembered the man's remark from the last time they'd met about having dinner with their wives sometime. Von Zandt must have known then that Anne would be working on his gardens. Reid's anger escalated to where he wanted to hit Von Zandt, but Anne took Reid's free hand in hers and looked up at him. Her face was melting into that sensual softness he loved, but, he wondered, had it begun when she saw him, or when Von Zandt was touching her arm?

Anne squeezed Reid's hand. "I'm so sorry, Walter. We really need to excuse ourselves. It's been a long week apart for us." She didn't even seem to notice the other man's eyes fixed intently on her.

Von Zandt turned to Reid, anger almost spitting out of his eyes. "We'll see each other again soon, Superintendent."

"I'm sure we will." Reid kept his voice neutral, but clutched Anne's hand.

"Good to see you again, Terrence." Jonas nodded at Anne. "Have a good weekend, Anne. We'll start work early Monday morning."

"I'll be there." She turned and whispered in Reid's ear as he led her away from the others. "I'm so happy to see you. I've been praying you'd call—but you coming is so much better."

Reid, not responding, guided his wife to the lift. He felt his control leave him and rage take its place, but he forced himself to wait. When they entered the lift, he finally spoke, his voice hard and clipped. "Are you really happy? I rather felt as if I were interrupting a party, Anne. You looked as if you were holding court." The lift doors shut behind them and he punched in the floor number. "That bastard Von Zandt looked as if he wanted to eat you up."

"Terrence, don't be silly. It wasn't a party, it was a business dinner. Jonas needed to take them to dinner—it's Walter's garden, and the other two men work for him. Jonas asked me along as I'm on the project, but I wouldn't have gone if I'd known you were coming." She smiled at him and rose up on her toes to kiss him. "I'm so glad you came. I've been so worried."

Jealousy surged through him riding on a wave of whiskey. "Why does Jonas have you come to a business dinner wearing something like this?" He crowded her against the back of the lift and slipped his hand down the front of her dress, cupping one of her breasts.

She looked up at him with surprise, although she didn't push him away and did nothing to stop his hands. In fact, she yielded entirely to him, as was her way, but unfortunately, he thought, only in sex.

"You've had quite a bit to drink, sweetheart, haven't you?" She nuzzled against him, her voice soft. "Terrence, I don't think we should do this here. Someone else might get on the elevator. Let's wait till we get to the room, okay?"

"I had a long wait while you were letting those men look at you in this dress." He put his mouth on her neck, kissing her savagely. "You shouldn't have worn a dress like this on a business dinner. This is not a business dress and you're my wife." He eased the skirt of her dress up past her bare legs, pushed aside the edges of her panties and found her.

"Yes, I am." Her arms went around his neck. She relaxed her legs and let his fingers enter her, her head tilting back as her eyes closed. Her voice came out in those lovely husky tones it took on when she was aroused, and she moved into his hand. "Shouldn't we wait until we get to the room? Someone else might get on." Her voice was breathless and he heard her desire.

He didn't answer her, but keeping one hand between her legs, unzipped her dress.

Dislodging her arms from around his neck, he took the top of her dress in his free hand and pulled it down to her waist. "There."

She half-heartedly tried to pull the dress back up, but he pinned her arms back with one hand, kissing her, and still moving his other hand inside her. She made a sound, somewhere between a moan and a sigh, her head leaning back against the lift's mirrored wall. His fingers worked quickly—he wanted to make her come right there, and he could tell it was near. It never took much with Anne; she was always so ready. He wanted to, needed to, hear her climax.

Suddenly the lift doors opened. Anne, startled out of her immersion in what he'd been doing to her, quickly pulled her arms free.

"Come on, my room is this way. Hurry, I'm so close." She grabbed the top of her dress and tried to slide her arms back into the straps. He reached for it and ripped it apart at the bodice.

"This is not a business dress, Anne. Not a business dress at all."

Her breath came out in labored efforts. "Let's just get into the room." She slid the plastic key card in the lock and opened the door.

He came in after her and closed the door. He pulled her around to him, grabbed the dress on each side and continued to rip it until the tearing stopped at the hem. Satisfied, he nodded, then stepped back and studied her. "There, now. You're not wearing this dress anymore."

She looked down at the remnants of her dress, a slight smile playing on her lips. "No, I guess not."

"You're mine. My wife."

"Yes, I'm yours. Just yours. Come to me, hurry." She held out her arms, but he stayed where he was.

"Not yet." He motioned to her. "Take off the rest of your clothes."

She unfastened the black lace bra and let it drop, then slid off the matching panties. She stood there in nothing but her high heels. He stared at her, awed as he always was with her perfection.

He exhaled the breath he hadn't realized he'd been holding. "Christ, you're beautiful. So bloody beautiful. And you're pregnant." He shook his head. "God, I need a drink."

"I don't think so—you've had enough of those. Finish what you started before I go crazy." She walked over to him, then pressed herself against him.

He kissed her, backing her over to the bed. Letting his pent-up need loose, he buried himself in her, feeling reassurance in her soft surrender.

"I love you, lassie. God, I love you so much."

She clung to him as he drove himself into her, again and again.

He heard a cry of surrender as he came, but didn't know if it was hers or his.

# SATURDAY, APRIL 11

# Chapter 43

**R**EID'S HEAD HURT when he woke up. He had been drunk, more drunk than he'd been in years, but not drunk enough not to remember stripping and groping Anne in the lift. He groaned, then sat up in bed. Anne was sitting at the little hotel table, placidly drinking something from a cup and studying her design notebook. Every once in a while, she made notations, her bottom lip caught tightly in her teeth in concentration.

He looked around the room. The offending black dress was stuffed in the small hotel rubbish bin, and a room service tray was sitting on the desk holding a pot of coffee, a smaller pot he assumed was her herbal tea, two glasses of juice, and two covered dishes.

She smiled at him mischievously. "How are you feeling?"

"Don't ask." He ran his hand through his hair. "My head is killing me." His eyes focused on her again. She wore a short white nightie that showed the cleavage he had objected to in her dress last night, as well as acres of tanned leg.

"God, Anne, you look so pretty."

She crossed over to the bed, kissed him and handed him two aspirin and a glass of water. "This might help." She went back to the desk, retrieved her cup, then came back and sat next to him on the bed cross-legged, watching him.

"Oh, girl, I'm sorry for how I acted. I was a total arse—drunk and crazy."

She tilted her head to the side and her golden hair shifted over her shoulders. "You were a bit drunk and definitely intense, but I enjoyed it quite a bit, as you may or may not remember." She took a drink of her tea, smiling. "I hope you remember. Perhaps when your head is better, and you've had some coffee and breakfast, I could do something to refresh your memory."

He just looked at her, trying to figure out this woman who'd totally turned his life upside down, over and over again.

She traced her fingers around his face. "You'd had a shock and you probably needed to get drunk. We definitely needed to make love—and we need to make love again."

He nodded. "Aye."

"But this time, let's keep everything inside the room—although that whole elevator thing was wildly exciting. Don't let's chance it again, though. I'd hate to end up in some tabloid in my underwear—or worse."

He swallowed the tablets she'd given him. "I still can't believe I did that. I've never lost control like that, and I can't remember the last time I was so drunk. Please tell me I didn't appear as drunk as I felt in front of Jonas and Von Zandt and the rest of your people."

"You were professional and elegant, as usual, at least until we got into the elevator."

"Thank Christ for that."

"Yes. Then you were . . ." She stopped and shook her head. "I can't even think about it until you're ready to make love to me again."

He knew immediately that she was aroused, which left him feeling gratified, but still a bit puzzled, and then, aroused himself. He gestured to the rubbish bin. "I ruined your dress."

"Totally. I guess you'll have to buy me a new one. And an ugly business dinner dress, too. But it was definitely worth it." She gave him a provocative slant-eyed grin. Her hand brushed between his legs over the sheet that covered him and he felt his cock instantly jump towards her under the sheet.

She glanced down and smiled. "Want coffee?"

He nodded, watched her uncross her long legs, get off of the bed, and walk over to the room service tray. She poured his coffee and brought it back to him, a luminous smile on her face. "I'm so glad you're here, that you came to me."

He shook his head and took the coffee. "I don't know how we're to do this, Anne. I've still got no answers. I just couldn't stay away. I love you so bloody much." He put the cup down on the table next to the bed.

"Let's not think about it right now." She sat back down beside him on the bed. Leaning over him, she hovered her lips over his and whispered, "As soon as your head can take it, let's pretend we're in the elevator again."

"Oh, girl." He laughed and pulled her down to him. "My head's just been outvoted by the rest of my body."

# Chapter 44

ON THE WAY back to Glasgow, Reid and Anne stopped at a chapel and attended Mass in honor of Holy Saturday. Then they picnicked on cold chicken and salad sitting on the floor of the lounge of the house on Aytoun Lane. Drop cloths to protect things from the painters covered almost every available surface. Both of their wine glasses held sparkling water instead of wine.

"The walls look great. It looks like the painters finished?"

He watched as her eyes traveled around the room, taking in the details. "Yes. Priscilla seems to have taken to heart my instruction that the job was a rush."

"Hmm. Do you pay more for rush jobs?"

"Probably."

Anne sipped her water. "I thought you'd probably have cancelled the work."

He took her hand. "That was the last thing on my mind. I've been imagining you here since I bought it. It's part of my dream for us, for our life."

"It's a lovely house. And it will be even lovelier when everything's finished."

"Are you warm enough? I've turned up the heat just in case you end up wearing less clothing than you have on now. Perhaps after we finish eating."

"Perhaps." She ran her fingers along his back. "It's perfect in here, but it is cold outside. When does it get warm? You know, for the spring—and summer?"

"The weather's not too bad just now, lassie, do you think? We've had quite a bit of sunshine."

She looked at him skeptically. "It's cold, Terrence. Are you saying this is normal?"

"Aye, for this time of year."

"Now, maybe, but in the summer?" She asked hopefully.

He laughed. "In the summer, sometimes we hit a little above what you'd know as seventy degrees. Fahrenheit, I'm talking, as you're used to that. Sometimes we'll even hit the eighties."

Anne's face showed her astonishment. "That's summer?"

"That's a very warm day in summer, girl."

"But what about at the beach? Scotland has lots of beaches, doesn't it?"

"Aye. But that's summer there, too."

"People surf here, though. I read that."

"Yes, but in wetsuits, lassie. Not in a bikini like you're used to doing."

She stared at him. "So never warm, not really? How did I not know that by now?"

"You've not been here much, and not in summer. We're considerably farther north than California."

"San Francisco's not all that warm."

"Warmer than here."

"I guess so." She didn't sound happy about it.

"If you're living here," He knew she would understand his meaning, and she nodded showing that she did. "If you are here, lassie, I'll take you on holidays to warm places—I promise—as much as we can get away. And you can drive me crazy wearing your little bikinis. Like on our honeymoon."

She leaned over to put her arms around him. "At least there's lots of rain. That's good for gardens, at least."

Reid reached out and idly picked up Anne's mobile phone, his casualness belying the jealousy that ate at him. "May I look?"

She raised her eyebrows, but nodded. "Go ahead. I don't have anything to hide."

He went to the call log and scrolled down. Between the calls that were clearly business and his own calls, were several calls from Andrew Grainger. He flipped the screen toward her.

"Grainger seems to be calling you often."

"He's just checking to make sure I'm okay."

"He's in love with you."

"Maybe, but I love you."

He put down the phone and took Anne's face in his hands. "The baby could be mine, couldn't it?" More than anything in the world, he wanted the child in Anne's body to be his.

"Yes, of course."

He got quiet. "My first son will be heir to Dunbaryn, and will be earl after me. If the child's not mine . . ."

"I know." Her eyes began to fill.

"If the child's Grainger's, you can't let it grow up in my house with that scandal hanging over its head. And you won't—can't—leave the child with him and stay with me. I couldn't ask that of you."

Tears started to fall down her cheeks. "I couldn't leave the baby. But I love you. I don't think I can live without you."

"You'll be fine, girl. You'll be fine. I'm not so sure about myself, but we'll not worry about that yet. Not just yet. For now, you're here with me."

She leaned over and they held each other tightly. He lifted his hand to wipe the tears from her cheeks.

"Terrence, I'm so sorry about all this."

"It wasn't just you. I'm to blame, as well." He tried to sound casual. "We'll do what we can." He brushed her hair back. "Tomorrow is Easter, you know."

"Yes, and our anniversary."

He smiled. "I wasn't sure you would remember, with all that was going on."

"A woman remembers her wedding anniversary." She kissed him. "I have something for you."

"And I for you. How shall we celebrate?"

"You think we should celebrate?"

"Yes." Whatever happened, she would be his only wife, and this might be the last wedding anniversary he'd have to celebrate. He wanted it to be something he could remember. "Would you like to go to dinner, my love?"

She nodded. "Let's not go any place where we'll need to worry about having our picture taken or running into people you know. This is complicated enough."

"I know a place. Let me take care of it and surprise you."

"Okay." She took his hand and raised it to her lips. "So, are you feeling . . . intense again, by any chance?"

"What did you have in mind exactly?"

"Well," She smiled wickedly. "I was thinking the stairs."

He laughed and took her hand. "Front stairs or back?"

"Front and you chase me–then I catch you."

"Oh, God, you're such a lovely girl."

\* \* \* \* \*

Later, lying on the floor of the empty lounge with a blanket covering them, they watched the shadows of the sun going down through the windows. Reid smoothed his hand over his wife's bare skin, thinking about how precious she was to him. Only with her had he ever been able to be so playful, but just now he needed them to be deadly serious.

"Anne, I need to talk to you about the Lynstrade Garden project and about Walter Von Zandt—and I need you to tell me how it came about that he came to Jonas about the job."

"Why?" Then, before he could answer, she leaned over and let her mouth start the caressing that he knew would sidetrack their conversation if he let her continue. He gently pulled her head back and she looked surprised.

"I can still listen."

"But I can't talk, my love." Where did a girl like this come from? She seemed to have an endless, effortless supply of passion.

She smiled, shrugged, and lay back. "Okay, talk then."

"This has to stay confidential." He knew he shouldn't be telling her anything, but there was no other way for him to explain why she couldn't take this job. Simple dislike for the man not only wouldn't be enough to sway her and might make her think he was doing what he'd done before: telling her how to run her own career.

"Okay."

"Walter Von Zandt is the target of the investigation I'm running right now."

"Walter?"

"Yes." He hated her using the man's first name, hated that Von Zandt had intentionally wormed his way into their lives.

Her expression changed. Suddenly she was no longer his soft, pliant playmate. He saw the stubborn look in her face that had kept her in the States while he was in Scotland. He sighed. Here we go again.

He took her face in his hands. "I would like you to turn the job down."

She pulled away from him. "What are you talking about? We've accepted it already."

He opened his palms in a placating gesture. "Anne, surely there are other gardens that need work in Scotland."

She shook her head. "Not ones like this. Jonas and I know this designer's work better than anyone else. It's an important project and, if it goes well, it will help me get more jobs like this here in Scotland."

He ran his hand through his hair, trying to think of way to make her understand.

"My love, I think he maneuvered things to have you on this project because of your connection with me."

She stared at him. "You're wrong. His wife told me she was the one who chose us."

"I'm sure he told his wife to say that."

"What do you mean?"

"I mean that he knows about the investigation, and he may feel having you working for him will affect the zeal in which I pursue that investigation with regard to him."

Her jaw set. This was not going well.

"If so, he's wrong. It shouldn't affect anything you do. Besides, I don't think you're right. Why can't Jonas and I being chosen for the job be just what it seems like? That we're the best choice for it?"

Reid knew with what was going on between them, he didn't have the right to interfere with her career, but he wanted her safe.

He kissed the seashell curve of her ear. "I'm not saying you two aren't the best for the job, I'm sure you are. I'm just saying he probably thinks having you working for him would give him an edge over me."

"I can't believe that. We're renovating the gardens. Gardens— plants, dirt, things like that. I don't see how that would interfere with you investigating for whatever financial crimes you suspect him of committing."

"It's too dangerous, Anne."

"Dangerous, how? We're talking about financial crimes, aren't we?"

"He deals with dangerous people. I can't really tell you more than that. Just trust me."

"Then you should trust me. I just don't see what possible advantage he could get from having me work on his garden. It isn't like any money he pays the firm can compromise you. I don't get any money directly and we're doing real work. Besides no one would be crazy enough to think any money I make would be enough to have an effect on you." She lifted her face to him, her voice teasing. "In case no one's ever told you, you're rich, Terrence. Rich with a capital R."

He closed his eyes, praying for patience. "I just don't think it's a good idea, Anne."

"And I don't think it would be fair to Jonas to turn down the job because of your investigation. He doesn't have any involvement in that. I don't even know how I could explain it to him. How am I going to get other jobs in Scotland if I turn down jobs as good as this one that's right here near you?"

"I'm not saying you have to turn down every job. Just this one."

"I need to be able to work. My work is just as important to me as yours is to you."

"I have no problem with that. Just with this job. Can't Jonas find someone else to work on it with him?"

"If I tell him to do that, how likely do you think it is he'll ask me again? It's not like Walter is going to shoot me or something. And he'd be stupid to think that he can get to you by being nice to me." She wrapped her arms around him and pulled him down to her. "Terrence, I want this job."

Reid sighed and kissed her. They had so little time left together; he didn't want to take the risk of losing her again by pitting himself against her work. Besides, a naked woman could be very persuasive. "All right, but you'll be careful, lassie? He's not a nice man, no matter how much charm he turns on when he talks to you. Promise me you'll be careful." He knew this was a terrible mistake, but he didn't know what else to do.

"I will." Her legs coiled around his own.

"Remember what I've told you. Have as little to do with him as possible. And keep others around you when you're near him. Don't be alone with him."

"I won't. I promise I'll be careful. But it's a job, a good job. And it's close to you. I need to be close to you as long as I can. I'm so scared, Terrence." She ran a finger along his face. "Scared we'll lose each other again."

He moved against her and felt himself becoming aroused again, but as he kissed her hair, she gave a little yawn. He suppressed a smile.

Pregnant women, he remembered from his sister Pippa, need naps. Even passionate pregnant women. He smoothed her hair as he held her. "You're tired. Let's get back to the flat and you can sleep a bit."

She yawned again. "I guess I could use a short nap. Then we can watch a movie or something. Eat popcorn. Do normal married stuff."

"Sounds good." He patted her bottom. "Let's get dressed, lassie."

# Chapter 45

HARRY PICKED UP his mobile, checking the screen to see who was calling him so late on a Saturday night.

"Guv?"

"Harry, I need to talk to you and it needs to be confidential." Reid's voice was low, as if he didn't want someone nearby to overhear.

"Of course."

"It's partly personal, partly to do with our operation."

"No worries, go on." There was a pause and then the Superintendent cleared his throat. Something must be wrong, Harry thought. His boss was never tentative like this.

"My wife—through the firm she works for—has taken a job renovating the gardens at Lynstrade Manor."

There was another pause. Harry let the quiet sit between them, not knowing where this was going. The last time his boss had mentioned his wife was two years ago when he'd come back from the States and matter-of-factly announced that he'd just gotten married and that he'd be out for two weeks on his honeymoon.

Finally, Reid spoke again. "Lynstrade Manor, it turns out, is owned by Walter Von Zandt."

"I see." But Harry didn't see. Was the woman daft? "Does she know who he is?"

"I've just told her, but she's already contracted to do the job. I'm afraid one of the reasons he hired her firm was because of her connection to me."

Harry searched around in his mind for the proper response. He could tell from Reid's voice that he was worried about his wife. She must really be a handful. As far as Harry could tell, she'd virtually disappeared from the guv's life after the honeymoon, then reappeared in that mess in California, involved with another man and a murder. Now this. He decided to respond to the worry and not provide any commentary.

"You'll be arranging for some kind of protection for her, guv?"

He heard Reid's sigh of relief at his reaction. "Aye. One of Stirling's companies is a private security firm. I'll call him and get something set up."

"You can't just ask her not to go there?" Harry tried to be delicate in his inquiry.

"I tried, but the contract's been signed, and I couldn't give her enough details to impress that upon her. She did promise to keep her distance from him. She doesn't understand what an evil bastard he is." He seemed at a loss to explain his wife's attitude, but Harry could tell that Reid was desperate to keep his wife safe. "It's hard to explain, Harry. She's from California."

"Oh, that explains it, sir. California." Harry spoke in a way meant to convey that he was not passing judgment on the other man's wife. "We'll just have to watch out for her, then."

"Thank you. I can't have anything happen to her." His boss's voice was quiet. "And I need this to be kept confidential. I'd rather not share this with the rest of the team or the brass unless it becomes necessary. I'll let Darby know, but other than that, let's keep it to ourselves."

"Aye, guv. I understand." Up until now, Harry thought, Reid's career had seemed bulletproof, but letting his wife get cozy with his chief suspect wasn't likely to be well received.

When his boss hung up, Harry shook his head, trying to fathom how a man who was so strong in everything else could let a woman twist his life around the way this one was doing. By now the Super should have kenned that the woman was bad news, even if she was as kick-your-cock-up hot as she looked in the tabloids. He leaned down to kiss the woman in his own bed. He liked Inez just fine, but if she left, he'd like someone else just as well. He hoped he never found anyone who made him feel the way the Superintendent felt about his wife.

# EASTER SUNDAY, APRIL 12

# Chapter 46

DARBY CARRIED her plate along the deliciously elaborate buffet line at the MacTavishes' elegant Glasgow townhome.

"A pity Terrence wasn't able to join us." John Stirling helped himself to juicy slices of the carved leg of lamb. "I had dinner with him Wednesday and tried to talk him into coming. He said work is too busy."

"He's busy, all right, but he's not working. At least not today."

Stirling raised his eyebrows. "Oh?" He smiled that tanned blond god smile that melted women's knickers. "Then he'd be with Anne, I'd guess."

"Yes." Darby tried to tone down the sourness in her voice.

"I was hoping that was the case. He could have brought her with him. But he must have wanted to keep her all to himself."

She made a face. She wouldn't break her promise about not telling that Anne was pregnant. But that didn't mean she had to pretend to like the woman. "I still don't know what he sees in her— other than the obvious. He's an absolute fool about her."

"You're a bit of a jealous baby sister."

"I don't like the way she treats him." And Darby didn't like what this was going to look like to her bosses. Helping Interpol take over an operation they should rightly be running in the first place was one thing, but she'd enjoyed the way people looked at her with respect when they'd found out Terrence Reid was her brother. Having her brother look like a complete fool wasn't going to do anything for her stock at work.

"He's well able to take care of himself. If he's with her, I'd say he doesn't think she's as much at fault as you seem to think she is." He grinned. "Besides, there aren't many men who wouldn't want her."

"Because she's pretty? Please." Darby rolled her eyes.

He gave a half laugh. "More like film-star gorgeous."

"You should know," she said, her tone dry. Stirling's name was always being linked to some beautiful celebrity or another.

"What can I say? I love women. All kinds of women."

She cut her eyes at him. "Anne?"

"God, no. She's my best friend's wife." Stirling paused, eyeing a colorful dish of red cabbage, then passed it by. "I wouldn't touch her if she were the last woman on earth. Even when they're fighting and apart, he worships her. And now, thank the gods, she's back here, and apparently, they're together. That should make him easier to live with."

"Don't be too thankful. I don't think things are going too well between them."

He turned his head to look at her and frowned. "No? I'd hoped with her finally here, they'd be good. That's all he's wanted."

"The sooner that whole thing ends, the better, in my opinion."

"Your father likes her."

Did Stirling know that the Earl wasn't really her father? Her face burned in mortification at the thought.

"He did before, but I don't think the Earl's thrilled with her now that she's flaunted her lover all over the tabloids. She's a slag."

Stirling touched his finger to Darby's lips. "Shh. Don't say that. Your brother's not likely to want to hear sentiments like that about Anne—even when he's mad at her. My stock reply to him is 'she's an angel from heaven' or variations of that, no matter what he says. So far, I'm still alive, so I'd recommend the same approach to you." He dropped his finger from her mouth, then took a serving fork and lifted a piece of glazed ham to Darby's plate.

She pulled her plate away. "No ham. I can't just act like it's okay with me if he has a wife that's going to ruin his life."

Stirling shrugged, and put the ham on his own plate. "Don't say I didn't warn you. Fish?"

She nodded, and he placed a lovely square of cod in what looked to be a buttery-sage sauce on her plate. Then reading her expression, he gave her another piece. That was one of the things that was so lovely about John Stirling. He really paid attention.

His golden head dipped down to look at the salads, then he whispered. "Salads are fillers. I'm skipping them."

She shook her head indulgently, then put a spoonful on her plate from each one of the salads on offer.

Stirling made a face. "That's a mistake. You need to leave room for the good stuff." He grabbed a roll, gestured toward her. "Like these. Want one?" She shook her head. He put the roll on his own plate. "Don't say I didn't warn you."

"I like to live dangerously."

Stirling indicated a sofa situated at the far side of the room, away from the thick of the party crowd. "Shall we sit there? Or do you want to eat and mingle?"

"No, that's good." Once they were settled, she took a deep breath, deciding to plunge in. Maybe he knew who her real father was. "John, I didn't go home for Easter, not just because I'm working, but I don't really feel like I fit in there anymore."

"I imagine it's always that way when you've grown up, having to develop a new relationship with your parents, you know, adult to adult." He scooped up a bit of potato cheese soufflé with his spoon, smiling with flicker of sadness rarely seen on his happy face. "Not such a bad problem to have, Darby."

She'd almost forgotten. John Stirling's parents had died in an automobile crash when he was a teenager; he probably wished he had parents to not fit in with when he went home. But she needed to know what he knew about her. She slid a glance to him. "I just meant, with the Earl not really being my father, and all. It's not really my home."

Stirling studied her while he took a drink of wine. She couldn't read what he was thinking, but he didn't look surprised.

She went on, "I don't think they know that I know."

Stirling speared a piece of asparagus, folded it into his mouth.

"You know, don't you?" She wouldn't drop her eyes from his face. She needed to know if he knew, if everyone knew.

He nodded.

"How long have you known?"

"I was at school with Terrence when it happened."

"So he told you?"

"Not him, actually."

"What do you mean?"

"Long story. Why don't you ask your brother? Or better yet, your mother?"

"Tell me, John. I had to find out from the bloke doing the deep background vetting on me for my promotion. I can't believe no one ever told me." Tears stung her eyes. Not here. She wouldn't cry here, not in front of John Stirling, not in the house of Terrence's bloody friends.

Stirling's voice was gentle. "We were at a school full of boys. Boys delight in tormenting each other, and the subject of a bloke's mother is always a way to deal a deathstar blow. The older boys explained it to us in excruciating detail."

She tried to swallow, but the burning lump in her throat ached too badly. Her voice came out in a whisper. "No one told me."

"Because it doesn't matter. Your parents love you and the Earl has always been your father, Darby. He dotes on you. You have to know that."

She bit her lip, thinking that pity could look like doting. "Do you know who my real father is?"

He shook his head. "No, but I'd say your real father is the Earl— the man who raised you. I was adopted, you know. My real parents were the people who raised me. I really believe that."

"Don't you ever wonder who your birth parents are?"

"Not seriously."

"Why didn't anyone tell me? I feel so stupid. Like everything I believed about my life was a lie." The words hurt like broken glass against her throat.

"I'm the wrong person to ask. Talk to your parents, Darby."

She nodded, but it would be a frigging freezing day in hell before she went back to Dunbaryn.

"Does everyone know? Am I the only one that didn't know?"

Stirling took his time before answering. "I'm not sure. I know, but I'm one of Terrence's closest friends. We were pretty young when your parents separated, so I'm not really sure what people knew or suspected."

Darby blinked hard, let out a breath. "Don't tell Terrence I know."

"You need to tell him."

"I will. Eventually." She pasted on a social smile. "Let's talk about something else. Work. Terrence said you're helping out on the investigation. Did he tell you Von Zandt has Anne renovating his gardens?"

"Aye."

"He thinks Von Zandt deliberately set it up so that Anne is there to get leverage on Terrence. Of course, instead of being furious at her, as he should be, he's worried about her." Darby felt an odd comfort in letting her enmity against Anne momentarily replace the pulsing ache that came when she thought about her family's betrayal.

"As any sensible man would be. Too much of a coincidence."

"You think she's in danger?" Darby was skeptical.

"Von Zandt never does anything without a reason. If he has something in mind that involves Anne, in some way it would be something directed against Terrence."

Darby considered, then said, "So you don't think he could have legitimately chosen her firm for this job?"

"I'm not saying that. I'm saying, knowing who she is should have been a good reason for Von Zandt not to hire her. That he did so anyway means he has something in mind, even if it's just goading your brother."

"I have my doubts as well, but my reasoning had more to do with why anyone would hire such a worthless bit of fluff for anything."

"I've not seen anything to indicate she's not as talented as your brother seems to think she is."

"The talents she has that interest him aren't in garden design."

He shook his head. "You're a heartless lass."

She clenched her jaw. "I know Terrence. Not that he hasn't had women in his life before, but he is that pigheaded that once he decided she was the one he'd been waiting for, he just won't let go, no matter how ridiculous a choice she's turned out to be."

"I think you're underestimating her, Darby girl. I've not had much interaction with her, but when I did, I had the impression she'd do anything for him."

Darby pressed her fork against her mouth, thinking. "Maybe you're right. Maybe she would."

And maybe Darby wasn't a real Reid, maybe she didn't have a real title, maybe she didn't have a real family, but she'd show them all that she was as good as, if not better than, their precious heir.

And she'd get rid of Anne at the same time.

# Chapter 47

THEY'D TAKEN their time that morning, gone to Easter Mass at a small church just outside town that Reid liked because the Mass was in Latin, which he found peaceful. The church required head coverings for women, so he'd brought along a delicate lace mantilla he'd bought for Anne. He liked the way she looked in it. She'd been a little surprised, but he didn't think she minded.

Afterwards, they stopped at a restaurant in the countryside not far from Anne's hotel. At Reid's request, they'd been seated at a table in the back, near a fireplace that held a warm, crackling fire. He smiled, looking across the table at his wife. Anne was wearing a long soft blue sweater dress that made him want to put his arms around her and hold her on his lap.

But of course, he didn't. Instead they ordered their luncheon: cream of morel soup, rack of lamb crusted in bleu cheese and pistachios, baby asparagus and new potatoes, to be followed by a chocolate soufflé. In deference to Anne's condition, instead of the wine the meal deserved, Reid ordered sparkling water.

After the waiter left, Anne whispered, "This is like our first date. Remember? You talked the waitress into giving us that table in the back by the fireplace even though it was reserved for someone else." Her face glowed, and Reid didn't think it was just from the flickering firelight.

"I didn't want anyone or anything to distract you from me. From my courting you."

"Courting? Not just trying to get me into bed?" Her smile showed the dimples he loved.

"No, definitely courting. We were going to bed—we both knew that from the first moment we saw each other. But courting meant my intentions were serious. And I wanted you to know they were."

"I guess so, since we were married in two weeks." She smiled, leaned over and put her arms around him. "I hardly made it through dinner that night, I wanted you so much."

"And I you."

"I love you."

"And I you," he repeated. Unwrapping her arms ever so slightly, he took a package from his pocket. The silver paper covering the box was sealed with a sparkling white ribbon. "Happy anniversary."

Anne slid her arms around him again, kissing him.

He laughed. "Take your present, lassie."

She did as he asked. "Can I open it now?"

"Please do."

He watched as she unfastened the ribbon and paper and opened the box. She lifted the intricate jeweled hair combs out of the box, her eyes widening as she felt their weight. Precious jewels winked from around paths of creamy pearls, set on a base of a bronze so dark it looked almost black.

"They're beautiful. Absolutely beautiful. How do you always know the perfect thing for me?"

He touched her hair, letting it ripple through his fingers. "It's you that's beautiful. I thought they would suit you—and your lovely hair. Try them on for me."

"Thank you. I love them." She kissed him. "I'll put them in and show you, but first, I have something for you, too. May I have the car keys? I hid your present in the back."

He watched as she ran out to the car and then returned, holding a large elaborately wrapped box. He noticed other diners watching them with that same reaction most people had when they saw Anne, especially when she was all but bubbling over with happiness. He hoped no one recognized them, but they had lost so much of their privacy in the past few months that he knew the odds of this moment staying private were not great. She was just too pretty not to stand out.

Nonetheless, he wouldn't have spoiled her pleasure for anything. He unwrapped the package, revealing an ornate chess set with carved replicas of predator birds serving as the chess pieces.

"Anne, this is spectacular. Where did you find it?"

She let out a sigh of relief. "Do you really like it? I got it from an antique store in Germany. I didn't go there, of course, but I ordered it from there. You are so hard to buy for. But I thought, with you raising falcons and owls, that this was perfect. It can go in your study in the new house."

He leaned over and kissed her. Privacy be damned. "I love it. My father will be so jealous. Will you play with me sometime?"

She shook her head. "You're too good. But your father said when I was here the next time that he'd teach me. If I get the chance, if I'm here," She paused. This, then, was the code they were using for if everything turned out and he was her child's father. "If I'm here, I think I'll take him up on that and then practice until I'm good enough to at least hold my own before I play chess with you."

"I can teach you, lassie."

She pressed her lips together, narrowing her eyes. "You'd have to promise to be nice."

He laughed, delighted with her. "Nice chess? Perhaps it's not your game, my love. Chess is a simulation of war."

She frowned. "It is?"

"Yes, but I'll promise to play nice if you'll play with me."

Her face was skeptical. "We'll see."

He smiled at her. "Please? I don't want my father to have all your attention."

She laughed. "No one but you will ever have all my attention."

"Promise?"

She pointed to her wedding ring. "I promised, and I promise. I'm yours and you're mine. Now let me go to the ladies' room and fix the combs in my hair so you can see."

"Aye, that would be grand." He watched her as she moved away and wished the day would never end. Then he picked up her mobile phone and quickly installed the tracking device he'd gotten from Stirling. Triangulating her mobile's signal would probably work if her phone was powered on, but the tracking device would allow him to fix on her location even if the phone was turned off or disabled, or the battery was removed.

Later, he left her at her hotel and drove back to the city, first making sure that the man from Stirling's security firm was discreetly in place to watch over her without her knowing she was being watched over. He didn't want to worry her any more than necessary, but he needed to know she was safe.

They agreed that on Friday he would come for her and bring her back to quietly spend next weekend with him. He would set it up so that she could meet with the designer on Saturday and give the next set of authorizations for the house furnishings. Perhaps they would start to make plans for the gardens. With it being spring, this was the time for it, and he was certain she would know exactly what she wanted done. He hoped there would be a lot of brilliant color and soft shades of green that would encircle their quiet haven and keep the world away.

He'd ordered a backyard grill, and thought that he'd try it out for her on the weekend. Steaks or chicken, or fish, for that matter, if that was what she fancied. He made a note to order patio furniture to be delivered before then. It wouldn't do to have her forever eating picnic-style until the house was furnished. And he'd prod the designer to get the selections for Anne to choose from for the kitchen table and chairs. Meanwhile, he'd get some of those patio gas heaters to keep her warm when they sat outside.

Whatever happened later, for now they were together.

# Chapter 48

DETECTIVE INSPECTOR MARK LAWRENCE looked over his shoulder as he passed through the entryway of his apartment building. He ran up the stairs, wrinkling his nose in distaste at the obnoxiously industrial smell of the cleaning product the landlady used on the floors. He'd been half afraid Reid would have someone following him, although he didn't really think the arsehole suspected him. He'd been hampered all week, however pleasantly, by having Darby teaming with him. He'd had a few moments of concern that she'd want them to work all day today, and he wouldn't be able to get away to do what he needed to do. But in the end, her la-di-da connections showed and she had announced she had plans for Easter and couldn't meet with him until nighttime.

Fucking Easter. He'd shaken off Shelley's invitation to go to her family's house by telling her he had to work all day and night. Bad luck that the woman he had to cozy up to in order to keep his pipeline to inside information at the upper echelons of CID, had to be not only uglier than mortal sin, but the worst tempered woman he'd ever met.

His ex-wife and children were spending the holiday at his parents' home. He'd been invited, but he'd be damned if he would show up and let Lottie tear after him in front of his own family. Her explanation of wanting to make sure the children spent time with both of them for Easter was a load of bitch swill. She certainly wouldn't have agreed to spend the day with him and the children alone. She wanted that buffer of his family so there would be no chance of him making any kind of move on her, or maybe she thought he'd hit her. As if that had happened more than the once. Well, bugger her. He didn't need the bitch making him look bad in front of his own family.

So instead, he'd spent the day at his friend Billy's house. Billy's wife was all right—she'd cooked a killer dinner, then left the men to talk and drink while she and the other women took care of the kids. That, topped off with sex, which he planned to get later tonight, was his idea of a perfect holiday.

He turned the key to his flat and went inside. He took a mental inventory of his liquor cabinet, satisfying himself that he could meet any reasonable request. Having drinks together would be a nice touch and perhaps make the bitter blackmail pill go down easier.

It rankled him that Darby hadn't invited him to go with her. Family friends, she'd said. Too good for the likes of him, she must have thought. Well, he had made his own plans, hadn't he? And later tonight, he'd be tumbling the snooty Lady Darby into bed. Why else would she want to meet with him so late on a holiday? Title or not, all women were about the same when they were naked and ready for a man to mount them. And Darby Reid looked like she knew both how to be ridden and to ride.

Right now, though, he had other business to take care of. Delicate business. Delicate, and lucrative. Not as lucrative as his association with Walter Von Zandt, but a little bit of icing on the cake, certainly. Icing that would allow him to wine and dine a woman like Lady Darby Reid in the manner in which she was accustomed, without having to touch what he'd already salted away. She was probably tired of the pasty-faced men she usually had panting after her. She'd be thankful to have a real man show her how a woman should be taken care of.

He'd use what he got from today's meet to pay for the damage to Billy's car and to take the high and mighty Lady Darby for a first class weekend break. Maybe they'd go to Ayr for the Coral Scottish Grand National next weekend. Champers and strawberries, if that was what she liked.

And if there was enough left over, he'd make sure young Parson's family was compensated for what happened to their son. It didn't need to be a lot. It wasn't as if the boy had a wife and kids. Besides, it had been Parson's own fault; the lad just wouldn't do as he was told. The idiot had had visions of Reid picking him to be on his team and just wouldn't pull his surveillance on Ramsey. Paid or not, he'd insisted on staying on the job until the morning shift took over. So

Lawrence had no choice but to borrow Billy's car and go out to where Parsons was watching Ramsey's house. He'd planned to tell the young cop that he'd take over the watch himself, and send him on his way home to mum.

Then Parsons had stepped into the road just as he drove up, and Lawrence had acted instinctively. After he'd dragged the body into the brush, he'd waited for Ramsey's Mercedes to leave, and followed it without his lights on. He'd pulled in behind a stand of trees near the railroad tracks and waited. Then he'd sat in breathless silence while the drama played out. He'd suspected Von Zandt had ordered the hit, but the man had denied it so vehemently that Lawrence believed him. Which meant the whole situation was a perfect set-up for blackmail.

Lawrence looked around to make sure he had the stage set for the meeting. He kept his flat tidy and he'd set it up as he imagined a bachelor's flat should look. Black leather, and plenty of stainless steel topped off with an enormous big screen telly. He'd not be ashamed to entertain Darby here. He took a deep breath, imagining her prancing around his flat naked, then her handcuffed to the bed, begging for him.

God, it was going to be a fucking fantastic Easter. He just needed to get this meeting over with first. Then he'd take Lady Darby on an Easter egg hunt she'd not soon forget.

The knock on the front door woke him from his imaginings. He assumed a nonchalant air and went to let his guest in. Playing the gracious host, he poured generous portions of whiskey. Whiskey was a good drink for business negotiations, providing both courage and relaxation. Not surprisingly, as they pinned down the terms of their mutual cooperation, his guest seemed to relax.

The second knock at the door took Lawrence by surprise. He hadn't been expecting another visitor. But when Lawrence looked through the Judas hole, he relaxed. This was no one either one of them needed to worry about. As he let the newest visitor in, he felt someone behind him, and too late, sensed danger. He saw the flash of something go over his head and then—quickly—the tightening of something hard and thin around his neck. Wire? He tried to fight, but first he needed to breathe. Gasping, he tried to raise his hands to tear away the awful thing choking him, cutting into his neck, but his hands were jerked away. He barely registered the clicking of handcuffs before he lost consciousness.

# Chapter 49

**D**ARBY WAS ANNOYED. No—more like royally pissed. She had expected Lawrence to be waiting for her call. She'd told him she would be busy for part of the day, but they'd agreed to meet later that night, Easter or not.

He was such a pain, thinking he was charming her when she could barely tolerate him. But Terrence had assigned her the job of keeping an eye on the arsehole, and she wasn't going to shirk her duties, no matter how she felt about her brother. And she was entitled to some time off, time to meet with friends and enjoy a part of the holiday. When she'd found out that John Stirling was going to be at the MacTavishes' party, her mind had been made up. Of course, she hadn't planned on confiding in Stirling; that had all just spilled out. Mortifying. She'd meant to seduce him, but now that would have to wait for another time.

She rang Lawrence again, first on his mobile, then on the telephone at his flat. Where the hell could he be? Darby suspected he was pouting that she hadn't invited him to go with her. He'd hinted, but she'd acted like she didn't understand. She certainly wasn't going to bring a dolt like Mark Lawrence to the MacTavish party. He was an idiot, but he was her assignment, and if he was up to something, she was going to find out what it was. She got out of the taxi in front of DI Lawrence's building. After asking the driver to wait, she opened the outer door and went upstairs to his flat. She knocked but got no answer, and knocked again. No answer.

Darby called out. "Lawrence, you prick, open the door."

Still no answer.

She reached out and tried the door. It wasn't locked. Some policeman. Leaves the bloody door unlocked. Well, then, she'd just go in; he would hardly complain. He'd been trying to get her in his flat since she came here. She'd have a drink and wait for him.

As soon as she opened the door, she knew something was terribly wrong. It was the smell. She instinctively knew what it was, although this was the first time she'd ever experienced it—the awful smell of death released when the body relaxed for the last time. She automatically looked for the body that had to be there.

She did not have far to look. DI Mark Lawrence lay sprawled out face down on the carpet near the front door. His hands were handcuffed behind him and he was unmistakably dead. A wire tight around his neck told all she needed to know right then. A sob escaped her. She wanted to vomit but forced herself to remain calm. She reached for her mobile and called Terrence.

# Chapter 50

FOR IT BEING EASTER NIGHT, the fish shop next to Reid's High Street offices was surprisingly busy. There were no tablecloths here, just battered linoleum topped tables with a condiment holder as the only table decoration, but no one seemed to mind. The smell of fried food and ale was heartening, and there was an easy neighborhood kind of atmosphere: loud and cheerful.

"We missed you at MacTavish's earlier." Stirling surveyed his fish supper platter: golden slabs of cod, bright green peas, and chips. "You were with Anne?"

"Mmm." Reid paused between bites. He had to set his features to avoid smiling. "It's our anniversary."

"Good reason, then."

"Two years."

"Much better than an Easter buffet." Stirling took a drink of his ale. "I'm surprised you're not still with her."

"Her big project gets fully underway tomorrow morning. She needs to get some rest. I collected her Friday night, so we had the weekend."

"You actually took the weekend off. She's good for you." Stirling sprinkled vinegar on his chips.

"She is, indeed." This time Reid couldn't conceal his smile. He took the bottle of vinegar Stirling passed him, then doused his own chips.

"Not a coincidence that Von Zandt hired her firm, is it, though?" Stirling showered salt liberally on his food, then passed the shaker to Reid.

"I don't think so, although if it hadn't been Von Zandt doing the hiring, it would have made sense. This garden is apparently some

particular type that Anne's boss has a great deal of experience with—
and Anne worked with him on a similar project for friends of Elisa
Von Zandt. But knowing Anne is my wife should have counted
against him hiring them."

"That was my thought as well. Does she know that he's the target
of your investigation?"

"Aye, I've told her. No details, though, just that his financial
dealings are under investigation."

Stirling picked up a chip and popped it in his mouth. "So what's
to be done now?"

"You're keeping one of your men nearby. That makes me feel
better."

"Aye. But he can't get too close unless you let her know,
Terrence."

"I will soon. I'm just not sure how she'll take it. Meanwhile, I feel
better having someone right there in case we need him. And I've
asked her to be careful, not to trust Von Zandt, and not to let herself
get into a situation where she's alone with him." Reid shook his head.
"Truth be told, I asked her not to do the job, but she's an
unbelievably stubborn lass."

Stirling started to laugh so hard he choked and his eyes teared up.
Sputtering, he pounded on his chest, still not able to talk.

Reid glared at him and motioned to the proprietor to bring
another round, then continued to eat, pretending to ignore his
friend's ongoing paroxysms of laughter.

Stirling finally recovering, said, "I'm sorry, Terrence, but the
thought of anyone being more stubborn than you just about undid
me." The gleam of amusement twinkling in Stirling's eyes told Reid
his friend wasn't truly repentant.

"I didn't say she was more stubborn than me. Just that she was
stubborn. She has this plan for her career and she just won't budge."

"As do you, although you'd probably not admit it." He pointed to
the mushy greens on his platter. "You're peas in a pod, you two."

Reid grunted. "You might be right. Not to change the subject,
although that's exactly what I intend to do, weren't we meeting
because you found something new?"

"Right." Stirling pulled a small notebook out of his pocket. "I've
some more information for you I gleaned from the coded
communications your people intercepted in the last twenty-four

hours—a list of offshore institutions that seem to be popular with these blokes." He handed Reid the list.

Reid studied the names Stirling had written down. "I'll get this information to my team and to MacTavish. Either he or Schilling may have contacts that can get us to the next level. If we can tie any of these to Von Zandt or the Nigerian faction, we'll be a lot closer to locating the accounts, even without the actual account numbers."

"Account numbers are beyond my powers, I'm afraid. No one transmits those, even in code."

"You've done more than enough. Thanks, John." Reid felt his mobile vibrate, and tried to suppress the goofy grin that was determined to spread itself across his face. "Just a moment. This will be Anne, I expect."

Stirling rolled his eyes in good natured mockery but Reid just shrugged, happy to have a wife back in his life to interrupt him with her calls. He moved outside the shop to answer so that he would be better able to hear her. When he heard Darby's voice instead of Anne's, he frowned.

# Chapter 51

**R**EID BOLTED UP THE STAIRS to Lawrence's flat two at a time. Darby was in the hall waiting for him outside of the flat's slightly ajar door. Another woman might have wanted comfort, but he knew his sister would think any such offer implied that he thought she was weak, so he simply met her eyes and nodded. "Rough?"

"I'm all right."

"The SOCO van just pulled up behind me. They'll process the scene. Tell me what you know, then you can leave."

"I'm fine." She swallowed, then spoke with considerable self-control. "We were to meet for a pub supper tonight, but he didn't call, and I couldn't reach him. I was aggravated as I didn't really want to have to babysit him, but as we were going to meet near here, I thought I might as well drop by his flat and see what was going on. The door was unlocked, and well—I found him. Garroted, it appears to me. No one else was here. I rang you and waited. End of story."

"Hard scene to walk in on."

"I'm fine."

"Of course you are." He nodded toward Lawrence's flat. "Did you touch anything?"

"The door handle when I let myself in. Nothing else."

"Did you check the rest of the flat to see if anyone else was there?"

"I don't think whoever killed him went to take a kip in the bedroom. So, no, I didn't. I didn't want to contaminate the scene."

Reid had been thinking more of the possibility of another victim or of the killer exiting out of a window or another door. But Darby was Interpol, not regular police, nor had she ever had that kind of experience. At least she hadn't interfered with the crime scene. And she'd called him.

"Good thinking."

Darby said, "Ta so much." Her voice was arrogant, but he knew she was upset, so he ignored it.

He got the times of her call and her arrival and the rest of the few details she knew.

"That's good for now, Darby. You don't have to stay."

She nodded, but made no move to leave.

He tried to determine how much she wanted or needed from him. "Anne's not at the flat. She'll be gone until the weekend. Do you want to stay there for a few nights?"

No one else would have seen it, that faint quiver of her lip as she hesitated.

He pressed her. "Come to the flat. Keep me company, why don't you?"

"Maybe. Just for tonight." Her tone had been grudging, but he could tell she was relieved not to have to be alone.

"Good. I'll see you back there. Go on with you, now." When she hesitated, he put his hand on her arm and pulled her into a quick hug. He heard her gulp back what he knew must be tears, then she pushed away from him.

When he saw her disappear down the stairs, he nudged the door open with an elbow and surveyed the grisly scene. He'd never liked DI Lawrence, but he'd never wished him dead, either. Especially not like this.

He turned, hearing the SOCO team coming up the stairs. Tilting his head to indicate the open door, he said, "In there, laddies." Recognizing two smaller figures in the pack, he amended, "and lassies."

Reid's thoughts went to DC Parsons and a chill skittered up his spine. What were the odds that Ramsey, Parsons, and Lawrence had been killed by different people? Reid answered his own question. Not good. Had Lawrence been the leak? If so, it was permanently plugged now. If he hadn't, what did that mean? Two cops working the same investigation had been killed. No, not just killed. Murdered. He'd warned his own team to be careful after DC Parsons had been killed, but Lawrence had been warned as well, and that hadn't seemed to do any good.

If Von Zandt was behind these murders, it showed how

completely ruthless the man was. To kill a cop was asking for trouble. To kill two cops was asking for war.

Reid doubted the man would blink an eye over killing a cop's wife.

# MONDAY, APRIL 13

# Chapter 52

REID SENT two uniforms to pick up Shelley Crichton and bring her to the interview room at Glasgow City Center station where Harry and he were waiting. She'd been at home, having understandably called off work that day. Everyone she worked with knew she'd been seeing DI Lawrence—apparently she'd made sure of that—and the news of his murder was all over town already, at least in the law enforcement community.

Harry had finished going through Lawrence's finances, and as Reid had suspected, the man had a great deal of unaccounted-for income. Reid didn't think it was coincidental that Lawrence's finances had soared astronomically since he'd been appointed to the task force. There'd been extra money coming in regularly before that, but not to the same degree. Reid would turn the information over to the unit responsible for internal inquiries, to do with whatever they wanted. Investigating a dirty cop who'd been murdered was a tricky business, and Reid was glad it wasn't his job. All he needed to know was how it impacted his investigation. He'd had Harry take a peek at DC Parson's finances, as well, but the most scandalous thing he'd found was a subscription to an online leadership course.

A woman police constable brought the tearful Shelley in when she finally arrived. Her acne-scarred face was studded by red-rimmed little eyes. When she realized who would be interviewing her, Reid saw her face turn from sodden grief to wariness. The wariness of someone who has something to hide. So she knew. This had been no inadvertent spilling of information from her desk to her boyfriend. She knew he'd been selling the information, and that it had to do with Reid's investigation.

Reid met Harry's eyes, gave a slight nod. Harry, getting the message that he was to take lead, motioned for the woman to sit down opposite him, while Reid remained standing against the wall.

"Couldn't you have come to my house? I'm in mourning, you know. Mark and I were practically engaged." Anger masking fear, Reid thought.

Harry shook his head. "We thought official would be better, considering the circumstances, luv."

"The circumstances? I know it's usual to talk to the family, but not like this unless . . ." She narrowed her eyes, and her tongue darted in and out of her mouth. "I'm not a suspect, am I?"

"If you know it's usual, then you'll know those closest to the victim are always suspects. But you've an alibi, I understand."

"Yes, I do." Her voice was indignant. "I was with my family all day. You can ask them. And Mark would have been with me, only he," here she pointed to Reid, "made him work. On Easter."

"We've checked on where you were, and we know about you being with your family all day."

"Then why am I here?"

"We thought, luv, that we could talk to you about a few other things. I'm going to turn on the recorder and caution you. Routine, you know."

Harry made the preliminary statements for the recording. Shelley's eyes kept flitting over to Reid, who stayed silent but kept his gaze on her.

"Shelley, as Chief Superintendent Steynton's admin, you see the things that go across his desk, don't you?"

"I guess."

"Including the ones marked confidential?"

She examined ragged fingernails, bit one, pulling a piece of it off with her teeth. "He likes me to open everything for him."

"And you've seen the confidential memos come through from the investigation into the financing of the university bombing plot, and the work Superintendent Reid's team has been doing."

"I guess." Shelley folded her arms across her wide chest. "What's this got to do with my Mark being murdered?" She squeezed her fat face together, and a few tears travelled down her cheek.

"You knew DI Lawrence was interested in those memos."

"I never told him anything."

"You knew he was interested."

"Of course, he would be. He should have been leading that task force. He would have been if it weren't for . . . politics." She glanced uneasily at Reid.

"You wanted to help him, didn't you?" Harry's voice was understanding.

"I never did anything wrong."

"But you talked with him about what you saw and heard?"

"We talked about work a little, of course we did. We were going to be married."

"He asked you to share what you knew with him." Harry kept his voice nonjudgmental.

"No."

"Come on, Shelley. That's natural between people as close as you two were."

"Well, maybe a little. There's no harm in that, is there? He's on the task force, too. Just because some were jealous of him, and tried to keep him in the dark, that doesn't make it right, does it?" She glared at Reid. "He should have been told in the first place."

"So you made sure he knew what was going on. From what you saw come across Chief Superintendent Steynton's desk."

She eyed Harry suspiciously, then looked over at Reid. "Sometimes, maybe. Just like you said, it was natural for us to talk about work."

"But you did more than that, didn't you? You copied memos and gave them to him."

"Why are you asking me this? What difference does it make? He's dead. You should be out there finding out who killed him, instead of slagging me off in my hour of grief." She sniffled.

"Shelley, luv, we think whoever DI Lawrence was giving the information to—the information he got from you—killed him."

Her mouth dropped open, revealing crooked rows of stained teeth. "Oh, God, no."

"And we think you might be in danger as well." Harry threw a sidelong glance at Reid, who nodded. "We're thinking we'll need to set up protection for you, but we need you to tell us what you know. What happened, what you told or gave Mark, so we can make sure we get the right people."

Her eyes opened wide. "They killed him?"

'Yes, luv. It was a horrible death. Did you hear how he died?

We've kept that detail quiet, but it was ugly." Harry clucked his tongue. "Garroted, he was." He motioned with his hands. "A thin wire around the neck, twisted tight till his eyes almost popped out. Cut deep into his throat as well."

She swallowed visibly, then glowered at Reid, resentment seething from her pores. "It's your fault. You and your money and your title. That should have been his job. You got him killed."

Reid stayed silent.

Harry took her hand. "Shelley, luv, we've gone through his bank accounts. Someone was paying him for the information you were giving him. You knew that, didn't you?"

She started to shake her head, then began to cry. "It was the money for us to get married, he said. He wanted to have enough so we could have a house and all. Babies."

"Who was it paying him?"

She spoke through her sobs. "I don't know. He didn't tell me that. He said there was no harm done, just sharing information with some that was happy to pay for it."

"Think, Shelley. We need to know who was paying him."

"I don't know."

"When did it begin? It looks like the money started coming in about eight months ago."

"Eight months ago? But that's when we started going out." She suddenly looked stricken. "Oh, God. You think that's why he went out with me, don't you? That I'm too ugly for him to have loved me. But he did. He was going to marry me."

"The men you two were getting the information for are involved in killing all those young people at the University in Heidelberg. You must know from what you've seen that we believe they're planning more attacks like that. You need to tell us whatever else you can remember so we can stop that from happening."

"Mark never would have helped those kinds of people. He couldn't have known that."

Harry leaned over and got right in the woman's face. "Shelley, we need to know everything he told you."

"He didn't tell me any more than that, and I didn't ask."

"You're sure you know nothing else?"

"I'm sure."

"Let's talk about the information you gave him, the memos, the conversations, everything, and I'll just write it down."

She pushed back in her chair. "I need a cuppa."

Harry looked at Reid. "Guv?"

Reid opened the door and sent one of the uniforms waiting outside in search of tea.

Harry continued, "Let's start, why don't we, luv, while we wait for the tea."

Shelley sniffed in exasperation, but nodded.

"Go ahead, then, tell us."

Shelley, nervously playing with her fingers, began to list what she remembered. "I kept a little file on it. In my desk drawer underneath my personal things."

The uniform brought in tea for all of them in paper cups, handed them around with whitener and sugar sachets, and left.

Reid opened the duffel bag they'd brought and pulled out a manila file, handing it to Harry, who then put it in front of Shelley.

"This it?"

Playing for time, Shelley poured tea and sugar into her cup, followed the sugar with two packets of whitener, all the while stealing glances at the file, apparently trying to decide what her reaction should be. She took a gulp of tea, then spoke, her tone offended. "You've been through my desk?" So she was going to play the innocent victim.

"Aye." Harry took a drink of his tea.

"That's an invasion of my privacy." Her voice was tentatively belligerent, as if she wasn't really committed to her argument.

Harry shrugged. "What can I say? No privacy in murder investigations."

Shelley's face set into a sullen pout. "I didn't do anything wrong."

"No? Well, we've been through the file as well. It looks like it's full of copies of confidential memos, and of notes you took on confidential phone calls. All things that were supposed to be destroyed after the CS read them."

"The originals were destroyed. Chief Superintendent Steynton shredded the originals after he read them."

"So these were extra copies you made?"

She gave a reluctant nod.

"For Mark?"

"I made two copies, one for Mark and one for my file."

"Why did you keep a copy in your file?"

She shrugged. "I don't know. Just in case, I guess."

"Right. So let's go through them, and you tell me how you got each one of these, and when you would have given them to Mark. Write it down."

"I'm not in trouble, am I?"

"Right now we just need your help. Do you want me to read the caution again? We can get you a solicitor if you think you need one."

She threw up her hands. "Hello? I'm a victim here, myself."

"Then you don't mind talking to us."

She bit the pen Harry handed her, then leaned over the paper in front of her and assiduously began to write.

After she finished her statement, Harry reviewed it, then shoved it back to her so she could sign it.

"Shelley, did Mark tell you how much he'd been paid?"

"No, just that it wasn't enough to get married yet."

Harry showed her a list of figures. "This is what we've calculated so far."

She shook her head. "It couldn't be that much. We'd have been able to get married long ago."

"S'truth. We verified the amount with the bank."

She sat back, obviously stunned. "You don't think he was going to marry me, do you?"

"What do you think?"

Her face crumpled with self-pity and grief. "What am I going to do now?"

"Time, I'd expect, luv. You're under arrest."

Reid opened the door and let the uniformed officers take her away.

# Chapter 53

REID DIRECTED Allison to grab a uniform from CID to accompany her to interview DI Lawrence's ex, and to sit in on the interview with her. He had no expectation that anything would come out of talking to Lottie Lawrence, but routine had to be followed.

The neighborhood canvas had turned up nothing. People had been out visiting for Easter, or been busy inside with their own families. Similarly, the SOCO report had elicited little. DI Lawrence lived a bit beyond his means for a man who had child support obligations, and who'd been through a financially punishing divorce. His flat was almost militarily neat, and other than a glass that had been washed before being put in the dishwasher, the only untidy thing was a matching glass of neat whiskey carrying only Lawrence's prints.

Besides the financial information on Lawrence's bank accounts, little personal paperwork had been found, an exception being a small address book which now lay on Reid's High Street office desk.

The entries were almost always just initials or one word—first or last name and then a number. He recognized a few entries: DI Lawrence's ex-wife, some cops' names, and the numbers for all of the stations in the Strathclyde police district, the district in which the Glasgow area was situated. Reid frowned. Frank Butterworth's ex's name was there, or at least that's who Reid guessed it was. Jill B. was all it said. He'd give Frank first dibs at talking to her, otherwise either he or Harry could do it.

Reid didn't know how Frank had gone through the break-up of his marriage with no more emotion than he'd have shown about changing banks, but in the last two years, he'd often envied his friend's detachment.

His eyes went back to another name that had caught his attention. Glynnis. No last name, just Glynnis and a telephone number.

Reid dialed the number. No answer. He let it ring until an answering machine clicked on.

You've reached Glynnis. Leave a message and I'll get back to you as soon as I can.

The voice was Glynnis Taylor's. Reid frowned. How had Lawrence known Glynnis Taylor? Probably through Von Zandt or Ramsey. There was nothing that looked like Richard Ramsey's number under the R's. But, under the tab for V, he found an entry with the initials HVZ. Henry's office number. So Lawrence had known both Glynnis and Henry. But oddly, whereas with Henry, it had been the office number, the number for Glynnis was apparently her home or mobile. It certainly wasn't her number at VZ Capital.

Not surprisingly, DI Lawrence's mobile was missing. They'd searched the man's flat so hard they'd have found a mouse's toenail, but there had been no sign of it.

"Harry, get the accounts for Lawrence's phones. His mobile and land line. And check to see if he had a personal mobile separate and apart from the department-issued one." Call records to any of the Von Zandts would show much than just a name in an address book. For one thing, the timing of any calls would tell them when the last time Lawrence had talked to them.

His sergeant gave him a pained look. Of course. Harry had already thought to do that.

Reid gave him a wry look. "All right, just let me know when they come in." Meanwhile, it was time to pay a visit to Henry Von Zandt's wife. Shake him up a bit.

# Chapter 54

REID WENT ALONE to interview Karin Von Zandt. He didn't expect to get much out of her, but one never knew. Perhaps she'd let something slip that she didn't even know was important.

Henry and Karin Von Zandt lived in a large home in one of Glasgow's more affluent suburbs. The house was new, as was the neighborhood. Reid opened the front garden gate and mounted the steps that led to the front door. Pressing the bell, he looked around. No sign of neighbors, no sign of children playing, in fact no sign of life at all from these houses that advertised that their owners had more money than taste.

A young woman wearing a pink track suit opened the door. The nanny, most likely, as she had two children hanging on her legs. When Reid showed his warrant card and asked for Karin Von Zandt, she let him into the foyer.

Speaking in a thick Czech accent, she said, "I'll get her." The nanny scooped up the smaller of the two children and took the other's hand, leaving Reid alone. The foyer, as well as the formal living and dining rooms to his left, looked as if they'd all been furnished in one fell swoop by an expensive furnishings shop. He guessed that even the artwork had come from the furnishings store— in fact, it had probably been part of the same store display as the furniture. The rooms contained no personal touches at all, as if the home's occupants were afraid to add anything that hadn't been in the store display for fear of putting a foot wrong.

He heard the click of heels on marble tiles and turned toward the sound. He'd seen Karin Von Zandt at the funeral, but here she looked in her element. Efficient wife and mother. Her short dark hair was perfectly styled. Above red high heels, she wore black stretch pants topped by a long red shirt.

She put out her hand. "Superintendent, what can I do for you?" Her voice was heavily accented. Northern Germany.

"I'm looking into the murder of Richard Ramsey, and of another man as well, a Detective Inspector Mark Lawrence."

She frowned. "And you want to talk to me? Why?"

"I assume you knew Mr. Ramsey."

"Ja, I met him a few times."

"Your husband gave you as his alibi for the night Mr. Ramsey died. After the birthday dinner for your mother-in-law. He told me I could ask you about it directly, so here I am." Reid smiled, but the woman regarded him with ill-disguised suspicion.

"Why would Henry need an alibi?"

"Just routine. Especially for people who benefit from the victim's death."

"Henry benefited?" Karin Von Zandt looked puzzled.

"VZ Capital benefited, Henry indirectly."

"Ach, I see." She thought for a moment, then said, "We went to Elisa's birthday dinner, then came home and went to bed. My husband stayed here with me all night."

That was a curious choice of words. Stayed here rather than was here. He wondered if, like his father, the son kept a flat in town, perhaps Glynnis's flat. Reid decided to take a chance. "He has a place in town, doesn't he?"

"No."

Reid pretended to think, took a little notebook out of his pocket, looked at something written there. "I thought . . ."

Karin Von Zandt puffed out her lips and Reid could tell he'd hit on a sore point. "That's not Henry's place. It's a guest flat for the company. He only stays there if he works too late for him to come home."

Reid nodded. "That's the place on . . ." He looked back at his notebook.

"That tall building next to the office," she filled in. "But, he was here."

"Right. The other man we're concerned about was killed on Sunday. Where was your husband Sunday?"

"Sunday?" She puckered her face in thought. "Sunday was Easter.

We took the children and went to Lynstrade Manor. We were there all day. All of us. The children, the nanny, Walter and Elisa, Frederick."

"All day?"

"Yes. From the morning, when we did an egg hunt until about eight at night. The children love it there." Recognition seemed to suddenly dawn on her. "Now I know who you are. I thought I recognized you. It is your wife that is working for Walter and Elisa on the gardens there, isn't it?"

He gave what he hoped was a proud husband smile, instead of the worried husband frown he actually felt. "Indeed it is."

She rested a finger on her cheek, and studied him. "So you're Lord Reid, not just Superintendent, right?"

He gave a slight nod.

"Walter and Elisa are very impressed with your wife. They say she's extremely talented."

"Aye, she's that."

Karin Von Zandt's face broke out into a smile. "You must come in to the den. Elisa's here. Come say hello to her, now that we have our alibis out of the way." Suddenly she seemed much younger and happier, on a more comfortable footing. "Why do you ask about Henry and this other man, this policeman? Are they supposed to know each other?"

"His name was Mark Lawrence. I found your husband's number in his address book."

"That's all?"

"And Henry's secretary's home number as well."

The smile turned to a scowl. "Glynnis?"

"Aye."

"Ach, that one's trouble." She pursed her lips. "You should talk to her."

"I imagine we'll have to, and everyone else in his address book, as well."

Karin glared. "What was the number he had for her? The telephone number?"

"I'd probably better not share that." Reid thought it would probably be unwise to give Glynnis's home phone number to her married lover's wife.

Karin snorted. "I know her number. She has a mobile, though, not a landline. Henry has to call her sometimes outside of work hours." She rattled off a number. "Is that the number you have?"

It wasn't, but he nodded. "Would you be able to give me the number of the company flat?"

"Of course. I'll write it down for you." She took a notepad from a drawer in the table in the entry way and wrote out a number. Reid examined it, thanked her and put the note in his pocket. The company flat number and the number DI Lawrence had in his book for Glynnis were identical.

"Now that we've gotten that out of the way, Lord Reid, come and say hello to Elisa." Karin led the way into a large room, with formal furnishings. Elisa Von Zandt sat on one of the sofas, a small black dog beside her.

"Elisa, look who's come to check Henry's alibi for Richard Ramsey's murder. Lady Anne's husband."

Reid went over and shook her hand. "Nice to see you again, Mrs. Von Zandt."

"And you as well, Lord Reid. Please be seated."

Karin excused herself to see to having tea sent in.

Reid gave Elisa a rueful smile and sat down. "I imagine that was what you were hinting to me at the funeral, that my wife was going to be working on your gardens?"

Elisa smiled faintly. "You didn't know. I didn't think so."

"Not at first."

"I'm surprised you let her work there."

"I'm surprised your husband allowed you to engage her."

"Jonas did a wonderful job on a similar garden for some friends of ours in England, and your wife worked with him on that. Jonas is wild about her."

"They work well together. Your friends' garden was another Russell Page garden, my wife tells me. Did you get Jonas and Anne's names from them?"

"Yes, but our estate manager researched it on his own as well. There are a few other designers with experience in Russell Page gardens, but Jonas and your wife are supposed to be the best."

"I believe they are. I hope you'll be pleased with the results."

"I'm certain we will be."

Reid was relieved to receive confirmation that Elisa Von Zandt had indeed been the catalyst, at least initially, in engaging the services of Anne and Jonas. Still, Von Zandt should have vetoed hiring them when he found out who Anne was.

He looked toward the door and then back to Mrs. Von Zandt. "Before Karin gets back, can you tell me what you know about Glynnis Taylor?"

"Henry's secretary?"

"Yes."

"As you didn't want to ask in front of Karin, I assume you know she's Henry's mistress?"

"Yes. Does Karin know?"

Elisa shrugged, puffed out her cheeks. "Probably, but she pretends not to. We wives always know even when we try not to. Karin thinks it's awful that I tolerate Moira. But I know Walter is not in love with Moira. Unfortunately, Henry is, I think, in love with Glynnis."

"But he stays with Karin?"

"Walter doesn't want Henry to divorce, so Henry stays. Glynnis has the company flat downtown. A peace of sorts."

Karin re-emerged, trailed by a maid carrying a tray of tea things, and the conversation between Reid and Elisa ended. Reid stayed only long enough to drink his tea, then headed out to his car.

Just as he opened his car door, a sleek black convertible pulled into the driveway behind him and an angry man got out. Henry Von Zandt's ears must have been burning or else someone in the house had told him Reid was there.

# Chapter 55

THE BUILDING where Jill Butterworth lived with DI Tony Grant was three stories high, with two flats on each floor. Harry hadn't known Frank when he was married to Jill, but he'd heard more than enough about her from scuttlebutt, although not from Frank. The gossip was that as soon as she found out that Frank's injuries were permanent, she'd started looking around for someone else. At least there were no children—but maybe that would have been better. Frank would have been left with something.

According to Frank, Jill had moved in with DI Grant a little over a year ago. She was a librarian, of all things. Harry had had a better impression of librarians until he heard that. As she worked the afternoon-to-evening shift today, she'd reluctantly agreed to have him come to the flat.

Jill Butterworth was pretty in that brittle way some women get when they get older, are too skinny, and smoke too much. Her hair was dark and short, but teased up on the top to give it a little height. The flat reeked of tobacco smoke, and Harry had to adjust his face not to show his distaste.

"Hello, Ms.—is it still Butterworth?"

She nodded. "Call me Jill. Come in."

The main living area was large enough, furnished with inexpensive furniture—Swedish style, Harry was fairly sure. He'd learned more than he wanted to know about furniture from a girl he'd dated who worked in a furnishings store. He had a ginormous hairball of random knowledge like that, things he'd absorbed from women through the years.

Jill motioned for him to sit down in one of the chairs. She took a seat on the adjoining sofa.

"Do you mind if I have a ciggy?" She started to take one out of the pack on the coffee table.

Harry nodded. "Actually, I'd rather you didn't. Asthma," he lied.

"Oh." She looked wistfully at the cigarette, then put it back in the pack.

"This shouldn't take long, then you can light up all you want. You probably heard about DI Mark Lawrence?"

"Tony told me. Murdered, right?"

"Aye. You knew him?"

Lips pursed into a tight line, she nodded.

"Your name and number were in his address book."

"I went out with him for a while before Tony."

"When exactly was that?"

"After Frank's accident." She flipped the cigarette package over, then flipped it back. "Since you work with Frank, you probably know I had a hard time dealing with his accident."

Bitch, Harry thought. Her husband was paralyzed in the line of duty and she'd had a hard time? But he kept his feelings out of his voice. "Actually, he's never mentioned you, but Superintendent Reid recognized your name in the book and asked me to talk to you. He said he'd met you back when you and Frank were still married."

"Yes, years ago." Her smile was stiff. "When we were all much younger."

"So when you were seeing DI Lawrence, were you still married?"

"Technically, I guess, but Frank and I weren't together anymore."

"When did you stop seeing Mark Lawrence?"

"A year and a half ago, I think." Her hands moved to take a cigarette again, but remembering, she pulled them back.

"Did you still talk to him after that?"

"Occasionally. If I ran into him or something."

"When's the last time you talked to him?"

She thought. "Last fall. He called me."

"About what?"

She picked up the pack of cigarettes and took one out, put it in her mouth, reached for her lighter, then remembered again and took the cigarette from her lips. She shook her head in apology. "Sorry, a habit. It was about Frank, actually."

"About Frank?"

"He asked if I knew anything about what Frank was doing now, you know, his work with the taskforce."

"Did he say why?"

"He said he was thinking of trying to get included on it, and wanted to know what I knew about it. And whether I thought Frank would hold the fact that we'd been together against him."

"What did you say?"

"The truth. I don't have any idea about what Frank's doing there." She met Harry's eyes. "I told Mark that Frank wouldn't care at all about him and me."

"Because?"

Her tone matter-of-fact, she said, "When things ended between us, they ended completely. Like it had never happened. There was none of that stuff you hear about, where the husband keeps calling the wife, asking her to come back, or being jealous of who she's with next, or anything like that. When I told Frank I wanted a divorce, he just agreed, and except for talking about a few details of the divorce papers, and what I wanted to take with me, we've never spoken again."

Harry tried to picture Frank with this empty woman, but he couldn't.

She played with the cigarette package. "Frank and I never had children. I didn't want them. I grew up taking care of six younger brothers and sisters. I never wanted to have to take care of anyone like that again. I wanted to take care of me. When Frank got hurt, I couldn't face having to take care of him for the rest of my life. I know that makes me sound like an awful person, but Frank never made me feel bad about it. He just let me go."

Harry nodded, concealing his contempt. Good riddance to bad rubbish. "You didn't tell Frank that Lawrence had been asking about the task force?"

"No. There was nothing to tell. And that's the last time I talked to Mark. So, Frank's doing all right?"

"Yes." Harry got up and moved toward the door.

"Is he seeing anyone?"

Harry wanted to slap her. "Why would I tell you?"

She shrugged. "No reason. I heard he's got his own place, drives himself around in a special van, and is working full time."

"Working more than full time."

She gave a twisted smile. "I guess he didn't need me after all."

"No, I don't think he did." He opened the door. Suddenly he couldn't get out of there fast enough.

"You hate me."

"Not me. You're not worth hating. And I've got a feeling Frank doesn't think you're worth missing."

# Chapter 56

HENRY VON ZANDT slammed the door of his car and marched over to Reid.

Reid raised his eyebrows. Maybe this visit would prove worthwhile after all. "Hello, Henry."

"What the fuck are you doing bothering my wife and my mother?"

Reid did his best insincere innocence act. "You told me I was welcome to check with your wife about your alibi for Richard Ramsey's death."

"I didn't mean come to my house unannounced."

"You didn't say that." Reid said, trying to sound injured. "Who called you?"

"What do you mean?"

"Who told you I was here?"

"What difference does it make?"

"I just find it interesting. I didn't get the impression from either your wife or your mother that they felt the need for you to come. I'm guessing it was the nanny. She spies on your wife for you?"

"None of your business." Harry spat out each word.

"Well, anyway, I'm glad you came home, as I have some more questions for you."

"I don't have to answer any of your questions."

Reid ignored the comment. "I asked both your mother and your wife, but neither one of them had any idea why your telephone number as well as your secretary's name with the number of the company flat was in DI Mark Lawrence's address book. Perhaps you can enlighten me."

"How would I know? I don't even know who you're talking

about."

"Just remember that we're getting his telephone records, so if your number or the company flat's number turns up, I'll know you're telling me a lie."

Henry faltered, then apparently reconsidering his decision to lie, asked, "Who did you say it was? A policeman?"

"DI Mark Lawrence, CID. He was murdered on Easter in his flat."

"Right. I didn't recognize the name at first. Yes, I'd met him through my secretary."

"When was that?"

"I don't know—a year ago, maybe."

"Was Ms. Taylor living at the company flat then?"

Henry narrowed his eyes. "Who says she lives there now?"

"That's the number by her name in his book."

Henry looked momentarily at a loss for words, so Reid went on. "Does she live there?"

"She's between places right now, so we're letting her use it. Temporarily."

"Nice of you. Does she pay rent?"

"What difference does that make?"

"None to me. Might make a difference to your wife."

"Then she can leave me, can't she? See if I give a flying fuck. None of your business, either." Then Henry's expression folded into a sneer. "From what I've heard, you might be better off paying attention to your own marriage."

Reid gave an acknowledging nod. "Always good advice. But my interest in you is professional. Why did Ms. Taylor introduce you?"

"I don't remember."

"Why did he have your number?"

"I'd consulted with him on some security matters."

"For the company?"

"Not that it's any of your business, but yes."

"What kind of security matters?"

"I don't remember."

"Think."

Henry waved his hand. "We had some money go missing. We thought perhaps we had an employee embezzling."

"And?"

"It turned out to be an accounting mistake, that's all."

"When was the last time you talked to him?"

Henry's shoulders went up in a casual shrug. "I can't remember. We talked once in a while when other things came up that I thought he could help with."

"I assume you paid him? So there'll be records?"

Henry clamped his mouth together and glared at Reid. He didn't seem to know what to say.

"Well?" Reid spoke amiably, enjoying Henry's discomfort. He reckoned Henry would be torn between saying he'd paid Lawrence and admitting it had been under the table, or spinning the unbelievable tale that Lawrence had worked for nothing.

"I'm not talking to you without a solicitor. And stay the bloody fuck away from my family." Henry got back in his car, made a flashy racecar driver turn, and headed back toward the city.

# TUESDAY, APRIL 14

# Chapter 57

REID LACED his running shoes tighter, then took off for his run through the park. Running cleared his head, helped get his blood moving, and readied his mind for Mass. He'd talked to Anne earlier that morning, wanting to touch base with her before she began her day. She'd sounded good, had gotten some sleep, and her nausea was . . . well, still there. As he ran, every time his left foot led, he silently prayed: let it be my child, let it be my child. Later, as he got into his stride, he thought about work, but underneath his thoughts deep inside of him, ran the prayerful conviction: it's my child, it's my child.

DI Lawrence's death, especially following so closely after DC Parsons, had CID in an upheaval. The loss of an officer was always taken personally, whether he was liked or not, and Reid had been inundated with cops volunteering to help with the investigation.

Reid had taken advantage of the offers and had uniforms scouring the neighborhood for any witnesses or other information. But his gut told him that Ramsey's murder and Lawrence's murder were connected, and that they weren't likely to get much joy from a door-to-door canvassing.

His feet pounded on down the path as he thought. Harry was working on going over Lawrence's finances—a move that would further incense CID if and when they found out. Proving a cop was dirty was something no one on the job liked to do, and their colleagues would resent it. Reid had a feeling they would find something in Lawrence's accounts that showed he'd been on someone's payroll, though he doubted they would be lucky enough to find anything implicating Von Zandt.

The morning was chilly, but he'd been pleased to see not just the forlorn little daffodils, but the beginnings of the other spring bulbs coming up in the park. There were bulbs coming up at the house as well, and this weekend he'd be there with Anne. They could have a cookout, just the two of them cocooned in their house, surrounded by the high stone walls that enclosed the garden.

He'd instructed the designer to keep moving forward as quickly as possible on getting the house finished. Anne had been pleased with how the painting had come out, and now the rest of changes she'd decided on—recessed lighting in some of the rooms, some changes in the shelving in the large walk in pantry, and changing out the fixtures in the downstairs powder room—could be started. Of course, there were a good many more decisions to be made, furniture to be selected, and when this next stage was completed, Anne could meet with the woman again and decide what she wanted.

He pushed the thought out of his mind of what would happen with the house if he lost Anne. He just wasn't going to think about that yet. They had months still. And with the house, they would have privacy until the baby was born—they could keep to themselves until they knew whose child it was. For now, they could just do what they were doing—tread water—and he would still have her with him.

Knowing it wasn't much of a plan, he put aside any doubts or thoughts of common sense and ran, forcing his mind to concentrate on work—specifically, back to whether, no, not whether, but how, the murders of DI Lawrence and Richard Ramsey were related.

Just before he reached his building, he noticed a slim figure in a long coat standing to the side, the face obscured by the overhang of the coat's hood. Reid slowly slipped his hand under his sweatshirt and felt for his gun. The figure turned toward him and let the hood down.

"It's Glynnis Taylor," she whispered. "I need to talk to you."

He felt chilled as perspiration from his run started to dry on his skin. "Then talk."

"I can't take the chance someone will see me. Can we go inside?"

Reid considered briefly. He didn't like to have people he didn't know in his flat, but he knew Glynnis was right. It could be dangerous for her to be seen with him like this. He nodded and quickly ushered her into the building.

He opened the door to his flat, put the electric teakettle on, and motioned for her to sit down. "How did you know where I live?"

"Walter has a file on you in the office."

Reid wasn't surprised. He assumed Von Zandt was doing at least that. But he wondered what else was in the file. More specifically, what was in the file about Anne?

"Don't you need to get to work, Glynnis?"

"Not until eight-thirty."

"Henry didn't stay in town last night?"

She shook her head. "He went home around eleven. His wife was upset with him, and she kept calling. He blamed you."

"Does he know you're here?"

"No."

The kettle whistled and Reid moved over to the counter to make tea. He brought the pot over, along with two mugs and let it steep, then went back to the refrigerator for milk. "White?"

She nodded. "But no sugar." He put the milk on the table so she could pour her own.

"I didn't tell her about you—or that the number in DI Mark Lawrence's address book he had for you was the company flat. I said it was your mobile number."

She gave a dry smile. "Clever."

He poured the tea into two mugs, then handed her one. "Why did he have your number?"

"Henry told me you asked that."

"So?"

"I went out with him, once." She added milk to her tea, stirred, then raised the cup to her lips.

"Once?"

"Believe me, once was enough."

"You were living in the company flat then?" Reid poured milk in his own tea, added a sugar, and stirred.

"You mean, was I with Henry?"

He nodded.

She stood up, taking her mug and walking through from the kitchen to the flat's main room, her eyes darting around, taking inventory. "I was in the flat, but not seeing Henry yet. Though I'm sure that's why he offered to let me stay there. I was unhappy with the flat I had—noisy, things like that. The company flat is quite nice. So I said okay, while I was looking for somewhere else. I just never left."

She picked up one of the framed photos of Anne from a side

table, examined it. Reid realized the mistake he'd made by letting her inside his flat. If Von Zandt had a file on him, now that file would contain the exact layout of his flat.

"How long have you worked for the company?" Reid wanted to snatch the photo out of her hand, but he stayed where he was.

"A little over two years. Richard set up an interview for me with Henry, and I got the job." She still held Anne's photo.

"Not just the job."

She acknowledged the implication with a nod. "I knew Henry was interested, but I fended him off for a long time. About a year and a half ago, I met Mark Lawrence at a club. I went out with him once. I didn't care for him, but he kept calling. I mentioned it to Henry, and that Lawrence was CID."

A little too convenient, Reid thought, but he gave a small go-on gesture.

"Henry asked me to make the intro. I did. That was it. Shortly after that, I let Henry start visiting me at the flat." She gestured to him with the photo she'd been examining. "This is her, right? Your wife?"

He nodded. "Why did Henry want the intro?"

"He said it was good to know cops." Looking around the room, she shook her head. "You certainly have a lot of photos of her, don't you?"

Reid ignored the remark, keeping on the subject. "That wasn't what Henry told me. He said it was because he had some security issues. Possible embezzlement."

Glynnis put the photo down suddenly and the unmistakable crack of glass breaking sounded. Obviously embarrassed, she looked at the broken picture, then at him. "Sorry."

"No worries. I'll get it fixed."

"What else did Henry say?"

"He said it turned out to be an accounting mistake."

Relief relaxed her face. "Oh, yes, of course. Now I remember."

Liar, Reid thought, but he asked, "Was Mark Lawrence giving Henry information about investigations?"

"I'm not sure. He called Henry sometimes, or sometimes Henry would tell me to get him on the line, but I never asked what it was about. Mark had stopped trying to chat me up. I think Henry warned him off."

Reid fixed her with his gaze. "Glynnis, why are you really here?"

"What do you mean?"

"Why did you come to my flat?"

"Because of what you said. About all of those young people being killed, and that if they weren't stopped, there would be more. I thought you should know about DI Lawrence. His connection with the Von Zandts."

"Frankly, that's not very helpful. I gleaned that much from the address book. Why not just call?"

"I don't know." She gestured, taking in his place. "I was curious about you. I wanted to see where you lived."

"So you could report back to your boyfriend?"

"Absolutely not. I can't tell him I've come here."

"Then why?"

"I guess I just wanted to see you again."

"I'm not sure what your game is, but I'm not playing. If you want to help, maybe you could start with telling me the truth about what Lawrence was doing for the Von Zandts."

She held out her hands in a gesture of surrender. "I don't know."

"I think you know more than you're telling."

"No, I don't."

"You know the kind of things Henry and Walter are involved with."

She shrugged. "There's nothing I can do about that."

"Glynnis, there are other jobs, other flats, you know. You're not Moira, and you're not Barbara. You can leave."

"That's what you think."

"You know what I think? I think Lawrence found out you were embezzling from the company and told Henry. Then Henry used the threat of prosecution to make you, as you say, start letting him visit you at the flat. And he holds that over your head."

Her mouth fell open. "How did you know?"

Reid shrugged. "Made sense from the timing."

She sat down on the sofa. "So, you see why I can't leave him."

"I don't think the Von Zandts would ever prosecute you. It would open the company's books up for examination from the police as well as your solicitor. They'd never do that."

She eyed him, as if she were trying to determine if he were telling her the truth. "Really?"

"Really. Of course, I don't know about what Henry would do instead. He may come after you. That I don't know, but you probably do. Have you paid the money back?"

"Yes, and Henry never told his father. He said he'd keep it just between us as long as I did what he wanted."

"So he'll not want to tell his father now that he'd kept this from him. Henry's in a bit of a spot himself."

"I never thought about it like that."

"Think about it. The Von Zandts have done so much harm to so many people. Standing by and saying there's nothing you can do doesn't cut it."

"What can I do?"

Reid took a deep breath. He decided to trust her, at least with one thing he needed done. "You know about their involvement in prostitution."

"Not really. At least, not much."

"There's a young girl whose life is being haunted by something she did when she was younger and desperate. Henry has films of her that he's holding over her head."

"What can I do?"

"Get the films. The originals and any copies."

Glynnis scowled. "How? Even if I found the films, how would I recognize the girl?"

"You've met her."

"I have?"

"She's Bert Ramsey's girlfriend. Patty Cady."

Glynnis's mouth fell open. "Does Bert know?"

"No, and she doesn't want him to find out."

She pursed her lips. "I can try."

"Thank you. I have something else I want to talk to you about."

"What?"

"I've asked you this before, but I need the truth. Did you have anything going on with Richard Ramsey?"

"Absolutely not."

"Did Richard ever do or say anything to indicate he was attracted to you?"

She smiled flirtatiously and put her hands on her hips. "Most men are attracted to me. You would be, if you'd let yourself."

"Did anything ever happen—did he ever make advances to you?"

Glynnis sighed. "You aren't comfortable with this subject, are you? The answer is no. He never approached me, and I never gave him any signal his interest would be returned. Oddly enough, considering how things turned out, he was in love with my sister, at least until her drinking got so bad. So if he was attracted to me, it was probably because I reminded him of her before she became such an incorrigible drunk."

Reid frowned. "When I first saw you at your sister's house, you said that Richard Ramsey didn't deserve to have his murder investigated. That he wasn't a nice man."

"Maybe that was a bit of an overstatement. What he did to Barbara destroyed her, but I don't think he meant for that to happen."

"What did he do to her?"

"She has such a talent. She's an incredible singer, and when they married, he stopped her performing. He didn't want to share her like that."

"What about Moira? Sending her to live with Walter Von Zandt?"

Glynnis smoothed her hand over her knee. "I like to blame Richard, but the truth is that was more Barbara than Richard."

"What do you mean?"

"If Barbara's voice is beautiful, Moira's is ten times more beautiful. But Barbara refused to allow Moira to have voice training or to do anything to pursue her talent. I hate to say it, but I think Barbara didn't want Moira to have what she couldn't. She was jealous of her own daughter. So she fell right in with Walter's suggestion that Moira be turned over to Walter, and packed her off without giving it a second thought. Richard went along with it, of course. He needed to keep Walter sweet to get that money in on the most favorable terms."

Reid tried to hide how stunned he was at this revelation. He remembered Moira scurrying away from the piano when her mother came into the room. Now he understood.

"I see. Thanks for telling me all this." He looked at his watch. "You'd best be going if you're going to get back before you need to be in the office. How did you get here?"

"Taxi, but I haven't finished my tea."

"All the same, you need to leave. Did the doorman at your building hear you say where you were going? I assume he reports to

Henry on your comings and goings."

"I pretended I was going for a walk and got a cab a few blocks down. I sometimes go for a walk in the morning when Henry doesn't stay over. But you're right." She stood, suddenly assuming a confident brusqueness. "He may come over before the office opens. I'll catch a cab around the corner." She waved and slipped out the door.

Reid took a clean kitchen cloth out of a drawer, went over to the framed picture of Anne that Glynnis had handled, and, using the cloth, picked it up. He took a paper bag from under the kitchen sink and placed the photograph inside. Finally, still using the cloth, he gingerly picked up the mug Glynnis had used, dumped the liquid, wrapped it in the cloth, and placed it in the bag with Anne's picture. He was fairly certain Glynnis hadn't been the woman with Richard Ramsey the night he'd been murdered, but one never knew. If any fingerprints or DNA surfaced, they'd be able to determine whether she'd been involved.

# Chapter 58

Harry LOOKED UP when Darby Reid leaned against the corner of his desk.

"Something I can help you with?"

"I thought we could talk. Do you have a minute?"

His guard went up. She was up to something. Harry knew exactly what she thought of him. She was rotten at hiding her disdain not only for him, but for the rest of the team. Except for her own brother, of course. Although even when Darby dealt with the guv, there was an undertone of something Harry couldn't identify in her manner, something he didn't like one bit.

"I'm all ears." He treated her to a display he'd learned as a boy, and wiggled his already prominent ears.

She ignored his little trick and gestured to the conference room. "Can we go somewhere more private to talk?"

"No need. There's no one else around, and I've just had my midmorning tea. Go ahead." He could tell that she didn't like not getting the reaction from him that he assumed she was used to getting from other men. Even though she didn't want him, she wanted him to want her. Too bad, Toots, he thought. Not going to happen.

She lowered her voice to an almost whisper. "I'm worried about Terrence."

"The guv can take care of himself." Harry didn't for one minute believe that Darby's concern was genuine.

"I agree that's usually true."

"Then what's the problem?"

She lifted her elegant arse to sit on his desk. "Anne. As always, Anne's the problem."

He couldn't think of a response to that. At least this one time, Darby might be right.

She leaned down to bring her face closer to his. "You and I are the only two here who know about her working for Von Zandt."

Harry shook his head slowly. "No, not quite. The guv knows."

"Of course, besides him." He could tell she was getting exasperated with him, but she managed to push it off. "Harry, I don't think he realizes what this could do to his career if people find out and he's still in charge of the operation. It could ruin him."

Ruin him? How ruined could the guv be? No matter what happened with the brass, Harry thought, Reid would still be the brilliant and immensely wealthy heir to an earldom.

"That's his problem, luv, isn't it? Or are you thinking of telling them?"

"No, of course not. I don't want his career destroyed." Her tone took on a hint of wheedling. "Maybe you could convince him."

"Convince him to do what?"

"To recommend that the operation be turned over to Interpol. If he's not in charge, Anne's working for Von Zandt won't be such a big deal."

Harry didn't even have to feign his surprise at that. "You've got to be daft."

"Terrence is acting like he's daft."

"The guv can take care of himself."

"You think so?" Darby's green eyes darkened. "Do you realize what would happen if people find out and he's still in charge of this investigation?"

"Above my pay grade, sweetums."

She slid from her perch on his desk and hissed, "They'll pull him off this operation."

"Then they'll pull him off. There are other operations. He's only got the one wife. She's certainly not working everywhere."

"Are you being deliberately obtuse, Harry? His career will be in shambles. And it won't do any of us any good if that happens."

Ah, that was what she was really worried about. Not her brother, but that her own career would be hurt.

"Yes, well, we peasants are sometimes a bit thick. It's our nature, we can't help it. Just like you can't help being a snobby bitch."

She raised her hand as if to slap him.

He grabbed her hand. "I wouldn't do that, sweetheart. I'm just ill-bred enough to slap you back."

"Swine."

He grinned as she flounced away, then picked up his ringing telephone. Harry only had to listen to the woman on the other line for two minutes before he knew it was important.

When he hung up, he went into the Superintendent's office. His boss was staring at his computer screen and frowning.

"Guv?"

Reid looked up, then made a notation on the paper in front of him. "Yes?"

"I just got an interesting call."

"From?"

"The wife of one of DI Lawrence's mates. She said Lawrence got her husband's car smashed up in an undercover operation. He promised to take care of getting it fixed, but never did. Now that Lawrence is dead, she'd like to know who's going to pay for the repairs."

Reid was quiet, then said, "Where's the car?"

"She said he told her husband that the car couldn't show up in a repair shop for a while because it would blow the operation, so Lawrence had her husband keep it hidden in a friend's garage."

"The repairs haven't been done yet?"

"She says no."

"What's the mate's name?"

"Billy Forester."

"Send someone to talk to her husband. And her. See if they'll agree to letting us search the car without a warrant. But before they do, get the address of the garage and I'll get a warrant request going, in case they won't agree. If we're lucky, SOCO will be able to get trace evidence linking the car to DC Parsons's murder."

Harry tasted bile in his throat. "DI Lawrence killed the kid, didn't he?"

Reid nodded. "Sounds like it. Or provided the car to someone else who did."

"Why?"

"The only thing that makes sense is that Lawrence wanted Parsons to leave off the surveillance of Ramsey and Parsons wouldn't agree."

"Do you think Lawrence killed Ramsey?"

"Maybe. Or maybe he was just tasked with making sure the surveillance was dropped so someone else could kill him."

"Then why was Lawrence killed? Why not just keep paying him off? He had to still be valuable even if just for the intel he was collecting through Shelley."

"Apparently Lawrence overestimated his worth." The Superintendent's voice was flat.

Harry grimaced. "Not for the first time, that."

# THURSDAY, APRIL 16

# Chapter 59

**R**EID APPROACHED the front desk of Anne's hotel. Smiling, he nodded a greeting at the young man behind the counter.

Instead of returning his smile, the desk clerk nervously avoided Reid's eyes, stammering. "Lord Reid, I don't think Lady Anne was expecting you tonight. She said you'd be here tomorrow to pick her up for the weekend."

Reid instantly got a bad feeling. He felt his face tighten. "Indeed, but here I am. My wife?"

The clerk looked down. "I could ring her room."

"Is that where she is?" When he got no response, Reid asked again, "Is she in her room?"

"I don't think so." The young man looked up, then quickly blinked and looked down again.

"Where is she?" The iron in Reid's voice sent a message that could not be ignored.

Without meeting his eyes, the clerk murmured, "The dining room, my lord."

"Thank you." Somewhere inside him he knew what he would find. Ice froze his heart as he walked into the dimly lit room and looked around.

Anne was not hard to spot. She was sitting at one of the elegantly appointed tables, a glass of sparkling water and a bowl of soup in front of her. Her golden hair shimmered in loose waves down her back. Across from her sat Andrew Grainger, drinking wine and gazing at her as if she held the soul of the universe in her eyes—or in her womb.

Reid debated whether to leave without saying anything or go over to the table and confront her. Anne's head suddenly turned toward him, as if she sensed his presence. The blood drained out of her face and her eyes got huge, like a mountain hare realizing a hawk's sights were fixed upon it.

She sprang up, dropping the napkin from her lap. Crossing over to where he stood, she reached out her hands to him. "Terrence."

Stepping back, he kept his voice low, his words sharp and clipped. "I see you keep busy when I'm away. No surprise there. Have you two been up to bed yet? His turn, I suppose." His words were cold, but a tremendous heat burned through his body. He wanted to knock over tables, throw things, hurt Anne, kill Andrew Grainger. He shoved his hands into his pockets to stop himself from doing violence.

"Of course not. He's just come to see how I'm doing."

"You neglected to mention he was coming." Digging his nails into his fisted palms, Reid tried to concentrate on keeping his hands in his pockets.

"I didn't know." Her voice was a plea.

From the corner of his eye, Reid saw the other man rise and move as if to come to Anne. Anne saw it too, and motioned to Grainger to stay away. The man stayed where he was, but did not sit down again. Reid thought, dare to come over here, you bastard, and I'll kill you. But Andrew Grainger stayed where he was.

Still keeping her voice low, she said, "I was telling him he needed to go. I don't know how he even knew where I was staying. He just found out and came."

"Don't tell him to go for me, Anne. I'm done with this." He took a deep breath and pulled his hands, now under control, out of his pockets.

Her face was taut with tension. "You don't mean that."

"Indeed, I do. I don't like the way the hotel clerk looked at me with pity when I asked where you were. I don't like the way I act when I see you with other men. I don't like the way I feel when I see you sitting there with your lover. I can easily understand how men kill in situations like this. I would like to kill Grainger right now. Him and, God help me, you. I won't because I'm civilized, but I can't do this anymore. I'm finished with this mess."

"Terrence." Tears shimmered in her beautiful eyes, but he'd seen them before, and his decimated heart couldn't feel sympathy for her.

"I'll have my lawyers draw up the papers, but it can wait until the child's born. On the off chance it's mine, we'll make sure it's born in wedlock. If you need anything from me in the meantime, perhaps you can have one of your sisters contact me. Give my best to Grainger." He smiled, a thin smile that held nothing but pain. "Actually, you already have, haven't you?"

"Please don't go." From somewhere far away in his head, he heard her plead with him, but he had to get out of there. He couldn't stand any more.

He turned to leave, and too late, saw the flash from the photographer's camera.

# Chapter 60

SHE'D GONE UP to bed right after she convinced Andrew to leave. The look on Terrence's face when he saw her with Andrew—and his words—haunted her. She'd fallen asleep once and woke up crying, dreaming of him walking away from her—saying he was finished with this mess, with her—then she slipped back into a restless sleep.

Close to midnight, she was awakened by the ringing of her cell phone. She picked it up quickly, only to be swamped with dismay when she realized it was Darby's voice on the other end.

"Anne, it's Darby. I need to talk to you."

"Goodbye, Darby."

"Don't hang up."

"Give me one good reason not to."

"I really need to talk to you."

Tired, Anne prompted her sister-in-law. "All right, go ahead, talk, I'm awake."

"No, not on the telephone. I'm not far from your hotel. I'll come there."

"Not tonight, Darby, I'm exhausted."

"It wasn't my idea to call you. Terrence asked me to."

Anne sat up, trying to make sense of what she was hearing. "Terrence? Why would he ask you?"

"I'll explain when I get there. I know we've had our differences, and I'm sorry about that, but I think you'll want to talk to me when you hear what I have to say."

Remembering her advice to herself earlier with regard to Darby to beware of Greeks bearing gifts, she was wary, but she needed to find out what Terrence wanted. "All right, we can talk. I'll tell the hotel to let you in."

She put on a robe and slippers and ordered tea from downstairs while she waited. She didn't have to wait long; Darby arrived just after the tea was delivered.

"The press has the place surrounded." Darby looked around the room, saw the tea and headed toward it. "Thank God, I'm parched."

"Help yourself. I had them send up regular and herbal."

"Definitely regular for me."

Anne inclined her head to the window in the direction of the press gauntlet. "It's been like that all night. The hotel's been good about not letting them inside, though." Anne waited until Darby had served herself before pouring a cup of the herbal mint tea. Taking her cup with her, she sat on the edge of the bed.

Darby took a drink of tea, then shook her head. "The press don't know me, so I had no problem getting through. Was it like this in California, as well?"

Anne nodded, wondering if she had the strength to go through again what she'd gone through with the press in California. Just the thought of it made her want to go back to bed, pull the covers over her head, and not move for a week. "For a while. Then they went away. These will as well—eventually. What did you need to talk to me about?"

"May I sit down?"

"Go ahead."

Darby sat in a chair by the little desk. "So are you still planning to stay in Scotland?"

"For now."

"Terrence was afraid you'd decided to go back to the States with the artist."

So that was why he hadn't called. "No. I have a job to finish."

Darby reached out and took Anne's hand. "I'm sorry I've not been very nice to you. I was wrong. I hope we can be friends."

Anne tried to hide her surprise. "Of course."

"I know I've been a right bitch to you. I've no excuse, but I want us to start over."

Finally, Anne thought. She'd tried so hard with Darby before, but nothing seemed to make a difference. Now, when she was at her lowest, her sister-in-law was finally accepting her.

She could let bygones be bygones. "I want that, too."

Darby released Anne's hand. "How much do you know about what Terrence is working on?"

"Not a lot. I know he's investigating Walter for some financial crimes."

"It's much worse than that." Darby explained the ties they suspected Von Zandt of having with the Heidelberg University bombing and terrorists plotting similar attacks.

Anne bit her lip. Why hadn't he told her any of that in the first place? "No wonder he wants me to quit working on the Lynstrade Manor gardens. Is that what you came to tell me?"

"No, actually, he's decided he needs your help. If you're agreeable."

"My help? With what?"

"The investigation. We've had no luck getting anyone inside Von Zandt's organization. He said that Von Zandt had earlier asked you and your boss to stay at his place, but you'd turned him down. Terrence suggested that you tell Von Zandt you've changed your mind, that you need to be somewhere the press isn't bothering you."

Anne frowned. "He wants me to stay at Walter's? I don't understand. He made me promise to stay away from him."

"He's changed his mind. We think you might be able to get some of the information we've been looking for."

"Don't you need a warrant or something?" Had he changed his mind because he no longer cared about her?

"Technically, we would, as we're law enforcement, but you're not, and if you're a guest, there's nothing stopping you from looking around, or paying attention to what's being said around you. Von Zandt can hardly say he doesn't know who you are—who you're married to."

Anne wasn't sure that made sense, but she knew little about the law, and certainly nothing about the law in Scotland. "Terrence usually has a fit if I suggest doing anything he thinks is dangerous."

"It won't be dangerous at all. Von Zandt isn't dangerous—he's just the money man. Besides, he shouldn't suspect a thing. All you're to do is look around, pay attention, listen, and report to us what you see and hear. Frankly, we're desperate. We're expecting another attack within the next two weeks, and it's likely to be worse than the last one."

"The next two weeks?"

"Before classes get out."

Still, Anne felt unsure. "Why didn't Terrence come talk to me himself? I've called him over and over and he won't even answer."

"He's in meetings with the brass. There's a lot of pressure on him right now." Darby gestured to the press outside. "Besides, he can't come here unobserved, and he thinks it's better if Von Zandt thinks the two of you are rowing. It will make him less likely to get suspicious that you're helping Terrence."

"But he's still upset with me?" Anne felt humiliated having to ask Darby, but she needed to know.

"I didn't ask him that. But he asked me to talk to you, so if he is, I think he'll get over it."

Anne wasn't so sure. "You think so?"

"He's gotten over worse from you, hasn't he?" A hint of the old snide Darby slid through her sister-in-law's voice, though Anne had to admit Darby was right.

"I guess so. And nothing happened."

"Right. So what do you want me to tell him?"

Anne didn't even hesitate. "Yes. Tell him yes. Of course, yes."

Darby smiled. "Great. I have DC Allison Muirhead downstairs waiting. She's a member of Terrence's team, and he sent her to help. I'm going to have her come up and fit you with the wire we want you to wear. She doesn't know anything about the personal situation between you and Terrence, so don't mention anything in front of her."

"Of course not. Will Terrence be calling me?" Anne felt her heartbeat speed up.

Darby shook her head. "He wants to, but he asked me to tell you to be patient. He needs to get Von Zandt packed away before he can think about anything else. There are too many lives at stake."

Anne nodded. Of course, stopping more terrorist attacks was more important that this silly misunderstanding about Andrew.

A knock sounded at the door, and Darby went to open it.

A young, fresh-faced woman came in, carrying a black case. She was dressed in jeans, a t-shirt, and a denim jacket. "Lady Anne, I'm DC Muirhead. I'm going to fit you up with a wire."

# FRIDAY, APRIL 17

# Chapter 61

ANNE'S LUGGAGE sat by the door of her hotel room waiting for the bellman. She'd had room service bring breakfast up so that she'd have more time to pack, but she hadn't been able to eat. She took her cell phone off the charger and rolled through the message list. There were messages from her mother, and her sisters. Nothing from Terrence, although she'd called him several times during the night and left messages for him to call her. She still wanted to talk to him about what she was doing. She wiggled her hand down her bra to check that her wire was in place.

A knock sounded on her hotel room door. The bellman had made it in record time. The hotel must be anxious to get rid of her, and to be honest, she didn't blame them. She let the man in to get her bags, then followed him down the hallway to the elevator, slipping her cell phone into her pocket.

She took a deep breath, dug out her sunglasses from her purse, and prepared herself for the gauntlet of the press waiting for her outside.

* * * * *

A stern looking woman with jet black hair and a German accent greeted Anne at Lynstrade Manor, introducing herself as the housekeeper. She led Anne to her suite of rooms through long hallways decorated with modern art instead of the ancestral portraits and landscapes more typical to these old homes. Anne thought the housekeeper's name was something like Hedda or Helga, but wasn't quite sure because the woman's accent was so thick.

Anne's rooms consisted of an elegant bedroom and a sitting

room, as well as a well-appointed bathroom. The furnishings were luxurious, replete with antiques and rich fabrics and, in Anne's opinion, a little over the top. Everything that could be gilt, was, and everything that could be covered with expensive silks and brocades, was. It looked like a courtesan's room, decorated lavishly for entertaining her guests. There was a small but well-stocked bar containing a small refrigerator, microwave, and coffee maker. There was no telephone and no television, but instead only a discreet sound system stocked with an inventory comprised almost entirely of classical music.

Anne felt her stomach grow queasy, whether from morning sickness or something else, she didn't know. For the first time since Darby had talked to her, Anne started to feel a little afraid. Would she really have enough freedom in the house to try to find the things they wanted her to look for? She was thankful Terrence trusted her to help, though, and she had to make sure she did the best she could for him. When Darby had told her that Walter was tied to the Heidelberg bombing and to plots for more attacks that were supposed to happen soon, Anne had been shocked. Terrence had said Walter was a dangerous man, but she hadn't understood the magnitude of what he'd meant.

"Dinner will be at eight, Lady Anne." The housekeeper cleared her throat, interrupting Anne's thoughts. "The family usually dresses for dinner."

"Thank you." Anne silently groaned. Great. She hadn't had time to replace the dress Terrence had ruined, and she hadn't packed anything else remotely suitable. "Actually, Hedda," she said the name quickly so that the woman wouldn't be able to tell if she'd gotten the name right, "I may not have anything appropriate to wear. I'm afraid I did not pack with dressing for dinner every night in mind when I left the States. Would you please ask Mr. Von Zandt if it would be all right if I just had something on a tray in my room?"

"Yes, my lady."

"Thank you."

When she was alone, Anne looked longingly at the bed. She really wanted to nap; the baby was making her so tired. After Darby had left, she'd tried to get back to sleep, but had only managed to fall asleep for short periods. As it turned out, she hadn't even had to call Walter to wrangle an invitation to stay at Lynstrade Manor. Elisa Von

Zandt had called first thing in the morning, right after she'd seen the papers, to offer Anne the use of a guest suite in their house.

The thought of the newspapers led Anne's thoughts back to one of the things that kept her up the night before. The photographer happening to be there at the exact wrong time—how had that happened? The desk clerk. It had to have been him. He'd been so nice, but Anne had the distinct impression that right after Terrence had shown up that first time, he'd put her name and face together with the stories from when Andrew's daughter was killed. He'd treated her differently after that, looking at her with that eager interest in everything she did that she'd come to know and dread. He must have called the press when Andrew showed up. He probably recognized Andrew as well. Their photos had been plastered all over the international news when Lenore had been murdered, and they'd been suspects. She'd meant to ask Andrew how he'd known where she was staying, but getting him to leave was all she could think of after Terrence stormed away.

As tired as she was, she needed to get out to the gardens and get to work. Jonas had probably already started work for the day. She would have to explain to him about what happened, and apologize for the whole thing with the press. At least the news stories she'd seen hadn't included any mention of her company's name. She couldn't afford to lose her job. If she was let go from such a prestigious firm, who would ever hire her again?

Then she thought of other people seeing the news stories. Terrence's family and his own bosses. Anne blinked away a flash of pain, remembering what Darby had said to her earlier about Anne embarrassing their family and hurting Terrence's career. But surely the people Terrence worked for wouldn't hold him responsible for any of this mess. Nor could his family blame him, though they must be appalled at her. Terrence had grown up in a family where things like this didn't happen. Perfect parents, perfect childhood, perfect career, perfect life. Until her.

She'd made so many mistakes. Anne circled two fingers around her stomach. Don't worry, baby. Your mama's not perfect, but she's trying and we'll be okay. No matter what, we'll be okay.

Anne changed into her gardening clothes, trying to figure out how one woman could attract so much trouble, then went outside to find Jonas.

# Chapter 62

REID SHOOK HIS HEAD. He couldn't have heard right. Holding his mobile phone steady against his ear, he said, "Tell me again?"

"She checked out of the hotel this morning, Lord Reid." The man from Stirling's security firm was clearly troubled, and more than a little nervous.

"Checked out? Where did she go?"

"I followed her taxi as far as I could, but the estate is gated, and I didn't think I should try to get past the gates."

His heart sank. "What estate?"

"Where she's working, my lord. Lynstrade Manor."

"She took her luggage?"

"Yes, my lord." The man cleared his throat. "What would you like me to do now?"

"I'll be in contact. Stay there, as close to the gates as you can without being spotted. Let me know immediately if you see her leave. And follow her." He paused. "But don't approach her unless it looks like she's in trouble. She doesn't know you're watching out for her."

"Yes, sir."

Reid ended the call. What the hell was Anne doing? It sounded as if she was staying at Von Zandt's. After what he'd told her about his fears that the man was using her to get to him, he couldn't fathom her reasoning.

The press. Perhaps she'd fled the hotel to get away from them. He knew from Stirling's man that they'd been camped around the hotel after the management had forbidden them to wait for her inside the building. The news stories, punctuated by the photographs of his own angry face directed at her pleading one, and others of her and

Grainger having their cozy dinner before he arrived, had been gleefully speculating on the love triangle—as they unimaginatively termed it. At least they hadn't heard what Anne and he had been saying to each other. There had been nothing in the news about the baby. He grimaced. That would have been a story the press would have been on like hungry hyenas tearing meat off their victims' bones.

Who had told the press that Anne was there at the hotel with Andrew Grainger? The hotel desk clerk? Reid clenched his jaw. It had to have been him. He'd kill the little shite. Of course, the desk clerk hadn't known Reid was going to change his plans and come a day earlier. It had just been an extra bonus to have the injured husband walk in and find the guilty couple huddled together in an intimate conversation.

In the few moments he'd watched Anne with Grainger that night, Reid had seen how well the two knew each other, and in Grainger's face, how much the man loved her. He'd not been able to see Anne's face, and for that he was glad. If he'd seen just a fraction of the feeling that showed in Grainger's face reflected in Anne's face, he didn't know if he could have survived it.

He was sure that the press was making Anne's life miserable, though they hadn't bothered him much. They were more circumspect with him, probably because, from time to time, they needed him. Reid had ignored multiple calls from Carolyn Caspary. Although he assumed she'd be sympathetic to him and offer to publish his version of events to refute this morning's stories, he didn't have a version of events to contradict what had been reported. He couldn't even imagine what Carolyn must be thinking about the pathetic gullibility he'd displayed during their conversation the other day.

Then he thought of McMurty and Shreve. And Nelson Schilling. If they read the papers or watched the semi-news, they'd now know by now about Anne working for Von Zandt. They'd be waiting for him to call, giving him the respect of turning himself in, so to speak. He'd be lucky if he wasn't brought up on charges, demoted, or just plain kicked off the job.

He forced himself to turn on the television. He wasn't sure if they'd gotten more pictures or film of Anne, or what exactly they were saying as he had studiously avoided the news reports or, indeed, any television at all. Perhaps he'd better check it out. He needed to know to what extent they were harassing his hapless bride.

Reid groaned as he watched the sleazy celebrity news show. As he'd feared, the press had surrounded Anne like hounds surrounding an unwary rabbit—and she'd fled. He watched the film as she left the hotel and got into the cab. She wore dark glasses and kept her face serene, not hurrying her pace in the least and ignoring the questions being thrown at her. As poised as she appeared, he knew the effort that charade took.

Anne was probably feeling humiliated and vulnerable. But to go to Von Zandt's house? To move there? Surely she wasn't planning to stay there for the duration of the project. He ran his hands through his hair, trying to determine what to do.

He hadn't left things between them in such a way that he could call her and just ask what the hell she was doing. He'd told her in no uncertain terms that it was over between them. And it was, but God knew, he didn't want her to come to harm. It was none of his business if she wanted to stay at Von Zandt's or Buckingham Palace for that matter. Nonetheless, if she was in danger from Von Zandt, it was because of him—because of any importance Von Zandt might think she had for him.

Reid closed his eyes. Nothing was ever uncomplicated with Anne. Nothing. He called Harry to let him know of the newest glitch.

"At his house, guv? Do you think Von Zandt did this to get at you?"

"Perhaps."

"And you've not been able to speak with Lady Anne?" Harry's voice was cautious and blessedly diplomatic.

"Things are a bit difficult right now with that." Reid knew Harry would have seen the newspapers or, God forbid, the television. He knew he should call Dunbaryn and reassure them that there was nothing to the stories, but he had no reassurances to give to them—or to himself.

"Right. And the security man you had on her?"

"He's outside the gates. Virtually useless." Reid held his mobile in one hand and rubbed his temples with the other. He couldn't explain this mess to anyone and have it make sense.

"But the homing device on her mobile is still in place?"

"I believe so. It shows up as being in his house."

"Does it seem strange to you that she would go there after what you've told her about Von Zandt, guv? I know she's, well, from California, as you said, and I admit I don't know her, but does it make sense to you that Lady Anne would do this?"

"Truth be told, it makes no sense to me, no matter what else is going on. I'm that worried about her. I can't fathom what happened." He couldn't tell Harry, but he was truly puzzled that she would put the baby at risk by going into what he'd told her could be a dangerous situation. Had she not been pregnant, he would not have been so surprised. His wife had an innocent confidence, a confidence bordering on recklessness, a confidence that allowed her to sail blithely into dangerous waters. He'd seen it before when they were in Bodega Bay and she'd boarded a yacht manned by an armed madman holding hostages. This was a woman who thought you could play nice chess.

He groaned. "Actually, Harry, the more I think about it, it might not make sense, but it is not really very far out of character for her."

Harry was quiet, probably trying to think of something nonjudgmental to say. Finally, he came up with, "Well, guv, I'm sure you know her best."

"That's debatable. In any event, I'm going to have to talk to the brass. Fall on my bloody sword and explain why my wife is not only working for the target of our investigation, but living in his house. You and the rest of the team had best keep clear of the situation. You may well have a different boss by noon, and I don't want you all to be out on the streets as well."

"I'll take my chances. Besides I've got a standing offer from your mate, John Stirling, to come work for him. So just let me know what you need me to do."

# Chapter 63

ALLISON GLANCED OVER to where Harry sat working at his computer, basking in the smug knowledge that she was in on a part of the operation that Harry wasn't. He always thought he knew everything the Super did, and truth be told, he usually did seem to be privy to things no one else was. This time, though, the roles were reversed. Harry was in the dark, and she was in the inner circle. No one else except Darby knew about the hush-hush operation the Superintendent had put together to get his wife into Von Zandt's house. Allison almost wished Harry knew so she could lord it over him. Diplomatically, of course. She wouldn't act like he did.

She was exhausted from being up most of the night before, but at the same time, she felt energized with a wonderful high, the high that came from knowing she was really valued at her job. The Superintendent's show of confidence thrilled Allison. He'd chosen her, just her, not any of the other members of his team.

Of course, surveillance devices were one of her specialties, so perhaps she'd been included more because of her skills than anything else. Allison was proud of the wire she'd fitted for Anne. A work of art, that. Explaining the intricacies of the device to a nonprofessional had been the hardest part, but the Super's wife caught on quickly. Darby would be monitoring the wire on her laptop herself. Allison had volunteered to help, but Darby had shaken her head, saying her brother wanted her to take care of it personally.

Allison stole another glance at Harry and was startled to see that he was looking right at her. She turned back to her computer, pretending like she hadn't noticed. She still had about a zillion leads to follow up on about the credit card records they'd linked to the explosives used at Heidelberg, but her lack of sleep was catching up on her. Columns of names and numbers danced in front of her eyes, and she yawned.

"Someone didn't get enough sleep last night." Harry's voice startled her, and she jerked to alert.

"I'm fine."

"How many times have I told you no carousing on school nights, kitten?"

She sent him what she hoped was a scathing look, while she scrabbled in her head for an explanation for her fatigue. He knew she didn't do what he called carousing even on weekend nights. Then his words registered, and she scowled. "Don't call me kitten."

"Sorry, sweetums. You still haven't told me what kept you from your snoozing time."

She huffed out her exasperation. Harry was so nosy and, unfortunately, so good at figuring out when there were things she didn't want to tell him, or that she was supposed to keep secret. She would have to be very careful.

"None of your business."

"Whoo-oo." Harry got up and came around to her desk. He examined what she had up on her screen, then leaned against her desk. "Let me guess. DC Michaud took you dancing and you twinkled and twined your toes together all night."

"Not hardly." She glanced over at the Super's office, making sure the door was closed. "You saw the papers this morning?"

"Aye. Hard to miss them."

The photos had been awful. Her mum had been muttering all morning about it, mad on behalf of Allison's boss, whom she approved of, even if he was a Catholic. Allison hadn't told her mother where she'd been last night or that she'd met the Super's wife. Lady Anne really did look like a film star, except that her eyes had been red from crying when Allison saw her. Well, she bleeding well should be crying, after what she'd done. From remarks Darby made on the drive to the hotel last night, Allison could tell that Darby did not care for her brother's wife. No surprise, when Lady Anne had been caught out by the press meeting her lover at the hotel.

"What do you think of her?" Allison couldn't resist the opportunity to get Harry's opinion on a subject that was rarely discussed within the team.

"Who?"

Allison blew out her breath in exasperation. "You know who. Don't be thick."

Harry's eyes widened. "Thick? Me?"

She rolled her eyes. "Yes, you. What do you think of the guv's wife?"

Harry wiggled his ears and raised his eyebrows up and down quickly. "I make it a point not to think about other men's wives."

Allison waved a hand at him. "Stop doing that. You look daft." Harry looked hurt, but Allison could tell he was having her on. "You know that's not what I mean. I mean, what do you think about them? About their marriage and all." It seemed like an extremely strange marriage. Allison was pretty sure the Reids didn't live together. The Superintendent didn't even have a photo of his wife on his desk, and he never talked about her. Harry, on the other hand, talked about his girls, not all the time, but often enough. Birds, he called them. The Super didn't seem to have anyone but this on again, off again, wife. So maybe he did love her. Who could ever understand men?

Harry grinned. "I definitely try not to think about marriage, even other people's marriages. Therein lies the path to disaster."

But Allison wasn't going to let him get away with not answering. If she had to talk to Harry, they would talk about something Allison wanted to talk about. Besides, it would keep him from asking her any dangerous questions that might give him a hint about the Superintendent secretly having his wife doing surveillance at Von Zandt's. "Do you think the Superintendent loves her?"

"What's not to love?"

Harry could be so exasperating. He understood exactly what she was asking but he refused to give a straight answer.

"Oh, never mind." Whether the Superintendent loved his wife or not, Allison still couldn't understand him sending her into Von Zandt's house wearing a wire. It was so dangerous. But then she remembered the stories about what had happened in California. The Super and his wife had caught the man that murdered her lover's little girl together. That had to have been dangerous, so maybe Lady Anne was more used to this kind of work than people realized.

She certainly hadn't seemed afraid. She'd nodded as Allison told her how to operate the wire and asked a few, actually good, questions.

Allison waved her hand to shoo Harry away. "Go back to your desk, kitten. I'm working." All he did was annoy her. He wouldn't even have an honest discussion with her about things. If this operation was successful, Allison had a feeling she'd be taking Harry's place as the Superintendent's right hand.

He scrutinized her, not seeming to care that she'd used the same silly name for him as he had for her. "Something's going on with you."

"I don't know what you're talking about, kitten." She was starting to enjoy this.

"No? I'm thinking there's something you're not sharing with your good mate."

"You're not my mate. Work colleagues is all, kitten."

He tilted his head and smirked with his maddening freckled face grin, clasping his hand against his heart. "You hurt me, girl. Haven't I worked hard to try to teach you the ropes?"

"What you want me to know and when you want to tell me. You aren't the only one who knows what they're doing, kitten."

"I am truly wounded. I've always been adamant that you are almost as good as me when I was . . ." He paused, then said, drawing his words out deliberately, "Weel, I'm thinking grammar school."

Allison cut her eyes at him. She had more brothers like him than she cared to think about. Then she remembered her plan to try to emulate Darby, and looked at him coolly. "I'm sure you're the most wonderful thing to hit the police force since…well, perhaps back to the beginning of Scotland." But, not that wonderful, she thought. The Super hadn't trusted Harry to be privy to his wife's infiltration of Von Zandt's house, and he had trusted her. Maybe he didn't want a ginger-haired idiot on something so delicate.

"You flatter me, girl."

She rolled her eyes. "You don't need me for that. You do such a good job of flattering yourself, kitten."

Harry lowered his mouth until he was right in front of her face. Then he pursed his lips and purred like a cat.

She slapped her hand in the air. "Go away."

# Chapter 64

"I'LL RELINQUISH the operation and you can assign someone to take my place." Reid looked from DCC Shreve back to McMurty, almost hoping they'd take him up on his offer. When he'd called to ask for this meeting, he'd known that they'd been waiting for his call. They'd given him the courtesy of letting him come to them on his own, instead of ordering him to a meeting and demanding an explanation. He knew he'd put them all in an uncomfortable position.

McMurty played with his ubiquitous unlit cigar. "Have you talked to Schilling?"

"Aye, this morning."

"What was his reaction?"

Reid shrugged. "He's leaving it to you."

Shreve took a drink of his tea. "So your wife won't give up the job?"

"No, and perhaps that's my fault. I haven't felt free to tell her enough so that she understood fully what's going on."

"This job is through her firm, and the person she works for is the one that took the job, not her?" McMurty got the point, thank God.

"Yes."

"But you certainly can't need her to work." Shreve put in.

Reid shook his head. "Perhaps not, but her career is important to her. And she was anxious to have work in Scotland."

McMurty said, "That's understandable. A long distance marriage couldn't have been easy for either of you."

"No."

McMurty nodded thoughtfully. "Probably part of what led to the events in California, I assume?"

Reid knew this subject couldn't be avoided any longer. "Aye. We were separated. I'd not been very understanding about the long distance thing. But we were trying again." He wasn't going to mention the pregnancy. "If you saw the tabloids this morning, you know it didn't work out." Reid didn't let his humiliation bleed through into his words. None of their business. Besides, he didn't need them, and he didn't need this job.

"You're not in contact with her now?" McMurty's tone was calm, dispassionate.

"No."

"Is she going back to the States?"

Reid shrugged. "I'd assume she will after this job is finished."

Shreve darted a censorious look in Reid's direction. "You should have told us about her working for Walter Von Zandt."

"Perhaps. But it took me by surprise, and I was trying to work it out with her."

Shreve glared at him. "Frankly, Reid, there's a lot of talk that the way you've run the investigation got DC Parsons and DI Lawrence killed."

Reid's head snapped up and he looked first at McMurty, then at Shreve. Shreve had a tendency to be a prick. Reid didn't take it personally, but neither did he appreciate it. "You well know that DI Lawrence was supervising Parsons. What's more, it certainly wasn't my idea to have Lawrence or his people included in the operation. If you remember, I came out strongly against it. And now, as you know, we have strong evidence that DI Lawrence himself was involved in DC Parsons's murder."

Shreve pouted in that infantile way that always made Reid want to put him in toddler time out. "I'm just telling you what I've heard."

"There's nothing I can do about idiotic gossip." Reid decided to go on the offensive. "Why don't you let people know that CID was responsible? And that you pushed me to accept their involvement? Or that a CID DI has been implicated in DC Parsons's murder?"

Shreve scowled. "No need to shoot the messenger, Reid. And we can't yet say for certain that DI Lawrence had anything to do with the constable's death. While we're on that subject though, you should know that Interpol has approached us, suggesting the operation be turned over to them. They say it looks bad for your wife to be consorting with Von Zandt, knowing he's under suspicion of providing money laundering services to terrorists."

"Consorting?" Reid felt like he'd gotten a hard boot kick to his gut, remembering what Harry had told him about Darby's suggestion that the investigation be turned over to Interpol. Had she really been worried about him, or had she been angling for that for some reason of her own? Had she been promised a larger role in the investigation if Interpol took over? Had she actually been conspiring against him? His own sister? No, he refused to believe that.

McMurty snorted and tapped the unlit cigar on the rim of his cup. "Interpol has a fat lot of nerve. Their own president resigned last year facing corruption charges."

"They emailed these photos to illustrate their point." Shreve turned his laptop toward Reid, displaying pictures of a smiling Anne sitting a restaurant table with Walter Von Zandt, Jonas, and the two other men Reid remembered from the night he'd first gone to her at her hotel. She was wearing the ill-fated black dress. Who'd taken those photographs? And who'd sent the photographs to Interpol?

Reid took a deep breath, let it out. "That was a business dinner. She was there with her boss." But who would believe Anne's relationship with Von Zandt was just business now that she was living in his home?

Shreve hit a key on his computer and another photo came on screen. "And how do you explain this one?" The photo showed Reid standing with Anne, Von Zandt, Jonas, and Von Zandt's estate manager, as well as the other man who'd been at dinner with Anne. The photograph captured the moment of false social niceties. He'd only been in the group for a few minutes before dragging Anne away and practically ravishing her in the elevator. Please God, don't let there be photographs of that. If there were, there was only one thing he could do. Resign.

"I renew my offer to step away from this investigation."

McMurty shook his head. "Absolutely not."

"For the record, I went to see Anne at her hotel and waited for her to return from a business dinner. I didn't find out until then that Von Zandt owned Lynstrade Manor. And my wife didn't know that Von Zandt was the subject of our investigation until after that night."

McMurty met Reid's eyes. "The only way to play this now is to make it clear that you and your wife have split up. The general public doesn't know Von Zandt is under investigation, but if the operation is successful, it will eventually become public knowledge. When that happens, Von Zandt's lawyers are going to try to scrape up whatever filth they can and dish it up to the press and the courts to get him off."

Shreve nodded. "And for God's sake, you've got to stay completely away from the woman. The break has to be clean. No calls, no visits, nothing."

Reid didn't bother to respond.

McMurty said, "If she's really only there to design his gardens, Terrence, there's no reason to think she's in danger. If she's there because there's something between her and Von Zandt, there's no reason to think she's in danger, either."

Reid swallowed. "There's nothing like that between them."

McMurty nodded. "So, to finish my thought on this, the only way she's in danger is if Von Zandt thinks you're using her to get to him."

"Which I'm not."

"Good, because if you put her in there as a plant, the rings Von Zandt's lawyers will be able to run around us will choke us till our eyes pop out."

"Don't be absurd. I'd never risk her safety like that."

McMurty raised his eyebrows, a glimmer of amusement in his eyes.

"Or the integrity of the investigation." Reid added, as the afterthought it was.

Shreve's mobile rang and he got up, walking to the other side of the room to take the call.

McMurty met Reid's eyes, and spoke in a low voice, a voice that held a hint of compassion and more than a hint of pity.

"Just let her go, lad."

# Chapter 65

ANNE WORKED until the light got too dim outside and the laborers were packing up to leave. Walter had visited multiple times during the day to watch the progress of the garden, displaying the book he'd bought about Russell Page. He'd eagerly discussed what he'd learned about the garden designer, and Anne had allowed him to tag along while he talked. He was certainly a quick study, and astutely identified the garden principles she and Jonas were using to adhere to Page's original garden plan.

She'd been relieved when finally, Jonas took Walter away to discuss some of the financial details of the project. As much as she enjoyed talking about the gardens, having an enthusiastic amateur dogging her heels slowed down her work.

Back in her room, she decided to take a bath, eat whatever they sent up on a tray for her, and go right to bed. Tomorrow she would try to do what Darby had outlined. Tonight she needed sleep. And food. She touched two fingers to her abdomen, gently pushing it in. Despite the emotional upheaval she'd gone through, the baby was making her hungry. She smiled to herself thinking of the little human being growing inside of her, making its demands known already.

She bathed, put on a robe and slippers and waited for her dinner tray to come. When she answered the knock on her door, however, it was not dinner but a young maid carrying an assortment of evening gowns. Anne's eyes widened in astonishment. The Von Zandts must keep extra clothes here for unprepared guests. Full service hosts.

Chattering an explanation that Anne should choose which she wanted to wear and then join the others at dinner, the maid put the dresses in the closet. The girl wanted to help her dress, but Anne, knowing putting on the wire would be impossible with the maid there, assured her that her help wasn't necessary, all but pushed the girl out the door.

Finally alone, Anne blew out a breath. Damn. All she wanted to do was to curl up and sleep and hope for no dreams—or at least no more dreams of Terrence leaving her. She sighed and went to the closet to examine the selections.

All of the dresses were Anne's size and appeared new, or at least in excellent condition. She selected one of the gowns, opting for an emerald green dress because it had the highest neckline, remembering Terrence's objections about business dinner wear. She put the wire back on, trying to make sure she did it exactly as she had been shown.

Even after her efforts determinedly tugging at the neckline, the dress still showed too much cleavage. Her pregnancy wasn't showing around her waist yet, but it was certainly making her breasts swell. She would have to go shopping for her own dresses to get some that were more modest if she was going to be staying here long. It wouldn't do if Terrence decided to come back to her and then left again because he thought she was being too . . . whatever. For a man who liked sex so much, he was a bit of a prude about things like this.

She turned to examine herself on all sides in the mirror, but there was no sign of the wire. No one would notice anything, even if they looked carefully.

Anne arranged her hair and make-up, took a deep breath, pasted a smile on her face, and went downstairs.

* * * * *

There was no one but Walter in the drawing room when she got downstairs. He had a drink in his hand and looked at her with frank appreciation.

"You look amazing, Anne."

"Thank you. I appreciate the use of the dress—and for the loan of the others, though I do intend to go shopping as soon as I can. I have to say, your home is certainly well prepared for unprepared guests." She looked around the elegantly appointed drawing room with its coldly formal furnishings and modern art, then took a breath. No sign of any other guests. Her skin began to prickle. This better not be what it felt like. "Walter, isn't Elisa coming down to dinner?"

He gave a small, sad smile. "Unfortunately, she was called away. Back to Germany."

"So suddenly? I hope it's nothing serious."

"Not at all."

"That's good. Will she be back soon?"

He shrugged. "I doubt it. She prefers Germany."

Anne eyed him, trying to figure out the situation. She was willing to help gather information for Terrence's investigation, but she needed to make sure Von Zandt didn't get the idea that she was available for anything else. She decided that the best way to handle things was to come right out and tell him her misgivings.

"Walter, you've been very kind, but I'm not comfortable staying here alone with you. I don't think it looks right for us to be staying in the same house by ourselves. I'll move back to the hotel. I'm sure the reporters have lost interest by now."

"No, no, please don't do that. And don't worry. When this sudden trip of Elisa's came up, I anticipated the need to make sure that the situation, however innocent, was not open to misinterpretation. So I spoke to Jonas this afternoon after you two finished your work and got him to agree to move here from the hotel. He's just settling into his rooms and will be down soon. My two sons, Henry and Frederick, will be here as well as a friend of mine, Moira Ramsey. I believe you may have met Moira before. She mentioned that she attended your wedding celebration at Dunbaryn."

A huge wave of relief washed over Anne. If he'd brought his mistress, he definitely did not have any designs on her.

"That makes me feel much better. I'm probably being overly cautious, but we both know how people can talk and things can get blown out of proportion. And right now, the press seems to have me in their sights."

Von Zandt nodded. "Indeed. This morning's story was reprehensible. I hope Lord Reid isn't still as displeased as he was last night."

"I'm afraid he is." Actually, Anne didn't know how Terrence felt, but Darby had said Anne needed to make sure Von Zandt thought that she and Terrence were not speaking. She'd tried to figure out if that meant that Terrence wasn't really still mad at her. Surely, he couldn't be as mad as before, or he wouldn't have wanted her to help with the investigation. Or maybe he'd just decided that his investigation was more important than what was going on between them. That was a depressing thought.

"And, forgive me, but the other gentleman? The artist?"

Anne's face burned. "I think he returned to California. Do you mind if we don't discuss that?"

"Of course, I'm sorry. We'll just enjoy the evening."

She decided to start a new subject for conversation. "It will be nice to see Moira again. I hope she's doing well." Anne couldn't actually remember having met the girl at the reception for Terrence and her wedding. She would have been, what, sixteen? There had been so many people at the reception and she'd known almost no one, so the names and faces were a blur. The only face she'd really cared about at that time was Terrence's.

"Yes." Von Zandt seemed uninterested in the topic of his mistress. Anne wondered how Elisa felt about her husband substituting the girl for her in her own house as soon as she left, and felt sorry for Elisa. Anne assumed the woman didn't have much say in what her husband did in that regard—or in any regard, for that matter.

Jonas entered just then, dressed in a tuxedo. He must have come to Scotland better prepared than she had. Of course, she had had the black dress. Shortly afterwards, Henry and Frederick Von Zandt joined them, followed by Moira, a very pretty young woman. Emphasis on the word young. Again Anne found herself wondering how this all worked. Did the sons not care that their father had another woman so openly? And wasn't Henry married? Where was his wife?

Moira eyed Anne warily, and only approached her after Von Zandt nodded at her, clearly urging her on.

"Lady Anne, I'm not sure you remember me . . ."

"Of course, Moira. Call me Anne, please. It's so nice to see you again. I was sorry to hear about your father."

"My stepfather, but thank you. Lord Reid was the one who notified us about it."

"Yes, he told me. How is your mother doing?"

"She's all right, I guess. I mean, it was a shock, but she'll be okay. My brother is there with her."

"I'm sure that's a comfort to her."

"I guess so." Moira looked around for Walter, and when her eyes found him talking to Jonas, she spoke quietly to Anne. "I saw the news. I hope things are all right between you and Lord Reid."

"Thank you."

"Walter said the reporters were bothering you. Are you and Lord Reid . . .?"

"It was a misunderstanding." Anne tried to think how to explain the mess she was in without telling too much. "But my husband reacted as most would, I suppose." She smiled with a confidence she was far from feeling. "He just needs time to calm down." This sounded so reasonable, she was almost convincing herself, although she knew she was not factoring in the impact of her pregnancy.

Moira screwed up her face and bit at a hangnail. "But you still love him? You want to stay married to him?"

"Absolutely."

"Walter thinks you're beautiful, you know."

"That's nice of him." Anne realized Moira was trying to assess whether Anne was a rival and decided to try to reassure her. "I'm sure he thinks you are even more so."

"He says you're the kind of woman men kill for."

Anne was momentarily speechless. Finally, she managed to respond. "That's ridiculous."

Their strange conversation was blessedly interrupted by the announcement of dinner.

\* \* \* \* \*

Reid was back in his flat before eleven. He counted himself lucky to have escaped the dinner party at the Spencer-Burkes at a decent hour. Going anywhere after the news stories today about Anne and him was difficult. Even the office had been hard, but going to a formal dinner party was excruciating. No one had been crass enough to mention seeing the photos and stories of him coming upon his wife in a tête-à-tête with her lover, but there was no question that it was foremost in everyone's mind.

Nevertheless, he needed to make these social appearances—for his family and for his work—and he refused to hide out as if he had something to be ashamed of. He was used to going out several nights a week for various obligatory occasions, and had kept it up even through these last two rough years. He always arrived at the end of the pre-dinner drinks and left as soon after coffee as he could. People sometimes asked him coy questions about his absent wife which he was generally able to deflect, but tonight no one had been stupid enough to try that.

Tonight's appearance was meant to send the message that he and Anne were over, and he thought he'd done a good job of making it clear without saying a derogatory word against her. He made a point of talking to the available women present, although it had been difficult.

He wondered what it would be like to have a wife to go with to these things. Maybe they would actually be fun. There'd be someone to discuss things with beforehand, smile across the table at, and go home with where they could talk over the night before falling into bed together. He'd found himself studying the couples at dinner, wondering what secrets they knew that let them successfully make a life together. Some touched hands as they stood together, but many didn't touch at all, only tying themselves together as if with invisible string. Some finished each other's sentences, as if they'd practiced their conversations ahead of time. Some listened to their spouses respectfully, even reverentially, while others laughed fondly or teased.

All day, ever since he'd learned of Anne's move to the Von Zandt estate, he'd hoped for news of her. He even thought she might call him again, but she hadn't. Despite what McMurty had said, he would take her call. But she probably thought, based on her experience from their other separations, and from last night as well, that he wouldn't answer her calls or talk to her. He'd been a hard man on that front, and now he was paying for it.

Surely she was fine. Von Zandt wouldn't be crazy enough to hurt Anne. At least not unless he was desperate, and there was no sign of that yet. No, Reid decided, he'd just have to sit tight and hope to get news.

He thought back to the call he'd gotten earlier that day from the decorator. He knew the news stories had prompted the call. Of course the woman would be concerned that, with Reid's marriage in tatters, her commission was no longer in play, or that he wouldn't be willing to keep paying for the work she was doing. He'd been annoyed, but, for reasons he could not even articulate to himself, he'd instructed her to go forward. To be safe though, and consistent with the instructions that he make it clear that he and Anne were finished, he said, "We'll be putting the house on the market but I want you to make all the changes my wife outlined. We'll get a better price if it's presented at its best."

The decorator had murmured her acquiescence, and he'd instructed her to get back to him when she'd finished.

He had no idea what he would do at that point, but he didn't have to think about it yet. What he was going to do with a house he had planned for Anne when he didn't have Anne anymore, he didn't know. He could not live in it without her. It would always feel empty without her. He looked around his flat. Even this blasted place felt empty without her, and she'd never even really lived here.

Maybe it was really just him that felt empty. And maybe he'd feel empty wherever he was.

He checked his messages. There was one from MacTavish getting back to him on some of the financial institutions Stirling had identified, and one from Harry saying he'd talked with MacTavish and was taking care of things, but there was nothing from or about Anne. He wanted to call her, but his instructions had been clear. No calls. But even if he called, what would he say?

He undressed, taking off the pleated white shirt, and laid the black pearl cuff links and studs on his dresser. Briefly, he wondered if he should call Grainger and see if the other man had heard from her. If he didn't hear from Anne soon, as humiliating as it was, he'd check with Grainger. Maybe Grainger could convince Anne to get out of Von Zandt's house.

# SATURDAY, APRIL 18

THE FIRST CUT

# Chapter 66

THE NEXT MORNING, Anne and Jonas were out on the property directing the workmen hired to do the heavy work. as well as the regular gardening staff.

She'd had the usual bout of morning sickness, but managed to get herself together and after some tea and toast, felt ready to work. She'd packed warm clothes and plenty of rain resistant gear, and that morning had piled on everything she could find to keep herself warm. The bitter spring Scottish wind seemed to penetrate clothing and flesh and go straight through to her bones. Luckily, when she got engrossed in her work, she forgot any discomfort from the weather. The project was challenging, but their experience at the prior Russell Page garden proved invaluable in unraveling the complexities of the design.

She'd managed to stop herself from calling Terrence yesterday or this morning, although it had not been easy. Darby had said not to use her cell phone, and Anne couldn't figure out what to do to get an outside line on the house phones. Even if Terrence had wanted to call her, he probably couldn't since he wouldn't want to interfere with what she was supposed to be doing at Lynstrade Manor. She needed to use restraint, as well. Soon they would be able to talk things over and she could explain about Andrew.

Noon came before she realized it. Walter had come out once again that morning to talk to her and watch the work, then again when the workmen had their tea break. She and Jonas had been given the use of an old granary conveniently located at the far side of the back garden to use as a working office, a place to lay out the plans and coordinate the work. Walter had sat with her there, having tea and asking questions about the design concept. He was funny and

315

charming, and she found herself laughing and intrigued. He treated them as guests rather than simply as contractors who had come to do a job. He'd left after the break, his eyes sparkling, and told her he would see her and Jonas at luncheon at one o'clock. She felt half-guilty when she thought about what she was doing to spy on him.

She sensed the potential danger in him that Terrence had told her about, but it seemed far away. Darby had assured her that Von Zandt was only a money man. That didn't change the fact that if what Darby said was true, the man was helping to perpetuate horrible evil, but she found it hard to believe. Surely Darby was wrong. Surely if Walter was as bad as Darby implied, he'd be behind bars already. And surely, if Walter was that evil, Terrence would not have asked Anne to move into his house to spy on him.

At luncheon, they ate the hearty fare Von Zandt's cook provided in a dining room medieval in architectural design, but on a sleek, modern table that was characteristic of Walter Von Zandt's style of furnishings. The contrast in styles was surprisingly effective, making Anne feel like she'd fallen into an issue of Architectural Digest magazine.

She was grateful that her stomach was stronger, because she was starving. The combination of exercise, fresh air, and being pregnant was a huge appetite enhancer, and she was happy they hadn't been given cold sandwiches, but rather some kind of delicious lamb stew. Henry Von Zandt had gone back to Glasgow, but Frederick remained, a quiet, almost skulking presence who hovered around the edges of the conversation. He rarely spoke, but when he did, it was generally only a few words, and most of those to Moira or his father.

As they ate, Anne could see through the large windows in the dining room that heavy gray clouds had crowded out the morning's sunshine. A sharp crack of thunder accompanied the lightning flashing in the suddenly darkening sky. The subsequent downpour did not bode well for the afternoon's outdoor work, but maybe now she'd be able to locate her host's office, or wherever it was that he likely kept the information Darby had specified.

When they'd finished eating, Von Zandt stood up from the table, smiling at Anne. He'd seated her next to him and spent the meal regaling her with stories of how he built his company when he was just a young man from the money he'd earned from gambling on horses.

"Allow me to make the library available for you and Jonas to work this afternoon. I assume that there are things you can do inside—planning and perhaps communications with suppliers and workmen? It will be more comfortable than forging your way through the rain to the granary."

Thus, Anne found herself in the library working on re-configuring some of the design diagrams and organizing plant orders while Jonas addressed other aspects of the project. She noticed Von Zandt going into his office which, she had learned, adjoined the library, followed by Frederick. That was, she guessed, where he would keep anything about his accounts or his activities. She was wearing the wire underneath her layers of clothes, and when she was alone she would relay the information about the office location to Darby. This one-way wire thing was strange. She could talk to Terrence's people, but they couldn't talk to her, and there was no way for her to tell if anyone heard her. She guessed that made sense because she couldn't exactly walk around with an earpiece and expect people not to notice.

What made everything more difficult was that Anne didn't quite understand what she was looking for. Darby's instructions had been so vague. If she could find a way to get into the nearby village later this week, she'd let Darby know via the wire where to meet her so that she could get more guidance.

Meanwhile, she'd just have to muddle through as well as she could. She checked her work email account and sent her mother and sisters each a quick message. Then she sent another one to Andrew letting him know she was fine. She thought of sending one to Terrence, but she doubted that would do any good. She'd already told him she hadn't invited Andrew, and if he chose not to believe her, that was his problem. So if he was interested in how she and the baby were doing, he could just ask Darby.

The thought of Darby brought Anne back to what she was supposed to be doing. She chewed on her pencil while she thought about exactly how to get the information she needed. Moira might be the best source. Certainly she would be a better prospect than the taciturn Frederick.

Almost as if she'd conjured Moira up, the girl appeared at the doorway of the library. Anne smiled, and motioned for her to come in, and turned her computer screen slightly in Moira's direction.

"Would you like to see what we're doing with the garden?"

"Why should I care? It's not my house."

"No reason. But it is a lovely garden. If you're interested, I can explain what the plan is—how we're bringing back the original vision of the garden design. If you're not doing anything else, that is. I don't mean to interrupt if you have other plans."

"I don't have anything I need to do right now. I'm taking classes part-time, but I'm caught up with my coursework."

"What are you studying?"

"IT."

Anne looked at her. "IT?"

"Information technology."

"Any particular area?"

"Information security. You know, on computers."

"Really?"

"What did you think I'd be studying? Cooking? Fashion?"

"I really hadn't thought. I would think information technology would be more useful than cooking or fashion—though there's nothing wrong with either of those. But I think what you've chosen is certainly more marketable."

Moira nodded, appeased. "I think so, too. And it's fun. You can do it anywhere. Walter likes me to go with him when he travels, so I need something I can work on wherever we are." She gave a typically teenage expression of exasperation. "He thinks I'm just playing computer games—that I'm just killing time, but I'm not. I'm really good at it."

Anne sighed. "I'm not. In fact, I'm just about ready to throw my laptop through the window."

"What's wrong?"

"I'm not really sure anything's wrong. It's probably me. Or maybe the software."

"What software?"

"It's for garden design. It's supposed to be the best, but for me, at least, it's clumsy to work with. I wish someone would design one that was friendlier to people like me whose talent doesn't lie in the technology, but who need desperately what the software is supposed to do."

Moira's face perked up with interest, and she flopped into a chair beside Anne where she could see the screen. "What do you mean, clumsy?"

"I'll show you." Anne explained the issues she was having, demonstrating on the program as she talked. "Generally, it works fine, but for these more tricky elements, it's a pain."

Moira nodded, then slid the laptop over to position it in front of her. She played with the program for a while, asking questions as she went. "Give me a moment." Not ten minutes later, Moira, wearing a self-satisfied smile, turned the computer screen back to Anne. "User error."

Anne frowned. "No way."

"Way. See here." Moira walked Anne through what she'd been doing wrong.

"You're right." Suddenly, the design clumsiness was gone; Anne realized she just hadn't been doing some of the steps correctly. Counterintuitive, some of this techno-geek stuff. "That's amazing. Thank you so much. This will be such a help."

"No problem." Moira tried to cover her pride with nonchalance. "Just let me know if you have any other problems with it."

"I will. I definitely will."

Moira lowered her voice to almost a whisper. "I was wondering if I could talk to you about something."

"Of course. What is it?"

"It's kind of personal, but I don't have anyone really I can talk to about things like this. My mum's hopeless and my Aunt Glynnis, well, she's in a worse position than me."

Anne tried to think where this was going, but she didn't have a clue. "Things like what?"

"Men."

Anne had to swallow a laugh. "I'm not sure I'm doing any better on that front right now. But I'm happy to help if I can."

"I think Walter is getting tired of me." Moira said, not making eye contact. "He treats me like I'm a servant or something. He tells me what we're doing, where we're going, but never asks if that's what I want. I mean, I want to go, but it would be nice to be asked, like he cared what I want, like I matter."

"I'm sure you matter."

"Lord Reid told me you choose the places you two go for vacation. That he goes wherever you want to go. I thought that was so romantic."

Anne almost swallowed her tongue. It was romantic, albeit completely untrue, and she wondered why he'd said such a thing to Moira. Besides their honeymoon, Terrence and she had never been on vacation together. But he must have had some reason for saying it, so she responded with just a smile.

Moira pressed her. "So how do you do it? Make him care about you like that?"

Anne couldn't think of an answer, the image flashing in her mind of how he'd looked at her at the hotel when he'd found her with Andrew, how he'd asked if she'd already had Andrew up in her bed, how he'd told her he was done with her.

She decided to just be honest. "I'm not sure he still does."

"He does. He wouldn't get so jealous if he didn't care. Walter would just be relieved if some handsome artist took me off his hands."

"I'm sure that's not true."

"I don't know what I'd do if he didn't want me anymore."

"Moira, a woman's life is important with or without a particular man."

"Maybe your life. Not mine." Moira gave a little-girl-lost smile and went over to knock on Walter's office door.

Anne heard a voice call out, then Moira opened the door and went in, closing the door behind her.

# Chapter 67

STANDING NEAR the main lily pond, Anne directed the workmen where to plant the various bushes and trees that had been delivered earlier that week. One part of her mind was on what she was doing, but the other part was pondering how to get into Walter's office and what she could do there if she did. If he kept everything electronically, she assumed it was password protected. Maybe he had hard copies of some of his records in the office, though. She could certainly look for those if she could just find an opportunity to get into his office when no one was around.

The lock was a problem. Walter seemed to be careful to keep the door to the office locked when he wasn't there. She decided to get herself invited inside the office so she could at least look around. That way she could plan how best to spend her time if and when she finally got the chance to get in there alone. Did he use a simple password like most of the rest of the world? She doubted it. Not if he was really involved with the things Terrence and Darby said. If he were that kind of a man, he wouldn't use a password that was the name of his wife or girlfriend, or his dog—if he'd had one. If the password was something tricky, and if she couldn't find it written down somewhere, she'd be out of luck.

If she couldn't find what she was looking for in Walter's office, she'd have to search the rest of the house. Where else would Walter keep incriminating evidence? It would have to be somewhere he considered safe. His bedroom? She tried to think whether he would be likely to keep a private stash of papers in his bedroom. Maybe. But Walter's bedroom was one room she definitely did not intend to go into unless she knew for sure that Walter was out of the house.

This spying was much harder than Darby made it out to be. So far no one at Lynstrade Manor was talking about secret accounts or terrorists, and she certainly never saw any confidential looking papers laying around. Anne couldn't think of anything to do to get the information they wanted other than getting access to Walter's computer or looking in his desk. She pressed her finger to her lips as she thought, wondering what Terrence would do if he were here. The realization came to her that she didn't actually know very much about what her husband did, or how he did it. How much did her husband know about what she did? Probably not much more than she did about his work.

Suddenly, Anne's attention was caught by something on the other side of the pond. She uttered a distressed cry and ran toward one of the workmen, stopping him just before he started trimming the roots of a rare variety of Japanese maple so he could stuff it into a too-small hole.

* * * * *

Anne got her chance to see Walter's office sooner than she'd thought. After dinner that night, he offered to take her on a tour of the house. Moira moved as if to join them, but he held up a staying hand.

"Moira, why don't you go call your mother and see how she's doing." It was an order, not a question.

The defiant look on Moira's face surprised Anne. She hadn't thought Moira capable of holding her own against Walter. "I called her this morning. Aunt Glynnis is staying there with her since Henry is here this weekend."

Anne wondered what Henry Von Zandt had to do with Moira's aunt.

The look Walter sent the girl was cold enough to freeze blood. "You're behaving like a spoiled child. Do as I told you. I'm going to show Lady Anne the house and the artwork. You've seen it all before and it bores you, as you've told me numerous times."

Anne tried to intervene. "I wouldn't mind if Moira came with us. She'll give another perspective."

Walter placed both hands on the table as if trying to contain his temper, but his eyes didn't leave the girl. "Moira has other things to do."

The unspoken threat in the man's voice sent a ripple of fear through Anne. Evil, she thought, and she wondered if Walter Von Zandt was really just a money man.

Moira's bottom lip went out in a pout, but she drew herself up and left the room, attempting a show of dignity.

Walter metamorphosed back into his role of charming gentleman of the manor, but his display of anger had scared Anne. This was unmistakably a man who could be dangerous. Until now, she realized, she hadn't really believed it.

Calling up every last scrap of acting ability she could muster, Anne acted her role of appreciative guest while he led her through the rooms of the first floor, expounding on the paintings and sculptures and the artists who'd created them. She murmured her admiration at the quality of the artwork, surprising not just Walter, but herself, with the knowledge she'd gained about art from having been a part of Andrew Grainger's life. He professed to be impressed by her familiarity with many of the artists, especially the American ones, some of whom she'd met with Andrew.

When they came to his office, Walter unlocked it and ushered her inside. This was what she'd been hoping for earlier, but now she just wanted to get away from him. She knew she couldn't do this much longer, no matter how much Terrence needed her help. She just didn't know what she was doing, and she was scared in a way she had never been before.

Walter didn't seem to notice her unease. "Please sit down."

Anne sat on a dark leather sofa and looked around, trying to memorize where everything was situated. For the time being, she was here, and as long as she was here, she might as well go on as she'd planned.

He went over to an intriguing drinks table that was a stunning, and no doubt expensive, variation on the trite world globe version. Walter Von Zandt's globe was composed of interlocking steel rings on which continents and islands floated. Through the network of the world, a mirrored surface shimmered like molten silver, and suspended in the silver sat an array of crystal decanters whose contents shimmered like the sunset.

"Would you like a cognac or would you prefer something else?"

She shook her head and smiled. "Nothing, thank you, but you go ahead."

"You do drink, don't you?" His voice was teasing, and he winked at her. "Beautiful women and wine go together like music and dancing."

She wanted to gag at the unoriginal remark, but she gave a little smile, trying to think of some reason, besides being pregnant, of course, for not drinking. "Actually, I'm not much of a drinker. It goes right to my head."

He laughed. "Then by all means, have a drink."

She kept her smile steady. "No, thank you."

Walter lifted a hand, indicating surrender. He opened the globe with a slight flourish, and poured himself a cognac. He sat on the sofa, far enough away from her so that she would not feel crowded, but close enough so that they could easily converse. Swirling the golden liquid around the high sides of the delicate glass, he fixed his gaze on her.

"I assume your husband has spoken of me to you." His eyes studied her intensely.

Ripples of panic skittered through Anne's chest. She willed her heart to slow down, then managed to answer in a surprisingly normal voice.

"Yes, he did. Briefly, that first night we had dinner."

"I suppose he told you he suspects some of my business dealings are . . . well, in word, illegal?"

She tried to look innocent but not stupid. "Terrence doesn't talk to me about his work. But he did say he'd rather I wasn't working for you."

"But still you agreed to do so." His words seemed to be asking something of her, something she couldn't quite understand.

"Yes. Jonas needed me, and I liked the challenge of your garden as well." Then she took a gamble, asking a question she wouldn't have asked if she were doing what she was doing. "So, are you involved in illegal activities?"

Von Zandt met her eyes. "Absolutely not."

She breathed out, nodded. "I didn't think so."

He moved a little closer to her on the sofa, not enough so that she could object, but enough to make her uneasy. "So, is it your habit not to honor your husband's wishes?" His oddly formal question wasn't accusatory, rather, it was as if he was trying to puzzle her out.

"This is my work. His work is his. I don't tell him how to run his career, and I don't let him tell me how to run mine. Do you think that's odd?"

He lifted his shoulders, smiled with a charm she no longer trusted. "Perhaps I'm old-fashioned. My wife does as I tell her."

Anne laughed, not so much because she thought he was funny, but in relief. He didn't know that Terrence had sent her here. "That is a bit old-fashioned, Walter. Or maybe it's just very male." Actually, Terrence and Walter had this in common, though she wasn't going to confide that to Walter. It was precisely her not doing what Terrence wanted that had caused the long estrangement between them. Old-fashioned as the attitude might be, it was certainly alive and well in the contemporary male population as far as she could tell.

"Your husband is just not the right man for you. With the right man, you'd want to do as he suggested." He laid one hand on the sofa between them and inched it slightly in her direction.

Anne felt her skin prickle all over, and her stomach contracted in an odd cramp. She concentrated on looking unruffled to keep her hand from going to her belly to reassure herself that the baby was okay. "I don't feel comfortable talking about my husband with you, Walter. Obviously, you two have some differences. That's between you and Terrence. But he is my husband, so let's talk about something else." She stood up and walked over to his desk. "Do you actually work here? Don't you have an office in Glasgow?"

Von Zandt leaned back against the sofa, obviously displeased both that she'd moved away from him, and that she'd changed the subject. But he recovered his equanimity quickly and a ghost of a smile teased his lips. "Yes, and in Frankfurt." He took a sip of his cognac, studying her as if he were a snake and she were a mouse he wanted very badly. "I work here sometimes when it is more convenient to me. Or at the flat in town."

"Where Moira lives."

He inclined his head in that way she'd thought elegant when she'd first met him. Now it made her feel like he was conserving energy for a deadly strike. "Temporarily."

Poor Moira. But she'd be better off without this asshole.

Anne decided right then that her own stay at Lynstrade Manor was going to be cut short. Very short. She'd use what time she had left here to get what she could for Terrence's investigation, then she was going to manufacture a reason to move back into the hotel.

Meanwhile, she needed more of an idea of what kind of thing she was looking for or she'd not be able to find anything, and this whole escapade would have been a waste of time.

"What is it that you do, exactly, Walter? I know you're in finance, but what does that mean?"

"To put it simply, I provide money for those who need capital. So I put investors together with various business enterprises. Capitalism at its best." He smiled and took another drink of his cognac, finishing the glass while not taking his eyes off of her.

Anne touched the top of the laptop computer on his desk. "Moira helped me with my computer earlier today. She's very good at it."

"Is she?" He sounded bored.

"Yes, she helped me with the software I use for garden design. She's very quick."

He looked as if he wanted to disagree, but thought she might not like it. He went over to the metal globe and poured himself another cognac. "I hope you don't mind me confiding in you." Instead of going back to the sofa, he came over to where she was standing.

Anne thought of her wire and was glad he'd come closer. Maybe he'd say something incriminating.

"Of course not, Walter."

"I've made some serious mistakes."

No kidding, Anne thought. "You mean in your business?"

He gave a small, sad shake of his head. "In my personal life. My marriage hasn't been happy. I should have done something earlier, not looked for comfort elsewhere. Especially with someone like Moira, someone so inappropriate."

Anne frowned, not able to think of anything to say. He knew she wasn't exactly in a position to judge people for extramarital affairs.

He continued, "I shouldn't have snapped at Moira tonight. I feel like a brute for doing that, and I sensed it upset you."

"It did a little." Perhaps she'd been overreacting. Perhaps he wasn't so bad. Perhaps she had just been witnessing the end of a love affair. No one was at their best at the end.

"I've come to a crossroads in my life. I wasn't quite honest with you about Elisa's departure. The sad news is that we're divorcing. We've grown apart, and it's for the best."

"That's too bad, Walter. I'm sorry for you both." He'd inched even closer, and she leaned away from him as far as she could without toppling over. One more step, buddy, she thought, and I'm going to knock your drink into you.

He seemed to realize he was intruding on her personal space, and leaned back against the desk, hitching one hip up to half-sit against it. "Getting involved with Moira was a mistake. She was wrong for me in many ways."

"Walter, I'm not sure I'm the right person for you to talk about this with."

He waved her concerns away. "I'm telling you all of this partly because I think we have a lot in common, and I feel like you may be in a similar position. I hope you feel like you can confide in me. I know your marriage hasn't been happy."

Anne decided that was enough. Even if she weren't wearing a wire that her sister-in-law was listening to, she wasn't discussing her personal life with Von Zandt.

"Walter, stop."

He straightened up from where he'd been leaning against the desk and was at her side before she realized it, taking her hand into his. She was so startled that at first she didn't know what to do. Then she snatched her hand away.

"Don't." She needed to head this off before it went any further.

He went on, as if she hadn't spoken. "I sense an affinity between us, and the potential for much more. But I don't want it to be sordid. I want to be clear to you about my feelings, and my intentions toward you."

"Walter, stop. I'm married."

"You've not been happy with him. If you had been, you'd never have been taken advantage of by that artist." She inwardly cringed at the thought that what Walter was saying was being recorded.

"Walter, I am very uncomfortable with this conversation. Please, let's talk about something else." He looked hurt, and if Anne hadn't known better, she might have felt sorry for him. She gave what she hoped was a placating smile. "Of course, we can be friends." At least until I get out of here, she thought.

He nodded. "Friends, then. For now. Perhaps later, when things are different . . ."

"Walter, please."

He smiled and held up his hands in surrender. "All right, friends."

But he would not give up so easily, she knew. She would have to be very careful.

# Chapter 68

REID POURED a substantial amount of whiskey into his glass, sat on the sofa in the lounge of his flat, and punched in Andrew Grainger's number on his mobile. By his calculations, it was about three in the afternoon in Bodega Bay. The first ring hadn't even ended before Andrew Grainger picked up.

"Terrence, what's wrong? Is Anne all right?"

Reid swallowed his pride along with the gulp of whiskey he'd taken. He hadn't expected the other man to answer so quickly. "Actually, I was going to ask whether you'd heard from her since you left."

There was a pause. "You haven't?"

"No."

Grainger said, "I haven't talked to her since that night you showed up at the hotel."

"Blast." Reid was torn between relief that she'd not contacted Grainger again, and worry that no one had heard from her, until Grainger spoke again.

"I did get an email from her earlier today. That would have been about noon her, and your, time."

Reid exhaled a breath of relief. "Was she all right?"

"I think so," Grainger said. "She said she was feeling better."

Reid wanted to ask more about what she'd written, but there was not only a line dividing their interests, but also Anne's privacy and what he was entitled to know, and he was afraid to cross it. He tried to think of something to say, how to ask for details without signaling his uneasiness about Von Zandt, or that the man was under investigation.

"Is there something I need to know? Is Anne in danger?" The

tension in Grainger's voice heightened Reid's own anxiety.

Reid made a decision he hoped he wouldn't regret. "The man whose house she's staying at, Walter Von Zandt, is the target of an investigation I'm heading. I've a suspicion he hired her firm to get to me."

There was a sharp intake of breath on the other end of the line. "Damn it, you should have warned her."

When Reid didn't answer, Grainger sighed. "You did, didn't you? And she wouldn't back down."

"Right." Reid swirled his glass, watching the butterscotch colors wash around the inside, thinking of how things had gotten to where his wife would email another man and not him. "But as you've heard from her, and all is well, I'll not worry."

"Do you want me to ask her to get in contact with you?" Grainger's voice didn't hide his reluctance.

"No need." Reid's innate good manners and humanity rose to the surface. "How are you doing? This has been a rough patch for you."

Grainger's voice suddenly sounded exhausted. "If you want to know the truth, it's been hell every day."

Shame washed over Reid, knowing his question had been pathetically inadequate. Losing a child to murder was a rough patch?

"I'm sorry, Andrew. I'm not good at expressing myself, but I can't imagine what you've been going through."

"No one can who hasn't lost a child."

"No."

Grainger cleared his throat. "Terrence?"

"Yes?"

"I just want you to know that if Anne is with me and the child's yours, you'll be welcome to visit in our home, or to have the child visit you when it's old enough. We won't do anything to restrict your access."

Reid's stomach clenched. "Thank you." He hung up the phone and drained his glass.

# SUNDAY, APRIL 19

# Chapter 69

ANNE HAD SEEN WHERE Von Zandt kept the key to his office. He hadn't even tried to hide it from her. Anne was beginning to think he wasn't the sharpest trowel in the shed where women were concerned. Or maybe he thought women were too dimwitted to worry about. When they'd left his office last night, he'd slipped the key under the foot of a statue in the hallway. At least Anne thought it was supposed to be a foot. The statue looked vaguely human, anyway.

Before she'd gone to bed, she'd reported the location of the key through her wire, wondering if the wire was even working. With no feedback, she couldn't tell. Today, after she spent a morning working on the gardens, she'd arranged to go into the village to have lunch and do some shopping for some personal items.

Walter was having his driver take her into town. She'd be dropped off, then when she wanted to be picked up, she could call the house and the driver would come back for her. Moira had told her there was a decent restaurant in town that had salads and quiche, so Anne had given Darby that name via the wire and asked her to meet with her there. She'd feel much better after they'd talked. At noon, Anne showered, changed into white wool pants and a matching sweater and jacket, and practically ran down the stairs to find the driver. The cramping she'd had the day before had stopped, and she actually felt good. No morning sickness, either.

Anne had another reason for wanting to be out of the house.

That morning when she'd woken, she'd been given a note from Jonas telling her that he'd been called away for a few days on a consultation for a problem with a project the firm was doing in France. With the workmen taking Sunday off, he thought she could handle things until he returned on Tuesday. As she'd never told him her misgivings about staying at Von Zandt's alone, and of course hadn't told him about what she was doing for Terrence's investigation, Jonas apparently hadn't thought twice about leaving her there alone. But at least Moira was still there.

In the restaurant, she toyed with her salad, trying to stretch the time out as she waited for Darby or someone else to come. She had some hope it would actually be Terrence who came, although she knew that, even if he had gotten over his anger at her, it would probably be taking too much of a chance. She looked around the prettily decorated room bordered with large pots of ferns, and listened idly to the classical music playing softly on the restaurant's sound system. She checked her watch again. It had been over an hour and a half. The waiter kept looking at her like he was hoping she'd leave so they could clean up her table. She'd finished her quiche ages ago and had already drank two pots of herbal tea.

Maybe Darby didn't think they really needed to meet. Surely that was it. Or perhaps the wire hadn't been working and Darby hadn't gotten the message. Or maybe it was too public a place. Perhaps she should have suggested they meet somewhere less visible, but she hadn't known the village and only had the name of the restaurant to suggest as a meeting place. But if Anne's wire wasn't working, surely they would have found some way to let her know.

Above all, she knew that Terrence wouldn't have asked her to stay there if he'd believed there was any danger. She wasn't so sure, but as long as she was there, she needed to keep trying to get Terrence the information he needed. Nothing she'd heard so far seemed even remotely to be what they were looking for. She had to try harder. She decided to stop in the ladies' room before she left the restaurant and try to contact Darby one more time, and then just go walking around the shops and try to find a public phone to call her sister-in-law, adhering to Darby's admonition not to use her cell.

After freshening up, she left the warm restaurant and walked slowly along the sidewalk, pausing to look into shop windows, all the while hoping Darby or someone else on Terrence's behalf would approach her. Several times, she caught a glimpse of a man watching her, and hoped he was someone Darby had sent to meet her. Deliberately, Anne had slowed her walk. However, despite her giving him several opportunities to catch up with her, he never did. Anne decided that it was her imagination, and that he was just following the same route as she was. She went back to her idea of calling Darby.

She spotted a phone and rushed over to it. Picking up the receiver, she dropped in coins, then dialed quickly. She listened, then frowned. No dial tone. She put the receiver down in disgust. Broken. Surely there must be another public telephone in this town. She would have to just keep trying until she found one.

But emerging from the phone booth, Anne bumped right into Moira.

# Chapter 70

DARBY ROLLED OVER in bed, listening to the sound of the shower, and smiled the smile of a woman who'd just been thoroughly shagged. After years of tagging along as the younger sister of his best friend, she'd finally gotten the delectable John Stirling to take her to bed.

She stretched out, feeling gloriously female. She'd used every muscle in her body, as well as every muscle in his body. It had been the most beautifully sensuous experience of her life. Sex with John Stirling was like being given every Christmas and birthday gift she'd ever wanted.

Getting him to agree had taken some effort, but she'd worked on it all week. Finally, she'd convinced him that she would treat it as he seemed to treat all of his relationships with women—wanting only the immediate pleasure with no emotional involvement. It had taken some heavy duty acting, because the truth was that she wanted him, and not just for a one night stand or a brief fling.

John didn't need to know yet that she would be different than his other women. She was determined that he would feel about her like . . . she hated to use the analogy, but like Terrence felt about that idiotic American woman. A momentary pang of guilt hit her as she remembered that she'd not bothered to listen to Anne's wire transmissions all weekend. She really should do that soon.

The shower continued to run. Darby didn't want John to think he needed to leave so she could work, but as long as he was in the shower anyway, she decided to quickly check the transmissions. She pulled her laptop out of her bag, powered it up, and hit the secure website to which the transmissions bounced. She listened, fast forwarding when the conversations were boring or routine, which was most of the time. Then she hit on a transmission from Anne in which she went on about a key to Von Zandt's office, and asked Darby to meet her in the village for lunch so that they could talk. Anne was talking about not feeling safe and wanting to give up and move back to the hotel.

As much as Darby didn't want to, she knew she'd better meet with Anne, even if it was just to convince the bitch to stay put. Darby looked at her watch. Only ten. She could get to the village easily by luncheon. John would probably be leaving soon anyway to return to Aberdeen. She needed to make sure they were together again soon. This was not a man you could leave unattended and expect that he would ignore other women.

The absence of sound finally hit her consciousness. He'd turned off the shower.

Quickly, she shut the computer, not taking the time to shut it down, and stuffed it back into her bag.

Looking up, she saw a toweled and deliciously sexy John Stirling emerge from the bathroom.

He smiled. "You're awake then."

"Aye. You left me."

"I needed to shower. I should be on my way." He sat down on the edge of the bed and tousled her hair. "I'm glad you talked with your parents."

"Me, too." She hadn't done anything of the sort, but she'd told him what he'd wanted to hear, and he seemed pleased she'd taken his advice. Men always liked it when you took their advice.

"And you feel better, don't you?"

"Mmm, much better." She pulled him to her, and he kissed her. "This was fun." She kept her voice light, wanting him to think she thought of it as casually as he did.

"You're not just Terrence's little sister anymore. All grown up." He ran his fingers down her body.

Her hands were as just as direct on his body, showing him that she wanted him right then, with no preliminaries. He took off the towel, and obliged her.

They had luncheon in bed, courtesy of room service. She was missing her meeting with Anne, but there was no way Darby was going to give up the opportunity to spend more time with the man she'd been chasing for years, now that she had finally had his attention.

Just after one o'clock that afternoon, he got out of bed. "Now I've really got to get on my way, girl."

"Back to Aberdeen?"

"Aye, for a while, then I'll be out of the country for a time."

She lay back, pulling the sheet up over her naked breasts. She tried to think of how to ask without seeming to cross the line of casual freedom he seemed to require.

"Oh? Where're you traveling?" She didn't let her voice sound too interested.

"I've some business in Greece. I'm taking my yacht and combining business with a bit of a pleasure trip."

"You're taking a holiday?" Darby thought quickly about how she could rearrange her schedule to go with him. She'd find a way; she just needed him to ask her. "When?"

"Two weeks from now. I've business to finish up so that I'm free to go."

"Greece is nice this time of year. A bit crowded with tourists."

"A bit."

She watched him as he dressed. "Your business is in Greece?"

"Aye. In Athens." He snapped on his watch.

"Surely you're not taking your hols in Athens? Greece is lovely, but Athens is a dreadful city this time of year—full of tourists and filthy with pollution."

"Just a day or two in the city, then I'll be off to one of the more private islands there." He was putting some things in an expensive but worn leather carryall. "You probably need to get going, as well? You must have things that have to be seen to, even on Sunday. From what Reid says, the investigation is a bit stretched."

She reached over to the floor to pick up her panties. "I should be finished here soon—or at least within a week or two. I'm not sure how long I can be spared from our Paris office, but I have some time off coming. In case you'd like company on your cruise." She made sure her voice showed that she didn't care one way or the other.

"That's a lovely offer, Darby girl, but I have company lined up already."

Darby felt like she'd been kicked in the gut with a steel-toed boot. Even though she'd told him this was to be a one-off, she'd done so just to get past his reluctance to do anything that would jeopardize his friendship with Terrence. She'd told him that she just was in the mood for sex, sex with no strings. She knew that he wouldn't have slept with his best friend's sister if he'd thought there would be complications.

Keeping up the pretense, but needing to know, she asked, "Oh, one of your young lovelies?"

"A woman from London. A barrister." He shook his head, smiling at her with what seemed to be admiration. "You're uncanny easy to be with. Having sex with a woman who thinks about it like most men do is refreshing. No strings, no games, no need for any kind of romance."

He clearly meant what he was saying to be a compliment, but Darby knew that it also meant that he had no thought that this had been anything more than a night of casual shagging—with no need to even buy her drinks or dinner. She wondered about the woman he was taking on the cruise to the Grecian Isles. Undoubtedly, that woman was more demanding, and she'd been invited on a cruise. Maybe Darby had made things too easy for him.

But it was too late now to tell him that she was like other women, that she wanted romance, and in particular, that she wanted him. So she smiled back. "I've known you all my life. I've no illusions about you. But I did think that you might be good in bed. I just wanted to see if you were."

"Did I meet your expectations?"

"You were tolerable." She gave an exaggerated yawn.

John's eyes twinkled. He knew he was good. "You're nothing like your brother, that's for certain. He doesn't know the meaning of casual sex. I tell him he doesn't know what he's missing."

"And look where it's gotten Mr. Perfect." Darby was barely able to keep the bitter edge out of her voice. "A wreck of a marriage and likely of a career, as well. He's got a blind spot as big as the bloody moon when it comes to her."

He raised his eyebrows. "You really think so? I'm not sure I believe those news stories. And Terrence's bosses must understand that a man can't tell his wife what to do."

"She's a whore."

"Darby, don't talk like that. There's no way you can know what's going on between them."

"She was in that hotel with her old lover, wasn't she? How else do you explain it? I don't see much difference between her and a whore, except that she limits her services to wealthy men. Terrence, then the artist. No coincidence that they're both rich. It's just a matter of time until it's someone else."

"You'd better never say these kinds of things to your brother about her."

Darby jerked her head in a defiant gesture. "He knows how I feel."

John crouched down beside the bed and took her face in his hands. "Darby girl, you'll be making a terrible mistake if you say that kind of thing to him. I've told you. He's not like you and me. This kind of thing," he motioned to the bed and her nakedness, "means something to him. It's not just fun and games for him. He's deadly serious about it—and about Anne. No matter what he says, or how often they split up, she's all there is for him."

Darby couldn't think of any way she could ever change the direction of what had happened between her and John Stirling. She wouldn't ever be able to tell him that she wanted him to think about her like Terrence thought about Anne. It was too late now.

She forced herself to smile. "You're right." Darby took his hands from her face. "Unless you have time to do it again, I guess I'll get dressed and get to work."

He gave a playful smile and tapped his watch. "It would have to be quick."

"Quick's good. I have things to do, as well." She pulled the sheet off of her body and started to rise. He pulled her to him, turned her around, opened his trousers, slipped on protection, and bent her over the bed.

Afterwards, on his way out the door, he turned and looked back at her. "I may be back next month, if you're not doing anything."

Darby shrugged. "We'll see."

"It's been fun. You're all grown up, Darby girl."

"Yes." The door shut behind him, and a cavern of emptiness engulfed her.

# Chapter 71

AFTER SWALLOWING HER SURPRISE, Anne took a deep breath, trying to control the hammering of her heart. Her first fear, that the girl had been sent to spy on her, was at least partially relieved when Moira announced that she and Frederick had been sent in place of Walter's driver to pick her up as they'd been going into town anyway. How long had they been watching her? Anne tried to appear pleased, while frantically reviewing what they might have seen. She'd had lunch alone, then tried to make a phone call. Nothing to worry about.

She decided not to mention, let alone try to explain, the aborted phone call. After all, she wasn't a prisoner. "I just finished lunch, and was going to visit the shops. I need to buy some clothes that are more suitable for dinners and things like that. I don't want to keeping borrowing dresses."

"Great," Moira said. "I'll come along. I love shopping, although I'm fairly certain this isn't a good town to do it in."

While they shopped, Anne kept her eye out for anyone who might have been trying to get into contact with her, but saw no one. Unfortunately, Moira turned out to be right about the town's shopping potential. There was only one actual dress shop in town. Moira wrinkled her nose when they went in, and after looking around, Anne was forced to agree with her.

The shop had nothing appropriate for dinner parties, not even something that rose to the level of the ugly business dinner dress that Terrence had specified. In fact, she'd never seen such a collection of drab dresses in her life. Surely Terrence wouldn't want her to wear something like this, even if the alternative was one of the gowns the Von Zandts were loaning her.

Moira fingered one of the shop's offerings and wrinkled her nose. In a voice that was trying too hard to be casual, the girl said, "Walter's divorcing Elisa. I heard him talking to his lawyer on the telephone." She beamed at Anne, with a shy hopefulness that broke Anne's heart. "I think that's a good sign for me. Maybe the gardens will be mine after all."

Anne managed a small smile that wanted to be a grimace. "Good news, then." Apparently Walter hadn't broken the news yet to Moira about ending their relationship—if he'd even been serious about that. It may have just been a ploy to get Anne to take his advances seriously. She was beginning to feel like she'd fallen headfirst into a soap opera or maybe some weird reality show.

Moira giggled. "Yes. At least I hope so. Why else would he do it now?"

"Good question." Hoping to end that subject, Anne held up another dress for Moira's inspection. "What about this one?"

Moira shuddered, and Anne nodded. "You're right. Hopeless."

Frederick Von Zandt, who was apparently otherwise perpetually unoccupied, drove them back to Lynstrade Manor when they'd given up on the shops. How strange it must be for him to have to interact with his father's mistress, a girl that was younger than he was. Did he think of her as a sister, Anne wondered briefly, or as a potential stepmother?

Moira yawned, leaning back against the headrest of the front seat. "I'm ready for a bit of a toes-up. At least we have a pass on dinner tonight." She turned around to look at Anne. "Walter and Henry have gone to meet with some people in Inverness. They won't be back until tomorrow." She made a face. "Tomorrow night is a dinner with some of Walter's business associates at the house. Very formal." Moira sighed. "And they're all foreign. Bleeding Arabs and Africans."

Frederick gave her a slightly reproachful look.

She slid her eyes sideways in a look of exasperation, but smiled. "You don't like them either, so don't look at me like that, pet." Moira patted him on the shoulder casually. He slid his eyes from the road to smile back at Moira, and Anne saw it: that man-in-love look.

"They're Father's clients, Moira." But his voice, full of affection, held no censure.

"Yes, I know. I'll be nice to them, Frederick. I always am." Moira kept her hand on his shoulder in the manner of two people who are comfortable with each other.

"I don't want to intrude on Walter's business dinner. I can just eat in my room." Anne would be relieved to be able to have two dinners in a row without the man, especially with Jonas still away.

Moira shook her head. "Oh, no. Walter definitely wants you to come."

"I'm sure not. I'll just have a sandwich and work on the design plans."

Frederick turned around in his seat and spoke to her directly for the first time. "Lady Anne, you have to come. He particularly wants you to be there."

Anne chewed on that for a moment. Maybe she should go. Maybe Terrence would want to know the names of the people Walter Von Zandt considered business associates. Arabs and Africans, Moira had said. They could be the connection to the terrorists Terrence was looking for. Of course, she needed to go. She hoped her wire was actually working. If not, she'd just have to remember anything important. "If I'm invited, then, I'll go."

"You are. My Aunt Glynnis will be there, too. With Henry. You absolutely have to come. This is the first time Walter's let me help plan the dinner. To be like a hostess, you know."

Anne was confused. "I thought Henry was married."

Frederick snorted, and Moira hit him on the shoulder.

"Be still, Freddie. He is, but Glynnis is his secretary and, well, you know. She's younger than my mum—thirty-three, I think."

"Thirty-four," Frederick corrected.

"Thirty-three, thirty-four, what's the difference? I've got the party favors for everyone." Moira gestured to a large shopping bag emblazoned with the name of a chocolate shop. "I found the most gorgeous chocolates in tiny boxes tied with ribbon." Moira's eagerness was touching. "Frederick tried them—he thought they were good. Didn't you?" She turned to the young man, who nodded and smiled at her as if she were made of chocolate.

Anne said, "Sounds wonderful. I can't wait to try them."

During the remainder of the drive, Anne listened and joined in when necessary to the back and forth of the conversation but her mind was busily making plans.

Tonight she'd be able to have the tray in her room she'd been hoping for yesterday, and she could go to bed early. But first, she'd get into Walter's office and see what she could find.

# Chapter 72

ANNE FROWNED at the extravagant arrangement of tulips she found waiting for her in her room, and at the note from Walter begging her forgiveness for having to leave on business, and promising to return soon. This wasn't normal behavior from a garden owner to someone who was working on his garden design, and she was sure Jonas wouldn't have received flowers. Walter was a hard man to discourage.

She changed into jeans, a sweater, and warm socks, and laid down for a nap. There'd been some cramping again when she'd gotten back from shopping, so maybe she'd overdone things a little. Anne had turned down Moira's offer to watch a movie with her and Frederick in the media room and have pizza, but was glad to know of their plans. That would tie the two of them up for a time.

Anne took a mental inventory of who else would still be in the house. The housekeeper, she supposed, whose name she'd finally confirmed was Hedda. Two maids and a butler-type also lived in, but the other maids seemed to be dailies, coming in from town every morning and leaving after dinner was cleared away. According to Moira, Henry Von Zandt had gone with his father, along with the chauffeur. The two bodyguard types that seemed to always be around Walter had left with them, as well. She was pretty sure that the guards that manned the gates and patrolled the grounds stayed in the gatehouse.

After her dinner tray was brought up might be the best time. Or maybe it would be better to wait until her tray was cleared away so the maid wouldn't have a reason to come into her room and find her gone. Better yet, Anne thought, she could volunteer to bring her own tray back downstairs to the kitchen. That would give her an excuse to be moving around the house. Anne didn't know if the staff would allow her to take this task on herself, but she was hoping that, with Walter gone, they might be happy to have one less chore to do.

The housekeeper looked surprised at Anne's offer, and dutifully protested, but Anne convinced her that it would be no trouble. She apologized for all the extra work caused by her staying in the house, and complimented Hedda on how wonderfully she ran everything.

Later, following the housekeeper's directions, Anne found the kitchen. It was a large, sterile-looking room: all stainless steel. The room looked like what Anne imagined a hospital kitchen might look. Surgery as well as cooking could be performed in this cold room. No one was there and the lights had been dimmed. Apparently the staff had taken advantage of a night without the boss, and retired to their own quarters early. As instructed, she left her tray on the counter next to the sink.

Anne wondered where the servants' quarters were. Surely they would not be too close to the main rooms. She decided not to worry too much about it. She could explain away being found in most of the main rooms—looking for a book, looking for a brandy, or looking for the media room to join Moira and Frederick. She would not, however, so easily be able to explain it if she were found in Walter's office. Well then, she just couldn't get caught in there.

She started toward where she remembered the library was, going through the dimly lit house as quietly as possible. She opened doors as she went along, praying she didn't open a door to a room and find one of the servants or, even worse, a security guard Walter had left behind.

As it turned out, finding the library was easy because the library door was standing open, although no lights were on inside the room. She entered the room and closed the door behind her. For a moment she just stood there in the dark. Outside the tall mullioned windows, spotlights illuminated the exterior of the house. There would be guards out there, Anne thought. Realizing that being in the room in the dark would look suspicious if she was discovered, she turned on a small lamp on a side table close to the statue where she'd seen Walter hide the key. Besides, she needed to be able to see what she was doing. She could make up a reason for being in the library at least, so she told herself she should feel relatively calm.

But no matter what she told herself, her nerves were on edge as she patted her hand around the statue's feet. Surprised when she felt nothing, she tried again. Nothing. She frowned. Surely it had to be here. Using both hands, she tried again. Again nothing.

With one hand, she tilted the lamp toward the statue, focusing the light on the figure's convoluted angles, while with the other hand she traced the base of the statue. She blew out a breath of relief when she felt something move against her prying fingers. The key lay against the side of the inside of the twisted foot's instep. Anne quickly palmed it.

She held herself still, listening for any signs that anyone might be coming to the library, but she couldn't hear anything. Outside, the spotlights continued their interlacing circles. Anne wondered if the guards were looking only for intruders or also were supposed to make sure that the people inside the house stayed there. Was she a de facto prisoner? What would happen if she decided to just leave? Just walk away? With Walter gone, would anyone try to stop her?

Leaving the remote estate in the middle of the night was probably more scary an idea than staying there was. No one had been anything less than kind to her at Lynstrade Manor. She hadn't been threatened or harmed in any way. She'd been treated like a queen. If she got in trouble here, it would be because she was acting like the worst sort of houseguest. A snoop, a liar, and ungrateful to boot.

Why not just go back upstairs and forget this stupid idea? What was she doing? She had no business doing this kind of thing. Why had Terrence decided to use her to help him? It was so unlike him to want to involve her in his work. Was he really that desperate?

She went over to the office door. If she got caught in there, would she really be in any danger? She shook her head. Of course she wasn't in danger. Terrence wouldn't have involved her if there was the slightest chance of something happening to her. If she were caught in Walter's office, she'd just make up a story about being lost, and have whoever found her point the way back to her room.

Somehow she wasn't convinced. She knew that if she got caught in Walter's office, there would be no going back, no way to put an innocent spin on what she was doing.

Anne closed her eyes and swallowed hard, curling her hand against her stomach. Love you. Then she made herself focus on what she was doing, and put the key in the door. She was carefully turning it to release the lock when she heard voices just outside the library.

Swiftly, she extracted the key from the door and scurried over to one of the bookcases. Pulling out a book without even looking at the title, she slipped the key into her jeans pocket.

The door to the library opened and Moira and Frederick entered.

Frederick fixed his watery eyes on Anne with suspicion, but Moira just looked startled.

"Anne, what are you doing in here?"

Anne smiled and held up the book in her hand. "Looking for something to read. I got bored in my room. I looked for the media room, but I couldn't find it, so I thought I would just get a book. Luckily, I remembered where the library was."

"The media room is downstairs, below ground. The cable went out—internet, too, so we lost our movie." Moira approached and took the book out of Anne's hand. She looked at the cover, then made a face. "Anna Karenina. We studied this book in school and it's not got a happy ending." Moira touched Frederick's arm in a sisterly gesture. "Have you read it, Freddie?"

He shook his head.

"It's about a married lady who has an affair and gets pregnant with the lover's child. She ends up committing suicide. It's a dreadful story. I cried for days."

Anne blanched, and suddenly felt faint.

Moira looked alarmed and moved toward her just as Anne felt her stomach seize into a tight cramp and her knees buckle. Frederick caught her and took her over to one of the sofas.

Moira's hand was on Anne's forehead. "Are you all right?"

"Yes, of course." Anne forced herself to smile. "Just a little dizzy for some reason. You two go on. I'll just lay here a moment, then I'll go back up to my room." She needed them to leave so she could return the key to its hiding place.

"I'll help you upstairs." Frederick's face had softened, and his voice was now solicitous.

"No, really, I feel so foolish. I'll be fine. I'll just lay here and rest."

"Let me bring you a brandy." Moira moved over to the drinks cabinet and poured a small snifter, and brought it over. Even though Anne knew that one drink wouldn't damage her baby, she couldn't bring herself to take the chance. She pretended to take a sip, then handed the glass back to Moira.

"I think I just need to get some sleep. I haven't been sleeping well."

Frederick, now insistent, led Anne out of the room and upstairs, flanked by a concerned Moira.

Later, in the middle of the night, Anne padded downstairs in her socks and replaced the key under the statue's foot just as she'd found it. She would make another attempt to get into the office later, but she just wasn't up to it again tonight.

# Chapter 73

DARBY COULDN'T BREATHE when she realized what Anne had said. Pausing the recording, she absorbed what she thought she'd heard, then hit the rewind button and listened again. She wanted to dance, to laugh, to shout. This was momentous.

If it were anyone other than Anne, Darby would want to kiss her. Maybe the woman wasn't brainless. At least she seemed to have the sense to realize that the dinner being planned for those clients of Von Zandt was important.

Darby took off her headphones. The universe didn't hate her after all. Fuck John Stirling and his Greek island cruise. Fuck John Stirling and his London barrister. Fuck him to hell. She didn't need him. She was going to be the one to get Von Zandt.

Her mind started making lists. They would need the names of the guests, and a description. She hoped Anne could figure that out herself since Darby had no way to contact her. The ban on Anne using her cell phone or having any phone contact at all had been a slight flaw in Darby's plan, but she'd wanted to make sure Anne didn't contact Terrence. Calling Anne now could risk the operation. If anyone checked Anne's mobile phone's call log, everything would be ruined. Darby considered sending Anne an email, but there was no way to make sure that wasn't seen either.

Until now, they'd believed all of Von Zandt's interactions with the terrorists and their financial backers were done through electronic transmissions. Who would have thought the man would have the temerity to have a meeting with them at his house? If that was actually what was happening. If it wasn't just ordinary business clients coming to dinner. If Anne didn't have it all backarsewards. No, she couldn't. This was just too perfect.

Ideally, they should set up surveillance of the house to see who arrived for the dinner and be ready to follow them as they left. Unfortunately, however, Darby on her own did not have the authority to order that kind of surveillance, and her superiors at Interpol would refuse to interfere to that extent without being invited by the authorities. For a fleeting moment Darby considered telling Terrence. No, thought Darby, he'd be furious. Besides, if she did it alone, she'd get all the credit. She deserved it; she'd planned everything and done all the work.

With Anne's wire running during the dinner, Darby would be able to figure out what exactly was going on. If it turned out the guests actually were the people involved in planning and financing the terrorist attacks, then she'd tell Terrence. They could still get the surveillance in place in time to follow the guests on their way out.

Then it would be Darby's operation, her success. She wasn't just Terrence's little sister any more.

As Stirling had said, she was all grown up.

# MONDAY, APRIL 20

# Chapter 74

ANNE HIT the alarm clock next to the bed, cursing its obnoxiously strident tone. Four a.m. Still dark outside, but she knew she needed to try again to get into the office before people got up and started moving around the house. This time she couldn't let herself be caught. She'd have no good explanation for wandering around the house this time of day. She gingerly touched her abdomen. The cramps seemed to have stopped. She breathed a sigh of deep relief. All was well, then.

She saw no one on the way to the library. Once inside, she closed the door behind her, ran to get the key, and quickly opened the office door. Then she locked it behind her. At least if someone tried to come in while she was there, she'd have some warning.

The room was totally dark and she realized she was going to have to turn on at least one light. She wondered if there was anyone outside watching the house who would notice. Finding the switch for the desk light, she hit it, illuminating the desktop.

The empty desktop. Walter's computer was gone.

She wanted to kick herself. How stupid of her. Of course he'd taken his laptop with him. She pulled at the top desk drawer handle but it didn't budge. Locked. Then she tried the bottom drawer, and although it opened, it contained nothing more interesting than paper and other supplies. She pursed her lips, thinking. Where would the key be? Walter didn't seem to be good with hiding keys if the office key was any indication. She looked under the desk blotter but found nothing.

Under the desk lamp. That's where she'd hide the key. She lifted it up and smiled to herself. There it was. Apparently, she wasn't too good at hiding keys either. Carefully turning the key in the desk drawer, she heard the snick of the lock release and pulled the drawer open. A checkbook and stamps. Perusing the checkbook, she saw that it appeared to be the household account; both Elisa's and Walter's names were on it, but most of the handwriting in the ledger looked feminine. This office was not where Walter kept his any of his illicit business stuff. No wonder he was so lackadaisical about hiding the key.

She scanned the room, but didn't see anywhere else where anything that she was looking for could be hidden. Disgusted, she locked the desk drawer and replaced the key, then slipped out of the office, locking that door as well and again replacing the key under the statue's foot.

What now? Where should she look next? Walter's room, perhaps? She wasn't sure where it was, but thought it was in the same wing as her own. How to find it? She couldn't just open every door. Moira would be in one room and Frederick in another. What if she chose the wrong door?

Anne pondered her dilemma as she went up the stairs back to her own room. This was crazy. No way was she going to search for Walter's room without a clue as to what she was doing. That would just be plain stupid. Doing any of this with so little guidance was stupid. This whole idea was beginning to strike Anne as incredibly stupid. She wouldn't even plant an herb garden with so little planning. It was amazing Terrence ever got anything done if this is the way he operated.

There was nothing she could do without more information. Despite it not having been any help so far, she was going to have to try communicating through the wire again. Back in her room, Anne got into bed and dictated into her wire everything she'd done and what she needed to know. After adding again that the dinner tonight might be important, she placed her hand on her tummy, gave it a pat, and went back to sleep.

# Chapter 75

HARRY LOOKED AT ALLISON, considering. The little bird was acting strange, no doubt about it. There was something going on. He needed to find out what it was, and he needed to find out quick. Difficult though, with Allison following the snooty Darby Reid around like she was the bleeding Queen. So he bided his time. When Darby received a call and left the building saying she would be back after lunch, Harry pounced.

"Allison, my pet, let's get lunch ourselves. No need to starve if our betters are eating. And we need to talk about your firearms training."

She studied him, faintly suspicious. "No, I can't. I've no time right now."

"Come on, ten minutes. We can get a killer Indian curry. If you're nice to me, I'll even buy you a pint to go with it."

He could tell she was hungry and interested. Allison loved Indian food, and this place his brother-in-law's family owned was super.

"Ten minutes? All right. But I can't do the pint, that'll just make me sleepy. I have work to do."

"Ten minutes, I promise." He grinned. "The best lamb, I promise you. So tender it will have your mouth praising its mum for giving it birth. And we really can't dally on getting your shooting up to par."

She caught up her jacket, smiling. "All right, then. I am a bit peckish. I could eat."

He smiled back. What are you up, luv?

While she headed for a table, Harry had a quick word with the proprietor, laying out exactly what he wanted, then followed behind her.

He pulled out his chair, sat down and signaled for the waiter. "I'll have a pint of Kingfisher and the lady will have?" He looked at Allison for an answer.

"A Coke."

The waiter went to get their drinks.

"I'll let you have a taste of my lager."

She tilted her face into a little smile. "I'll not say no to a little taste."

The waiter came with her Coke and Harry's pint, then left.

"Aren't we going to order our food?"

"I ordered for us when we came in. One of my sister's husband's family owns this place. We're getting a sampler menu." He drank his ale. "Ah, perfect. And it's all on the house. Even better."

Allison rolled her eyes. "I should have known you weren't really paying."

"Don't look a free lunch in the mouth." Harry wasn't ashamed of his reputation for being thrifty. He had plans for his money. "The food here is great." He pushed his glass toward her. She took a sip, then nodded in approval.

"Want one?"

She hesitated, then smiled. "Maybe a little one."

He got the waiter's attention and pointed to his glass.

"Harry, no. Only a half. I can't drink a whole pint at lunch."

"I'll finish what you don't want."

"Why are you being so nice to me?"

"I'm always nice to you. So let's get down to business. I'm thinking we start your firearms training next week. I can get time at the range evenings between six and seven."

"I can do that." She took a drink of her Coke, and Harry could sense her excitement. "Will I get my gun issued to me right away, then?"

"Next week, I'm guessing. I'll check with Frank."

The waiter arrived with the pint for Allison, and Harry handed him the Coke to take away.

She gave a slight frown. "I could have still used the Coke."

"Doesn't go with the lager." Harry pulled out his pocket diary and scribbled in the training times. He pointed to her with his pen. "You'd better write down the times as well. I don't want to stand around waiting with my gun all ready to go and no one to play with."

She looked at him suspiciously, as if trying to ascertain if he'd meant that as a double entendre. He kept his face innocent, and her face relaxed into a smile. "I won't forget. I can't wait."

"You might not like it."

"I'll like it," she said.

Another waiter came with a small plate of lamb vindaloo for each of them. Allison ate a few bites, then took a drink of lager. "Spicy."

Harry nodded. "A little." He ate, watching her. They both cleaned their plates. By that time, Allison's pint was half empty.

She waved her hand in front of her mouth, as if trying to put out flames. "That was the hottest bloody vindaloo I've ever had."

"Good, though?"

"Good."

The waiter took their plates away, replacing them with two small plates of shrimp curry.

Harry gestured to the curry. "This is milder. It might seem spicy at first bite, but eat quickly and it mellows out."

"Really?" She took another gulp of lager.

"Really. Some kind of odd cooking voodoo."

"I'll try it. Mild would be good." She picked up her fork. "You've hardly drank anything. Isn't your mouth on fire? I can hardly feel my lips." She put a finger to her lips. "They're numb."

He considered her lips, considered feeling her lips, considered. The thought made him uncomfortable. She was practically a baby. Besides, she was up to something.

"It's maybe a little hot. But this curry will calm your mouth down. You'll see. I've gotten expert on eating Indian food since Marla got married." He watched as Allison took his advice, taking quick bites of shrimp curry. He ate his own more slowly, though he didn't have to worry. He'd given instructions for Allison's dishes to be prepared differently than his, using the hottest spices they had.

Allison's eyes got huge and she drained her pint as if trying to extinguish a raging fire, then put her glass down and reached for his. He held it away. She waved frantically to the waiter who pretended not to see her.

"Harry, get me something to drink. I'm dying."

Harry shook his head, then took a slow drink of his lager. "Not until you tell me what you're up to."

"What? Give me a drink." Her hand went to her throat.

"Not until you tell me what's going on."

"I can't tell you."

"Why not?"

"It's a secret." Her words came choking out through hoarse coughs.

"A secret from who exactly? Or should I say with who?"

She reached for his glass. "Please, Harry."

He held it away from her. "Tell me?"

She nodded and he put his glass it to her mouth, allowing her one small sip, then jerked it away again.

"Who?"

"Darby. And the Super."

He gave her one more sip. "No, Allison. Whatever she's doing, Darby's doing it on her own."

"No." Allison's tone was incredulous. "She'd never do that."

"Yes, she would. You know very well that the Super doesn't have secrets from me about work."

Realization seemed to hit Allison in a rush. "Oh, shite."

"Tell me."

"Get me a Coke, Harry. Please. I'll tell you."

"Everything?"

"Yes, yes."

He waved to the waiter. By the time Allison was halfway through the Coke, he had the story. He hid his fury long enough to put some money on the table. Then he yanked her arm up, grabbed the glass away, and slammed it down on the table.

"We're off to see the guv, darling. You've got a lot of explaining to do."

\* \* \* \* \*

Reid shook his head and looked at her with disappointment.

"Allison, did you forget to whom you report?"

"Sir, I thought you knew. Darby said that this was your idea but that you just didn't want to talk about it . . ." and here she had the grace to blush, "with what was going on with you and your wife."

"You should know better. I do not give orders like that. My wife is not a police officer. She's a garden designer. Garden designers have no training for this kind of work. Do you understand the kind of danger my wife is in now with this hare-brained scheme of Darby's?

A harebrained scheme in which you assisted?"

Allison was crying and nodding, but Reid had little sympathy for her at this point. He planned worse for Darby when he got his hands on her.

"DC Muirhead, you may leave. I'll consider what to do about your role in this when my wife is safe."

The young woman went white. "I'm so sorry, guv. I'll do whatever I can to make this up."

"Right now we need to get my wife out of Von Zandt's house unharmed." Reid motioned with his head toward Harry who took the cue.

Harry took Allison by the elbow gently, leading her out of Reid's office. "Tell us exactly what happened, luv, so we can do what we can to help Lady Anne get out of there safely."

# Chapter 76

REID WATCHED through the glass that surrounded his office for Darby to return from her lunch. When she waltzed in through the vestibule, he got up, went to his office door, and opened it. "Darby, a word."

She went toward him, and he motioned for her to come in.

At first, she seemed unconcerned and her manner was breezy. But when he closed the door, he saw her start to hesitate, as if finally registering the fury vibrating through him.

Darby tried to act casual. "Something wrong?" Her eyes flickered over to Harry who stared back at her.

Reid nodded. "Aye. Something's wrong."

"What?"

"Think about it. You know."

"I do? Well, sorry to disappoint you, but I don't."

He eyed her coldly. "Anne."

She jutted out her chin. "What about her?"

"You had her go into Van Zandt's house? Wear a fucking wire."

She flinched, but in typical Darby fashion, refused to be contrite.

"So? I put her in there to see what she could find out about Von Zandt. She went willingly." Her arrogance appalled him.

"What the hell do you mean, you put her in there? This is my operation."

He grabbed his sister by the arms. There was a cold fear in her face, but being Darby, she did not back down.

"Back off, Terrence. Interpol has an interest in this investigation, too. Anne's wired and she's fine. We've been monitoring her."

"What the fuck do you mean she's fine? He could kill her before you even got a blip on your goddamn monitors."

Darby shook his hands off. "Why would he? There's no reason for him to suspect."

"Why her, Darby? Why Anne?"

"I knew Von Zandt would offer for her to stay there after the story hit. The press was bothering her at the hotel. It was a priceless opportunity. She's working on his gardens, and it makes sense for her to stay there. You've never had anyone else get inside his organization. It was too good to pass up."

"It makes sense? Are you out of your mind? He knows she's my wife and that I'm hunting him. You have got to be a total idiot to serve Anne up to him like that."

"Your connection to Anne isn't an issue. He can't think you care about her. He knows you told her to go to blazes. Why are you even worried about her?"

"You're an idiot. He's a man—a vile man—but a man nonetheless. He knows I care about her or I wouldn't be so bloody jealous of her. And, aye, he wants her himself. I know. I saw him around her. And he's seen me around her."

"She wanted to do it, Terrence. I didn't force her. I just asked her and she agreed. She didn't hesitate at all."

"How did you even come to be talking to her? You've never tried to be a friend to her." When his sister didn't answer, he asked again. "Answer me."

Darby's voice was sullen and she kept her gaze averted away from him. "I called her at the hotel."

"When?"

"I don't remember exactly."

"Don't lie to me. I can find out."

"Thursday night."

"Thursday night?" He tried to make sense of that. "But you couldn't have known about what happened with Grainger until the next morning when the story came out."

She looked away from him, setting her lips together tightly, then gestured at Harry. "Do we really have to have him here for this discussion?"

"Yes, we do. To keep me from killing you." Reid felt the truth of his own words. "So you knew about what happened before you saw it in the papers? How?"

Darby crossed her arms against her chest. "I have my sources."

"What sources?"

"I don't have to tell you." She unfolded her arms.

"Yes, you bloody well do."

She threw up her hands. "The photographer. He called me."

"Why would he call you?"

"I guess he thought I'd be interested."

"How do you know him?" Darby was lying, Reid could tell.

"I get around."

"Let me get this straight. You called Anne after you got a call from the photographer because you realized there would be stories in the morning tabloids?"

She nodded, and he saw her quickly conceal her relief. That wasn't what she'd been afraid he'd find out. There was something else, and whatever it was, it was worse. He motioned to Harry. "Take her mobile."

Harry slid his hand in her back pocket and got the phone before she could stop him. She tried to slap his hands away but he paid no attention.

Darby's phone in hand, Harry sat down and started scrolling through her call logs. "Doesn't go back far enough, guv."

"Get the records."

Darby looked from Reid to Harry. "What are you looking for? Why don't you just ask me?"

Reid said, "Because you lie."

"Just tell me. What do you want to know?"

"When did you first speak to the photographer?"

The cornered look on her face gave him his answer.

"I thought so. You arranged for the photographer to be there." Reid stared at her. "How did you know Grainger would be there? Anne said she didn't even know he was coming until he got there—and she didn't even know how he found out the name of the hotel where she was staying."

"And you believe her?"

"Anne doesn't lie."

"No, she's a bloody angel." Sarcasm dripped from Darby's voice.

"Tell me how you knew Andrew Grainger would be there." Reid's words were slow and deliberate, and his eyes never left his sister's face.

Darby was silent.

Realization began to dawn on him as to the enormity of Darby's perfidy. "You arranged it all. Grainger and the photographer as well." He wondered if he'd ever hated anyone as much as he hated his sister right then.

Darby scowled at him defiantly. "So what? I was doing you a favor. I got her lover's number from her mobile. I called him and told him she needed him. I figured whatever happened would be best for you. I didn't know you'd be at the hotel when it happened, but what difference does it make?"

"What do you mean what difference does it make?"

"She's been making a fool of you since you met her. Just like our mother did to the Earl." Darby's last words were muttered under her breath.

When what Darby had said registered, Reid motioned for Harry to leave. After the door closed, Reid said, his voice low, "You know."

"Yes, I know. No thanks to you, brother. Instead, I had it thrown in my face during a security interview."

"Poor you. I had it thrown in my face when I was eight years old. Get over it. Right now we need to concentrate on getting Anne out. How did you get her to do this?"

Darby sat mute.

"Tell me, or so help me, God, Darby…"

She glared at him like a cornered rodent. "I called her and told her I needed to talk to her. That you wanted me to call. When I got there, I said you wanted her help. I told her you expected Von Zandt to offer to have her stay at his house to get away from the press, and that you wanted her to accept so she could get in there to look around. And if he didn't offer, I told her you wanted her to ask him herself."

Reid concentrated on breathing evenly. "And the wire?"

"I took little Allison with me. I had her fit Anne with the wire and teach her how to use it."

"You're out of your mind."

"It worked, didn't it? The next morning Elisa Von Zandt called her, and offered for Anne to go stay there. That man she works for is there as well."

"Jonas is there?" Relief flooded him, and Reid let his head fall into his hands. "Thank God."

For the first time, Darby looked shaken. "Not now, but he was.

He left Sunday morning, but he's supposed to be back Tuesday or Wednesday."

When what she'd said sunk in, Reid had to fight back the urge to throw his sister out of his office. "I can't believe you did this. Any of this. Not to mention that you sent her in there even knowing she's pregnant." Sweat dampened his body as absolute fear filled him. "Sweet Jesus. We have to get her out of there."

Darby pursed her lips, giving a slight shake of her head. "We can't. Not now. There's a dinner tonight that's critical. From what she's reported, I believe Von Zandt has the men responsible for funding several terrorist groups meeting there. There's bound to be some information that Anne will be able to get to us through the wire."

"Tonight? Why is this the first I've heard of this dinner? What else did you tell her to do? There has to be more." He went to grab her again, but Darby backed away.

She shook her head. "No, that's all."

"You're lying. What else?"

Darby let out an exasperated sigh. "She's looking around, all right? To see if she can find anything that can lead us to the ties with the terrorists. Anything on communications, accounts, or payments. The only way to cut the snake's head off is at the money connection. You've said that yourself."

"Anne doesn't have the slightest idea how to do that, and certainly not how to do it so that Von Zandt doesn't suspect."

"She's not a child, Terrence. I told her where to look. She's already gotten into his office but she didn't find anything. She's still looking around. It's not that hard. I'm sure she can take care of herself."

"She's a gardener, Darby. What do you expect her to do? Defend herself with a garden spade?"

"Don't be melodramatic. No one will hurt your precious Anne."

"Who else is there? His wife you said? Tell me Elisa's there. A buffer for Anne against him?"

Darby looked sullen. "His wife went back to Germany."

"When?"

"Friday."

"The same day Anne moved in? Darby, you're so stupid. He wants Anne and he sent his wife away so the way would be clear to pursue her." Reid could tell there was something else Darby wasn't telling him. He grabbed her. "I'm right, aren't I?"

She tightened her lips and stared at him.

"Tell me."

"All right, yes. He told Anne he was getting a divorce."

"Shite." He thrust his hands through his hair. "Oh, God, oh, blessed God, have mercy. And you left her in there? What else?" He wanted to throttle her, but instead grabbed his mug from the desk and threw it against the wall, shattering it. "What else, you stupid bitch?"

"All right, all right, Terrence." Finally, she seemed to have the sense to be scared. "Moira. He told Anne he was ending things with Moira."

"Why? Why would he tell Anne things like that?"

She looked up at him, her face telling him the truth. "You know why."

"Fuck."

"Terrence, you can't think much of her devotion to you if you think she would let him . . ."

"Anne's fidelity to me is the least of my worries right now. You don't know Von Zandt like I do. If he finds that wire on her, he'll kill her. And in a way that you won't be able to prove he did it." Then, he saw the whole picture of what his sister had done and why she had done it, and a cold hatred filled him. "If you sent her in as a sacrificial lamb, which I suspect you did, you'll not even be able to pin her death on him. You did this on purpose, you heartless bitch." He turned away. "I'm going in to get her."

Darby looked pale and her eyes filled with rare tears. "I wouldn't try to get her killed. You can't think that about me."

He spat the words out. "I don't know what to think. But right now, I don't give a fuck about you. I need to get her out of there. Tell me everything you know about what's going on there tonight. Right now."

"No—you'll ruin everything. Von Zandt won't hurt her. I've been listening. She's good at fending off his advances." Darby seemed to regain some of her confidence. "And Moira's still there."

Reid shook his head. "That means nothing. Moira's inconsequential. A convenience. No protection for Anne." He picked up his mobile. "You're off this operation, Darby. I want an immediate briefing on everything you've done and everything you know. I want to know everything that's been said, every bloody thing." He opened the door and called to Harry. "Get in here. And bring DC Muirhead."

Reid looked at Darby, barely controlling his fury and disgust. "Suffice it to say, I hope I never see you again after this is over."

# Chapter 77

"HARRY, take over the monitoring of the transmissions Anne's sending. I want to know if anything happens. Who's been monitoring them, Darby?" His sister's name tasted like acid on his tongue.

"Me. I checked them in the morning and once later at night."

He shot her a look sharp enough to scathe her skin off. "That's not the same as monitoring them."

Unwisely, Darby let her voice become derisive. "Generally, it's been a scintillating discussion of garden work with some workmen."

"And what was she supposed to do if she got into trouble?"

Darby said nothing.

"When's the last time you checked on her wire?"

"Last night."

"Last night?" You bitch, you bitch, you fucking bitch, he thought. My wife and her baby. God, please let them be okay. He wanted to scream, to cry in desperation, but he kept his face immobile.

"I've been busy."

He said a silent prayer that nothing had happened since then. "Harry, can you feed the transmission to an earpiece for me?"

"No problem. Give me a second to program it."

"Be quick."

Harry raised his eyebrows as he finished fiddling with the apparatus. "Okay, your earpiece is ready. But, guv, there are no transmissions coming in right now. The wire's not on. I scrolled back through the recordings and have the last one coming in at about six tonight. She's talking and there's someone with her. Another woman."

"Nothing coming through now? There's no action? Or it's not on?"

Harry shook his head. "It's not on at all."

"We need to get in contact with her." Reid whirled around and fixed his gaze on his sister. "Darby, how were you communicating with Anne? Not her mobile, I hope."

"No, we didn't want the calls to show up in case anyone saw her call log."

"So how?"

"She was to tell me when to meet her if she had anything important to tell me. Through the wire."

"And did she?"

Darby was quiet, then admitted, "She wanted me to meet her in the village yesterday."

"And?"

"I was busy."

"Doing what? You weren't working."

She was silent.

"What was so important you ignored Anne's needing to see you?"

"None of your business."

He waited until she finally spoke, her voice grudging.

"I was with John Stirling."

Sick at his sister's selfishness, he asked, "Did you send anyone to see what she needed, to meet with her?" His heart ached for Anne's isolation.

Darby scowled. "No."

He didn't think he even knew this woman who was supposed to be his sister. "So how do we get hold of her? To tell her to get out? Or that we're coming?"

Darby just looked at him, her face a blank.

"Don't tell me we don't have any way to get hold of her." He heard the anguish in his own voice, and saw that this, at least, seemed to move Darby.

"She's fine, Terrence. You're making too much of this."

"Shut your mouth."

Harry broke in. "Guv, here's the last transmission that came in. That was an hour ago. It's Lady Anne talking to Moira. I'll put it on the speaker, guv, if that's all right."

Reid nodded.

"Is that what you're wearing tonight?"

"I guess so. The maid brought it up for me earlier today, and took all the others away."

"Walter bought it for you."

There was a pause. "Bought it? I just assumed they had extra clothes here for guests."

"No, he's had all the dresses for you sent over from a shop he likes. This one's beautiful, don't you think?"

"It's a bit bare. What are you wearing?"

"An evening gown I already had. He didn't send me a new dress. Actually, ever since you came, he's had nothing to do with me. And he talks about you all the time."

"Moira, don't be ridiculous. We've talked about this. I'm married and I'm in love with my husband."

"Walter told me I'm to keep the two Nigerians entertained tonight."

"Entertained?"

"That's what he said. I think he means . . ."

The recording paused again, then resumed.

"No, he couldn't possibly have meant anything like that."

"I think maybe he did. But it's not your fault. I know you don't want him. He may not be able to tell, but I can. Here, let me help you get ready." There was a sigh. "It's really a beautiful gown. Take off your robe and I'll slip it over your head so it doesn't snag."

"I don't need help. Moira, stop . . ."

A space of crackling silence, then Moira spoke again. "What's this wire for? Then a laugh. "Uh oh, Walter's not going to like this."

Static played over the transmission and the wire went dead. The implications of what had happened registered with each one of them, and a momentary silence sat heavily over them.

Finally, Harry spoke. "The wire's not just off, it's been disconnected."

Reid stood up, a cold dread in his stomach. "We have to go in now. Get things set up, Harry. Pull the house plans for Lynstrade Manor." He motioned to the door. "Darby, get out of here. You can decide for now how to tell your agency why you're no longer working with us. I'll be talking with them later. If I have anything to say about it, your career with Interpol is over."

His sister looked as if she was going to speak, but he shook his head. "Don't say a word. Just get out. Now."

After Darby left, Reid looked over at Allison, whose face showed that she fully understood the seriousness of the situation and the role she'd played, however unwittingly. "Pull up my calendar and tell me where I'm supposed to be tonight, DC Muirhead."

The young woman started at his use of her rank and last name, apparently recognizing from that, and from his tone, that their relationship had, at least for now, changed. Chastened, she hit some buttons on the computer. "A dinner party at Lord Stergus's house, sir."

"I'll wear a dinner jacket then." His glance was distracted. "I'll be the jealous husband going to collect my wife to take her with me to the party. After the news stories last week, no one will doubt my jealousy, or my wife's unfortunate habit of getting herself into situations where other men are paying too much attention to her."

Allison looked away, obviously not knowing what the appropriate response, if any, was to a comment like that. Reid registered Harry sending her a glance warning her to be silent.

Reid went into his office, closed and locked the door, and pulled the blinds. He changed clothes, putting on the dinner jacket he kept in the office closet, and quickly armed himself with his service firearm, as well as his own personal firearm, which he strapped to his ankle. In his pocket he placed a switchblade.

# Chapter 78

"GOOD THING IT WAS ME that found this, and not Walter's men. You must be crazy to come in here with a wire on. He'll kill you." Moira shook her head.

Anne was so scared she didn't know what to do or say. She felt an urgent and inconvenient urge to pee. She didn't say anything, just watched Moira for cues. If she had to go past Moira to get away, she'd just have to do her best.

Oddly, enough, Moira didn't seem to be particularly upset or outraged. "They do an electronics sweep before a dinner like this looking for anything that transmits a signal. And a weapons scan, of course. You don't have a weapon, do you?"

Closing her eyes for a second, Anne shook her head. "No." But if she got out of this, she was going to take some kind of self-defense lessons and learn to use a gun. How could she have agreed to do this idiotic thing with no protection? How could she have put her baby at risk like this? Suddenly she wondered if Darby hated her enough to have deliberately put her in danger, even knowing she was pregnant. Surely not. Then she remembered that she'd asked Darby for someone to meet her yesterday, and no one came. The truth of her situation came to her, as clear as if a fog that had been obscuring her vision, had suddenly lifted.

She'd been left here on her own, wearing a wire that could get her killed. She doubted now that Terrence even knew she was here. He would never leave her in a situation like this with no support—and she realized, suddenly, she'd been an idiot. He would never have put her in this situation in the first place—no matter how desperate he was. She was pretty sure he didn't even know she was here, and she was absolutely sure that Darby didn't care.

Moira's face concentrated in thought. "That's good. I'll keep the wire in my things. They search your room every night when you're at dinner, but they don't search mine anymore. I'm sure Walter's expecting to be in your room tonight."

Anne felt herself go pale. "What do you mean?"

"He wants you. He's not going to wait much longer. I know. He looked at me that way when we first met. He won't stop until he gets you."

Anne swallowed, fear edging like a razor against her chest. "No, Moira. I've told him that's not possible. I'm married."

"Well, he knows that didn't matter at least once before for you. You know, the artist."

"But Terrence and I had been separated for a long time when that happened."

Moira shrugged. "I'm just saying what I'm sure he thinks. So why were you wearing the wire?"

"Because I'm an idiot. My sister-in-law, who hates me, told me it would help Terrence's investigation, and that he wanted me to help and I believed her. I think she lied to me."

"Investigation of Walter?"

Anne nodded. At this point, she was at Moira's mercy. What did she have to lose now? There was no innocent explanation for wearing a surveillance wire. "It has something to do with funding terrorists. I was hoping if I found something that helped him, Terrence would forgive me."

Moira looked at her suspiciously. "Forgive you for what?"

Anne decided to just go with the truth. Nothing else could explain the dilemma she was in. "For getting pregnant."

"You're pregnant?" Moira was clearly surprised and whistled. "Shite." Then her eyes got huge. "That's why what I told you about that book upset you. It's the artist's kid?"

"Maybe. I don't know." Anne couldn't wait any longer. It wasn't very glamorous, but when you have to go you have to go. "Do you mind if I go to the bathroom? I really have to go."

Moira waved her hand. "Go ahead."

When Anne returned, Moira was sitting on the bed. "So, what are you going to do?"

"I'm going to have my baby." If I live, she thought.

"I mean about your husband—and the artist?"

"I'm hoping my husband will be with me either way. If not, well, I don't know right now. That's as far as I've gotten."

"But you don't want Walter?"

"Of course not." Anne had to smile. "Why would I want to add another man to the mix?"

Moira giggled. "And Walter wouldn't want another man's baby." Then the girl's brow furrowed, and her mouth formed a grim smile. "So he's sending me to sleep with the Nigerians, and he's going to end up sleeping alone. Serves him right."

"Has he done this before?"

Moira shook her head. "Never. That's why I know he's serious about you. And he's tired of me, I can tell."

Anne's mind was racing. She had to get out of here. She needed to get a message to Terrence. Without the wire, she had no choice but to use the cell phone. She would wait until Moira left, and then make the call.

"Moira, I need to rest. We have at least an hour until dinner. Do you mind if I take a short nap? Being pregnant makes me so tired."

The young woman nodded and went to the door. "I'll wake you up in time to get ready. We can go downstairs together."

"Okay. Thanks. You won't tell, will you?"

"No, but I won't give the wire back to you either. I love Walter, even as awful as he's being right now. I don't want him to go to jail. Without him, I have nobody."

"Thank you." But Anne didn't entirely trust Moira. She had to assume that the girl would change her mind and go to Walter. She had to figure out how get out of here on her own.

As soon as the door shut, Anne went through her bag and found her cell phone. She pushed the power button and waited. Nothing happened. She pushed it again, and again nothing happened. Her heart sank. Her cell phone was completely out of power. She scrabbled through her suitcase for the charger. Where had she seen it last? Then she remembered. The hotel. She'd left her charger in the outlet when the bellman came to get her bags. She sat down hard on the bed, trying to hold back the sinking sense of despair that threatened to overcome her.

She was completely on her own.

# Chapter 79

ANNE HEARD a rapid knocking on her door. Her stomach clenched into a knot so tight she could hardly walk. She grasped the paring knife she'd taken from her room's refreshment bar. It wasn't big; it must be meant for cutting lemons or limes for drinks. But it was something, and it was sharp.

If Moira had broken her promise and told about the wire, then whoever was on the other side of that door would be coming to . . . what? Surely not to hurt her. How could they? Someone would have to explain what had happened to her. People knew she was here, didn't they? She ran through her head who knew she was here besides the Von Zandts and Moira, all of whom she assumed would lie if they had to. Jonas. He knew. But they could tell him she'd left on her own. Jonas hadn't been here to see her suddenly disappear.

Darby knew she was here. Anne put her head in her hands and realized what a fool she'd been on so many levels. Darby hated her. Why had she been so ready to believe that Darby's feelings toward her had changed? If something happened to her, and Darby knew that admitting she knew Anne was here would implicate her in what happened, Anne had no doubt that Darby would lie. Stupid, stupid, she told herself.

She had to get out and make sure her baby would be safe, despite the fact that it obviously had a very foolish mother.

The knocking became more insistent, and Moira's voice hissed into the room through the door. "Anne, wake up. It's time for dinner."

Warily, she opened the door, relieved beyond belief to see that the girl was alone. Moira wore a long form-fitting beige lace dress that was cut low in the front, exposing a substantial amount of snowy white cleavage. Around her neck was a diamond choker, and from her ears hung diamond earrings.

"Being pregnant must really make you knackered. I thought you'd never answer the door." Moira scrutinized her face. "Are you all right?"

"Did you tell?"

"I won't tell. I like you." Moira smiled. "And I really, really like your husband."

Anne started to cry with relief, and Moira put her arms around her.

"Stop crying. Even someone who looks like you isn't going to look good after you've been crying." She took Anne's face in her hand. "Stop it. Really."

Anne sniffled and looked up, nodding.

"I brought you something. You can have it if you promise you won't sleep with Walter. No matter what."

Anne laughed, making a small strangled sound. "That's not hard."

Moira's voice was stern. "Promise."

"I promise. What is it?"

Moira held up a small piece of metal.

Anne examined it, puzzled. "A flashdrive?"

"Right. I took the information on the accounts that feed the money to where you were talking about—those organizations—and copied them on to this. You can have it, but then you have to leave. You can't stay here anymore. Walter isn't going to leave you alone if you're here, and I want him to come back to me." She looked at Anne, her gaze keen. "Do you promise?"

"Yes, I promise. I'll leave tomorrow. I'd leave tonight if I could figure out how."

Moira pondered that. "That would be hard. Just don't let him in here."

"I won't." A little embarrassed, Anne pulled out the knife. "I'll use this if I have to."

The young woman looked at the little knife, appraising. "That's not much of a weapon. I'll get you a bigger knife than that before you go to bed. I've no doubt he will come to you, and I don't think he'll take no for an answer. Don't hurt him though—just scare him away. Make him know you mean it. Then tomorrow we'll get you out of here."

Anne nodded. "Okay."

"I'll try to distract him from you when dinner's over so you can get up to your room."

"Thank you. I tried to use my cell to call my husband, but it's dead. And the internet's still down, so I couldn't use email. Do you think it's safe to use the telephones here? There isn't one in here, but maybe I could use one of the telephones downstairs."

Moira shook her head. "No, they're locked with a password and even if you ask to have it unlocked, they're monitored by the security guards. Walter is the only one that can use them without them being monitored. I think the internet is down on purpose because of tonight. I'd let you use my mobile, but they've all been collected for security. I'm surprised yours wasn't taken, too. They'd know you have one from going through your things."

"I guess they could tell it was dead and didn't find a charger either." Anne finished getting ready. "I'd say we could send a message out on that wire for someone to come help me, but I did that already and no one came. So it either isn't working or no one's listening to it."

"You're kidding?"

"I wish I was. My sister-in-law is the one who was supposed to be listening. I can't believe I trusted her. I just seem to do one dumb thing after the other."

Moira goggled at her. "Your sister-in-law must be a right bitch."

"You said it."

Moira shook her head. "It's nice to see that even someone like you can make mistakes and have problems."

Anne started to laugh. "Moira, that's so funny. You can't believe how many mistakes I've made—big ones—and the problems are equally impressive."

The girl looked at her quizzically. "I really do like you. Maybe it's that you're American that makes you seem so strange. Lord Reid must be totally gone on you, you know, to be so jealous." She eyed Anne, and Anne felt as if she were being dissected. "You're probably not easy to be married to—for a lot of reasons. Anyway, get dressed and let's go down." Moira pointed to the flashdrive. "You can't leave that in here when you go downstairs. You need to put it somewhere else."

"All right. I'll think of somewhere. But how did you get it? Are you sure it's the right accounts?"

"I'm not as dumb as Walter thinks I am. I've watched him put in his passwords when he thought I was too empty-headed to worry about hiding it from me. I know more than he thinks I do. Those accounts aren't actually in his name, but it's the accounts he uses for those shites downstairs. The ones he wants me to sleep with for him."

"Won't he know you've taken the information?"

"No, I only copied the data—he won't be able to tell unless he really looks, and there's no reason for him to do that."

"Will you be safe if he finds out?"

"He won't find out. Don't worry about me. I have my own plans." The look on Moira's face promised retribution. "He's not treating me like some kind of a whore he can pass around."

Anne didn't know what to say, so she changed the subject. "You said there'll be scanners tonight. Will this flashdrive set them off if I have it on me?"

"Not the scanners because it's not giving off a signal. But the weapons screening will register the metal."

"Oh." She thought. "That's a problem, then, but I'll figure something out. Thank you so much, Moira." Anne put her arms around the girl and hugged her.

"That's all right. He asked for it. Get dressed now and let's go downstairs." Moira glanced toward the door. "We don't want them to come looking for us."

"Give me ten minutes and I'll be ready."

"I'll wait for you here." Moira sat on the bed and looked over at the table next to the bed. She picked up Anne's copy of the design notes and photographs of the Aytoun Lane house. "What's this?"

Anne looked over as she finished fixing her hair, and seeing the notebook, smiled. "That's the house he bought for us—before I told him about the baby. We were furnishing it for us." She sat on the bed next to Moira. "It's on a lovely little cul-de-sac called Aytoun Lane. It's close enough for him to not have too much of a drive to work, and has a lovely garden, and room for children." At that, she started to cry again.

Moira shushed her in the manner of a much older woman rather than the very young woman she was. "Stop. We have to go downstairs and look smashing. Finish getting ready. I'll meet you at the top of the stairs in ten minutes. Don't worry, you'll have your house on Aytoun Lane with Lord Reid."

# Chapter 80

TWISTING AROUND to see the back of herself in the bathroom mirror, the first thought Anne had was that she was glad Terrence wasn't there to see her in this dress. He would be furious— it was not a business dinner dress at all. The narrow straps flowed into a fitted bodice that plunged deeply in front and was nonexistent in the back. A slit ran up the front of the black lacy fabric to mid-thigh and then down to the elegant five-inch high-heeled sandals that had arrived with the dress.

The dress was beautiful, but definitely not modest, fitting her closely, and leaving little room to hide anything. She would have had trouble hiding the wire even if she'd still had it. She could hide the flashdrive somewhere in the dress but it might still trigger the metal detector. Perhaps the scanning device wouldn't be that sensitive; the flashdrive was small—certainly not the size a weapon would be. She tucked it inside her backless, strapless bra. She could pretend it was part of the underwire, and no one would look any further. She thought about it, then unzipped her dress and rearranged herself.

Then she scrutinized her hair. She'd arranged it on top of her head and secured it with the heavy jeweled combs Terrence had given her for their anniversary. She turned and caught sight of them. Ornately fashioned metal lavishly studded with diamonds, emeralds and rubies. For a man with simple tastes, Terrence certainly knew how to pick out jewelry, she thought, looking down at her wedding ring, a large diamond surrounded by constellation of diamonds and sapphires.

Tomorrow, she and Moira would have to figure out how to get her out of here. She'd given up on any help from Darby who, Anne realized, had abandoned her here, even after hearing that the wire had been discovered. Of course, that assumed that Darby had even really ever had the wire monitored.

She just needed to make it through the night. Tomorrow, if she was still alive, she'd find a way out of this mess. She slid the knife under the pillow in her bed, hoping Moira would come through on her promise of a bigger knife.

Anne had no doubt she could use it. She kissed two fingers and touched them to her belly. She would keep her baby safe, even if it meant she'd have to kill someone.

# Chapter 81

MOIRA WENT THROUGH the screening ahead of Anne. Anne watched, hiding her nervousness with the look her sisters called her ice princess face, a look generally reserved for when she needed to erect a barrier between her and unwanted attentions from whatever quarter.

First, a wand swept Moira from head to toe, scanning for wires or any electronic transmissions. The man, one of the bodyguards Anne had seen before, moved the device slowly down the girl's back, then up her front, then on each side of her. Moira looked bored but tolerant. Then a metal detector replaced the wand and swept slowly upwards starting at the five-inch heels. The detector beeped, and Moira had to remove her shoes which must have had a metal heel component. The shoes were scanned through a machine by one of the other bodyguards while the one wielding the metal detector continued his way up her dress. Anne watched nervously as the wand reached Moira's breasts, knowing the girl would also be wearing a bra with an underwire for this type of dress. The metal detector beeped again, and Moira rolled her eyes. The man handed her a robe which she put over her shoulders.

"Can I have her unzip me?" Moira motioned to Anne.

The guard nodded.

"Anne, unzip me so I can take off this stupid bra and have them scan me without it. I told you these things set it off. I'm never wearing one again. This is just bloody ridiculous." Moira glared at the guards as she spoke. "I think these arseholes just do this to get off."

Moving to help Moira, Anne could hardly breathe for the fear that had settled in her chest. With this kind of thoroughness, the security guards would certainly find the flashdrive on her when it was her turn. She tried to control the panic she felt rising through her as she unzipped Moira's dress. Moira pulled the bra out and handed it over to be scanned. The other guard ran the wand over Moira's body.

The bra was then handed back to Anne, who helped Moira put it back on under the robe.

When Moira had rearranged herself, she stood back to help Anne for her turn.

Anne stood quietly as the scanners passed across her body. The scan for electronic transmissions went quickly and without incident, as she'd expected. She handed her shoes over to the guard who'd checked Moira's shoes. Then the other guard handed her the robe so he could do the metal detection scan on her body.

Anne shook her head and refused to take it. "I'm so sorry, but I can't. My husband would never tolerate me undressing in front of you gentlemen, or allowing you to handle my lingerie. I've already gotten in enough trouble with him this week."

The guard looked at Moira, too unfamiliar with Anne to feel comfortable asking her the question. Moira nodded and quietly spoke in Anne's ear. Anne whispered her response, feeling her face redden.

Moira slanted her eyes to the guard. "She doesn't think she'll need the robe. She's not wearing a bra. Go ahead and do the scan."

The guard swallowed and nodded self-consciously, starting his slow scan of Anne's body for metal. As the wand rode up along her body, she prayed. Reaching her breasts, there was no signal. He paused and nodded, indicating that Moira had been right, then continued running the metal detector where he'd left off, moving upwards toward Anne's head. When he reached her elaborately coiffed hair, her jeweled combs set the machine off.

"I'll have to ask you to remove your hair ornaments, Lady Anne."

She gave a big sigh. "All right, but my hair will fall down. It took forever for me to arrange it." Anne reached up and started to unfasten the combs, then noticed Walter Von Zandt watching her intently from just inside the dining room. She waved and smiled at him. "I may be a while, Walter. I'm going to need a mirror and some time to redo my hair after this."

Von Zandt came forward, shaking his head at the guard. "She's fine. We don't want Lady Anne's beautiful hair to be disturbed." The guard backed away and Walter took Anne's arm to lead her in to dinner. "My dear, I'm sorry about all these security precautions. It's just necessary these days."

"I understand." She could feel Moira's eyes burning into her back. She stopped, turned, and reached her hand out to the girl behind her. "Thank you for waiting for me, Moira. Come on. I can't wait to see the table arrangements. Walter, Moira's worked so hard on everything. I'm sure you'll be pleased."

Von Zandt managed to readjust his face to hide his dismay, but Moira smiled and Anne felt safer; she could not afford for Moira to become alienated from her right now. She squeezed Moira's hand.

# Chapter 82

VON ZANDT SAT at the head of the long, elegant table with Anne to his right. In addition to Von Zandt's two sons and Moira, Anne counted seven other dinner guests, all men. Five men who seemed to be of Arabic origin, two Nigerians, and Cyrus Rothman, Walter's solicitor. Moira was seated between the two Nigerians and seemed to be doing her best to be pleasant to them. Moira's aunt had not come after all, and when Moira asked Henry about where Glynnis was, he'd brushed her off.

Covertly, Anne watched Von Zandt nod toward Moira, then to the two men next to her in an admonishment for her to pay attention to them. Moira's face held a hint of defiance, but under his harsh gaze she did as she was told, and entertained the two men with what appeared to be amusing conversation. Anne wondered if Walter actually meant for Moira's entertainment duties to go so far as to take them to bed. Anne did not think Moira would be so obliging, no matter what Von Zandt thought.

Von Zandt had turned on his overwhelming charm, and had the table engaged in an animated discussion of world affairs. With Anne, he was solicitous and attentive, without being overly aggressive. His hand would touch Anne's arm, though, and occasionally, he would cover her hand with his. The smell of his expensive cologne hung lightly in the air between them. When he spoke to her, his face was too close, and she felt his breath on her. Anne recognized the signs of a man making a serious move on her, even when those moves were covered by a layer of finesse. Moira was right; she would have to get away to her room right after dinner.

She tried to think of a way to get out of the house tonight. Not only did she need to get the flashdrive to Terrence, but she was more afraid than she wanted to admit that Moira would turn on her. Unfortunately, no brilliant plan came to her.

Anne had busied herself during the pre-dinner cocktail hour trying to commit the guests' names to memory, and then throughout dinner trying to link comments about where they were from, and what they discussed, to their names, so she could report the information once she got out of there. About half of the guests chose non-alcoholic drinks, and Anne surmised that they must be more devout Muslims than the others. Careful to not look too interested in the dinner guests, and recognizing that most of the men there were not used to casual conversation with unrelated women, she took care to behave demurely, and was quiet most of the time unless a remark was directed at her.

A manservant served the appetizer which was some kind of mushroom and eggplant dish, then cleared the plates away and brought a light, almost Asian soup. The menu seemed to have been designed to cater to the stricter of the guests' Muslim dietary requirements, and the dishes, although unfamiliar to Anne, were delicious.

Walter was solicitous of his guests' preferences, but did not try to adhere to them himself. Wine was served with each course for those who wanted it, and, of course, he had included both Anne and Moira in the dinner party, which would not have been acceptable in certain Muslim countries, especially dressed in gowns that showed so much bare flesh. Clearly, Walter had his limits about how far he was willing to alter his own behavior to accommodate his business associates.

The solicitor, Cyrus Rothman, eyed everyone and spoke very little. Anne studied him so she could report about him as well. He was a thin man with almost exaggerated features; his nose was large, as were his lips and ears. His graying hair was combed thinly back from his receding hairline. His tuxedo was close-fitting and expensive and he wore a silver wedding ring.

Rothman caught her looking at him, and returned her gaze, letting his mouth curve into what he must use for a smile. Anne knew better than to look away and pretend she hadn't been looking him over. Instead, she returned his smile with one of her own at full wattage. He blinked in surprise and actually blushed. She casually turned back to listen to Von Zandt with wide-eyed interest.

Von Zandt, catching only Rothman's side of the exchange, eyed his solicitor with displeasure. Rothman looked uneasy as he tried to regain his composure. Von Zandt leaned possessively toward Anne, not pausing his conversation with his business colleagues.

Anne resisted the impulse to smile at the lawyer's discomfort, and instead went back to her interrupted observations of the guests and conversation. The names of the men were so difficult. She had tried to put together an acronym to remember them, but couldn't for the life of her think of one. Faruq, Hakim, Asim, Hashim, Kadir were the ones she thought of as Arabs. The Nigerians were Abejide and Jaja. Their surnames were even more difficult, so those she silently chanted to herself to make herself remember them. She wished for her worthless wire so that she wouldn't have to do this. She decided to think of the men as plants, so many of which had difficult names. She put a different plant together in her mind with each one, and tried to think of drawing each one of them.

That seemed to work, and it was something she could do as she listened to the conversation. Maybe I'm not half bad at this covert operation stuff, she thought.

The butler entered, approached Von Zandt, and whispered something in his ear. Walter looked annoyed, shook his head, but then responded sharply with words Anne could not hear. Von Zandt's eyes landed on Anne, narrowing. Her heart stopped as terror seized her.

He knew.

# Chapter 83

REID DROVE UP to the gates of Lynstrade Manor in the sleek black Mercedes he generally used only for social occasions. With no warrant, he couldn't very well push his way in. Of course, he was not coming under his official capacity, but as a husband looking for his errant wife. If Von Zandt refused him entrance, he would have to figure out another approach.

Two guards were posted at the stone gate stations, both armed. One approached his car. Reid hit the button to roll down his window. "Lord Reid. I'm here to see my wife, Lady Anne."

"I'm sorry, sir, but we don't have your name as authorized to enter this evening. We'll have to check with the house." The guard looked back at his counterpart who nodded and went into the small guardhouse.

Reid shrugged, assuming the persona of privileged aristocrat. "If you must."

The guard who'd gone in to make the call, came back out, and went over to the car. "Lord Reid, I'm sorry, but Mr. Von Zandt is giving a dinner party tonight and regrets that this is not a convenient time for visitors."

Reid made himself look annoyed and arrogant, as he thought these guards would expect from someone like him. "I'm not bloody visiting him. I'm here to get my wife."

The guard cleared his throat. "Sir, I believe Lady Anne is attending the dinner."

"She bloody well isn't. She's coming with me." He narrowed his eyes. "Is Andrew Grainger here with her? She damn well better not be meeting him here." Reid assumed these guards were up on the gossip about Anne. The story had to have been irresistible when they had the pretty star attraction of the tabloids staying right here under their noses. "I'll not leave until I make sure that American bastard isn't here sniffing around her. You tell Von Zandt I want to see my wife right now. By God, he'd better not be letting her meet that bastard here."

The guard, surprised by the vehemence of Reid's rant, went back into the guardhouse to call again. When he came out, he said, "Mr. Von Zandt said you can go through. He'll meet with you alone. But he wanted me to remind you that he has guests for dinner, and that he cannot spare much time."

"I don't want his bloody time. I want my wife." Reid drove through to the front drive, too fast, abruptly stopping the car on the gravel drive.

The door was answered by a manservant dressed in a traditional formal black suit. From the man's physique, Reid was fairly certain that the man was also one of Von Zandt's bodyguards. His half-bald head was fronted by the face of a belligerent bulldog.

"I'm Lord Reid, here to see Lady Anne. My wife."

"Yes, my lord. I'll get Mr. Von Zandt for you."

"I don't need to see him. Just my wife. We have an engagement for a dinner party with Lord and Lady Stergus, and I expect her to join me." He made his words slur a little as if he'd had just a little too much to drink.

"Lady Anne is dining with Mr. Von Zandt and his guests."

"No, she's not. She's dining with me."

"Mr. Von Zandt asked me to tell you that he'll meet with you. I'll get him now. If you'll wait here, please, my lord."

"You don't need to trouble yourself. I'll get the bloody woman myself. The dining room is this way?"

The man scurried after Reid as if he were going to try to stop him.

Reid turned back, his face hard, and bit his words out. "You don't want to interfere. I am getting my wife, and she will be coming with me."

He opened the door of the dining room and the room became quiet. Five guards who had been stationed around the table drew automatic weapons and pointed them at Reid. The servant apologized to Von Zandt who stood up and silenced the man by raising a hand, then motioned for the guards to stand down.

"Lord Reid, if you'll wait a moment, we can talk."

"I don't want to talk to you. I've come for my wife."

Anne, seated to Von Zandt's right and across the table from the door, found his eyes, and he saw relief register in her face. She'd known she was in danger.

Silently sending her thoughts of reassurance and entreaties to play along with him, he motioned with his head toward the door. His voice was rough. "Get up, Anne. I've had enough of this kind of behavior from you. We're leaving."

Her eyes downcast, she rose from the table. Reid, watching and keeping his gaze disapproving, was momentarily struck anew by her startling beauty. She wore an exquisite, but revealing, black evening gown, and her hair was drawn up in the jeweled combs he'd given her.

Von Zandt put his hand on her arm to stop her from going, the possessive gesture not escaping Reid.

Reid felt a low growl rumble up from his chest. "Anne, let's go. Now."

Von Zandt drew himself up, his eyes like knives. "You've been drinking. I'm concerned for her safety if she leaves with you." He moved his arm to encircle Anne, and his voice gentled. "My dear, you don't have to go with him. You are welcome to stay here as long as you wish."

Reid kept his eyes fixed on his wife, willing her to move away from the man and the danger. "Anne, come here right now." His voice was harsh and authoritative in a way he'd never spoken to her before, no matter how heated their arguments had gotten.

Appearing almost hypnotized, she started to move away from Von Zandt and toward him. Von Zandt, however, kept his arm around her and walked with her out of the dining room, motioning for Reid to follow.

After the door to the dining room closed, Reid spoke through clenched teeth, keeping his voice low but menacing. "Von Zandt, take your fucking hands off of my wife before I break them off. Anne, come with me." His speech, though still clipped, had the slight slur of someone who had imbibed too much alcohol. He wanted to appear just inebriated enough to explain his impulsive behavior, but not enough to look vulnerable to being fended off.

Von Zandt, momentarily startled by being spoken to in such a way, released her. Anne moved toward Reid, but Von Zandt seemed to recover himself, and put his hand out to grab her again. "Anne."

"I mean it, Von Zandt. Back off. Anne, get over here."

She nodded, and shook her head at Von Zandt. "Walter, please." Then she looked back at Reid, her voice placating. "I'm coming, Terrence, but you have to let me drive. You've definitely been drinking too much for that. I'll take you home."

"We're not going home. We've a dinner to attend. And I think I can be excused for drinking a little when I have a wife that won't stay where she's supposed to be."

She huffed in an excellent rendition of an exasperated wife. "Okay, but you have to let me drive."

Reid motioned for her to come, and let impatience and annoyance flash across his face. "Bloody hell, woman. Drive if you want. Just come on."

"Terrence, let me have a minute to say goodbye to my host."

Reid's eyes bore down on her. "One minute—that's all. I'll wait right here, and he'd best keep his hands to himself. I've had enough of this. No one will be touching you but me. And I'm listening, mind you, so watch that pretty mouth."

"Calm down. Just give me one minute." Anne held up one finger, then went over to Von Zandt whose face was full of concern. Reid watched and listened as she talked to him, keeping his own face impatient and angry, while his heart pounded almost out of control.

"Walter, I'm so sorry we've disrupted your dinner party. I need to go with my husband."

"Are you sure you'll be safe?" Von Zandt looked over at him. "He won't get violent?"

Reid felt another growl roll from his chest and out through his throat. "If I got violent every time the bloody woman caused me trouble..." He shook his head with frustrated temper.

Anne's face was a perfect study in wifely annoyance. "Please, Terrence." She turned back to Von Zandt. "No, he won't hurt me. Thank you for your hospitality, Walter. You've been so kind. Can you have someone send my things over to the hotel tomorrow?"

"If you really want me to."

"Please."

"But you'll still be here to finish my gardens?"

"Yes, of course." She lowered her voice to a whisper. "I just don't think it's wise if I stay here."

"I understand. Let me know if there is anything I can do. Frankly, I'm concerned for your safety." Von Zandt looked at Reid warily, but his tone to Anne was still solicitous.

Reid glared at him, and only part of his behavior was an act. "Fuck you, Von Zandt. She's my wife. I'll worry about her."

Anne shook her head at his outburst. "Really, Terrence, please be civil. Walter, don't worry. He won't hurt me. We've just been going through some difficult times. I'm so sorry to have involved you."

Von Zandt nodded. "If you're sure."

"I'm sure."

"Please let me know if you need anything."

"Thank you, Walter."

She put out her hand to Reid. Taking it quickly, he pulled her close to him. He squeezed her hand tightly with relief at almost having her out of there. Then he put his arm around her and guided her to the car. She put out her hands for the keys and Reid, putting on a show of annoyance for the man watching at the top of the stairs, took them out of his pocket and handed them to her.

From the corner of his eye, Reid saw someone running toward him. He slid his hand into his jacket, ready to grab his weapon. Then he saw it was a smiling Moira, and he momentarily relaxed. She handed him a small box wrapped with black satin ribbon and kissed him on the cheek. Startled, he took the box from her.

"Chocolates, Lord Reid. All the guests get a box. These are Lady Anne's."

"Thank you, Moira." He put them in his pocket and got into the car.

The girl turned and ran back to the house. Looking back, Reid saw Von Zandt scowl and say something to her.

As they drove away, Reid let himself breathe.

THE FIRST CUT

# Chapter 84

**W**HEN THEY GOT OUTSIDE the gates of the estate, Reid expelled the breath he'd been holding and pounded his fist against the dashboard. "Oh, Christ Jesus, thank you, thank you, God." He heard the raw relief in his own voice.

She swallowed, and he saw the extent of the danger she had been in register with her.

"Good girl. Just keep driving. Pull over ahead when I give you the signal. I've an armed team waiting there in case they needed to come in to help get you out."

She nodded. "I was so glad to see you. You know Moira found the wire, then? I'd hoped whoever was listening heard that."

"Yes."

"She said she wouldn't tell him, but I was afraid that she'd change her mind. She took the wire and I had no way to talk to anyone. Darby told me not to use my cell phone, and when I finally decided I had to, it had no power. I guess I left the charger back at the hotel. The regular phones at Walter's are all passworded and monitored. Then the internet was down. I didn't have any way to contact anyone."

"I could kill Darby for sending you in there—especially with a wire."

"Darby said you wanted me to do it."

"I only found out about it tonight, after you'd already stopped transmitting. Then I heard the recording and realized what had happened. It's a miracle Von Zandt's people didn't find it before Moira did. They must not have been doing scans."

"They hadn't been. I gather they were doing them tonight because of the guests they had there. If Moira hadn't found the wire

391

earlier, they would have caught me with it."

He expelled a sigh of relief. "Thank God for Moira, then. And she didn't tell?"

Anne shook her head. "No. She's mad at Walter."

"I suppose she wasn't happy about his attentions to you."

"No."

"And the wire? Where is it?"

"She took it to her room because she said they searched mine every day."

"You kept it on you the whole time then? Until she found it?"

Anne nodded. "I was so scared she'd change her mind and tell about me having the wire. She's a little unstable. I was worried that if she decided to blame me instead of Walter for him being . . . you know, interested in me, that she'd tell him. I was so relieved to see you."

Reid was just barely able to control his own relief at getting Anne out safely, and didn't trust himself to speak more than the bare minimum. "Me, too."

"I should have realized right away you wouldn't have wanted me to do this. I'm sorry. Are you mad at me?"

"No. Not at you."

"Darby said you thought it was too good an opportunity to pass up."

"Even if Darby asked you, why would you agree? Not just your safety was at issue, but what about the baby?"

"Darby said it wouldn't be dangerous, and I wanted to help you." Her eyes, so full of emotion, almost sank him. "I told Andrew not to come, you know. But when he came, I couldn't not talk to him."

"It's all right, Anne. As long as you're safe, everything's fine." He felt numb. Nothing was all right and he doubted if it would ever be again. His wife was almost certainly having another man's child. The time Reid had been allowing himself with her—time for them to pretend to make a home, to make love and be together as if their lives weren't destined to be apart—was over.

She quickly took her eyes off the road to look at him. "I've been so worried, thinking you'd never forgive me. I really didn't tell him to come."

"I know. Darby arranged it. She also set up the photographer."

Anne rubbed her temples. "God, she must really hate me."

"I'm so sorry. I should have kept her away from you."

"It's not your fault. It hurt you, too."

He was quiet, not able to speak over the lump that had stuck in his throat.

Anne glanced at him, then spoke, her voice tentative. "Terrence, I haven't had a chance to explain things to you. I only agreed to meet with Andrew in the hotel dining room because I didn't think I should take him upstairs to my room. I had to talk with him, and I thought it would be much better to do it out in the open—in public."

"I know, Anne. It doesn't matter." But he could tell she didn't understand what he was saying. He could have kicked himself for causing the hope he saw spring up in her.

She smiled and happily went on talking, with the giddiness that often follows a near escape from danger. "I'm so glad to be out of there. I'll be fine finishing the work with Jonas, but there is no way I'm setting foot in that house ever again. I was so scared. I don't know how you do what you do." Anne reached her hand over and placed it on his leg. At her touch, an electric current shot through him, but he caught her hand and put it back on the wheel.

"Best watch the road, girl."

She steered the car around a curve, concentrating on what she was doing. "I felt so isolated. Not being able to even tell if anyone was listening to whatever I said on the wire was unnerving."

"Yes." He indicated a van parked in a leeway. "Pull over here."

When the car came to a stop, Harry emerged from the van. Reid held up his hand to signal for him to wait before approaching them. He needed another moment to finish things with her.

"Anne, you can't go back to Lynstrade Manor. If Von Zandt finds out what you were doing, you'll not be safe. I can't protect you in there. I had one of Stirling's men outside the gate watching out for you, but he couldn't go in past the gates."

Her mouth fell open. "You did?"

"It wasn't much good, as he could only watch you if you left the estate."

She nodded. "I think I saw him the day I tried to set up a meeting with Darby." Anne frowned. "Did she say why she didn't come?"

"Apparently she finally got Stirling to go to bed with her, and she was not willing to leave to make sure you were okay. I'm so sorry. If I'd known . . ."

Anne waved her hand. "It's not your fault. But I do have to go back and finish the job with Jonas. I can't leave it unfinished."

"You can't go back."

"I have to."

"Anne, please. I am begging you not to go back to Von Zandt's."

"I can't let Jonas down. I'll be really careful. I won't go anywhere near the house, and I'll have nothing to do with Walter."

"That's not good enough. If Moira tells Von Zandt what you were doing, you won't be safe there. And it's not just your safety at stake. It's the baby's."

"If he finds out, I promise I'll leave the job, finished or not, right away."

"That's crazy."

"No, it isn't. How would I explain to Jonas or anyone else why I left a job unfinished? Walter's not been arrested or anything. As far as anyone knows, everything is normal. All that's happened is that my husband didn't want me staying at the house, and came to get me."

"Anne, damn it, be sensible."

"I promise I'll be careful."

He shook his head in defeat. The woman was impossibly stubborn. Maybe even criminally stubborn, if there were such a thing.

She reached out and put her hand on his arm with a hesitant, tentative touch. "Terrence, those guests of Von Zandt's—do you want their names?"

He turned and stared at her. "You have them?"

She nodded. "I think I can write them down. Do you have some paper?"

He took a pen and a small pad out of a nook in the car, and handed them to her.

"Thanks. Don't talk while I do this, okay? The names are difficult, so I need to concentrate to write them out."

He nodded and watched as she wrote. When she finished, she handed him the list.

Reid looked it over and shook his head in amazement. "You're sure you got their names right?"

"Yes. But you should have them followed when they leave."

He set his jaw. "I fully intend to."

"Good." She motioned to her list. "I put where they were from there, too. I think I can give a good description as well if you have someone who can draw them. I could try, though I'm better with plants than people."

Reid stopped himself from gaping at his wife in astonishment. "That's all right. We'll get someone to draw them from your description."

"Okay."

"After that, one of my men will drive you back to Aytoun Lane. I've had things set up so that you can stay there. Make-shift, but it should work. Sheets, blankets, all that. I'd prefer you stay there if you insist on finishing the project here."

She turned in her seat and beamed at him. "Thanks, Terrence."

Averting his face from her, he went on. "I'll have one of Stirling's men drive you to and from the job—that way you can rest in the back of the car on the way there and back. He'll also be with you during the day while you're there. If anyone asks, he works for you and Jonas. He'll be happy to act as one of your workmen, as long as his work is always right by your side."

Uncharacteristically, Anne didn't fight him on this. "Okay. I'll think of something to tell Jonas about him."

"Good. As long as Moira doesn't tell, and you act like nothing has happened, Von Zandt shouldn't suspect you. If things change, you'll leave the job immediately." He locked eyes with her, determined to get her agreement on this point.

She nodded. "I will, I promise."

He cleared his throat. "Good, then."

"Terrence, I know you have things to do right now, but do you think you'll be able to come back to the house later tonight?" She leaned toward him, starting to put her arms around him, but he caught her hands and kept them in his.

"No, Anne." He took a deep breath. "I'll be staying at the flat. And when your job is finished here, I think it's best if you go back to California."

She flashed a stunned face in his direction, pulling her hands back. "You won't be staying with me?"

He shook his head.

"Why not?"

"Anne, let's not do this."

"But you said you knew I didn't have anything to do with Andrew coming. And that you understood why I was talking to him."

He made himself go on, looking out the window as he spoke. "I do, Anne, but it doesn't change things for us."

Her gaze went down to her hands where she had placed them in her lap. She raised them and put them on the steering wheel. She looked straight ahead at nothing.

Reid, not looking at her, cleared his throat and quickly went on. "I know how you feel about finishing the project. As you know, I'd rather you didn't. You really should be on a plane away from here tomorrow morning."

She just sat without speaking.

"There'll be a man guarding the house while you're there. He and the man that accompanies you during the day will be there for your protection. They won't report to me unless something's wrong. You're entitled to your privacy. You can see whoever you like. Anyone. I mean that." He pressed a card into her hand, letting the tips of his finger touch her briefly. "These are Harry's numbers. Just let him know if anything seems off, or if you need anything."

"Tell Harry. Not you?" Her voice was dull, defeated. He wanted to comfort her but he had no comfort to give.

"It's better that way."

"I see. Thank you." She looked down, but not before he saw the tears swimming in her eyes.

He put distance between them with his voice. "Use me as your excuse to avoid Von Zandt if you need to. You can tell him that you think I have a private investigator watching you. If he won't give up, tell him you're pregnant, and say I'm the father. That will likely end him bothering you."

There was a long silence between them before she finally spoke.

"Great. Right. I'm sorry for all the trouble I've caused, Terrence."

"It's fine. As long as you're safe, it's fine."

She blinked, then her head snapped around. "I almost forgot. I have something for you." She fumbled with her hair combs, pulling something out, while her hair tumbled down around her lovely bare shoulders. Watching her, he wanted her, loved her, ached for her, all over again.

Her face impassive, she handed him a small metal device.

Reid looked at her, puzzled. "What's this, then?"

Her voice was tired. "A flashdrive. Moira gave it to me—she copied information from Walter's records, his bank account information for the terrorist group funding. I hid it behind my combs. When they used the metal detector on me, they thought it was my combs that set it off and didn't make me take my hair down to check if there was anything behind them."

His heart rose to his throat with sheer terror at the danger she had been in. "Sweet Jesus, lassie. Von Zandt would have killed you for doing that. He will, if Moira tells him she gave it to you."

Anne showed no reaction, and Reid knew he didn't have her attention anymore. She was still back on what was going on—or not going on—between the two of them. Her voice was detached. "I don't think she'll tell."

"If he confronts her, she might. He's an evil, vindictive man, and he won't tolerate betrayal. Anne, you can't go back there. If he finds out . . ."

"I'll be careful."

He sighed and slipped the flashdrive into his pocket, frustrated. "How much longer will the project take?"

"About a month. I'll call . . . Harry, is it? I'll call him if anything seems wrong."

"All right." Reid motioned over to a young officer coming out of the van. "There's Simpson. He'll drive you to have the sketches made, then home. You'll need to switch sides with him." He reached for the car door to get out.

She spoke, her voice soft and devoid of hope. "I won't be with Andrew if you want me. No matter whose child it is." She looked over at him for a response, but he could tell she didn't actually expect to receive any reassurance from him. She knew him, after all.

He shook his head. "No, you need to do what's best for the child. It's got nothing to do with what I want."

"Don't you love me?" The tears brimming in her eyes hovered there one last instant, then started to fall.

His heart ripped apart, and he closed his eyes, swallowing his grief. "I love you so much this is killing me."

"Me, too. Oh, God, me too." She put her face in her hands and cried.

He knew she wanted him to take her into his arms, and more than anything else in the world, he wanted to do just that. But if he did, he didn't think he would be able to ever let her go. So he opened the car door and started to get out. Then he turned back to her, pulled out his handkerchief and handed it to her. She took it from him and wiped her eyes.

"Anne."

"Yes?" She was crying and put her face in the handkerchief to muffle the sounds.

"Look at me."

She kept her face in the handkerchief and shook her head.

"Anne, look at me."

She shook her head again.

"Please."

She raised her head up and turned to him. "What?"

He forced himself to smile. "That's not an ugly business dinner dress, my love."

She sniffled and looked down at the provocative black gown as if it had suddenly appeared on her, then looked back up at him. Seeing his smile, she returned it with a tremulous one of her own. "You're right. I'll burn it."

"I'd appreciate that."

# Chapter 85

REID PACED as he watched Harry scan the information from the flashdrive on his computer screen.

"So, does it look genuine?"

Harry held up a hand. "Just give me a bleeding minute, guv. I've got tracers going through the lines to see if the accounts are legit, and if they're channeling money to the targets from the Nigerians."

"Could you hurry? I've got McMurty sitting by the telephone in his pajamas, I'm sure, ready to get the authorization to pull the plug on the accounts if they're the right ones. MI5, Interpol and the FBI as well will need to be notified."

Harry ignored him and kept working. Reid looked at his watch. Almost half ten. They needed to get this finished before Von Zandt's dinner party ended. The man might check his accounts before retiring for the night. If he noticed anything wrong, he might do something to stop them from closing the accounts down. But bothering Harry to make him hurry was counterproductive.

Frustrated, Reid looked over at Allison, who was listening to the recordings of the transmissions sent from Anne's wire and taking notes, while running searches on the computer of the names on the list of dinner guests. He started to talk to her, but she pointed to her earphones and shook her head.

He went to the office's little kitchen and poured himself a cup of coffee, as well as others for Allison, Oscar, and Harry. He had sent Frank home already; the man had been entirely exhausted. His stamina wasn't what it was pre-injury, and Reid did not want to compromise Frank's health when there was really nothing for him to do here right now. Frank would be there first thing in the morning, Reid knew, when, with any luck, the rest of them would still be asleep.

Allison took off her earphones when he brought the coffee over. "Thanks, guv. I've the data on the two Nigerians." She handed him her notes, and pointed to two of the names. "The printer should have what I got on these two, if you want to look them over while I finish with the other guests."

Reid went over and pulled the papers off the printer and started to read them. Then he exhaled, suddenly inflated with hope. "We've got a hit. These two have to be the ones we want. But what the hell was Von Zandt doing inviting Anne to a dinner these slime would be at? Why would he take such a chance that she'd tell someone their names?"

Allison took a drink of coffee, staring at her computer screen. "Typical man. He wasn't thinking with his big head. On the tapes, Moira said he wanted to show Lady Anne off like she was his girlfriend or something." As if realizing what she'd said, Allison's eyes got huge and she put her hand over her mouth.

"Were there any biscuits, guv?" Harry quickly interrupted, and out of the corner of his eye, Reid saw him shaking his head at Allison to be quiet.

Reid pretended not to notice the exchange. "Is this what I'm relegated to now? Getting coffee and biscuits?" He grumbled. "There aren't any biscuits. But I do have chocolates." He patted his jacket pocket, drawing out the small box. He tossed them to Allison. "Moira gave them to me—actually they were intended for my wife, but they ended up in my pocket. Apparently they're a party favor or something."

"Wonderful." Allison opened the box. There was a silence, then she said, "Guv?"

"What?"

"These aren't chocolates." She pulled out a mass of wires. "This is the wire I fitted up for Lady Anne."

\* \* \* \* \*

There was already a watch at all exit points from the United Kingdom for the men using the names Anne had given, and as soon as the police artist finished with the drawings from Anne's descriptions, they'd broadcast those as well. Reid wanted all of the men picked up if they were still in the country, but if they'd already left, he'd need help finding them from Interpol. He picked up the telephone and started to dial.

After Reid had relayed the information and been assured that all possible measures would be taken to apprehend the men, he went over to Allison's desk. He picked up the wire and the chocolate box and put them into his pocket, then checked on Oscar's progress accessing the accounts that were to receive the midnight transfer of funds, as well as the account that had received the transfer earlier that day.

The only noise in the room was the sound of light tapping on keyboards and soft curses coming from Harry as he worked. Then, suddenly, a crow of triumph erupted, and Harry shot up from his seat. "These accounts are the genuine article, guv. I've just gotten confirmation."

"You're sure?" Reid was almost afraid to believe they had finally done it.

"Positive. Eight accounts funneling millions from the Nigerian extremists to offshore accounts that are in turn going to the financing of the jihads involved."

"Bravo, Harry. Good job. I'll make the call for authorization, then. You can divert the funds?"

"Yeah, and shut the accounts down, or at least zero them out. But they've got transactions scheduled to occur at midnight, so unless you want to take a chance at ending up holding the bag after the money's flown away, we'd better do it soon. As I mentioned before, someone already transferred four million pounds out early this evening. Though I'm thinking if we act quickly, we might still be able to get that back."

"How?"

"Reverse the transaction. Unless it's been moved again, in which case we're out of luck."

"Try."

"Just give me the word and I'll get on it."

Reid picked up the telephone, and again spoke quietly into it. He held the receiver, waiting for McMurty to come back on the line with the authorization to seize the accounts. He covered the receiver, and asked Harry, "Millions? How many?"

Harry stared at the screen, did some mental calculations, screwing up his face as he thought. "Looks like about sixty million pounds all together."

Reid raised his eyebrows and told McMurty the number. There was another wait, then McMurty spoke, giving him the go ahead. He broke the connection and nodded to Harry.

"Go for it. Clean them out and get back any transfers you can."

Harry grinned and went to work.

Reid went over to Allison and handed her the printouts on the two Nigerians. "As there are no photos of these men, when we get the identikit drawings, if the men haven't been picked up, I want the drawings on the news. Good job on this, Allison." He patted her shoulder before moving on to see what Oscar had found.

Allison, seeming to register his return to the use of her first name, and what that meant, said quietly, "Thanks, guv."

Harry turned to her, put his thumb up and winked.

Reid pretended not to see her nod back with a small, relieved smile.

# Chapter 86

"YOU'RE JUST IN A ROTTEN MOOD because Anne's gone." Moira kicked off her shoes and helped herself to a vodka from the small refrigerator camouflaged to look like just another of the cupboards of the bookcases in Walter's office. Walter hadn't said anything when Moira had taken Anne's place next to him at the table after Lord Reid had taken Anne away, or when Moira had refused to have anything more to do with the Nigerians, but she was expecting she'd hear about it now. Bringing up Anne might take his mind off her own disobedience.

Walter took his own drink over to the desk, sat down, and opened his laptop computer, not even bothering to look at her. Uneasiness skittered along her spine. She'd done some risky things when she was mad about the Nigerians. Not only had she given Anne the account information, but first, she'd scheduled a transfer of four million pounds to her own account, an account she'd set up simultaneously in another name.

If he was planning to check his accounts, he might see what she'd done. It wasn't yet midnight, but if he was checking on his own scheduled transfers, he'd likely discover what she'd done. She didn't regret it, thinking of what he'd wanted her to do with the Nigerians, but she didn't want him to find out, either. She needed to distract him.

"Walter, don't work. Can't we just spend some time together alone?"

"Don't be tiresome, Moira. I have work to do. Go up to bed."

"Come with me." Usually, after a party like this, he wanted sex. Heavy sex, and if he was in a bad mood, mean sex. His mean sex could leave her exhausted, but she needed to keep him away from the computer, and it wasn't like she hadn't done it before. She had to keep him distracted until she decided what to do. The way she saw it, she had two choices. She could either reverse the transfer before he found out, or let it go forward and make sure she was long gone when Walter found out.

"Not tonight." He turned on his computer, and the screen went through its usual machinations while the system booted up.

"You're mad at me about those Nigerians, aren't you?" If he didn't want sex, she was going to have to make him fight with her to get him away from the computer.

Walter waved his hand as if to shoo her away, and drained the contents of his glass. "Go to bed. You're bothering me."

This wasn't like him. He wanted her to either obey him mindlessly, or disobey so he could punish her. Ignoring her disobedience was something he'd never done before.

She just needed to push him a little more to get him angry enough to decide he needed to discipline her. "That's so bloody unfair. It's bad enough that you'd want me to sleep with another man, but with both of them? That's twisted." She leaned against the desk, trying to put herself between him and the computer.

He pushed her away trying to reach the computer. "Don't be ridiculous. I simply asked that you entertain them. I never said anything about you having sex with them. I'd already arranged to have women brought in and waiting in their rooms for them. If you want to know the truth, they insisted on virgins, so you didn't even qualify. Rebecca sent over some girls she's just acquired. I'm sure they're being well-taken care of even as we speak."

She felt a deep, raw relief at the same time she realized what a terrible mistake she'd made. "Oh, my God. And I thought . . ."

Walter held up his empty glass, commanding service, but still not looking at her. "I can't even imagine where you would come up with such an idiotic idea."

Moira took his glass from his hand and refilled it from the cognac decanter in the globe drinks table. Her mind was racing. She'd been such an idiot. Of course he hadn't wanted her to be with another man. They loved each other. She closed her eyes, thinking about what she'd done giving the account information to Anne. She needed to warn him that Anne now had his financial information. But not until she could come up with a story that didn't implicate herself, and not until she undid the transfer to her account, because there was no way to explain that. She could do it from any computer, but not if he was logged into his accounts.

She padded over to him and handed him the cognac, kissing him on the top of his head. He accepted the refilled glass without a word of thanks. She sat down on the arm of his chair and put her arms around him. Easing one hand down his chest, she began to unbutton his shirt. If he wouldn't fight, she'd have to try again to distract him with sex. He untangled himself from her, swatting her hand away, and pushed her off his chair. "You're going to make me spill my drink. Go up to bed."

"What's wrong?" Had he already found out what she'd done? Did he have something awful already planned for her? Was one of his men waiting for her when she left him? Terror seized Moira's chest and her mind searched for a new plan. Maybe she should just confess. She'd confess, and he'd punish her, then he'd forgive her because she'd only done it because she loved him and she'd been hurt thinking he wanted to share her.

"Just go up to bed, Moira. We'll talk tomorrow."

But by tomorrow he'd know about the transfer, unless she kept him away from the computer long enough to cancel it. Whatever it took, she had to keep him away from the computer.

"Let's talk tonight." She gave him her best I-really-need-you-to-fuck-me face. "In bed."

He looked at her as if she were some dirty beggar on the street asking for spare change. "Moira, I don't want to have this conversation tonight."

"What conversation?" Her mouth went dry. He had found out. He was just going to make her squirm all night, then he'd have her killed.

He glared at her. "All right, if you insist, we'll do it now."

She swallowed, waiting for what could be her death sentence.

But he just gave an annoyed sigh. "The time has come for us to go our separate ways."

Moira felt her face tighten and go numb with an odd combination of relief and surprise. "What?"

"I'm finished with you." His voice was completely impersonal. Impersonal, not furious. So he didn't know about what she'd done. He was, what? Breaking up with her?

His next words almost knocked her off her feet.

"But you don't need to worry. Frederick wants you."

"Frederick?" She choked out the name. "Freddie?"

"He seems to think he's in love with you."

"Freddie? Walter, are you crazy?"

He shot her a quelling look. "It makes perfect sense. You'd be financially comfortable and he'll be devoted to you. He assures me that he would be able to put your liaison with me out of his mind. What's more, he's willing to take you, not as a mistress, but as his wife."

"Willing to take me? Walter, are you saying you'd be able to see me with your son and not care?" This was almost worse than him wanting her to do a one-time thing with the Nigerians.

"Don't be absurd. Why would I care?"

Moira shook her head, not believing what she was hearing. "But I love you."

Walter flipped his hand up as if to indicate that her feelings didn't matter. "You'll get over it."

"Don't you love me at all?"

"Don't be a child. I enjoyed you for a time, but that's all." His tone signaled his boredom with the topic. "Frederick will make you a good husband, Moira, and, frankly, you're bloody lucky he wants you."

Moira tried to control the panic pulsing through her. She had to think. "You seem sure I'll agree." She barely managed to keep the tremble out of her voice.

"It's your best option. You and Frederick are friends, he wants you, and you'll both be comfortable financially. That's not a bad foundation for a marriage."

She would not bring up Frederick's disabilities. Even now, she knew better than to imply his son was anything less than a desirable marriage partner.

"You also seem to work well together," he added, smiling for the first time since this horrendous conversation had started.

"Work well together? The only work we did together was for you."

Walter's smile vanished. "I have no idea what you're talking about."

Anger rushed through her, almost pushing out her fear. "I'm

talking about taking care of Richard and that cop. You told Freddie what to do, but you knew he couldn't do it by himself. I helped him, but it was for you, not for him."

"I have no idea what you're talking about, Moira." He went on, his voice completely empty of emotion. "I'm offering you a simple choice. It's up to you. If you accept Frederick's proposal, the two of you can stay in the flat. If you decide not to accept Frederick's proposal, you have until the end of the month to vacate the flat and figure out a way to replace the allowance I've been giving you." He bared his teeth in a cold, scary smile. "I'm sure I could get you a job in one of Rebecca's whorehouses."

"You bastard."

"Don't be dramatic, Moira. Frederick is your best alternative and I strongly suggest you take him. Now get out. I still have work to do and it's close to midnight. Shut the door when you leave."

\* \* \* \* \*

When the door slammed behind Moira, Walter Von Zandt picked up the house phone and called Frederick's room. Things were coming together as well as could be expected. A few setbacks—Reid showing up, Anne leaving the house temporarily—but the dinner had gone well, and he was rid of Elisa and Moira. As an added bonus, if Moira accepted Frederick's offer, his son would be happy.

As for his own plans, he'd talk with Anne again when she came back to work. He'd convince her that he would give her a much better life, a much happier life, than she'd ever have with her idiot of a husband. He allowed himself a brief moment to think about Anne coming to him before Frederick's voice came on the other end of the line.

"Father?"

"I've told Moira about your offer. You need to go to her."

"Now? I thought you said tomorrow." Frederick's voice was agitated in that odd way he had. "I'm not prepared. I wanted to have flowers, the ring."

"That can wait. Just go to her. She's on her way to her room right now."

"Father? What did she say?"

Von Zandt considered his response. "She was surprised, but I think she likes the idea."

"Really?" Frederick's words trembled with excitement.

"She may play hard to get for a while, but don't worry about it. She's yours. Just go to her. If she gives you any trouble, let me know." He hung up, then pulled up his accounts to ensure that the scheduled transfers for the next phase of the Nigerians' operation went through.

# Chapter 87

MOIRA NEEDED time to think. Walter had been getting on to his computer even as she was leaving. What if he found out she took the money? Or worse, even, found out she'd copied all the account information and given it to Anne? Even marrying Frederick wouldn't save her then.

He'd kill her.

She couldn't be anywhere within his reach when he found out. She had to get away fast, and she had to do it without any help from anyone, especially not from her mother. Her mother was totally dependent on Walter now for financial support. Besides, she remembered how her mother had ignored her pleas not to be sent to Walter in the first place.

Actually, her situation then had been similar to the one she was in today. Her mother had told her that for the good of the family she needed to go to Walter, and that she needed to make him want to keep her as long as possible. She was to do whatever he wanted. Richard and her mother had made it clear that if she didn't, they'd have nothing else to do with her. So she'd gone, and she'd not really regretted it until now, because she'd fallen in love with Walter.

Moira thought about her options.

If she somehow got the transfer cancelled before Walter realized what she'd done, she could stay. But not with Walter. The bastard had basically ordered her to marry Freddie. Fury mixed with humiliation pulsed through her veins. She'd been doing what Walter wanted since she was sixteen, and she'd tried so hard to please him. How could he want her to marry Freddie? To sleep with Freddie the rest of her life? Freddie was nice, but sort of . . . weird. And she was definitely not attracted to him. That watery eye was all right for a friend, but for a lover? Ick.

No, this time she wasn't going to do what Walter wanted. If he didn't love her, she sure wasn't going to let him tell her how to live her life. She would have her own money now, and she could do what she wanted.

Moira opened her bedroom door, her mind still planning the steps of her escape. She drew in her breath in surprise when she saw the lamp by the bed was on. She was sure she'd turned it off when she'd gone down to dinner with Anne.

The guards must have searched her room after all and left the light on. But they wouldn't have found anything. Moira had made sure of that. She closed her bedroom door and reached around her back to unzip her dress, just as she registered someone else's presence. She spun around, and her hand went to her throat in shock, until she realized who it was. A beaming Frederick stood leaning against the wall, watching her. He looked more nervous than she'd ever seen him.

He straightened up, moving toward her. "Are you all right, Moira? Did I startle you?"

She made herself smile. "A little, but it's all right. I just wasn't expecting you to be here."

Freddie stammered. "My father said he told you how I feel about you?"

"Yes." Quickly she assessed her options—truth or deception?

Gingerly, put his arms around her. She felt him trembling and knew he was worried about her reaction. "Moira, I want to marry you. I know this is sudden for you, but I've loved you for so long." She let him hold her while she thought, resting her head against his chest, nor did she protest when he started to kiss her neck.

She decided on deception. She couldn't afford to alienate Walter or Frederick until she was safely away with her money. Making her voice affectionate, she said, "I feel the same way about you, Freddie."

He blew out a breath of relief, then held her even more tightly against his chest. "I can't believe it. I didn't think I had much of a chance."

She kissed him full on the lips. "Silly. How could I not love you, Freddie?"

Excitement all but bubbled out of him, and his words fell over each other on their way out. "I've got a ring picked out for you, but it's being sized at the jewelers. I thought I'd have until tomorrow. Sooner is better, of course, but I'd wanted to propose with flowers, champagne, and a ring. This is wonderful!" He gave a hoot of delight.

"You're so sweet." Moira smiled, tracing her finger along his face, trying not to flinch when her finger passed over one of his many pimples. "I don't need a ring tonight. I just need you."

He grinned. "All right, but I want to do this right. I want to propose properly."

She gave him a flirtatious look. "Okay, then, do it."

"Moira Ramsey, will you do me the great honor of marrying me?"

She took his face in her hands and smiled. "Of course. I've been in love with you for so long. I just didn't know how to tell you or what to do about . . . your father, or how you'd feel about . . . my past."

He put a finger over her mouth. "That was another life. We'll never talk about that again. I love you, and you're going to be my wife." His face looked transfixed with his feelings for her, and she felt a little guilty, but now self-preservation was her only concern.

"You'll make love to me tonight, Frederick, won't you?"

He blushed. "If you're ready for that. I know this is sudden for you. I've wanted you so long, but I can wait a little longer, if it's too soon for you."

She untied his tie and started to unbutton his shirt. "I don't want to wait a minute longer."

Later, after Frederick was asleep, Moira carefully moved away from him to go to the bathroom and clean up. He'd been telling the truth; he'd obviously been wanting her. He hadn't lasted two minutes the first time, and had been ready to go again ten minutes later. It was a funny sensation, being adored like that. With Walter, she'd been the one who loved, and he'd been the one who'd, sometimes grudgingly, allowed her to love him. She didn't know which way was worse.

# TUESDAY, APRIL 21

# Chapter 88

**R**EID HADN'T GOTTEN BACK to his flat until after three o'clock that morning. He was awakened not four hours later by the incessant ringing of the telephone. Fifteen minutes later he was on the way to Lynstrade Manor on the report that Frederick Von Zandt had been murdered, and that Moira Ramsey was missing, presumed to have done the deed.

The gates to Lynstrade Manor were open when he drove up. There were three police cars in the driveway as well as the coroner's vehicle and a scene of crime van.

Frederick Von Zandt apparently had been killed by way of a large knife in the heart. He'd been found naked in bed in a room Reid was told had been occupied by Moira Ramsey. Blood thoroughly soaked the area of the bed near his chest. It appeared Frederick had been asleep and had likely not even known he'd been stabbed. The medical examiner had preliminarily opined that the man had been dead approximately six to seven hours.

Reid gave instructions to the scene of crime operatives, then gave the nod to the medical examiner to have the body removed after the photographing and videotaping was completed. He walked down the front staircase to join Walter Von Zandt in his study.

Von Zandt sat behind his desk. He appeared composed and motioned for Reid to sit down in one of the chairs opposite him. Reid's eyes registered two other men sitting on the leather sofa, Henry Von Zandt and Von Zandt's lawyer, Cyrus Rothman, and he nodded a greeting.

"I hadn't thought to see you again so soon, Lord Reid. I trust Lady Anne is all right?" The man's eyes searched his face, and Reid was startled to see what seemed to be genuine concern.

For Christ's sake, Reid thought, realizing Von Zandt was more concerned for Anne than he was for his murdered son. "She's fine. She won't be coming in to work today, of course, with what's happened." He'd made a call earlier to make sure Anne was not driven to Lynstrade Manor today and to make sure she stayed at home.

"I hadn't expected her today, in any event, after last night. I'll have her things sent to the hotel, of course, as she asked. I would have had it done already, but . . ." Von Zandt gestured around him, indicating the chaos things were in.

Reid met the man's gaze. "She won't be staying there. I'll take her things with me."

Von Zandt pursed his lips, clearly unhappy.

Reid said, "I've been advised that your guests are no longer here. I'll need their names. We'll need to interview them about the events of last night."

Von Zandt splayed his hands out in front of him in a gesture of helplessness. "They left right after dinner so I don't think they'll be able to help. However, we anticipated your questions and Cyrus has prepared a list of their names. I'm afraid I don't have their addresses." He passed a piece of paper across the desk to Reid.

"I understand they left by helicopter." So, of course Reid's people hadn't been able to follow them. Reid had had cars waiting to follow Von Zandt's guests when they left Lynstrade Manor, but when he'd gotten reports that a helicopter had come and gone in the middle of the night, he'd guessed they'd all absconded. Efforts to locate the helicopter had been futile. Of course, at that time, they hadn't known Frederick had been murdered.

"Yes."

Scanning the list of names, Reid realized they'd been fabricated. The names were close enough to the actual names so that if Anne had reported the names of the men she'd met, she'd be excused by a Westerner's inability to distinguish one foreign name from another, but off enough so that it would have been impossible to locate the men using the fabricated names. Reid didn't let on that he knew he was being deceived or press for the correct contact information, deciding to let Von Zandt think that his deception had been successful, and that Reid's people would be chasing their tails looking for the wrong men.

He asked, "Why was your son in Moira's room? In her bed? She was your mistress, wasn't she?"

Von Zandt sighed. "Frederick was in love with Moira. When I realized that, I broke things off with Moira. He wanted to marry her. I believed Moira returned his feelings. I don't know what happened between them last night."

"How was his body found?"

"The housekeeper found him."

"What time was that?"

"It was early. You need to ask her to get an exact time. She said she'd gone to get Moira's dress so it could be sent to be cleaned this morning. She found my son, told me, and I called the police."

"After you emptied the house of your guests."

Von Zandt looked appalled. "Absolutely not. They'd left already. Otherwise, of course I would have insisted they stay."

"Of course." Reid barely bit back the urge to make a sarcastic remark. "Did you recognize the knife?"

"I did. It appears to have come from our kitchen. The cook has no idea why Moira would have it upstairs."

There was a knock on the door and, at Von Zandt's permission, the door opened and a manservant came in with a tray of coffee. Reid declined, even though he badly needed the caffeine.

He stood up to go. It didn't matter how many questions he asked. He was being fed a load of swill for answers. "We need to search the flat where Moira lives. I believe you're the owner of record. Do you have any objection?"

"No, of course not. We want you to find the girl before she hurts anyone else."

Von Zandt's cooperative attitude rang false. He knew Von Zandt had taken control of this situation long before a call to the police had been made. Reid suspected he'd already had someone visit the flat to make sure the police didn't find anything he didn't want found. And perhaps to make sure they found what Von Zandt did want found.

"We'll need to interview your housekeeper."

"Of course. She's available. A little shaken, but still here."

"And the rest of the staff. Including the guards at the gate."

He nodded. "They'll cooperate."

"Good. We'll get on with it, then. Meanwhile, please have someone get my wife's things together."

Von Zandt narrowed his eyes, and for the first time that morning Reid felt like he was seeing the man behind the façade. "You don't deserve her."

Reid stared back, making sure his eyes were flat and cold. "Neither do you."

\* \* \* \* \*

Later, after the interviews of the household staff were completed and the search of the pertinent areas of the house finished, Reid touched base with Allison on the status of the search for Moira Ramsey. A watch had been put on her mother's house as well as on the flat, but so far nothing indicated she'd been to either place. Reid wouldn't have put it past Walter Von Zandt to have killed the girl and his son, and set it up to make it look like Moira had killed Frederick.

The search of Moira's flat did bring some developments. A wig of dark, real, hair, was found to match the hairs found in Richard Ramsey's car. Also, she'd apparently been unsophisticated enough to have neglected to delete two voicemails from DI Lawrence. One made the clear implication that he'd seen her go with her stepfather the night he'd been killed, and the other confirmed the meeting at which DI Lawrence ended up garroted.

Moira couldn't have acted alone, though, and the more Reid mulled it over, the more it made sense that the young man besotted enough to buy an engagement ring for a woman who was still having sex with his father, would have been her logical accomplice. Any personal motive Moira might have had for killing her stepfather was unclear. Reid assumed it had been to stop him from giving evidence against Von Zandt. But the explanation that DI Lawrence was killed just because of the blackmail seemed a little too easy. Reid still suspected that Lawrence had been the leak that was feeding information to Von Zandt.

Everything made sense if Von Zandt was behind the killings, but without Moira, Reid had no evidence to support his theory. Frederick would not be talking, but Moira might if she were still alive, and if he could find her. Of course, Von Zandt would do everything in his power to make sure she did not tell what she knew.

They needed to find Moira Ramsey before Von Zandt did.

"Sir, come take a look."

One of the young officers conducting the search pointed to a display over the fireplace. Two bullfighter's swords were crossed in the center, and on each side was a shorter, narrow and rounded dagger. Reid remembered Moira talking about the trip to Toledo. Toledo, the Spanish city known for its high-quality swords and knives.

Reid shook his head. None were the right shape. "Not those. What we're looking for will be long and thin." He paused. "And it will be in her room." Von Zandt would have made sure of that.

Minutes later, the officer returned, a deadly looking black and gold handled stiletto held between two gloved fingers. "This what you were thinking of, guv?"

He nodded. "Exactly that. Get it tested for blood, prints, DNA."

The officer grinned and bounded out of the room, full of barely suppressed delight.

Outside the building, Reid found his car where he'd left it, parked in front of a fire hydrant. But now, a big grungy orange cat was perched on the bonnet, watching Reid with sleepy eyes. He stroked the animal's back and looked around.

The slightly portly cop stationed at the door of the apartment building waved his hand to indicate the cat. "The lady who takes care of the building says it belongs to Moira Ramsey, but when she tried to take it back, the man that answered the door said it was a stray." One of Walter Von Zandt's men, no doubt.

Reid nodded, scooped up the cat and put it in the passenger seat beside him. He gave it one more pat before turning the ignition. "If only you could talk."

# Chapter 89

MUCH OF WALTER VON ZANDT'S STORY seemed to check out. The jeweler who was sizing an engagement ring for Frederick verified that he'd had the order for a week and that the young man seemed excited about it. If they hadn't gotten the account from Anne of what Moira had told her last night, and of what they'd talked about while Anne stayed at Lynstrade Manor, as well as what had been on the recordings, Reid might have been more likely to believe the version of facts being fed to him.

As it was, Harry, who'd called Anne, told him Anne was sure Moira had had no idea that she and Frederick were expected to get married. Armed with that knowledge, Reid was confident that he was still missing many of the facts about what happened to Frederick and to Moira.

He was enlightened, however, by a review of the seized accounts, and by the failed transfer from one of Von Zandt's terrorist-feeding accounts to an account Moira Ramsey had opened under another name. From what they'd pieced together, the girl must have scheduled the transfer before she brought the flashdrive to Anne.

Moira would have to have planned on leaving Lynstrade Manor before Von Zandt found out what she'd done. But if she really was the one who'd killed Frederick, why? Perhaps it had been something as obvious as Frederick having forced himself on her and she tried to protect herself. Anne's explanation about Moira promising to get the knife for her explained why Moira had the knife, but not why she'd used it. Reid tried not to think about how afraid Anne must have been to need to arm herself with a kitchen knife for protection, and the story about the paring knife she'd first planned to use had almost broken his heart.

Walter Von Zandt's name had not been linked to any of the accounts on the flashdrive. In fact, they'd all been traced, through a labyrinth of other accounts and names, to accounts originating in Frederick Von Zandt's name. Walter had apparently set up his expendable son to take the fall for him if the accounts were ever discovered. Even though Reid knew there was no way Frederick could have been behind the money laundering operation, every document and other piece of evidence led to Frederick. Reid wondered if Frederick's death hadn't been in Von Zandt's mind all along—maybe not when it happened, but whenever it became necessary.

Walter Von Zandt's laptop computer showed no trace of ever accessing the accounts, and Reid strongly suspected it wasn't even the same computer the man had been using when Moira copied the account information. Perhaps the helicopter that escaped Lynstrade Manor had taken away more than just people.

Frederick taking the fall and dying before he could talk was a tidy solution for Von Zandt's legal problems, but for his plan to work, Moira could not be allowed to testify. Moira was a dangerous loose end for Von Zandt and he couldn't let her live.

When Reid went to talk to Barbara Ramsey about Moira's whereabouts, Walter Von Zandt was just leaving. They acknowledged each other briefly as they passed, Von Zandt seeming to be as unwilling to cross swords at that particular moment as was Reid.

Barbara Ramsey was pouring herself a drink when the maid ushered Reid into the drawing room. He could tell from the woman's wobbly movements that this wouldn't be the first drink she'd had that day.

"Mrs. Ramsey?"

Barbara Ramsey turned, apparently trying to focus on who he was.

"Terrence Reid," he reminded her.

"Oh, yes, Lord Reid." Her voice was vague. "Would you like a drink?"

"Not just yet, thank you. Can I have a few moments of your time?"

"Of course. I have nothing but time. Please sit down." She plopped into a chair, slightly sloshing her drink over the rim of the glass.

He sat across from her, trying to get her eyes to meet his. "I want to talk to you about Moira. We need your help to try to find her."

Barbara Ramsey shook her head. "No."

"No?"

"Walter told me that Moira killed my husband."

"We don't know that for sure. There are things we need her to explain. If we find her, we can help her."

She crossed her legs, taking a long swallow of her drink. "I don't want to help her."

"Has she tried to contact you?"

Barbara Ramsey shook her head, a little unsteadily. "Walter told me to tell him if she did, but she hasn't."

"Barbara, if Moira gets in touch with you, call me. Whatever you do, don't let Walter Von Zandt know. This is police business."

"Walter says he'll take care of me. That I can trust him. He said that Richard made him the trustee of his estate because he trusted him to take care of me." She giggled. "Makes sense. Trustee trusted."

"Where is Bert, Mrs. Ramsey?"

"At work. But Walter says the company is his now." She nodded. "So Bert works for Walter. Walter is going to take care of both of us."

"I'm going to talk to Bert. Maybe I can find someone to help him stop Walter Von Zandt from taking everything your husband left."

But Barbara Ramsey wasn't paying attention. "Glynnis is gone, you know."

"Gone?"

"She was supposed to go with Henry to that dinner Moira went to at Lynstrade Manor. But she didn't go, and no one's seen her since then."

Reid frowned. "When did you see her last?"

"Friday night. She stayed with me because Henry was out of town on business with Walter. Then Saturday morning, she left to go back to her flat. She called me once that afternoon, but I haven't heard from her since. Do you know where she is?" Tears filled the woman's bleary eyes.

"No." Reid tried to think what this meant. "Henry said he hadn't seen her either?"

She nodded. "He's frantic."

"Do you think something's happened to her?"

"Yes, of course. She wouldn't just disappear. She wouldn't just leave Henry."

"Perhaps she did." Reid remembered his advice to Glynnis Taylor. He hoped she'd left on her own, and that nothing had happened to her. "I'll make some inquiries. Meanwhile, I'll talk to Bert about your husband's will. Will you be all right here?"

"Yes. I'll just go upstairs to bed." She pointed up and wobbled. "If you'll excuse me."

Reid took her arm; he didn't want the woman negotiating the stairs in her condition. He found the maid waiting out in the hall and instructed her to take Barbara Ramsey up to bed, then left to find Bert Ramsey.

Von Zandt could not be allowed to take over Ramsey International.

# Chapter 90

REID ADJUSTED the headphones on the surveillance monitor. He kicked his feet against the bottom of the seat across from where he sat in the van. They had parked close enough to get immediate reception, but hidden in a stand of trees.

Walter Von Zandt's voice sounded disgusted. "The bitch betrayed me."

Henry said something in response, but Reid couldn't make it out.

The elder Von Zandt spoke again. "She should have been watched more carefully."

Henry Von Zandt's voice, now audible, registered the rebuke. "I thought we had things covered."

"Apparently you were wrong."

Reid had neither requested nor received authority to plant the listening devices at Lynstrade Manor that he'd gotten from John Stirling. Nonetheless, during the investigation into Frederick's murder, he and Harry had planted scan-resistant bugs in various places inside the house. Anne's bodyguard, who was pretending to be one of Jonas and Anne's workmen, had placed additional directional microphones outside in strategic spots. Nothing they heard via these devices could be used in a legal prosecution, but Reid didn't care about that so much as he cared about making sure he knew if Anne was in danger.

"Yes." Henry's voice again.

"You've determined how she did it?"

"The account data was transferred and copied from the computer in your office to some sort of removable disk or flashdrive shortly before dinner—when you were meeting with your guests in the secure conference room. Before the women joined us."

"I should have known when Reid came in with his jealous husband act that something was up. That has to be when she gave him the information. I wouldn't have been so ready to believe his act if I hadn't seen him act the same way about Anne before." Walter Von Zandt's voice paused, then resumed. "So she must have had it with her when we went into dinner. God damn it, the security scans should have found whatever she copied the data on to if she had it on her then."

The first part of Henry Von Zandt's response was inaudible, but the next words were clear. "How do you think she got into your computer?"

Walter Von Zandt sounded disgusted. "I never made any secret within the house about where the key to the office was, but the computer was password protected."

"She figured out your password?"

"She must have done. I could kill her with my bare hands, the little bitch."

Panic thudded through Reid's lungs. He needed to get Anne away from Lynstrade Manor's grounds right away. He checked the time. Half three. Was she there right now? What if something had already happened to her? Reid knew he shouldn't have allowed her to continue working there. He should have insisted, kidnapped her, had her visa pulled, anything.

He punched in the number of the man assigned to guard Anne on his mobile, and waited while it rang, his attention still focused on the conversation over the wire transmission. It was Walter Von Zandt's voice again.

"The little cunt handed him the data right in front of me—chocolates, she said. I thought nothing of it because she had made such a production of putting together those stupid boxes of chocolates."

Reid closed his eyes in relief, and his heart slowed down to almost normal. Von Zandt wasn't talking about Anne, but rather Moira. Anne's bodyguard answered with a quiet, "All's well here."

"Thank you." Reid hung up, just as Henry Von Zandt spoke again.

"Why would Moira help Reid?"

"Who the fuck knows?" That from Walter.

Henry asked the obvious question. "Do you think Reid's wife was in on it?"

Once again Reid's heartbeat quickened, and he was suspended in terror while he waited for the answer.

Walter's voice softened. "No, not Anne. I can't imagine Reid allowing her to get involved. He's protective of her and insanely jealous. It was obvious he didn't like her being in my house or even working for me. And if she had been involved, he'd never have allowed her to come back here to finish my gardens."

Harry looked over at Reid and gave a thumbs up.

Reid felt a hundred years old as he put down his earphones. "We have to find Moira."

# WEDNESDAY, APRIL 22

# Chapter 91

"WE SHOULD have no problem getting the will set aside. Cyrus Rothman had a conflict so large it could swallow the sun. I should be surprised if Rothman isn't warned off, as well, and not be allowed to practice law anymore. The bar does not look kindly on members who do things like this." Ronald Hitchcock not only looked the part of a formidable solicitor, with a bushy head of graying hair and serious eyes covered by metal-rimmed glasses, but he came with impressive credentials. What's more, he'd immediately made time in his busy schedule for Reid and Bert Ramsey to meet him in his offices.

The small conference room of the exclusive Gordon Street offices of one of the largest law firms in Scotland was kitted out in such a fashion as to give clients the message that they were part of an exclusive, privileged clientèle. Rich wine-colored leather upholstered chairs sat around the sleek round mahogany table, and the modern art that adorned the walls was obviously original.

Reid nodded, satisfied that they had the right man for the job. He'd gotten the recommendation for Ronald Hitchcock for Bert from his own family's solicitors. He was going to make sure this prize as well as the money from the accounts was snatched out of Von Zandt's greedy paws, if it was the last thing he did. "Bert, do you want to challenge it?"

Bert Ramsey looked at the solicitor. "How much of a difference would it make?"

Hitchcock steepled his fingers. "The difference between nothing and millions. Although, of course, you and your mother could decide not to challenge the will, and to instead rely on Walter Von Zandt's generosity."

Bert shook his head. "No f'ng way. What happens now?"

"It's a significant enough estate to motivate the putative beneficiary, in this case, Walter Von Zandt, to fight our efforts to set aside the will. If he doesn't, he'll lose both your father's personal assets and Ramsey International. Additionally, I'd advise you to petition to have the Ramsey stock transfers to Von Zandt reversed. Of course, if the will is set aside, the estate will have to pay whatever portion of the loan is still outstanding, but that amount is negligible. The rest of the loan has been paid back with interest, so the court is likely to simply set aside the other conditions of the loan, such as the seats on the board and the stock that was given with the loan, because Rothman's conflict of interest is so flagrant as to basically constitute fraud."

Bert tapped his pen on the pad of paper in front of him. "Then the stock will still belong to the estate, and go to my mother, I presume?"

"Yes. There'll be no trust and no trusteeship for Von Zandt." The solicitor adjusted his glasses. "Was there a prior will?"

Bert nodded. "I don't know if we even still have a copy. It had some bequests to my sister and me, but other than that, everything went to my mother."

"Good. You've a strong case, as I've said. That being said, the conservative approach would be to strike a deal with Von Zandt to avoid years of litigation. Decide what you're willing to give up and what you aren't, and make a trade in exchange for dropping the will challenge." Nothing in Hitchcock's demeanor gave a clue as to whether he was recommending making such a deal or was just identifying options. Reid thought the solicitor would make a formidable poker player.

Bert frowned. "If he doesn't back down, and we lose in court, Walter could possibly get my father's whole estate and control of the company?"

Hitchcock considered. "It's possible."

Hitchcock's suggestion was reasonable, but the solicitor wasn't aware of all the implications of Von Zandt getting control of any part of Ramsey International.

Reid shook his head. "Von Zandt won't dare engage in a civil suit over the will. He knows what an investigation into his accounts and business dealings would reveal. He'll fold up his tent and slink away if you challenge it."

Bert nodded, setting his jaw. "You're right. We won't settle."

Reid exhaled the breath he hadn't realized he'd been holding.

"What about my sister?" Bert turned to Hitchcock for an answer.

"She'll not be entitled to anything from the estate if it's true that she killed your stepfather."

"But if I want to make sure she has enough money for her legal defense? Can I do that with money from the estate?"

"That's entirely up to you and your mother."

"I have my mother's power of attorney. I want to make sure Moira's got enough for whatever she needs." Bert's face suddenly seemed much older. "They used her, you know. All of them—Richard, my mother, Von Zandt. She was just sixteen. He's such an evil bastard and they sold her to him."

Hitchcock made a note. "Very well, then. We'll make sure she's taken care of."

Fuck you, Von Zandt, Reid thought. Fuck you.

* * * * *

Reid was back in his office by midmorning. The search for Moira Ramsey had continued with no luck. She seemed to have just vanished. Reid knew they had to move quickly if they were to beat her executioners to their task, and Von Zandt had the advantage of knowing his prey better than Reid and his people did.

But there was no sign of the girl anywhere. And Glynnis Taylor was still missing as well. Reid wondered if the two of them were still alive. Maybe they were together. He hoped they were. Moira would have a better chance of surviving with her aunt's help.

He looked away from his computer when he heard children's voices outside his office. That was a first. He didn't remember ever seeing children in the office before. None of his team had any, and it wasn't exactly a child friendly environment.

Puzzled, Reid went to his office door to investigate. Smiling, he recognized his sister Pippa's two eldest children just as they were hurtling toward him. Pippa was coming up behind them, all smiles. Pippa, unlike Darby, was petite like their mother, but like her brothers and their father, her hair was almost black with eyes to match. Pippa's children, however, were sturdily built blue-eyed towheads like their father. Nobody who didn't know them would guess they were even related to their mother.

"We're here to kidnap you for lunch."

"Great." He hugged the children, then his sister. "Where's the little one?"

"She's home with nanny. Two-year-olds don't travel well and I needed some time with these two hellions."

He smiled, rubbing the children's heads fondly. "Where shall we go?"

Pippa grinned. "Someplace they don't want to skewer noisy brats."

He pretended to ponder. "Hmm. No brat-skewering places. That narrows down our choices." He waggled his eyebrows at the children and they laughed.

"Funny." Pippa punched his arm and he pretended to flinch.

"Ow! Tough girl."

"Don't you forget it." She waved her hand toward her children who had wandered away, commandeering Reid's desk chair, and spinning it around.

"Stop that right now, you two."

"They're fine, let them play," Reid said.

"It's your office. Don't say I didn't warn you."

"I'll consider myself warned." He took his jacket from the hook behind his door and put it on.

"Is Darby still in town?" Pippa asked. "Perhaps we should see if she wants to join us?"

"No."

"No, she's not in town anymore, or no, you don't want her to join us?"

"I don't think she's in town, but I don't want to see her if she is."

"Well, then." Pippa's voice was bright and matter-of-fact. "The children and I will have you all to ourselves."

They settled on a restaurant on the edge of a park, and were sitting at one of the outside tables as, for once, the weather was fine. Reid was charmed by his niece and nephew and freshly reminded of his fondness for this softer sister of his. Although younger than him, Pippa was well settled in her marriage and with her small brood, neither of which Reid could say for himself.

He listened as Pippa entertained him with stories of the family back at Dunbaryn, and what was going on with the family's distillery business where she worked with her husband.

"The folks miss you, you know. You need to visit. You haven't been home since Christmas."

He ran a hand through his hair, looking away from her. "I know. I can't just yet."

"They're worried about you."

"Aye, I guessed that. They call."

"And Anne? Where is she in all this?"

"She's here in Scotland, as I'm sure you know as you would have seen the latest bit in the gossip sheets."

Pippa ate a chip. "Perhaps I did see something. Are you not together, then?"

He shook his head. "It's a bit complicated."

"Always is with you two, isn't it?"

He twisted his lips in what tried to be a smile.

"So Anne's here, but not with you. What's she doing in Scotland?" Pippa reached over quickly and stopped a cup of milk from being overturned by her son, then turned her attention back to her brother.

"She's on a job. A garden renovation outside of Glasgow."

"Is she with that other man?" Pippa asked, her voice trying too hard to be casual. "The one from California?"

He shook his head. "No, she's not. At least not right now." They were silent for a moment.

"I'll order ice creams for the children, but I fancy a Guinness. You'll join me, won't you, Terrence?"

He nodded, although he rarely drank at lunch. "That would be good."

She beckoned the waitress over and gave their order. "So tell me what's going on. Darby knows, apparently?"

"Part of it. She sussed it out on her own."

"Just tell me if you want me to mind my own business. I won't, of course. I'll just worry." She stopped talking as the waitress approached with their drinks and the ice creams, then nodded her thanks. She settled her children with their treats, not taking her attention from Reid. Her eyes signaled she was willing to wait as long as it took for an answer.

"No, it's all right." He took a long drink of ale. "I need to talk about it to someone I can trust."

Pippa put her hand on his. "That's the nicest thing you could say to me. I'm always coming to you with my problems, but this is the first time you've confided in me. Thank you for that, for trusting me. What is it, then?"

He looked down at his sister's hand where it covered his. "She's going to have a baby."

"Oh, Terrence, how wonderful."

Then he looked up and saw her face change as she read the problem in his tortured face. "I see. A baby, you said. Not your baby?"

He held out his hands in a gesture of helplessness. "We don't know. It's a possibility, but more than likely not mine."

She lowered her voice as she watched her children. "Well, excuse my language but, shite."

He shook his head and gave a small, mirthless laugh. "My sentiments exactly."

"What happened? I mean, I can figure out the basics, but you know."

"It's complicated, as I said. When I went to her in California, she broke things off with the other man, and we reconciled." He looked down at his glass. "But somewhere right in there—well, she's pregnant and the timing makes it anyone's guess right now whose baby it is." He took another long drink. "But the odds are against me."

"Oh, dear God, I'm so sorry. So where is she staying?"

"I bought a house for us here in town. She's there. I'm at the flat. She'll only be here until the job's finished; then she'll go back to the States."

"No, Terrence, that's awful. Is that what she wants?"

He grimaced. "No, nor what I want. But there's not much for it. If the baby's his, Andrew Grainger would not be willing to let the child grow up thinking it was mine; and the child would know that his mother had conceived him with his father when she was married to me. His life would be constant explanations and his classmates, well, his life would be hell. Not a good way for a child to grow up."

"But wouldn't that be true even if she was with the artist? Children adjust."

"When they have to. More fair for the adults in the child's life to make the adjustments. And if our marriage is over and she's married to the baby's father, it will make things more settled for the child. More defensible to playground teasing, at least. And I think it's less likely to make a difference over there." Not only wouldn't Anne be swimming in a fishbowl of publicity because of her titled status, but surely the crowd of people that artists associated with were less rigid than the ones Reid encountered both in his work and his private life.

Pippa worried her lower lip. "You're sure the other man will want the child?"

"Positive. He wants the child and he wants Anne."

"What about Anne? Would she actually marry him for the sake of the child—and lose you?"

"I think she knows that it would be the best thing for the child."

"I don't think you should give up each other like this, Terrence. You've never loved any other woman. What will you do without her?"

"We can't let what we want ruin the child's life. Anne's close to Grainger, probably closer than she'd ever admit to me, and he loves her. It won't be a bad life for her."

Pippa made a face. "Shite, shite, shite."

He nodded, staring hollowly at nothing.

"How far along is she?"

"About three months."

"How is she feeling?"

He blew out a breath and sent her a look of relieved gratitude. "God bless you for asking—for not just hating her on my behalf. She's all right, I think. Morning sickness, though, last I heard. We don't talk, but I have people watching out for her."

"You still love her."

He nodded.

"And she still loves you?"

"I think so."

"Oh, Terrence, I'm so sorry."

They were both quiet for a moment, then he asked, "Will you do me a favor? Will you visit her? I'm afraid she's lonely in that house by herself at night. You could take the children and just distract her a bit. Maybe for dinner tonight if you're not going back just yet?"

"Of course, I'd be happy to."

"I'd appreciate it if you don't tell anyone else about her being pregnant."

"I won't. Give me her number."

He wrote it out along with the house address.

"She's out in the country working on the job until about six-thirty each night. If she is up for seeing you, perhaps you could pick up some food and take it so she won't feel the need to cook? She's tired with the job and just from being pregnant. It's making her a bit worn out."

"I will. I know how that is."

"I know you do. Thanks for that, then."

"You can't join us?"

"No. We're not seeing each other. But if you would let me know if there's anything you notice she needs, I'd appreciate it."

"Of course." Pippa got up and put her arms around him. "I'll call you after and let you know how she is."

He held his sister as tightly as he could. "Thank you."

# Chapter 92

ANNE GAVE A NOD to the workman on the other side of the pond, signaling him to turn on the waterfalls on both ends. Water streamed like sheets of glass over the angular stone slabs and down into the pond. She turned and smiled at Walter Von Zandt, though she wanted to throw him in the pond and hold his head under.

"What do you think?"

"Spectacular. They're lighted at night?"

She nodded with satisfaction. With the completion of the waterfalls, the project was almost finished and the firm would get their money. Jonas, with his acute financial acumen, had set up the payment of their services through funds safely put in escrow at the inception of the project, portions of which were paid out as certain benchmarks were reached. All that was left now were some finishing touches, then the last, smallest payment would be released.

"Maybe you can stay until after it gets dark tonight and show me." He glanced over at the man who was busily doing something with measuring instruments close enough to be in earshot. He lowered his voice. "Does that man ever do anything that isn't right beside you? I can never talk to you in private anymore. Can you tell him to do something somewhere else?"

She shook her head. Even if she wanted him to, which she didn't, she doubted the bodyguard pretending to be one of her workmen would listen. He stuck to her like sap on pine bark from the time they got to the garden every morning until she got back in the car to go back to Aytoun Lane, even hanging around outside when she went to use the restroom. She'd told him he was taking his instructions too seriously, but he acted like he didn't understand. He was obviously more worried about getting on the wrong side of Terrence than he was about annoying her. Likewise, the man blandly ignored Walter's pointed remarks suggesting he occupy himself away from Anne.

She motioned for Walter to sit beside her on the stone bench that faced the pond, and loudly explained to him how the original waterfalls had been improved upon with invisible modern technology. He nodded, listening. Then she whispered, pretending to be worried. "I think he reports what I do to my husband, Walter. I have to be careful." Anne was more grateful than she could say for Terrence giving her this protection, especially as nothing else she did seemed to discourage Walter's attentions.

"Reid's spying on you?"

"I think so. You saw how Terrence is, and now he's even more jealous."

"This is no way for you to live, Anne."

He tried to put his arms around her, but she shook her head and moved away.

She was tired of fending him off and decided the time had come to play her strongest card. "Walter, you don't understand. I'm pregnant."

His eyes flew open and his face seized up with tension as if he'd sustained a grievous blow. Clearly Terrence had been right about the effect that her news would have on Walter. Unlike the simple complication of her being married, her being pregnant with someone else's child instantly made her undesirable. In this, Walter and her husband were alike.

She saw Walter's jaw set and his eyes harden into flint.

"How long have you known?"

Anne tried to sound innocently unaware of the effect her revelation was having on him. "Since right before I came here."

He expelled a long breath and shook his head. "Why didn't you say anything?"

She widened her eyes. "Why would I? It has nothing to do with the job."

"So he has you. Damn him to hell. He's won this, as well." He spat out his words, and Anne saw an undisguised malevolence in the man's face that made her skin prickle.

"I don't know what you're talking about."

"No, you wouldn't. But he does." He stood up, but his face softened as he looked at her. "I'll let you get back to work, Anne.

Take care of yourself."

* * * * *

The car Terrence had hired for Anne, driven by the bodyguard who never said a word beyond what was absolutely necessary, took her home each afternoon after she finished work and retrieved her each morning at the Aytoun Lane house. Someone came during the day to clean and sometimes they left a dinner for her to eat when she got home. By the magic of unseen hands, the kitchen was kept stocked with foods she liked to eat and her clothes were cleaned and pressed so she didn't have to spend time taking care of those details.

And every day the decorator left a notebook with questions and options on the new kitchen table for Anne. When Anne returned home in the evenings, she indicated her choices in the notebook and left it on the table for the decorator to see the next day. It was kind of a dream world. Choosing things for a life they would have had if so many things hadn't gone awry. Would Terrence live here when she left, she wondered. Or would he sell the house?

At night, she would drink her herbal tea and walk around the house and think, what would he like here, what would be comfortable for him there. In the bookcase of the study they had planned would be his, she put the whiskey and brandy he liked and a few volumes of books that she thought he might like, books she'd bought during her rare shopping excursions. She imagined him sitting in the study, having a brandy and looking over some of his work papers or maybe studying the screen of his laptop at the end of a day after they'd had a casual dinner together. His new chess set would be set up, and maybe she'd have the courage to play with him. Or maybe she would be curled up on the sofa reading a book to be close to him, with the baby next to her.

Then she would shake herself back to reality and wonder where he really was, what he was doing as she stayed alone in the big house. She knew she couldn't call him again. She'd tried so many times, got only his voice mail, left messages and never heard back from him. Every time she called him and didn't leave a message, Harry called her right away to make sure nothing was wrong. That was a bit embarrassing, as obviously Terrence had him call her to see what she wanted, so Harry had to know that she'd called her husband and he just didn't want to talk to her. So she'd stopped calling without leaving a message. She'd almost stopped calling and leaving messages, as well. Now she only called when she couldn't stop herself.

But tonight she would have company. Pippa and the children.

# SUNDAY, MAY 10

# Chapter 93

HARRY DROVE into the Aytoun Lane house driveway. He'd taken the task of looking after Lady Anne seriously, as he knew the guv expected, and popped round to check on her a few times a week. He telephoned every morning and every evening, even if he had to leave whatever dolly bird he was with to do so. He'd sussed that Sundays were particularly hard for her, so he always came to see her on Sunday afternoons.

She opened the front door even before he'd turned off the engine, the orange cat in her arms. Waiting, she'd been. As always, he saw her scan the car he arrived in to see if he was alone. He always was, but that hadn't stopped her from hoping she'd see the guv. Still, she smiled at him and waved. She was lonely enough to settle for seeing him.

"I thought you might come. I've made tea."

"Tea sounds fine, Lady Anne."

She made a face. "I wish you'd call me Anne."

"Nah, it just wouldn't feel right to me." They'd had this discussion before.

She gave a resigned smile. "All right, then." She led him into the kitchen. "Don't faint, but I've made a cake."

"Brilliant. This morning?"

She nodded.

"You were feeling good this morning then? You're not always one for facing food in the morning." They never discussed what he was almost positive was her condition. She always claimed to have a bit of flu, or an upset stomach. Sometimes she'd say she must have eaten something that was off. But he'd had three sisters who'd gotten preggers when they were still in school and he was living at home, and he was fairly sure Lady Anne was expecting. He didn't know if the guv knew, but Harry wasn't going to be the one to tell him.

"I feel good. Yesterday and today both. I think I'm finally getting over that bit of flu. I had eggs for breakfast today. So then I thought I would bake a cake in case you came by for tea. It's chocolate. You like chocolate, don't you?"

"Indeed I do."

She put the cat down and brewed two pots of tea—one regular and one the awful herbal stuff he teased her about drinking. Then she busied herself cutting slices of cake. When she had everything ready, she poured the tea.

She wiggled a hand in his direction. "Go ahead. Try the cake. Tell me if you like it. This is a recipe of my sister Jeanne's, the one that runs a bed and breakfast."

He took a bite and closed his eyes as he tasted it with what he'd planned to be exaggerated pleasure, surprised to discover that it really was good. "Delicious. Lady Anne, you've made me a happy man."

She laughed. "I'm so glad you like it. I just wanted to do something to thank you for all you do. I know watching over me must be a horrible nuisance for you."

"Not at all. It's a pleasure. And with the cake, we're definitely even." He watched as he saw her face suddenly get serious, and her eyes drop down to where her hands surrounded her tea cup. He knew what was coming. What always came about now with her.

"How is he? I never see him, you know." Tears swam in her eyes. "He won't see me, or even talk to me." She gave a small, self-deprecating laugh. "Of course, you know that."

The first time this had happened, he'd been surprised, shocked even, but now he was used to it. It had taken Harry some time to get used to the idea that this beautifully elegant wife of his superior officer was really just a girl sick at heart for a man who wouldn't have anything to do with her.

Harry knew the guv wouldn't want him to tell her anything that would worry her, so he wouldn't tell her what Reid had gone through to explain to his superiors what had happened. If things hadn't turned out so well, Harry didn't know what would have happened to Reid's career. But Harry said nothing about that to her. Even though the Superintendent kept his distance from her himself, he obviously wanted his wife protected from as much as he could manage to protect her.

"He's fine, Lady Anne. Works all the time, but that's normal for him. Things are busy at the office." That was the truth, of course, but the guv was working much harder than necessary.

She sighed. "Still no sign of Moira?"

"No, nothing."

"Do you think she's dead? That Walter's had her killed?"

"Either that or she's just doing a good job at not being found."

"I hope she's okay. You'll let me know if you hear anything before I leave?"

"Aye. Count on it."

She was quiet, then took a sip of her tea. "I never heard if there was anything helpful on that flashdrive Moira gave me. Was it a total fizzle?"

Harry was taken aback. He'd assumed she'd at least known how important what she'd risked so much for had been. But of course, everything had been kept confidential, and only a handful of people knew of her involvement. Keeping her name out of all of the reports so there would be less chance of retaliation against her had been an unbreakable order. But she was entitled to know a little, he decided.

"No, not a fizzle at all. The information you got helped us get millions and millions of pounds out of the hands of terrorists."

"Oh." She looked surprised.

We were able to show not only that they were involved in ordering the Heidelberg bombing, but up to their necks in a conspiracy to bomb almost a dozen universities in the UK and Europe. The information MI5 got out of them saved many lives, I daresay."

She nodded. "I saw that part in the newspaper."

"You did a fine job giving the descriptions for the sketches of the suspects. Of course, there's been no mention of your part in things, as the guv doesn't want anyone to know you were involved. To keep you safe."

"Of course."

"We weren't able to get enough to arrest Von Zandt yet, but eventually, we'll get him."

"I wish I could have helped more with that."

"What you did helped a lot and the guv is uncommonly proud of you. He just wants to make sure no one comes after you, to, you know, retaliate or something."

Tears fell down her beautiful cheeks. "He's nice that way, isn't he?"

"He doesn't want anything to happen to you."

"I'm a dreadful wife for a man like him."

Now Harry didn't know what to say. He'd gotten better at navigating these talks with her—the first time had flummoxed him—but this one was tricky. In spite of himself, he had become genuinely fond of her, but she had caused the guv more than a fair amount of trouble. He was fairly certain that despite the Superintendent being so crazy about her, she actually was a dreadful wife for a man like him.

She laughed, while at the same time wiping away her tears with her hand. "You should see your face."

He stammered, trying to regroup. "No, not at all, I was going to say."

"No, you weren't." She got up and took her cup over to the sink. "Would you like more cake?"

He'd cleaned his plate. "Don't mind if I do. It's a lovely cake." He brightened. "You do know how to cook."

She smiled. "Thank you. I'll have to work on the rest of the wife things."

"That's the spirit." Whew. They'd gotten through it again.

She brought him another piece of cake. "Did you get a chance to ask if he'd found the things I'm missing in his flat? My perfume and the nightgown? I'm getting packed and still can't find them."

"Aye. He said no, that you must have left them in the hotel."

# Chapter 94

ANNE WALKED OUT TO THE CAR to see Harry off, then went back into the house, knowing she would face another lonely Sunday evening. Other than the one visit from Pippa, Harry had been her only visitor while she'd been living there. She felt a little like she was in exile, but her work days were long, and she was usually tired at night. Besides, she wasn't really feeling too sociable, so it was probably for the best.

All of her weekend chores were finished and she was ready for her last week of work at Lynstrade Manor. The gardens would be finished by Wednesday, or Thursday at the latest. Friday she would be leaving to go back to California. Jonas had offered her another project, this one in Dallas, and she'd given him her tentative acceptance. She'd have two weeks in between projects. Two weeks to visit her family, see her doctor, and rest. The cramps hadn't come back, but she wanted to be careful. Also, she'd promised Andrew she'd help with ideas for the foundation he'd set up in Lenore's memory.

She closed the front door and went through to the patio outside of the living room to get the book she'd left on the table by the lounge chair before she'd heard Harry drive up. The sun had gone under a blanket of clouds and it was already getting too chilly to stay outside. From the look of things, there would be another May shower this evening. She grabbed her book and went back into the house, locking the door for the night. The man who watched the house generally took a break when Harry was there, and she hadn't seen him get back yet. She thought maybe she'd take him some of the cake when he reappeared.

Anne slipped off her shoes and headed for the kitchen to put the tea things away. She looked around, wondering where the cat had gotten to. He usually stayed close, and never went outside unless she made him. He had to be curled up in some corner taking a nap. After she took the cake to the security man, she would take a bath and then spend the rest of the night in bed with her book.

Her thoughts already on the next week's work, she entered the kitchen and immediately knew she wasn't alone. Fear sucked the breath from her chest in a violent thrust. She tried to think of something she could use as a weapon, something to protect herself, to save her baby. Her heart pounding in her chest, she lunged toward the counter where she'd left the cake knife, grabbing it, then spun around to face the table.

Moira Ramsey sat there looking at Anne in astonishment. Her clothes were dirty, and her hair was limp and needed washing. She was stroking the cat, eating a piece of chocolate cake and had a glass half full of a dark golden liquid in front of her.

Anne clapped her hand to her chest. "God, Moira, you almost gave me a heart attack." She dropped the knife on to the counter. "You scared me to death. Where on earth did you come from?"

Moira grinned, "That was fierce. You and your knives." She motioned her head to the patio door. "I thought he'd never leave. I was waiting outside. Who is he?"

"Harry Ross. He works for my husband." Anne wrinkled her nose. "What are you drinking?"

"Brandy. I found it in the other room. The only choices were brandy or whiskey, and I needed a drink. You don't have any wine or anything else around that I could find."

"Sorry, I can't drink because of the baby, so I just don't keep anything much here."

"So what was he doing here?"

"Harry? He just keeps an eye on me for Terrence."

"Lord Reid's still cheesed off at you?"

Anne made a face. "I wouldn't say that, but he doesn't think we have much of a chance at a future together."

"That's why you're living alone, I guess."

"That's why. I've been worried about you." Anne went over to Moira, and clasped her in her arms. "Where have you been? You must know the police are looking for you."

Moira hugged her back, sniffling. "I know. The police and

Walter's men, both."

"Don't cry. I'll make sure you're okay."

"I knew I had to find you."

"And you did. You know there's a guard here?" Anne released Moira gently to go to check the window. She peered out, but couldn't see any sign of him. "At least, there usually is. Somewhere out there."

"Yeah, I know. He wasn't there just now, though, so I came over the garden wall." Moira got up and went to the refrigerator, opening the freezer compartment. "Okay if I have some ice cream? I'm starving."

"How about if I cook something like a real meal for you? Cake and ice cream and brandy aren't very nourishing."

"What have you got?"

Anne thought, then said, "I could make hamburgers and French fries? Or chicken with pasta?"

"Cheeseburgers? You're hungry, too, aren't you? You've got to eat for the baby, right?"

"Sure." Anne started to get the things out she needed to begin cooking. Keeping her voice casual, she asked, "Where have you been all this time?"

"Just here and there." Moira nuzzled her face against the cat. "How'd you get Tiger?"

"Terrence found him outside your flat."

"Figures. Walter hates Tiger. He probably threw him out and hoped he'd starve to death. Just like me."

"Haven't you been eating?"

Moira shook her head. "Not much. I ran out of money. I thought I'd be fine because when I got those account numbers for you, I got the bright idea to transfer some money to myself." She took a drink of her brandy. "So I did. Four million pounds. I was mad at Walter because I thought he wanted me to sleep with those Nigerians. I wasn't going to put up with being treated like that."

"Of course not. Who would?" Anne put two frozen hamburger patties in the skillet, then eyed Moira and added another one. She started the oil for fries in another pan as she listened.

"So I thought I'd have quite a bit of money I could use when I left." She shrugged. "But I guess whatever Lord Reid did to those accounts did something to any scheduled transfers, and my money was gone when I tried to get it." She screwed up her face. "To do it right, I guess I needed to move it out of that account right away to another one. But I didn't realize that until it was too late." She went to the refrigerator and took out the milk, holding it up to Anne, who nodded and pointed to the cupboard that held glasses. Moira poured a glass for Anne and one for herself, and went on. "I didn't have any money but what I had on me. It's been rough."

"Your mother?"

Moira shook her head. "I didn't even try. She'd never help me. My brother, either. They're too afraid of Walter. I tried my Aunt Glynnis, but her mobile's been disconnected."

"You need to turn yourself in, Moira. That would be the best thing for you. It would show cooperation, I would think."

Moira came over to the stove and stared at the food in the pan, but Anne knew the girl was seeing something else entirely.

"I'm scared." Tears welled up in Moira's eyes. "I did some things. Bad things. Really bad things. And I'm afraid."

Anne took Moira into her arms again and let the girl cry. After Moira's tears had subsided, Anne whispered, "Shall I call Terrence?"

Moira wiped her arm across her face. "I guess so. But I want to eat first. It smells so good."

Anne nodded. "Let me get these fries before they burn. And we'll have a salad."

"Not fries. Chips. If you're to be a proper Scottish wife, they're called chips."

"Chips, then, though my status as a Scottish wife is up in the air, and I hardly think I can be called proper." Anne made a wry face and Moira laughed.

When the food was ready, Anne dished up their plates and they ate companionably at the kitchen table. Anne did not feel any fear of Moira, no matter what she'd done. It wasn't that she doubted Moira had done what she was supposed to have done; she could just tell that Moira was not going to do anything to her. They didn't talk about what had happened; Anne decided it was better that she let someone who knew what they were doing get Moira's story, and she wanted to keep the girl calm until the police came.

Afterwards, Moira took a badly needed shower and Anne called Terrence—twice. She wasn't really surprised that he didn't answer. So she called Harry, who answered immediately.

# Chapter 95

SITTING IN HIS OFFICE, Reid watched the screen on his mobile as it rang.

It had been two weeks since the last time Anne had tried calling him. He knew Harry had gone over there this afternoon, and things were fine. Although he was hungry for news of her, he knew he had to wean himself from that need. He had been careful never to appear receptive to even the brief reports Harry had tried giving him in the beginning, so now he rarely heard anything more from Harry except that things were fine. Not even that she was fine. Harry always said only "things are fine" and that nothing was needed.

She called twice in rapid succession, but he could tell she didn't leave a message. He pressed in Harry's number to tell him to call her and make sure nothing was wrong. Nothing ever was, she was just lonely. Sundays were the worst, he knew, for her as well as for him.

Looking at his watch, he held the phone to his ear and started shutting down his computer. Time to go home—if an empty flat is a home. He'd come to High Street after Mass that morning and stayed all day, not bothering to eat. No one else was in, so it was quiet and he'd been able to work undisturbed. He'd get something to eat on the way home if he decided it was worth the trouble.

He left his office, shutting off the light. His mobile rang again. God, Anne, have mercy. How many times did he have to resist temptation? Automatically, he checked the screen. Not Anne, Harry.

His heart lurched with terror. He dropped his computer bag and hit the talk button.

"What's happened, Harry? Is she all right?"

"Moira got into the house. She's with Lady Anne, guv."

"Is she armed? Is Anne all right?" As he talked, he ran for the front door. "I'm on my way from High Street. Tell me for Christ's sake, is Anne all right?"

"She called me just after you did. She says she's all right. Moira's all right, too. In the shower, your lady says." Harry gave a little laugh. "She made them cheeseburgers and then Moira went to take a shower and wait for you to come get her. Lady Anne says the girl trusts you and that she's sure there'll be no trouble."

Reid shut the front door of the offices behind him, heard the click as the automatic lock engaged, then ran to where his car was parked, just as the skies opened up with a pelting rain. "I'm on my way. Meet me there."

The security guard outside the house on Aytoun Lane waved him through. Where the fucking hell was he when a murderess got into the house? He'd deal with the man later. Harry's car was already in the front driveway, so Reid pulled up behind him and ran up the front steps, ignoring the rain. The door was unlocked and he rushed in, his eyes scanning for Anne.

"We're in the kitchen, guv." Harry's voice called out.

Reid brushed the rain from his face as he quickly walked to the back of the house. Moira Ramsey, hair still slightly damp, sat at the kitchen table in jeans and a pink shirt he recognized as Anne's. Next to her sat Harry. They were both eating chocolate cake topped with vanilla ice cream. Reid shot a question at Harry with his eyes.

"She's upstairs, guv. She didn't want to interfere with police business." Reid detected a note of pride in his sergeant's voice.

"Oh." He hid his disappointment. "Good, then." Reid forced himself to focus on Moira. Sitting down next to her, he said, "Moira, I've been looking for you."

She nodded. "I know."

"We need to talk."

"I know."

"I need to caution you about your rights."

She nodded her head toward Harry. "He did already. He had me sign that paper."

Harry held up the signed acknowledgement of rights and then took his plate to the sink. "You finished eating, Moira?" She nodded and he cleared her plate as well.

Reid said, "Your brother wants to help you. He'll pay for a solicitor for you. He's having your father's will set aside so nothing will go to Walter."

"But he wants to help me? After everything I've done?"

"And after everything that was done to you."

Moira nodded, tears starting to pool in her eyes. "I'm ready to go now, Lord Reid. I don't need to be handcuffed, do I?"

"I don't think that's necessary, do you?"

"No. I'm tired of running and I'm afraid of Walter's men. And besides, I've got nowhere else to go. I ran out of money a week ago."

"Why did you come here?"

"I knew Anne would help me. I've been trying to get in here to see her, but there was always some guard around. Until this afternoon. I was so hungry." She seemed like such a child right then, not a cold-blooded murderess. Nineteen. Just nineteen.

"Did you get dinner then? Not just cake?"

"We had cheeseburgers, chips, and salad. Anne cooked. She's a good cook."

"Aye, she is that. All right then, shall we go?"

Moira's eyes searched his. "Don't you even want to see her?"

Startled, Reid couldn't think of anything to say. He swallowed, recovering his composure. "Later, perhaps. Just now I need to take care of you."

"Can I go up and say goodbye to her? I need to do that."

He nodded. "Harry, you go on up with Moira. I'll wait outside in the car."

# Chapter 96

MOIRA KNEW MORE than she thought she knew, and the Procurator Fiscal's office, which would be responsible for prosecuting Von Zandt, was optimistic about being able to bring charges and eventually getting a conviction based on her information. Not only could she implicate Walter Von Zandt in Ramsey's and DI Lawrence's deaths, but she would be able to give them enough to tie him to the terrorists. She remembered dates of meetings, names of his associates. Not only that, but she was able to provide information about the places they went at times that tied Von Zandt to being in multiple locations at the same time as the men funding the university bombing plot.

Her testimony would be critical, the piece that held everything together. The solicitor hired for her by Bert Ramsey secured a promise from the government for her freedom in exchange for her cooperation, with the proviso that she undergo psychiatric treatment in a secure facility after the trial was over. But the Procurator Fiscal insisted that she be kept incarcerated until the trial. For her safety, she was put in a private cell and kept away from the other prisoners. Her brother visited her every day, although her mother would not.

Moira confessed that when DI Lawrence told Walter Von Zandt that Richard Ramsey was talking to Reid, Walter had ordered Frederick to take care of Ramsey. Frederick had come to Moira and they worked out how to do it together. DI Lawrence had been responsible for making sure Parsons dropped the surveillance detail on Ramsey. Moira said that they hadn't known until afterwards when Lawrence tried to blackmail them, that he'd taken Parsons' place and had kept watch himself.

Reid asked, "So where'd you meet up with Richard that night?"

Moira pulled at a hangnail with her teeth while she answered

Reid's questions. "I never actually left the house after dinner that night. I just pretended to leave when Frederick came for me. He left by himself and waited where we'd arranged to meet. Instead, I let myself into Richard's car and laid down in the back seat waiting for him. I actually fell asleep for a while."

"Did Richard expect you to be waiting for him?"

"Duh. We'd planned it." She left off on the finger that had started to bleed and started nibbling on the next one in line. "I knew he wanted me, but he waited for me to make the first move. So I did. Easy peasy."

"Why the wig?"

With the smile of a naughty child who thought she'd done something very clever, Moira said, "Freddie watched something on television about people leaving hair at a crime scene, so we decided on a wig to keep my hair tucked away. That was my idea."

"When did you put it on?"

"In the garage while I waited for him to come out. I brought it in my rucksack, along with the blade. Richard loved the wig." She reached up and folded her hair to make it appear shorter. "It was short like this. The way Mum's hair was when they first met."

Reid was beginning to understand. "And Freddie?"

"Freddie followed us when we left the gates, then waited while I did what I needed to do. Then he helped me get Richard on the tracks afterwards." Her teeth went back to work on her fingers.

"What about DI Lawrence?"

"Walter was mad when Freddie told him that the cop was trying to blackmail us. The idiot thought Freddie and I had gotten rid of Richard on our own or something. That Walter didn't know." She shook her head like she was disappointed in DI Lawrence's stupidity. "As if. Walter told Freddie the man was past his sell-by date. Freddie didn't understand that, but I explained." She started to put a finger up to her mouth, but then seemed to catch herself, and put her hands behind her back, keeping the tempting finger treats away from her voracious teeth.

"What happened after Walter found out DI Lawrence was trying to blackmail you and Freddie?"

She shrugged. "Walter told me and Freddie to take care of him. So we did. We acted like we were going to pay the money, then at the meeting, Freddie twisted a wire thing around the guy's neck."

"And the young cop?"

She released her hands from behind her back and brought them forward in a "not me" gesture. "No frigging idea."

Reid nodded.

Moira added, "Though if I had to give it a guess, my money would be on the slimy haired cop."

Reid thought Moira's money would have been safe with that guess.

# TUESDAY, MAY 12

# Chapter 97

HE DREAMED OF HER AGAIN, and as always, he was grateful for the dream, although even in his sleep, he was conscious it was only a dream. He loved these dreams when he could be with her, and every time he woke after having one of them, he just wanted to go back to sleep and be with her again.

He seemed to have missed the beginning of this dream, though, and tried to make it start over again from the beginning, when he would see her and she would smile and he would tell her all the things he wanted to say to her. He would hear her laugh, then watch her think as he told her something serious. He needed all of the first part of the dream, as well as this part, to get him through his lonely waking hours. This dream was hurtling by too quickly. He was surrounded by the feel of her mouth in his dream when he suddenly woke and, at the same time, came with exquisite, agonizing pleasure. He heard himself groan with his release.

After he could breathe again, he realized with a start that he could still feel her touch. He looked down and saw her golden hair in the faint moonlight from the window, then her face and the smooth skin of her naked body as she moved up to lay in his arms.

His heart pounded rapidly, torn between what he wanted and what was right. "Anne . . ."

She put her finger over his lips. "I'll leave before morning. I need one more night with you before I go. I need it, Terrence. You don't have to talk. I don't want to hear any logic or what's best for any of us. I just need this night. And besides, you can't make me leave now, not when it's my turn. That wouldn't be fair."

He smiled. "No, I'd never do that. Not when it's your turn." He kissed her, and ran his hands along her curves, feeling her body shudder in response. "Waking up like that could kill a man, lassie. But dying like that would be worth it." He moved from her side and turned her body so he could see the long beautiful nakedness.

"I've missed you so much, Terrence."

"Lassie, you don't know what missing is."

"Show me." She lay back and let him begin his pleasuring of her.

He started with his mouth on her neck and moved down slowly to her breasts. He took his time, loving the way this part made her arch up in desire, her body looking for his. That would come, but not yet. He trailed his tongue down past her still-tight abdomen and found her center, continuing his caresses. He wanted to feel her desire get her to that point he loved, where she begged him to finish her. His mouth still buried in her, he glanced up to see her face. Almost there, you're almost there, my love.

Her voice, husky and desperate, broke out. "Terrence, have mercy. Please, please."

He released her and she flew off her cliff, crying out.

Afterwards, he moved up to lie beside her and let his fingers gently draw swirls around her breasts. "Now we're starting off even."

She smiled. "I like the sound of that—starting off. Come be inside me."

"Not yet. You're still in that earthquake aftershock region. Any touch will take you over again, and the male body's not quite as resilient—at least not at my age. We've hours."

She placed a hand on his chest. "Don't fall asleep."

"No, no sleeping." He drew her to him. "I'm going to kiss you for a while."

"Mm-m."

He kissed her hair, smoothing it down with one hand. "How did you get here?"

"The security guard, Brian. I told him you'd called me." She smiled. "I think he blushed all the way over here."

"I can imagine. Where is he now?"

"Parked downstairs. I told him to take a nap, that I'd be down again before morning."

"He'll probably never be able to look either one of us in the face again."

"I don't care."

"Nor do I." He kissed the valley between her breasts.

"Earthquake region quiet?"

"Quiet enough. Come be inside me."

"Truthfully quiet, lassie? I want you to last more than five seconds."

She considered. "Maybe you should just keep kissing for a while, then. I'm probably still in the five-second range."

He spread her legs apart and eased into her. "I have a better idea. Let's just get this series of earthquakes over with, and then start again."

She started to say something, but instantly got caught up in a tremor. He moved inside her, just enough to transition her from one to the next, loving the way she cried out with each eruption, saving his own for when they started again from the beginning.

He fell asleep just before dawn. When he woke up, she was gone. On the table beside his bed she'd left a gift-wrapped package with a small card on top. Next to it was her key to his flat.

He'd forgotten it was his birthday. Opening the card slowly, he read the words she'd written, words that impaled his heart with their simple message.

# FRIDAY, MAY 15

# Chapter 98

REID WATCHED as Anne boarded the plane for the States, taking care that she did not see him. He'd gone through security with his police credentials and been given a secluded place where he could observe her flight being boarded. She wore jeans and carried her worn leather carryall. Her hair lay loose around her shoulders. She looked impossibly young, but also determined. He was glad to see that; she would need that determination.

On the other end of her journey there would be someone from Stirling's security force to watch over her, at least for the next couple of months, in case Walter Von Zandt found out what she'd done and decided to come after her. The fact that Reid and Anne weren't together would help avert any suspicion that she had helped Reid's task force, and hopefully lessen the odds that she would become a target for Von Zandt's revenge.

But that wasn't why they weren't together, and he wasn't going to pretend it was. If things were different, he'd have kept her here in Scotland with him no matter what. He would have protected her, but he'd have had her with him.

Things weren't different, however.

Masochistically, he'd tried to calculate the number of nights Andrew Grainger had slept with Anne as compared to the nights she'd been with him. Even being generous with the count on his own side, he estimated that Grainger had spent at least five times as many nights with Anne as Reid had during their entire marriage. And what made it absolutely unbearable was that all of the nights Grainger had with Anne were nights when she'd been Reid's wife—nights they'd been apart because of Reid's own stubbornness. It hurt, but in the hurting, he told himself, eventually he would find freedom from loving her.

Sometimes he wondered about Andrew Grainger. Did the man spend nights lying awake, as Reid himself did, wondering about the child Anne carried? With his own child murdered only months ago, did Grainger see this child as a chance for hope again? Reid felt guilty for coveting the other man the coming child, but it didn't stop him from doing it.

He knew Anne could be happy with Grainger; she had been happy with him before Reid had come back into her life. If Reid stayed away, she'd be happy with Grainger again, especially now that the two of them would share a child, be a family.

The pain was unbelievably excruciating. All he could do was to pray that the passage of time would eventually fill the gaping hole that losing Anne was leaving inside of him, and that someday he wouldn't ache for her with every breath he took. He thought about the words she'd written on the card. Only six words, but maybe enough for him to live on:

*If you want me, I'll wait.*

He watched until the plane rose in the sky and disappeared from view, then headed to the office.

* * * * *

Reid handed the pile of disks to Harry. There were a dozen copies all told. They'd arrived that morning with no note, but he knew who they were from. Somehow Glynnis Taylor must had gotten a hold of the films Henry Von Zandt had been using to torment Patty Cady.

"Get rid of them. Burn them, shred them, whatever. Then call Patty and tell her."

Harry nodded. "I'll take care of it."

Harry left, and Reid sat thinking. The orange cat sat on one of his office chairs, looking sleepily back at him. The intercom buzzed, but the cat didn't even blink.

Reid hit the button, and Frank's voice came through. "Walter Von Zandt is at the front door. He says he wants to talk to you."

"Let him in."

Reid didn't bother to stand up as the elegantly dressed snake entered his office.

"Have a seat."

Von Zandt looked around, narrowing his eyes with distaste when he saw the cat. He pulled the other guest chair well away and sat down. "Nice to see that you're not wasting taxpayer dollars on your surroundings. This place is a dump."

"Did you come here to give decorating advice?"

"Aren't you going to offer me coffee?"

"Sure. You want coffee?"

"Please. Black."

Reid buzzed Frank and asked him to bring coffee.

"At least you have a good location." Von Zandt conceded.

"It's convenient."

Frank brought the coffee and shut the door behind him when he left.

Von Zandt took a drink from the mug. "Not bad. Police-issue coffee?"

Reid shook his head. "We buy our own coffee. They're particular about that, my team. But I suspect you didn't come here to talk about coffee, either. What can I do for you?"

"You've been interfering in my business."

Reid raised his eyebrows. "Me?"

"Ramsey International."

"Ah."

"I saw your hand in that."

"Good eye."

"That and other things." Von Zandt wouldn't come right out and tell him that the money from the seized accounts had been his, not Frederick's, but they both knew. Likely Von Zandt had a great deal of other money stashed away that they hadn't been able to find, but he'd need to use at least part of it to compensate the dangerous people whose money he'd lost.

Reid pretended false modesty. "Just doing my job."

"I think it's more personal than that."

"You can think what you like."

Von Zandt gestured at the desk and around the room. "No photo of Lady Anne."

"More decorating advice?"

"An observation. I heard she's gone back to the States."

Reid felt a chill go through him. "And just who did you hear that from?"

Von Zandt flashed a shark-toothed smile. "She and Jonas did a brilliant job on my garden. It was expensive, but you get what you pay for. No regrets on the expense at all."

"Speaking of finances, I hear you may be having difficulties in that arena."

Von Zandt shrugged. "I'm going through a divorce. Sometimes it's preferable not to appear to be too flush until after the settlement is finalized. You may want to keep that in mind."

"Really?"

Von Zandt's response was matter-of-fact. "It doesn't take much to conclude that things aren't promising for the two of you. She's moved back to California. You live here. Her lover lives there. In fact, according to my sources, he met her plane when it arrived. I have a feeling he doesn't care if she came back to him carrying your child."

Reid took a deep breath to stop himself from killing Von Zandt. "Let me see. So far you've given me decorating advice, analyzed my coffee, and now you're giving me marital advice. Why are you really here?"

"We have unfinished business."

"Now on that, we're in total agreement. I confess I won't be happy until you're in prison."

Von Zandt clucked his tongue. "That smacks of a personal vendetta."

"Nothing personal at all, I assure you."

"As I told you before, I am a legitimate businessman. And personal vendettas can go both ways. I was hoping we could agree to stay out of each other's way."

"Sorry. Not possible."

Von Zandt stood up. "I'm afraid you're about to find out that you've no case against me."

"That's where you and I disagree."

"Moira won't testify against me."

"Don't be so sure."

Von Zandt put on his coat, opened Reid's office door to leave, then turned back, "Jail can be a dangerous place."

Harry suddenly appeared in the doorway behind the man, breathless from running. Reid took one look at his sergeant's face

and knew.
    Moira was dead.

**Author's Note: On Scientific Advances**

Doubtless many readers will be aware (especially if they've read the first book in this series) that a reliable and relatively risk-free in utero test for paternity, Cell-free fetal DNA testing, is now available. This prenatal screening tool, which was first developed and used to detect potential health issues in the fetus, involves taking a blood sample from the woman and the potential father(s) and is 98% accurate for paternity. Unfortunately for Anne, this story takes place in 2009, a little too early for Anne's physician to have offered the test to her.

# ABOUT THE AUTHOR

Mary Birk lives in Colorado. Before embarking on writing fiction, she authored the *Colorado Pretrial Handbook*, published in 2008, and reissued in 2011 by Bradford Publishing Company. She has been named a Library Journal SELF-E Select author.

*The First Cut*, the second book in the Terrence Reid/Anne Michaels series, won the Rocky Mountain Fiction Writers Colorado Gold Award in the mystery/suspense category in 2014. The first book in the Terrence Reid/Anne Michaels series, *Mermaids of Bodega Bay*, was a finalist for the Rocky Mountain Fiction Writers Colorado Gold award in 2013, and was named by *Library Journal* as a SELF-e Top Book of the Year for 2016.

**Mary Birk on Social Media:**

Website: http://marybirk.com
Facebook - https://www.facebook.com/authormarybirk
Twitter - @marypricebirk
Pinterest -marypricebirk

Made in United States
North Haven, CT
26 October 2021